SIEGE

GUSTAVO BONDONI

SEVERED PRESS
HOBART TASMANIA

SIEGE

CHAPTER 1

Maybe, just maybe, we'd have been better off not knowing.
Kan looked through the scout craft's visor. The heavily tinted and shielded crystal revealed a sky out of the worst nightmares of a hyperactive stak addict. Purple dust clouds warred and lost with the dark edges of the accretion disk, with only a few stars dimly visible through the murk. But these were the only skies available to humanity now.

She tore her eyes away from the view. She'd seen it before, more times than she could count, and from all the angles available. Her instruments were showing her something much more interesting, and much more portentous. Something that might signify the end of human civilization in that sector of the galaxy, and, unless there were remnants the high command on Crystallia was unaware of, probably everywhere else as well.

There was nothing for her to do but watch. Even tightly focused laser communication was forbidden – a lesson that had been painfully learned. So she watched.

It seemed innocent enough: just some random piece of space debris, about a cubic meter in size, radiating nothing, just moving through space on a trajectory that it had followed since the early days of the galaxy.

But there was nothing innocent about it. The very fact that it was drifting along in this part of space was a dead giveaway. There was no way a random piece of debris would have been able to navigate the maze between the accretion disk and multiple black holes that would soon join the supermassive one at the center of the Milky Way. But even if this had, against all odds, been overlooked by earlier surveying missions, there was no way to account for the fact that it had, within the past four hours, corrected its flight path twice – neither change due to any natural phenomenon.

There was no doubt that it was an artificial artifact. And that meant that it was an enemy artifact. All that remained now was to see what it would do next, and to keep hiding. It seemed almost impossible that the artifact was there by chance.

Kan waited and watched, and waited and watched. Her tiny reconnaissance ship might be nearly invisible among the rocklets that made up the rings, but it wasn't completely invisible. She would only be allowed to move when the planet came between her craft and the anomaly, four days hence.

Being a Recon Leader was lonely work.

***

As she neared Crystallia, Kan felt her heart in her throat. Had she been seen? Was some unseen, unimaginably advanced enemy following her at that very moment? Would she be the one to bring death to the colony? She'd taken every possible precaution, of course, but it would be impossible to know for certain before it was much too late.

There was still one last trick she could use, however. The world on which Crystallia was located had not been chosen at random. It was a medium-sized rocky planet with an atmosphere consisting mainly of carbon dioxide, with perhaps five percent oxygen. The beauty of the world was that it was still extremely active geologically, and dust from the constant eruptions made the sky opaque enough that all flying had to be done by instruments. To any outside observer, the evasive path programmed into her Recon craft would be impossible to follow under normal conditions.

Crystallia base itself was also well concealed, lying under a kilometer of rock in one of the few geographically inert areas of the planet. A perfect forward base for humanity's colonies at the center of the galaxy.

Kan concentrated on her breathing, trying to get her heart rate under control. There would be no time to relax, not even time to shower, before her presentation before the Council. Even before she landed, the ground crew would ask her whether all was well. Her answer would see her whisked straight to the conference room, where the colony's leaders – many pulled unceremoniously from other activities – would be waiting to hear her report. She consoled herself with the thought that the military leaders of Crystallia were accustomed to encountering disheveled military pilots.

What they weren't used to was the kind of dire, desperate news she brought with her.

After what seemed like an endless series of evasive maneuvers in the atmosphere, her ship finally darted straight down. The ground came up to meet her, and then she was through the camouflaged blast doors. Once they closed behind her, radio silence could be broken.

"Welcome back, Recon Tau Osella. Is all well?"

"No," she replied grimly. "Not at all." It was all she was allowed to say, all they would expect.

"I see." The voice on the other end of the communication had changed, the tone going from welcoming to flat. "Engaging debrief protocol."

"Thank you."

She sat in silence as the ship negotiated the winding tunnel, designed with defensibility in mind more than with ease of entry and exit. Eventually, her little Recon ship entered a huge hangar, and parked beside a cluster of enormous, heavily armored evacuation shuttles – long tubes built for speed that would barely clear the tunnel with a meter to each side in the curves.

As she landed, a group of black-clad techs swarmed over her ship like ants. The crew leader, a Recon lieutenant himself, opened the hatch and helped her out of the cockpit.

"Did you bring a bag?" he asked.

"In the lounge," she replied, pointing towards the back of the ship, where a tiny cot and shielded entertainment system allowed a crewman to stretch out after a long day's scouting. The space was so small that some unnamed Recon wag had taken one look and immediately christened it the lounge – a name which had stuck.

He nodded. "I've left orders for everything to be taken to your rooms. Please come with me." Only then did she notice his eyes, cold and hard, with none of the 'welcome back' warmth usually reserved for pilots returning from the unfriendly depths of space. He knew where she was going.

She motioned for him to wait a moment, and pulled the recording memory chip from the control panel. He noticed the movement, and his eyes fell, but he said nothing.

They walked through a long white corridor. It was well-lit, and the walls were smooth stone, offering no concealment in case of an invasion. A shiver ran through her, thinking that, pretty soon, all the arguments about the absolute invulnerability of the Crystallia stronghold would be put to the test.

But Kan knew that she still had to do her duty, still had one last briefing before everyone was put on a war footing. The thought made her smile – the Recon team was always on a war footing, and the millions of civilians in the lower levels of the colony would, probably, be less than useless if they were discovered by hostile forces. Still, every effort would be made, every chink in the armor repaired.

They came to a blast door set in the corridor wall, and the lieutenant stopped in front of it. "This is as far as I go," he informed her.

His eyes searched her face for any trace of the information she brought with her. If not the actual data, then at least some inkling about how serious it was. She returned his gaze, impassive. He swallowed and nodded towards the door. "Good luck in there." What he really meant, Kan knew, was 'try not to give us any news we can't survive in there.'

She returned the nod, and he moved off. The door slid towards her right, the foot thick layer of reinforced steel and concrete swishing silently, ending flush with the wall itself. Beyond the door was nothing but a large meeting room with no other exits, but an invading enemy wouldn't know that, and would have to take the time to knock down the door and investigate. They couldn't risk having the colony launch a counter-strike out of a hidden corridor. This far into the complex, many of the blast doors hid precisely that kind of corridor.

"Well met, Recon Leader Tau Osella."

Since her eyes were unaccustomed to the sudden gloom of the meeting room, Kan couldn't tell which of the men seated at the table had spoken. It seemed to her that the voice belonged to a white-haired Recon general near the end of the table opposite her, but it didn't matter. She knew she was in a place no one wanted to be – hell, no one wanted *anyone* to be here.

"Well met," she replied, the formula serving to calm her down as well as allowing her to have a look at the other people seated around the table. Military uniforms mixed with civilian dress approximately evenly – it had been decided that the council would be a joint enterprise, ostensibly to keep the military from taking unnecessary risks with civilian lives. In reality, the Recon Force often spoke with the voice of caution, never forgetting that the first priority was to avoid detection, and that the soldiers would be the first to suffer if this wasn't achieved.

A wrinkled woman with steel-colored hair wearing a brown dress spoke next. Kan identified her as Rima Centauri Han, the elected spokesperson for the civilian contingent. Her voice showed that she was used to command – Kan could almost feel the centuries of Han family history in that imperious tone. "Sit down, Tau Osella," the woman said. "Please report your findings."

Kan sat and, trying to keep all emotion from her voice, began her report. "On the second day of my patrol, my instruments picked up a small unidentified mass, approaching from above the ecliptic. Both its speed and its direction led my instruments to classify it as possibly artificial. A pair of course corrections confirmed that it was self-powered."

Many of the silent, elderly faces in the room turned pale when they heard this, but Rima nodded for her to continue, as if she'd heard nothing she wasn't expecting.

"I continued to observe its passage until my movement brought the planet between it and my sensors."

"Is there any chance you might have been observed?" The question came from a blocky man in uniform who should have known better. But she supposed it was understandable – everyone was on edge, and his days flying Recon ships were long gone. He probably didn't remember the endless protocols, the determination to keep the colony safe, no matter what.

"No, sir," she replied. "I followed the manual to the letter. Passive observation only and my ship was powered down the whole time. The only thing I did was drift with the rocks in Crystallia's rings. There was no way I could have been detected unless the object was using some kind of active surveillance we are unaware of. My sensors picked up nothing out of the ordinary on any of the quantum or electromagnetic bands."

A few heads nodded around the table, but everyone knew that the fact that her instruments hadn't picked anything up was meaningless. The reason the colony was hidden there, in the most inhospitable wastelands of the galaxy and under a kilometer of rock, was precisely because they knew that their technology could never measure up against that employed by any of the enemies they knew about – and likely those they were unaware of as well. For all they knew, incredibly advanced scanners had located her ship, the hidden colony, and the colonies at Tonswell and Hammersmith 214. Hell, there was no reason that they wouldn't have found the cloud colonies as well.

"Was it a human artifact?"

She swallowed. "It was about a cubic meter in size." They all knew what that meant – no human could cross the interstellar void in a craft that size; there simply wasn't enough room inside for a person and the apparatus to keep a person alive. Which meant that it was either a probe or a nanofactory. Or something even worse.

"Thank you, Recon Leader Tau Osella. I suppose I don't need to remind you that you cannot speak to anyone outside this room about what you've seen?" the blocky general asked her.

"Of course not, sir."

"Good. Please leave your recording chip on the table."

She saluted and left.

***

Kan lowered herself into the steaming, bubbling bath and let out a sigh that was part released tension, part anxiety about what was coming, but mostly just pure physical happiness. The grime and sour, fearful sweat accumulated over the past four days had been weighing on her consciousness since she'd landed. The Recon vessel was equipped with an ultrasound bar and chemical cleansers, but it simply wasn't large enough to carry the water required for bathing. She appreciated the tact of the council of elders, who'd made no mention of the way she must have smelled.

So she luxuriated in the water, leaving her worry aside for the moment. She let her hair out of its captivity, felt the weight of the long dark tresses as they became waterlogged, felt the past few days melting away. She was proud of her hair, and expressed her vanity with an assortment of treatment products that most of her friends in the force tended to view with contempt – or at least bemusement. But then again, most of the other women on the force tended to be humorless fanatics who wore their hair cropped as close as the men, another group of humorless fanatics.

She supposed they'd joined the force because of some overblown sense of responsibility, a feeling that humanity wouldn't be able to survive without them. They were people who were able to ignore or belittle any mention of the Out Programs and explain at tortuous length the reason the Recon Force was so important.

Kan smiled and slathered conditioner into her hair. She swore she could feel the stuff being sucked into the strands. Pure pleasure.

And now the soap, something she'd been thinking about for nearly three days. Not bothering with lather, she simply passed the bar directly over her caramel-colored skin. It wasn't as though she would be sharing that soap with anyone, after all.

At that thought, a wave of guilt came over her. She'd promised to comm Wilde as soon as she landed. While that had been impossible for obvious reasons, she felt that, at the very least, she should have let him know she was back after the council meeting. Well, too late now. She was actually better off this way. He would have wanted to come over, to go out or something, and she just wasn't in the mood for his attention – he was sweet, but could be overly clingy.

She realized that her thoughts of Wilde had ruined the state of bliss, and a hard knot was threatening to form in her shoulder blades, and she forced herself to think about nothing other than the feel of the water against her skin.

But it was no use. There was an undercurrent of nameless dread which, no matter how Kan positioned herself in the water, no matter what she did with the control for the water jets, stubbornly refused to disappear. So she gave in and tried to understand what was driving it.

She came to the conclusion that what she knew, what was happening beyond the atmosphere, beyond the comforting kilometer of rock above her head, would never let her feel peace until she did something about it. She just couldn't know what she did and remain inert, letting someone else deal with it. It went against her training, against everything she'd been taught. But most of all, it went against who she was.

"Crap," she said to the empty bathroom, as she pushed herself out of the tub. "There are people handling this. The council will be in meetings. There are procedures. People with experience, not twenty-five-year-old Recon Leaders, no matter how many tours of open-space duty they might have under their belts."

But it was no use. Maybe Wilde was right, and she needed to get a new job.

If this blew over, she would think about it but, in the meantime, she forgot about sleep and headed towards the Recon control center. Maybe the news had filtered far enough that, even though she wasn't permitted to talk about it, she might be able to hear the latest speculation.

***

Greg shifted the weight from his left leg on to the right. His shift was nearly over, and he'd been standing at his post for seven and a half hours. More than enough to make his legs stiff, but nowhere near enough for him to need a break or to admit to the discomfort. He was a Marine, after all, and he wasn't just showing his own toughness; the pride of the entire corps was at stake in his every action. He was one, but he represented many.

Especially here. The Recon people were always going on about how ground troops were obsolete, how true war was fought in the icy depths of space or in the ferocious gravity wells of gas giants. They seemed to take some kind of perverse pleasure in stressing that, if a ground war was necessary, everything was already lost.

Evidence, of course, tended to support this view. Over the past three centuries, human ground troops had been markedly ineffective against all enemies, whether they be insectoid Brillans, Blobs, or even Uploaders. Not only had they been massacred, but in the more recent engagements, they'd been unable to buy enough time to allow even partial evacuations. The services had been reorganized and merged into the Interstellar Marines, and tactics and weapons had come a long way since then, but the attitude towards them still hadn't changed: they were cannon fodder useful only as a delaying tactic.

Even so, there were a few good things about working security in the Recon Rooms. In the first place, he could always lord it over Recon's own security personnel – soft cases relieved every six hours who were really little more than gussied-up civilians and promoted members of the ground crews. Knowing there was a real soldier on duty allowed them to fall asleep, take walks to stretch their legs, and even, much to Greg's amusement, borrow a chair to sit in while on duty.

Another benefit, more important, was the respect the pilots gave him. They might think that the Marines as an institution were an obsolete dinosaur, draining resources from where they would do most good, but they respected individual Marines for their bravery, knowing that, if it came to war, they would have what amounted to a suicide mission to keep the rest of the colony as safe as they could. Recon pilots, despite their superior attitude, understood bravery and respected it. He wasn't required to salute officers of the Recon Force, but made an exception for the flyers.

But the main reason he actually looked forward to guard duty here was now approaching, her long strides eating up great chunks of terrain as she advanced down the stark white corridor. Her hair, loose and perfect today, swayed to the rhythm of her body.

Kan Tau Osella was, to Greg's eye, the ideal Recon officer. Not only was she rumored to be on the fast track towards generalhood – she was already the youngest Recon Leader in the history of the Force – but she did it without seeming to care. She was brilliant without having to suck up, respected without having to take things to an extreme. She was the only woman in the force with long hair, the one who smiled most often, and the only one who ever gave him more than a short greeting. He told himself that the fact that she was a beautiful woman had nothing to do with it, which, of course, was a lie.

"Good Morning, Recon Leader Tau Osella," he said, giving her a crisp salute.

She stopped in front of him. "Is it morning already?"

"Yes, four o'clock," he replied, trying to avoid sounding concerned.

His worry must have gotten through anyway, because she smiled ruefully. "I'm fine. I just got in from a mission, had a bath, and came over. I didn't really stop to think about the time."

"Sounds reasonable," he replied, impassive. It wasn't unheard of for pilots to return from the timeless emptiness of space and not know what time the arbitrary clock in the base said it was, but it just didn't seem like something Kan would do. The scanner to his left had already checked and verified her identity, so he moved out of the way to let her in, but she hesitated.

"How are you today?" she asked him.

"I'm fine. It was a bit of a slow night until about ten minutes ago. Six people came in during that time." *And now you*, he didn't say. He wanted to ask whether something was wrong, whether he should be afraid, but he knew better than that. He would be told what he needed to know, when he needed to know it.

"Did the colonel come in?" she asked.

"Just ahead of you," he replied.

"Thank you." She saluted him and walked past.

Greg now knew that something was very, very wrong. It wasn't the salute itself, although it was unusual that any Recon Force officer would salute a Marine, especially just a grunt, but it was her eyes. Her eyes had been sad, downturned, and had said much more than she had probably intended.

Kan Tau Osella had been saying goodbye.

CHAPTER 2

The silence, a certain sign that everyone in the lab was concentrating on a specific issue, was broken.

Trienne gave a small exclamation and, had her dignity allowed it, would have run to where Hamak was hand typing the results of the latest batch of tests he'd conducted. Trienne being Trienne, there was no running involved, just a dignified stride. Nevertheless, there was no doubt she was excited. Her face, normally a shade of white that only the families from the old Luyten colony could ever manage, was flushed nearly beet red.

"Look at this," she exclaimed, waving a sheaf of cellulose printout in front of his face. "I think we've got it!"

Hamak gently pried the sheaf from her hands and studied the figures. At first, he expected to see just a slight improvement of the indexes with regards to the tests they'd run the week before, so he scanned the data without much hope. Luytens were a fiery, excitable bunch.

But as he read, his attention increased. He perused in absolute silence for nearly fifteen minutes as Trienne fidgeted. Finally, he looked up at her. "Are you absolutely certain that there are no errors in this report?"

"All the instruments gave the same reading, and I double-checked every one of the calculations. Unless the underlying theory is wrong, or I'm missing something, the results are accurate."

Hamak nodded. That was all he needed to hear: Trienne might be flighty at times, but she was absolutely reliable with numbers – much more, in fact, than he was. There would be no mistakes in the calculations.

He looked around the lab. The other research teams seemed completely unconcerned by their breakthrough. Hell, most of them had no idea what anyone else was working on, much less what stage the research was at. None had taken any notice of his conversation with Trienne beyond a sharp look of irritation when she shouted. The silence had returned after that as each went back to his or her work. All Hamak could hear was the hum of the ventilation system pumping dry air into the room.

Good. The less everyone else knew about what they were doing, the better. Even Trienne had been kept in the dark. She believed that the experiments were aimed at creating a completely safe way to recycle all the colony's waste – whether organic, plastic, or metallic – without generating heat that might be detectable from space. Nanomachines that dissolved everything into stable molecular prime materials but could recognize human DNA well enough to avoid attacking it.

It was a perfectly reasonable cover story, of course. The colony was always looking for new ways to recycle everything, and tearing things down to component molecules which could be reused was a great way to avoid having to dig deeper pits into the planet's crust. The machines used for excavation work could be detected from space, so it was a risk the colony really couldn't afford to continue to take.

The tests showed that the new process now worked perfectly. No more adjustments needed. All her hypothesis had proved correct.

"I am amazed. This is a great breakthrough. One of the best pieces of applied nanoengineering I've ever seen," he said.

She pulled herself up to her full height. "Thank you, sir. Coming from you, that is truly significant."

He smiled. "I think it's time you got to lead your own team, Trienne. I'll put in the recommendation once we finish checking these results."

She beamed. "Thank you, sir."

"Now, it seems we have no more work to do today. I just need to look over this before announcing the success. I trust your work, of course, but I can't sign off on anything that I haven't reviewed."

"I understand."

"So, go on home. I'll comm if I have any questions. I'll also text as soon as I've sent it along to the review board, but don't wait up. It might be a few hours. Remember not to tell anyone about this until the review board gives us the green light."

"Of course not." She nodded, hesitated for one moment, and then gave him a hug before walking off, a proud spring in her step.

He watched her go, sadness warring with the pride. He'd developed her from a raw lab assistant with nothing to her name but potential, had groomed her to become the best nanoengineer on the colony – as far as he knew, the best nanoengineer in human space.

But that was over. He'd not maneuvered himself into this position, into running this particular project just because he wanted to teach young scientists how to develop new things.

No. There were more important issues at stake, years of work which couldn't be abandoned just because he'd grown fond of his lab assistant. Certain principles would always be more important than any one individual.

Or even any one species, even if that species – like all others – felt it was the only one that had the right to survive.

So with some regret, he made a single copy of the formulas and techniques he and Trienne had developed over the past couple of years on a storage bar and placed it carefully inside a carbon fiber messenger's folder. Then he erased his computer's memory drive.

Then he walked to Trienne's computer, erased the contents of her memory, and walked calmly towards the door, carrying the folder with him.

Hamak turned to look at the lab one last time. Other scientists, the men and women he'd called colleagues since taking the position, were hard at work developing new strains of nanomachines, mainly for medical purposes. The colony would never allow them to see the light of day, except for tightly controlled off-planet military uses, of course.

But it no longer mattered. The research they were doing there would never be completed.

As he walked down the corridor with tears streaming down his face, Hamak pressed a button. Behind him, dozens of vats of nanoculture he'd been working on exploded, igniting jars placed in strategic positions all over the lab. The inferno took less than a second to cover the entire area, and less than ten seconds to burn itself out.

Hamak walked on. He'd done the calculations, and was confident that there would be no survivors.

***

Wilde was not happy. He knew for a fact that Kan was supposed to get in that night, and understood enough about the way Recon was done – all fixed trajectories and precisely timed orbits – to know that she would never be late. Also, if anything had happened to her, it would have been all over the news.

So the fact that she hadn't called was a slap in the face. He could understand that she might want to take a shower before calling him, but she'd been back at least for a couple of hours, and he knew he wouldn't be receiving a call that night.

In the end, Wilde did the only logical thing he could think of: he commed a couple of friends and went bar-hopping.

That had been four hours previously. His friends, citing early rising on the following day, had all drifted off to their various houses, but that didn't matter. He'd made a bunch of new friends during the course of the night – great folks and a lot more entertaining than his usual bunch.

He wondered how, on a colony as small as Crystallia, he'd never met them before. They were such great listeners!

"These soldiers," he said, concentrating on getting the words out without slurring. "They all think they're better than the rest of us, you know?"

Despite the fact that he was talking into his drink, heads nodded around the table.

"They all think that they're the only ones who matter on the whole colony. That their job is to protect us, and that our only function is to survive so that the human race doesn't go extinct." He looked up to find his audience, or at least the three people nearest him along the gently curving bar, listening closely. He raised the hand not holding his glass to encompass the rest of the bar, and the entire civilian population of Crystallia. "So what are we? Just animals in a zoo they have to keep alive?"

He thought about it for a minute. "Are we cattle?"

One of the guys in his audience responded. "I don't think so. They ain't eating us."

Everyone laughed uproariously. It was definitely the funniest thing Wilde had heard in years. But he suddenly grew serious again. "I mean it. Look at us. We're only allowed to work in the entertainment industry without a military rank. Even if we do nothing, they feed us, clothe us, and give us medical care. Half of the military personnel are dedicated to keeping us alive." He paused for effect and to take another drink. "Even my girlfriend looks down on me. She can't even be bothered to call me when she gets back from a Recon run. I've been missing her for four days, and she doesn't even bother to call me!" He couldn't hold it back any longer, and began to cry. "We've been together for two years, and I never felt like I was important to her at all. She would always be getting paged in the middle of the night, or writing reports instead of going out with me. Like her life was her job, and I was just a distraction for when she couldn't be doing Recon stuff."

Murmurs of assent rippled across the bar. Every civilian on Crystallia, man or woman, had had a similar experience. Even though fully half of the million or so people in the colony were civilians, they'd always been treated as second-class citizens. Off to his right, Wilde saw that he had another new friend. A blond guy drinking a non-alcoholic fruit cocktail sat a couple of stools away, seemingly already listening closely.

Wilde saluted him with his drink, and waited for the guy to return it before going on. "I mean, think about it. It's been nearly seventy years since we had to fight a battle. Do you really think the Blobs are going to come after us here in the middle of nowhere? What could they possibly gain?" Seeing that no one was attempting to answer his question, he continued. "And still, we can't start building a new society because the military threat assessments are always skewed towards the alarmist side. But what do you expect? If they ever say 'we think the danger's passed, you can all go on with your lives,' they'll lose the power they have over us!"

The new guy took a calm sip of his juice and met Wilde's gaze. "That's not the worst part," he said mildly. "The worst part is that they're not even making any attempt to negotiate a peace treaty. The party line seems to be that anyone who isn't human deserves no quarter, and therefore, we will offer them none."

Something about this seemed wrong to Wilde, but he didn't want to offend any of his wonderful new friends. He thought about it for a second before he was able to put his finger on it. "But didn't the Blobs attack us first? Didn't they depopulate three complete colonies before we even knew what was happening?"

"That's the official story, yes."

But Wilde wasn't finished. "And they ate everyone. That was the problem with the Blobs. They use us for protein. Everyone says so, not just the military."

"Even if that were true, what about the Brillans and the Uploaders? They don't eat people. Why do they have to die? Don't you think it would be better to try to come to terms? To share the galaxy?"

"How? The Brillans hate us. They kill us for fun. And the Uploaders think we're not human until we upload too."

The blond guy shook his head. "Do you really believe that? Have they done such a great job teaching us what they want us to know? How do you know these things?"

"From history files."

"*Censored* history files," the other man spat. "And do you know who censors them?"

Another guy in the crowd spoke up then. "The military does. But they do it for security reasons, and for the greater good."

Blond guy laughed. "That's what they tell us, sure. But look at the evidence. All these so-called security measures are doing two things. The first is keeping the general population away from information we might need. The second is to maintain the status quo. And the status quo means that they rule us and tell us what to do at all times. Like you said before, my friend, we act like cattle."

Wilde wasn't certain about this. "I don't know," he said dubiously. "My girlfriend actually seems real worried about the things that can happen to us if they find us. I don't think she's lying."

"Don't think she's lying? Why not? You already said she didn't really seem to care about you one way or the other. Why wouldn't she put on an act just to keep you from guessing the truth?"

"She just wouldn't."

"Yeah. She sounds like a really nice girl, the kind that worries about our safety all the time. But wouldn't a girl like that call you when she gets back from a long mission?"

Wilde said nothing.

"And if she can be so heartless in one thing, isn't it obvious that it's all an act, that she's lying to you in everything else?" He leaned back to include the rest of the audience in his question. "Come on! Haven't the rest of you been lied to by your supposed friends in the military? Don't you always feel that you're the last priority in their lives?"

The mood, which had been jovial and comradely, suddenly turned dark as an angry mutter went around the bar. The blond man looked around, nodded once, and turned back to Wilde. "Don't let her fool you. I think you can help the whole colony learn the truth. Give me a call." Pulling out his comm, he buzzed his contact details over to Wilde's handset and pushed his way through the crowded bar to the corridor.

For some reason, Wilde no longer felt like drinking.

***

Kan watched the newsfeed, feet propped on the table in front of her, as she sipped stimcaff. A couple of Recon ensigns lounged on chairs to one side of the couch, looking just as relaxed as she knew she did. And yet, a slight tightness of their features, a slight darting of the eyes revealed that dark emotions were stirring under the surface. Kan herself was aghast.

The anchor, a typical civilian with nothing better to do with her time than stand in front of a camera reading official government press releases, the only kind of news that was permitted other than entertainment industry gossip, was misinforming the civilians as ghastly images of a burnt-out lab played on an endless loop. "…there were no survivors," the middle-aged woman was saying. "Investigators are looking into the causes of the accident, which bears some similarities to the propulsion lab disaster that destroyed a large military research complex just a few months ago. I'm here with Dr. Spren Proxima DeNetri, head of nanoresearch for the Armed Forces."

The scientist, a nervous-looking guy with a receding hairline and long sideburns, spoke haltingly, as if trying to remember his lines. "In the first place, I'd like to extend my deepest condolences to the loved ones of the victims. We lost many of the best and brightest researchers in Crystallia, and it is a tragedy the likes of which we hope will never be repeated.

"Having said this, I need to remind everyone that the research being conducted here is for the good of mankind. We simply don't have the option of slowing down the pace of research for safety reasons. We are thousands of years behind our enemies, and we have to fix that if we're to have any reasonable hope of surviving as a species. You often encounter surprises when dealing with cutting edge technology."

He paused, ran a hand through the remains of his hair, and went on, not quite looking straight into the camera. "Nevertheless, we are extremely pleased with how well the explosion was contained by our security walls. Once again, despite taking risks, all civilian lives were perfectly safe at all times. We…"

Kan tuned him out. She knew that both the scientist and the newswoman were lying. He was lying consciously, and it showed, while she was just repeating what she'd been told.

Even if it hadn't been obvious from his expression, Kan would have deduced it from events she'd witnessed – her grade wasn't high enough for her to participate – in the headquarters chambers that morning. Although she'd been expecting plenty of excitement involving Recon general staff and senior field commanders, which had indeed been the scene when she came in, pretty soon one of the generals was called away for an emergency meeting. She was sitting on the same sofa, watching an inane talk show when the man left, worry written all over his face.

By the time he returned, he'd managed to pick up an escort of Crystallia Security Force members. While the CSF was a competent enough force in and of itself, it dealt only with issues regarding the civilian population of the colony. They would never see enemy fire, and would certainly not be brought into the loop for something involving a possible pitched battle in space against one of the many factions vying for control of the galaxy.

Something else was up, and this report and the hastily prepared official explanation went a long way towards telling her what it was.

One of the ensigns shifted in his chair. "Bullshit," he said. "What do you think, Miss Osella?"

She had to smile; so young, so earnest, so polite to a superior officer, and yet vulgar without even noticing it. Typical of the breed, and she'd probably been the same. "I've been watching the same thing you have, flyboy. What makes you think I have any idea what's going on?"

"Well, you're an officer. Of course you know stuff they aren't telling us."

Also typical. But fair enough, considering that she knew that the one thing every human on Crystallia, every human in the galaxy, feared most had come to pass and she had no intention of letting them know. They had a right to know, as they would be the ones to die – probably the first of many – but she still wouldn't be the one to tell them. "I'm sure they'll tell us all about it in their own sweet time."

As if on cue, the parade of CSF officers poured out of the meeting room, posted a printout of a photo of a brown-haired guy with longish hair and a full beard on the bulletin board, and left. A caption under the photo identified him as Hamak Wolf Pendalai, and issued the instructions that if he was spotted by any military personnel, he was to be taken into custody immediately for questioning.

The three Recon pilots walked over to study the image.

Kan chuckled. "There's your answer. Recognize him?"

The younger pilots shook their heads, and Kan realized with a start that one of them was actually a woman. The short hair and the fact that all ensigns looked the same to her – young and clueless – had caused her to miss it originally. She just couldn't understand why the girls insisted on wearing their hair short. There was nothing in the rulebook that forbade anyone, male or female, from wearing their hair any way they wanted to.

Maybe it was a way to differentiate themselves from the civilian population, a group that everyone in the military had always looked at with thinly concealed disgust. To anyone involved in the extremely serious business of defending the scattered colonies in these inhospitable wastes, people who deliberately turned their back on that need were seen as little more than parasites, freeloaders, and a source of easy sex.

Kan didn't feel that way, but then, she'd always been different.

The three were pulled from their silence by the door of the meeting room being pushed open once again. Colonel Jackson, Kan's superior officer, peered out at them. When he saw Kan sitting there, he rolled his eyes. "Why am I not surprised? Do you actually know the meaning of downtime, Recon Leader?"

"Couldn't sleep, sir," she responded brightly.

He scowled, but said, "I guess I can't really blame you. You might as well come in. Smith and Al Aama, you guys come in as well."

Kan dutifully entered, followed by the two younger pilots. The meeting room was packed with high-ranking officers, most from the Recon Force, although some were Marines. Although she could hear the air-conditioning going strong, the air in the room smelled of many nervous people.

Jackson addressed the room. "This is Recon Leader Kan Tau Osella. Most of you met her a few hours ago, and for those who weren't there, she's the one who discovered the object. The other two pilots are Mr. Smith and Ms. Al Aama, two of the best young pilots in the force, and the only two currently on base rated for deepscan technology."

Kan was about to tell him that she was also rated for deepscan, but held back. The colonel was perfectly aware of it, and if he preferred not to tell the rest of the officers, it was for a reason.

"The two ensigns will be launching immediately to confirm and refine Leader Tau Osella's readings." The ensigns' expressions conveyed that this was news to them, but Jackson continued, oblivious. "We have a favorable window in an hour and a half. The secondary moon will be blocking sight lines from the object's trajectory. The major will continue the briefing. I hope you'll excuse me, but I need to coordinate some more vehicle movements." He made a beeline for the door, motioning Kan to follow him.

They approached his office in silence, and only after closing the door did Jackson speak. "If it were anyone else, I'd ask if you were sure of what you saw. But in your case..." He just left the phrase hanging and opened a cabinet. He poured two glasses of an amber fluid and pushed one across his desk before sitting down. "Tell me about it."

"It wasn't a rock, that's for sure. Two course corrections in a few hours. Not big enough to be a manned human ship either."

"What would you guess?" He'd seen the readings, probably heard more analysis and had more information than she did, but Kan knew that Jackson was an old-school guy. He would always listen to the word of the soldier on the ground, even if that meant trusting gut feelings instead of cold analysis.

"Uploaders. Even the Brillans can't get anything useful into a spacecraft that small."

Jackson nodded and smiled, seemingly relieved. "The analysts agree with you. They're pointing at what look like design similarities with some of the Uploader vehicles we've got on file. The resolution at that distance means they aren't anywhere near certain, and those bastards wouldn't put their asses on the line anyway, but the preliminary guess is that we're talking Uploaders."

The news could have been a lot worse. Uploaders, at least, had never seemed to want to kill humans outright. Of course, who knew what Uploaders were thinking, anyway. The electronic society, the Upload, was possibly the most alien of the enemies out there, and the fact that humanity was responsible for its creation and most of its composition made it worse, not better. She shuddered. "Can we run?"

"Where to? The rest of the known galaxy belongs to them, and only the tidal nightmare here at the core has kept them from looking for us earlier." Jackson gave her an odd glance. "You knew the answer to that one. What's on your mind?"

"I'm just wondering why you sent a couple of kids out to do a woman's work, and why you brought me here. I have a feeling there's a connection between the two."

He laughed, a hearty, deep sound. "And here I thought I was being all sneaky." He turned serious. "You're grounded for the foreseeable future." He held up a hand, interrupting her protest. "I know you love to fly, but I need someone down here who will think things through and won't tell me just what I need to know. Someone involved in the planning sessions who, if needed, can fly out there and take action. The rest of the pilots are great — as pilots. I need someone who thinks about things, and isn't afraid to make a pain of herself if we need to move stuff around."

"A ground-hugger?"

"An officer. A major. And don't bother arguing. It's gonna happen whether you like it or not. The colony comes first." He gestured towards her drink. "Now, bottoms up, and go get some rest. That's an order. I want you back here in eight hours – we might have more info by then."

CHAPTER 3

Less than ten astronomical units from the Crystallia colony, a massive gas giant orbited the same star. The star itself had no name. It had been invisible to earth's astronomers in the maelstrom of the galactic core and had only been discovered because of its gravitational effect on a nearby dust cloud. It had a catalogue number which no one remembered, and the humans on the colony just called it 'the star,' and ignored it – it wasn't relevant to their lives, since they lived a kilometer underground.

The gas giant was less relevant still. Even the Recon troopers just referred to it as G6, which stood for the gas giant occupying the sixth orbit out from the star.

But the planet had a system of moons, and it was on one of these that the object Kan had observed impacted. It wasn't so much a landing as a controlled spear-thrust deep into a lake of liquid methane. Deep enough to reach the rocky bottom of the lake.

As soon as the object lodged into the lake bottom, the automated systems revived one of the minds that inhabited the object, and began putting it up to speed. They reported an uneventful space crossing, no sighting of any enemy vehicles, and a successful landing in a suitable location.

Define suitable.

Organic compounds in nearly pure form already liquid, while the surface contained metal oxides in abundance. The current location had been selected because it had access to both liquid organics and the solids and oxygen from the surface.

Good. Proceed with the construction. Wake me again when the first body is ready to use.

The mind went back into stasis, the terabytes of information that made it up simply inactive for the moment. That wouldn't last, of course. The tiny nanofactory in the vehicle was extremely efficient at what it did. In a matter of hours, it would have been able to tear down countless molecules from both the surrounding liquid and the moon's surface and create everything its masters needed to survive, including bodies for them to inhabit. But this time, its instructions were different: the first thing it had to do was to build a copy of itself.

***

A hooded figure watched from an open blast door as people began exiting the funeral room, the weight of an adapted mining laser pushing heavily on both his body and his soul. The chamber was a large cavern carved out of sheer bedrock, supposedly to give it a spiritual feel, to drive home the connection between the death of the body and Oneness with the planet, or some such nonsense. Essentially, anything that could make the grieving families and friends forget that their loved ones would soon be recycled into the colony's supply of raw materials.

The crowd paying their respects to the victims of the lab fire was larger than usual, which was both a risk and an opportunity for the gunman.

The risk was self-evident. A larger crowd meant that he would have less chance to operate unseen – although the laser had been disguised inside a cardboard tube. Being seen was not an insurmountable obstacle if he could make good his escape, however. Judicious use of cosmetics had turned him into a black-haired individual with light skin and freckles. But if he was caught…

He wouldn't be caught. Somewhere in the crowd was a person with a transmitter. The transmitter controlled a small bomb implanted somewhere in the gunman's body. If it looked like he was going to be caught, the bomb would be detonated. The military oppressors would get nothing from him.

The opportunity was worth the risk, however. After the lab blast, the government cover-up had been a thing of beauty. Even the leaders of the movement admitted that the military had done a better job than expected at keeping the civilian population in the dark. But the cover-up had been expected and the movement had kept an ace up their sleeves just in case. A backup plan that would leave the government no choice but to admit that the fire at the lab had been deliberately set, and to explain the reasons behind it. When the objective was to put things into the public consciousness, the more witnesses, the better.

That ace was Trienne, the sole survivor of the blast. In some ways, the instigator of the blast. Her discovery had forced the movement's hand – there was no way they could allow a weapon of that magnitude to fall into the hands of the corrupt military establishment.

His target had yet to emerge, which was unsurprising. As one of the few surviving scientists, she would be more deeply affected by the deaths, need more time to overcome the shock. Not to mention that many people would want to ask her what had happened, to see if she could give them any new information, any insight to their loved ones' last moments.

Then there would be the others, the resentful ones. People who'd lost someone and wished that he or she had survived in Trienne's place. They would give her unfriendly glances, unaware of what they were doing but hurting her all the same. It would be these people who'd finally force the researcher from the funeral chamber, out into the relative open of the underground passages.

Where he was waiting for her.

In order to fulfill his mission, the assassin needed to make a positive identification, and the crowd exiting the large chamber had been getting thicker by the minute. He would only have one chance, and it was imperative that he not miss. If he missed, the government would know that Trienne was valuable to them. Hell, they probably already suspected it anyway. Unless they were completely incompetent, they'd be aware that Hamak was missing, and that only his most senior assistant had survived.

Suddenly, a flash of unmistakable color burst through the crowd. A burst of hair so blonde it was nearly white, and skin so pale it was translucent. This had to be Trienne, her Luyten ancestry plain to see: her coloring contrasting starkly with her black jumpsuit.

The man moved quickly. Time was of the essence, since the window in which Trienne would be in his line of fire, but far enough away that he could make good his escape would be very narrow.

He placed the tube on his shoulder, as if he were just moving a load to a more comfortable position to carry it home. Then he toggled his visual implants. These were highly illegal, and would get him executed without a trial if they were discovered, but they were a risk he was willing to take for the greater good.

The implants, connected to the laser's targeting system, showed him where the beam would strike. A red dot appeared, overwritten on Trienne's arm. He moved the tube a fraction of a centimeter so that the dot appeared on her chest and pressed the firing stud.

He'd expected the laser to take a few moments to burn through her clothing, but the results shocked him. As soon as his finger closed the circuit, he saw a plume of vapor rise from the woman. A fraction of a second later, her scream reached his ears, cut off in mid-shriek, and she began to topple to one side.

The people around her immediately went to her aid. A man caught her before she reached the ground, another instinctively took her hand. The rest of the crowd milled about in confusion.

But one man, dressed in a tan jumpsuit that stood out like a sore thumb among the dark colors of the mourners, wasn't confused. He cast a glance at Trienne, but decided immediately that there was nothing he could do to help. Then he turned his attention to the surroundings.

By the man's movements, it was obvious that he was a member of some security force or other. He quickly scanned and discarded two groups of people approaching from the left before his eyes finally found the gunman. Less than two seconds had passed since the shot.

The assassin, who'd been watching the effects of his shot in a kind of daze, realized that he was in danger. Time began to move at its normal pace. He jerked the tube towards the man in the tan jumpsuit and pressed the stud again.

It was far too late. The man had already dived off to one side, rolling to avoid the shot. A plume of smoke issued from one of the walls behind him.

Despite his earlier lapse, the gunman knew exactly what he had to do. He dropped the weapon and walked quickly through the blast door. The door led into a short corridor that connected to a major walkway. He dropped the cloak in the corridor and merged into the crowd with time to spare. The security guy would never see him.

Once clear, he let out a sigh. He wouldn't die on this day after all. While it was likely that he'd already made his most important contribution to the cause, he was happy to know that, if needed, he could make a few more.

***

As promised, Kan – Major Osella now – was back in the headquarters chamber. Colonel Jackson gave her a sour look, but she just raised an eyebrow at him, silently asking him whether *he'd* gotten any rest. The man grinned ruefully and shook his head. They had an understanding.

"So, what's up?" she asked.

"Seems like you are, despite orders to the contrary." He called her attention to a schematic of the planetary system. "From the data we picked out of your ship's recorders, we've narrowed down our unidentified friend's possible destinations. It's going to land on one of G6's moons – either the big one with the methane lakes or the smaller ball of water ice. We're guessing the big one because it's easier for a nanofactory to build things there. To get metals out of the ball of ice would mean mining for ages. There are only traces of anything heavy in that moon."

"So you're convinced that the intruder is an Uploader?"

"Yeah. Unless the others have completely changed the way they explore space, Uploaders are the best bet on a craft that small."

"If that's who they are, the size of the ship won't make much difference. We'll be up to our asses in avatars in a couple of weeks." She thought about it for a minute. "Do they know we're here?"

Jackson sighed. "We aren't really sure. We think they probably know we're somewhere in the area. I don't think they know where our colonies are – it's a bit hard to do any sensor readings from the other side of those black holes."

Kan could hear what her superior had left unsaid: now that they were here, the Uploaders wouldn't take all that long to pinpoint their location. Their tech had already been good enough to make short work of concealment such as Crystallia's the last time the two races had met, decades ago. There was no reason to assume that they'd lost any capability since then – and many reasons to believe that they'd extended their advantage appreciably. Uploaders weren't hamstrung by the need to avoid certain highly advanced machines. They embraced technology, and were in turn absorbed by it.

"What are we doing about it?"

"Right now? Not a hell of a lot. The meeting you walked into earlier was supposed to define our course of action in response to any number of scenarios." He shook his head in disgust.

"I take it it didn't work out that way."

"Of course not. The civilians, and even the retired officers on the council, are dragging their feet. They seem to think that, if we keep using passive surveillance, whatever is out there won't stop to try to find us, thereby giving us more time to plan an evacuation."

"That's not out of the question. After all, we can't be certain they're here because of us." Kan decided that, if she was going to be grounded, she might as well make herself useful. At the moment, that meant playing devil's advocate.

"How can you even say that? Why else would the Uploaders have sent a ship?"

She grinned. "Just pulling your chain, but we do need to be careful of assumptions that might not be justified. Who knows? Maybe the Uploaders decided to have a look at what this empty, mysterious sector actually holds. Maybe it's a research probe sent out before quantum drives were invented. Maybe it belongs to some poor race that no one's encountered yet. A sad group who, when they come and say their big hello to the galaxy are going to find it already occupied by a whole bunch of species hell-bent on wiping each other out." She thought for a moment. "There's no real harm in letting the kids you sent out make a report. A few days won't make all that much difference."

"We need to be getting ready to attack right away. If it's a nanofactory, we just might be able to blow it to pieces before it builds defenses."

"It's probably already too late for that. Besides, we can't launch until we know for certain where it landed."

The colonel shook his head. "We should have launched as soon as you made contact. With two fleets, one for each moon. That way, we'd have a lot more time to evacuate. There's no way the rest of them, whoever they are, could get here in less than six months – even quantum drives get distorted by the gravity around those black holes. That would have given us six months that we aren't going to get, now, thanks to these assholes."

Kan shrugged. He was right, but there was nothing she could do about it other than help him make the best of a bad situation. "So what do we do now?"

"We need a plan to defend the colony, as well as a plan to attack the enemy."

Repeating that they weren't even certain that an enemy existed would be pointless. She got down to business, counting on her fingers. "We know that the Recon mission won't send word back for at least a day. We also know that it will take us a week to get out to G6 and into position. By that time, the nanofactory will have copied itself a number of times, and the copies will have had time to build defenses. Depending on how much their tech has advanced, it's possible we'll run into a force that we just can't handle."

"So attacking them on the moon is a waste of time?" the colonel asked her.

"Maybe. Maybe not. It depends on what the evacuation plan is. What did the council decide about evacuating Crystallia?" Kan knew that, though the colony was very large, there was a fleet of ships buried under the living quarters, always kept at the ready by maintenance crews. Not everyone would be able to leave, but most of the colony could make a run for it.

Jackson snorted. "Nothing. What did you expect? They say they'll decide once we have a clearer picture, and, in the meantime, they don't want to create a panic."

"So they're not planning on telling the civilians?"

"They're not planning on anything. They seem to think that, if they just hope hard enough, the problem will turn out to be something trivial. They just don't want to deal with it."

"So what do we do?"

"All we can do is plan for the inevitable. They may be wrong, but they still have the last word."

As the ground officers trickled in, they began to lay down the groundwork, first generating the assumptions as to where the enemy would be located, and the strength of their force. Then they began to assign forces to each scenario. There would likely be changes to each, but it would be much quicker to modify existing plans and simulations than to start from scratch each time new information came in.

And time was of the essence.

***

Janine Espilon Al-Aama looked out over the surface of the G6's moon. The yellowish-orange surface of the methane seas told her absolutely nothing about what went on beneath. All they'd been told was that Recon Leader Osella had discovered an anomaly in the system that was presumably heading towards one of the large moons.

That was it. Other than a strict admonition to keep their mouths shut and not to speculate about what they were doing out here, neither she nor Everard had received any information. So, of course, they'd spent the entire trip out here trying to figure out what the object could be.

At first, Janine was adamant that it had to be an alien craft. Or maybe something, it was anyone's guess as to what, built by the Uploaders.

Everard had laughed. His reasoning was that if it were something that vital to the safety of the colony, they would have sent out a more experienced crew. They both knew something big was going on – they were able to recognize most general officers on sight, and there had been quite a few in that meeting room – but eventually concluded that the mission they were on was just a decoy, and that Kan Tau Osella would probably be doing the fancy flying to look into whatever serious threat faced them.

Then Everard had raised the possibility that they were being sent out as bait, just to see what would bite them. That hadn't helped Janine sleep all that well.

But by the second day, she'd forgotten her reservations. By then, Crystallia was difficult to spot with the naked eye, and she spent the hours looking into the empty depths of space. A huge dust cloud obscured the stars above the ecliptic, and the sheer sense of not having a large planet to anchor them was startling. Neither had ever been this far from the colony.

Upon reaching G6 three days later, she felt completely at peace with the vast, empty galaxy.

Then her sensors detected something under the surface of the methane seas, something she couldn't see, and began to chime insistently.

"Everard," she called back, "I think we've got something."

He rushed into the cockpit just as a recording activated. "Crew is instructed to make the following course correction." A series of numbers rolled across the readout. Neither Janine nor Everard were surprised that it instructed them to make a close pass at the moon. What was surprising was that the system had been preprogrammed to react to the sensor's findings. That kind of computer power was unheard of among the Crystallians – it came very close to Uploader tech.

"Wow. They're going all out for this one."

She just nodded. "Maybe we're not just bait after all."

"I guess that's what they want us to think. But remember that we weren't the only people at that meeting. One of Recon's best pilots was there too. I wouldn't be surprised if she was behind us, commanding a fleet and waiting to see what we stir up."

"Man, you're just a bundle of sunshine today, aren't you? I've already entered the course correction and my authorization. Punch in your code so we can get going."

They zeroed towards the surface, watching entranced as the tiny brownish ball in space got bigger and bigger, and Janine found herself looking at the surface of the moon. Liquid methane went peacefully on its way there, but the instruments told her that the innocent-looking surface was hiding a huge amount of activity. Energy readings were off the chart. If she hadn't been looking at a flat, peaceful sea, Janine would have bet that someone beneath the surface was setting off thermonuclear devices.

Suddenly, unexpectedly, the speakers boomed again. "Crew is instructed to send data collected to Crystallia. Tight-beam protocol. Standard encryption."

"That can't be right," Everard said. "We're never supposed to send any transmissions. Ever. That's basic ensign-level instruction."

Janine was already preparing the comm. "At least with a tight-beam, it's nearly impossible that anyone will overhear us." She looked his way. "I suppose you understand what this means? How important it must be for them to order us to break the single most important rule in the book?"

He swallowed and nodded. "We're right in the middle of something, aren't we? Something huge."

"Everard, I think they've finally found us."

CHAPTER 4

Wilde couldn't believe that his head could hurt so much. But then again, if someone had told him that he'd been up drinking all night and most of the following morning before taking a "power nap" until ten in the evening, he would have predicted dire results for that person. So he couldn't really complain.

He took a couple of analgesic tablets, and he wished he had something for the queasiness in his stomach. It was simply incredible that a race able to fly between stars didn't have among its technologies a simple cure-all hangover medicine. He wished he could just crawl under something and die.

Looking in the mirror to see if his face showed how he looked, he was unsurprised to find that, if anything, he looked even worse. His dusky skin was sallow and greenish, not the glowing olive color that he was so proud of, but a dull tone that called to mind the veins below the surface. Argh. He'd never realized just how bad he could look. No wonder Kan Hadn't called him when she got in.

Kan! That was why he'd been drinking the night before in the first place.

Ignoring his throbbing temples, he ran to his comm unit, to see if she'd left him any messages. Nothing. He pounded the desk with a fist and dropped dejectedly into his chair.

He'd heard the stories often. A perfectly decent civilian – solid, reliable, not given to flights of fancy – would begin a relationship with a pilot on the Recon Force (there were sad stories that involved members of the other forces, but Recon seemed to be the worst offenders, for some reason). Their love would grow and mature, soon becoming something important.

And the hammer would fall. The pilot would 'go out on a mission' and never call again, and often not even return calls. No reason would be given, and inquiries would show that the absent partner was in perfectly good health, just no longer interested in the relationship. As simple as that.

You heard about it, but you never thought it would happen to you. Until it did.

But why? What was it that made people in the military use civilians for a while and then discard them like used underwear? The most common explanation was that they were simply too immature and irresponsible to be trusted. Unlike most civilians, who could be counted on to act in a responsible, predictable way, the men and women of the Recon Force seemed to want nothing more than to zip around the planetary system pretending to be doing something important. They were anachronisms, from a time when humanity was a warlike race, and couldn't be trusted.

Wilde had thought, truly believed, that Kan was an exception. That she was a bit less egocentric, a little more human. He couldn't believe that she would let everything they had go, just on a whim, because she felt the call of the wild.

But, in the stories, they all thought that.

His sadness hardened, part of the inevitable cycle he was living. What made her think she had the right to treat him this way?

He'd been over this before, alternate bouts of self-pity, hope that she'd call and anger at the knowledge that she wouldn't. This time, he pulled the card that the stranger had given him out of his pocket. The man had made sense, but what he'd said was also taboo in the colony – there were some things that simply weren't said in a society in which over half the population was dedicated to planetary defense.

He was about to order his comm to connect to the code on the card. But he thought better of it and put the thin plastic sheet back in his pocket. There was probably a perfectly reasonable explanation for her absence.

***

Deep beneath the surface of a methane sea, a structure created out of woven strands of carbon sealed itself, becoming impregnable to the surrounding liquid. Mechanical pumps, also made of carbon, began flushing the liquid out of the habitat and into the surrounding ocean. Nitrogen was pumped in in its place.

When only traces of methane remained, tiny mouse-like robots separated themselves from the walls and spread along every surface, removing the last traces of the flammable liquid. Only when the cleansing was complete did the structure fill itself, expending some of its precious oxygen. Then the heaters came on, bringing the room to a temperature suitable for human life.

By this time, the nanofactory in the middle of the room had nearly completed a more complex construct, one of the most complicated in its database: a perfect reproduction of a male human body, grafted to a brain composed of ceramic superconductors. Moments after the temperature reached the human comfort zone, the body popped out. It looked to be about thirty years of age, thin but well-muscled with bronzed skin and dark hair.

A thick cable pulled by one of the mouse-like machines snaked towards the head and one end inserted itself with surgical precision into a socket at the base of the skull. The data transfer could easily have been achieved by electromagnetic transmission, but speed was of the essence, and transmitters, even the ones available to the species that had built the habitat, were never quite as quick as superconductive hard-wiring.

As soon as the cable was secure, the body on the floor began to twitch and shudder. The brain was being uploaded bit by bit, first automatic control functions, followed by motor control centers, memory. When everything else had tested correctly, and the body had stabilized, breathing normally, the consciousness was transferred.

Eyes popped open. The head moved to one side and then the other. The body sat up jerkily and looked back towards the machine that had produced it.

Another body popped out of the nanofactory onto the floor beside the sitting figure. This one was a female that looked about twenty-five years old, with proportions as perfect as that of the male. She had lighter skin, and lighter colored hair, and her features had a slightly Asian cast to them. The cable snaked towards her head.

The man waited for the test process to conclude. He showed obvious signs of impatience: first he drummed his fingers, then he stood and walked tentatively around the room, before finally sitting down with a frustrated look on his face and drumming his fingers again.

After two minutes, the woman's eyes opened.

"Finally," the man blurted. "I thought I would go into sensory deprivation shock. How do corporeal humans deal with the boredom?"

The woman looked towards him. "How long have I been inert?" she asked, alarm creeping into her voice.

"A hundred and twenty thousand cycles," the man replied. "Eternity."

"Oh," she replied, relief evident. "No problem, then. That's well within operating parameters. I thought you were all right with this."

He grinned sheepishly. "You're right, of course. It was just the shock of it, I guess. Don't worry about me – I'll be fine now."

"Good. Have the corporeals made any attempt to communicate with us?"

"I haven't checked."

She strode to the control interface, their only link to the cybernetic world of endless information they were accustomed to. She understood how he felt – the walk to the panel took nearly five thousand cycles, and the feeling of missing out on infinite information was deeply disturbing. No communications had been received, and corporeal activity was about what they'd predicted: a single probe and not much else. The nearest planet – a military base of some sort – was presumably being prepared for an attack, but sensors were unable to penetrate the surface deeply enough to understand what, precisely, the nature of the preparations were.

"Are you certain that this is the proper human clock speed?" the man asked her.

"Positive."

"Wow. How can they get anything done?"

"Slowly. But that's not the issue. We're here to talk to them, and we need to convince them to help. So, in answer to your next question: no, we can't speed up our own clocks, even a little. We need them to understand that we're human too, so we need to act like them."

"So what next?"

"We wait. If you want, you can pass the time picking out a human name. Mindnet coordinates probably won't get us too far with the corporeals." She smirked at him. "Plus, you're no longer in the mindnet."

He shuddered.

***

"We've pinpointed their location, and uploaded it onto the navigation systems in each immersion vehicle."

Murmurs greeted this announcement – no one enjoyed having to share such a tight space with the kind of electronics that could be used to run a positioning system – but no one raised a hand. The intelligence analyst who'd been tasked with giving the briefing nodded once and continued.

"Your insertion craft will be a modified troop carrier flown by Major Tau Osella." He nodded to Kan who was standing at the back of the briefing room. A large schematic appeared on the wall behind him, showing the relative positions of the planet, the moon, and the Crystallia fleet. "The main body of the fleet will come around the back side of the moon relative to the enemy and go into orbit around the moon in position to bomb the factory. A smaller force will land about a hundred kilometers inland, on this methane ice formation here."

He paused and the screen behind him showed an animation. As the fleet went around the back of the moon, a tiny yellow dot separated from the main body and began to orbit in the opposite direction. "Your carrier will attack from the opposite side. Using the moon as cover, Major Osella will drop to a height of thirty meters over the surface and go around the moon in the other direction. Once you reach the far shore of the liquid methane in which the enemy's facility is located, you will drop in. Hopefully, the distance to the objective, as well as the curvature of the surface, will keep you hidden, and the obvious attack from above will distract them long enough for you to take them out. Any questions?"

There wouldn't be, Kan knew. They'd been running this scenario in simulations since setting out from Crystallia, two days before. They knew it back to front.

To her surprise, a Marine at the front of the room – one of the regular headquarters guards, she saw – raised his hand. "Just one, sir. Could you tell us what kind of enemy we'll be dealing with? That seems to be the only thing no one wants to talk about.

The intelligence officer seemed to be about to respond – and he would have said no – when Kan spoke up. "We think they're Uploaders, Marine."

"Thank you, ma'am." His was steady, concerned but unafraid.

"All right, then," the officer in charge of the briefing said. "Your transport leaves in an hour, the submersibles will be deployed in three. I wish you the best of luck." He saluted them and left.

The Marines got up unhurriedly. The briefing had been scheduled so that they would be able to board the transport without rushing – but without giving them enough time to obsess about what they were about to do. They would have just enough time to grab their things and get into their vehicles.

Kan watched them file out, feeling like a mother hen despite the fact that many of the troops were much older than she was. Even though they had as much combat experience as she did – none whatsoever – she felt that her time had, at least, been spent on the front lines. She was also the only person on board who's actually seen the enemy with her own eyes. Many of the Marines met her gaze, some of them saluting as they passed, or mouthing, 'Ma'am.' The lieutenant in charge even stopped to shake her hand and thank her for volunteering to take them in.

Eventually, she stopped the Marine who'd asked about the enemy – the same guard she'd conversed with on guard duty the night after she'd discovered the enemy. "It's Greg, isn't it?"

The man saluted. "Yes, ma'am."

"Why was it so important to know who the enemy was? It won't make any difference in the preparation – we have no idea how any of the factions would fight this kind of battle. Hell, we don't even know if the enemies are still the same ones we left behind when we went into hiding."

"I know." He paused a few moments. "I just felt it was important somehow, to know who we were fighting."

Kan said nothing, but she thought she understood. If you were going to die, you might as well know what had killed you. She saluted. "Good luck, Marine."

"Thank you, ma'am." He walked off, straight, proud, and ready to die.

***

Greg wriggled, trying to get comfortable in the cramped quarters. The submersible was a tight fit, and his broad shoulders were wedged into the harness with no room to spare. But his arms were free to move and his head had an unobstructed view for three-hundred-and-sixty degrees – it protruded into the clear dome that made up the nose of the immersion craft.

At the moment, however, there wasn't much to see. As the vehicle's diagnostics ran, a few status reports were projected brightly onto the shaped diamond canopy, but the outside world was cut off completely by the sub's outer casing. The sheath that surrounded the immersion craft was made of carbon composites strong enough to withstand impact with the surface at nearly five hundred kilometers per hour. It was also shaped in such a way as to disperse most electromagnetic radiation and coated in energy-absorbent polymers in order to ensure that it reflected everything it couldn't absorb.

The casing was designed to split open right after impact, liberating the submersible, which would then take a pre-assigned path to the target. Each of the twenty vehicles would hug the ocean floor, taking advantage of the natural cover in an attempt to reach the objective undetected. Their lives, and the success of the mission, might depend on stealth, as they knew nearly nothing about the technology they would encounter.

Greg thought about that. In the course of his training, they'd watched all the Tri-D's of mankind's previous encounters with other races, of course. In theory, Crystallia's tech should be more than a match for anything the Brillans, the Blobs, or the Uploaders could throw their way. But those recordings were over a hundred years old. The enemy had presumably also been busy developing new tech – and they had the advantage of being in constant contact with each other, while humanity had been in hiding.

So stealth was probably the best bet, especially if they really were dealing with Uploaders. The mere thought made Greg shudder. While Blobs and Brillans were each terrifying in their own way – Blobs were adapted to nearly the same environments and used human planets after first wiping out the original inhabitants and Brillans used humans as slaves after suitable lobotomies – nothing was as frightening as the Uploaders.

Uploader society had, like humanity, originated on Earth. They were, in fact, technically human. But while regular humanity had conquered the stars, the first Uploaders had decided that human bodies were a cumbersome nuisance and simply done away with them. They'd scanned their minds and personalities onto colossal computer systems and created their own society, separate from the rest of mankind. In a matter of decades, Earth was one huge computer simulation.

Human colonies, led by the Tau Ceti system, had tried to retake the mother planet for humanity, but had been soundly beaten back. That had marked the end of humanity's glory. Running from the Uploaders, they'd encountered first the Blobs and then the Brillans. These two races had been at war with each other for centuries, and were millennia ahead of humanity technology-wise. A messy four-way war had ensued, with no winner, and only one clear loser: corporeal humans.

The Uploaders had been able to develop technology quickly enough that they were able to generate a stalemate against the aliens. And they easily conquered and uploaded any human colony they encountered.

That was one of the things that made them frightening. They wouldn't kill humans if they could avoid it. They uploaded *everyone* – prisoners, willing subjects, men, women, children. The only choice one had at their hands was death or an eternity in their nightmarish, unreal twilight existence.

The other terror-inducing aspect of Uploader culture was something that was not confirmed, but only a rumor. It was whispered among Marines that the post-humans in their cybernetic worlds could increase the speed at which their minds worked, making them capable of living several human lifetimes every year. This was supposed to be the reason they'd become invincible in battle: human decision processes working at supercomputer speeds. If this were true, no mere human would ever be able to resist them.

Greg felt his submersible shudder. Good. That meant that they'd come into position and the transport taking them to Sonic Major, the moon on which the enemy had established their foothold, had disengaged from the carrier. They were on their way.

A quick glance at the diagnostics flashing in front of him told him that all was well, and nothing needed his attention. In a way, he was disappointed – not only did this make him nothing more than a passenger, it also gave him even more time to think. According to the information on the screen, it was still two hours before launch.

This was the worst part of the trip. For all he knew, locked inside the cocoon, they might have been detected. Even now, the enemy could be taking defensive steps, launching everything they had at the single, lightly armored transport. He could be dead, a desiccated hunk of flash-frozen flesh floating in orbit for the rest of eternity, before he was even aware of what was going on.

But that was his job. He had no choice. None of the Marines had a choice. They'd signed up to be front-line combat troops with the implicit understanding that there was no such thing as an optional mission. Even suicide missions planned to gain the civilian population an hour or so of precious time – and there were a depressing number of these in the playbook – were compulsory. One did what one was told.

But the pilot, this Major Osella, was a volunteer. What would make someone willingly fly a sluggish troop carrier into the jaws of an Uploader bastion? She could easily have gotten a position flying an evacuation ship. But then again, that woman – not really much more than a girl – seemed to have liquid hydrogen running in her veins. Greg was sure she'd seen right through his tough guy act and realized just how scared he was. He should have kept his big mouth shut at the briefing.

The next couple of hours passed in much the same way. Bouts of self-recrimination interspersed with completely unnecessary checks to see if the harnesses were tight. Strangely enough, his fear had lessened after the first few minutes that the troop transport had disengaged from the carrier.

Before he knew it, his timer read ten seconds. Five. Suddenly, the submersible bucked hard and he was in free fall, and he braced instinctively. The quiet surprised him – he'd expected to hear a loud roar as the moon's atmosphere rushed by – but the surprise lasted only a second. He remembered that the satellite's atmosphere was extremely thin.

The clock on his head's up display was no longer showing the time to launch. It now displayed time to impact. *What a poor choice of words*, he thought. He focused on it as it neared zero and tensed for the splashdown.

A split second after the timer hit zero – long enough for him to wonder whether something had gone horribly wrong – the universe exploded around him. The vehicle suddenly seemed to *stop*, as if it had hit a brick wall. The harness strained and Greg felt one of the restraining belts pop, but it managed to hold him in place and keep him from slamming into the windshield.

Blood sprayed from his nose, obscuring his g-counter, which was probably just as well. Gravity took hold immediately and his vision narrowed and Greg had to fight to keep himself conscious.

After an eternity, the craft steadied. It was obvious that someone, somewhere, had seriously miscalculated. They couldn't have meant for the submersibles to hit that hard, could they? The outer shells finally fell away, and in the soft light filtering in from the surface, he could see that they were ragged, torn.

But, except for one big red square on his head's up display warning about the failure of a backup system, everything was green. The sub was good to go.

Greg powered the engines up, cautiously picking up speed. Each submersible was built to carry one man, and most of the rest of the craft consisted of weapons and engines. The vehicles were armed with a combination of energy weapons, such as long-distance laser burners and what they called contact weaponry: underwater rocket-powered missiles. Most of the projectiles had antimatter warheads but, considering the nature of the enemy, Greg thought he might try his luck with an EMP blast first, to soften up the defenses.

Likewise, the engines were extremely powerful. Each was a water-jet five meters long engineered for both speed and silence. When combined with the submersibles' slippery shape, the engines could drive the vehicle to a top speed of a hundred and fifty kilometers per hour in liquid methane. All of this power was under the command of Greg's right hand, while his left was free to select weapons options from the menus that were projected onto the clear canopy in front of him.

One thing he couldn't do was communicate with his teammates, even assuming anyone else had survived the unexpectedly violent immersion. Human science had yet to develop a mode of communication that was effective in liquids that couldn't be detected by enemy sensors so, if the mission was to remain undetected, radio silence was a must.

His instruments told him that he was still ten meters above the bottom: an unacceptably exposed position. He dove to a meter above the ocean floor and took his bearings. He was far enough from the surface that there was very little light making its way down. All he could see in the dim light that made its way out of the cockpit was a dark reddish sludge. A sudden wave of claustrophobia washed over him, a feeling that he was buried in mud.

Greg pushed it aside. He had a job to do.

His head's up display showed the topography of the sea floor in front of him, suggested a path through the dips and valleys. He followed the line as best he could, since the submersible didn't have an automated navigation system and watched as the objective came ever closer. He could feel the diamond canopy absorbing the heat from the cabin, although that was not really a problem – as long as the pile was running, he would have more heat than he needed.

The submersible inched towards the target. Had they managed to get in undetected? Or was he driving towards his death? There was nothing he could do about it anyhow. He could feel the moisture under his arms despite the cool temperature in the cabin.

A chime indicated that he was in missile range, making him jump. He quickly activated two projectiles – one antimatter missile and one EMP, and moved towards the surface, in order to get a clear shot over a ridge in front of him.

There! The head's up display indicated that there were no more obstacles.

But suddenly, alarms lit up all over his canopy, and the submersible began to creak ominously. The view out the front became even more clouded with some white mixing in the muddy red. It was very obvious that something was going on outside.

But what? He checked his readings for clues. The only thing moving was the temperature gauge, an animated thermometer, and that indicated that the sea outside was getting colder and colder. A blue line on the display marked the melting point of methane, and, as the simulated mercury moved beneath it, a loud groan came from the engine, followed by a sickening snap. This was followed only by silence and a large number of error messages.

As far as Greg could tell, the sea two meters to every side of his submersible had frozen solid. He checked and rechecked, but the message was still the same. He was locked in a cube of methane ice, unable to activate his weapons, and even if his engine hadn't suffered some catastrophic failure, he wouldn't be able to move.

Greg, the submersible, and the huge block of ice around it, sank slowly back to the ocean floor.

CHAPTER 5

Two figures appeared on the screen. If it wasn't for the fact that the transmission was clearly coming from the enemy position on the moon, Kan would have sworn that the image she was viewing was simply two humans – from Crystallia or one of the other hidden colonies. On the other hand, they were both naked, and they both seemed to be perfect specimens of human form – which indicated that they weren't what they seemed.

But the truth was more sinister. At the moment, the comm screen was the only system working on her ship. They were drifting in space, engines off, guidance systems disabled, weapons non-responsive. Even life-support was gone, but that was not immediately serious; the air would be fine for a few hours.

"Greetings, humans," the female of the pair said. "I am Mika Bina, and this is Rester Appins. We have come to you with a message from the Federation of Universal Purity."

Kan had no idea what the federation was. She thumbed her transmission button, but to no avail.

The woman went on. "This transmission is reaching the entire fleet sent to attack us, and we are not, at present, allowing you to transmit to us. We will permit this after we have finished telling you what we feel it is necessary for you to know. Please be patient."

Kan's stomach sank. They had managed to immobilize the entire fleet? It was obvious that Uploader tech had advanced to the point in which it was indistinguishable from magic, as the old saying went.

"We understand why you felt the need to launch a preemptive strike on our position. Relations between our civilizations have not exactly been cordial over the course of history. For this reason, we have made every effort not to harm any of the attacking troops. The only casualties thus far were submersible pilots who succumbed to the deceleration on impact. We regret these losses, but remind you that we had nothing whatsoever to do with them.

"The message we bring is a simple one. We have reevaluated the role that corporeal humanity must play in the future of the galaxy, and have decided that our previously stated goal of uploading every human being in the galaxy to form a part of the mindnet was misguided.

"We would like to offer humanity a truce. We will still allow any who wish to upload the chance to do so, of course, but it will no longer be mandatory. Corporeal humans will be welcome to share our planets and our resources, as well as benefit from the protection we can offer you against the Brillans and Krllt.

"We shall open a channel to the largest ship in the fleet in one standard hour, to hear your reply.

"Thank you."

Kan couldn't believe her eyes or her ears. The Uploaders had decided not to subsume them? How could that be?

"It's a trick," she heard one of the crew mutter under his breath.

She turned to look at him. "What would they gain from a trick like that? They can just keep us immobilized here and upload us at their pleasure."

He returned her gaze, unflinching. "I don't know what they hope to gain. But trust me. These sick computer people need something from us, and when they get it, we're as good as uploaded."

Kan said nothing. She wasn't going to get into an argument with a subordinate. And besides, there was every possibility the man was right. Even if the Uploaders were telling the truth, there was certainly something else going on, and she sat down to wait until she found out what it was. She tried to use body language to convey her preference for silence, but her crew was having none of it, and she didn't feel that in their situation – adrift and at the mercy of the Uploaders – she could order them to sit in silence and contemplate their future. The hour passed with the speculation getting wilder by the minute. By the time the Uploaders reappeared on her screen, Kan was ready to accept any treaty whatsoever just to make her crew shut up.

Not that it was her decision, of course.

To her relief, her bridge crew fell silent immediately when the first signs of a transmission appeared on the screen. The two Uploaders stood, as far as she could tell, precisely in the same positions as they had occupied previously. "Do you have a reply?" the woman, Mika Bina, asked without preamble.

"Er … we have some questions." Despite the unaccustomed hesitation and notes of panic, Kan immediately recognized the voice as belonging to the Recon Force general in charge of the fleet.

The woman's image nodded once, a curt, efficient gesture.

"In the first place, we don't really have the power to negotiate a truce for the whole system, and much less for the other colonies. All we can really promise at this time is that we won't attempt to attack you if you return power to our systems."

The woman seemed to take a long time to digest this information. The man beside her was about to speak, but she raised a hand. "That seems reasonable," she said.

"Oh. Well, as commanding officer of this fleet, I pledge that if you allow us to regroup, we will not take any action whatsoever against your position." Despite the relief in his voice, even Kan knew that the Uploaders had already shown that they had nothing to fear from the human fleet in orbit around the moon.

The woman looked back impassively. When she spoke, it wasn't the answer they were awaiting. "You said you had questions for us?"

"Yes." The general hesitated again. "I would like to know what guarantees you can give us that you will not attack the system when we are stood down."

She didn't even blink. "None whatsoever. But the fact that you're still alive should be enough for now." The man beside her pushed some buttons on a console that was not in the camera's view. An expression that looked like extreme distaste crossed his features, but he nodded to the woman. "Your ships are now free to move. I am sending you the coordinates of your incursion troops. I'm afraid less than half of them survived the drop, and only four remain conscious. We will contact you again to discuss a meeting with your leaders."

***

Wilde looked over the table at the other man. He couldn't believe what he was hearing. All this time, the possibility of rebellion, of turning the tables had been just around the corner. As he went about his life, anguished by the fact that Crystallian society offered him no chance to do anything meaningful, he'd never suspected that it was possible to create a new order in the colony.

But the blond guy sitting across the table from him assured him that not only was it possible, but that there was a whole organization which dedicated itself to achieving that very goal. To say that Wilde was shocked at the news would have been quite the understatement.

The moment when Wilde caved and called the blond man had been when one of his friends in Recon had informed him that Kan had shipped off again. At that moment, it became obvious that she had no interest in ever seeing him again. He'd been ready to do anything to get back at her, but was completely powerless to do so.

The card, as always, had been in his thoughts. The man who'd given it to him seemed to feel confident that he would understand Wilde's problems, could help him. It hadn't felt like a pickup attempt –

just another guy who felt that it was unfair to treat the general public this way.

But there was also a touch of the sinister in it. Why was there no name on the card, just a comm code? Why use a card in the first place? They were unwieldy and inefficient – it was much easier just to sync comms.

But in the end, raging against Kan and everything she represented, he'd connected to the code on the card, not really sure what he would say, but certain that there was no way he could feel worse than he already did.

A man's voice had answered after fifteen seconds, just when he'd been about to disconnect – it was really unusual for a call to take so long to get through. Wilde had no way of knowing whether it was the same man he's spoken to before, and the video privacy option was on, so he couldn't see the person on the other side. It was a sign of his anger that Wilde didn't disconnect directly at this further sign of secrecy.

"Yes, hello. This is Wilde Tau Bennet. We met at Hillman's the other night, and you asked me to call you."

The voice on the other end seemed to brighten, gaining enthusiasm. It was hard to tell, since there more static than Wilde had ever experienced on the Crystallia comm net. "Oh, yes. Mr. Tau Bennet, how nice to hear from you. I was beginning to believe that your Recon pilot had called you after all, and that things were back to normal!"

"Not by a long shot. They tell me she shipped out again a couple of days ago, and no one seems to know just when she'll be back."

"Ah. We know just how you feel. So typical. These Recon people sometimes forget that the people they're always working so hard to protect have feelings beyond the simple wish to survive."

"Exactly. They act as if the only important thing is security."

"I can tell that you're unhappy with her right now."

"Furious."

"We might be able to help you deal with that." The man on the other end of the communication paused. "Would you be able to get together with me this afternoon?"

Wilde hesitated, but then remembered how Kan had promised she'd call. "Sure," he said. "When and where?"

The Hanbar, it must be admitted, was a dive. It wasn't the cleanest place he'd ever seen, and it was nearly empty. Both of these things were unusual for an establishment in Crystallia, and probably had to do more with the location of the bar in the lower levels, near the evacuation fleet hangars, than anything else – after all, there was no crime to speak of in the colony. Other than that, the place was perfectly ordinary.

Fluorescent panels gave a bright white glare and shiny plastic tables and countertops reflected the same light back into Wilde's eyes.

On one wall, a strip of Newscast monitors blinked silently from one celebrity story to the next.

The blond man from the previous night was already there when Wilde arrived, and was easy to recognize despite the fact that Wilde had only seen him a few minutes, and that he'd been drunk at the time. The man, despite being tall and robust, seemed somehow delicate. His features were thin and pointed, blue veins clearly visible under extremely pallid skin. Even his hair, though short, seemed too thin. It fell lifelessly to the sides of his head. Watery blue eyes followed Wilde's entrance, and then lingered on the entrance, as if waiting to see whether anyone followed him in.

On reaching the table, Wilde stood beside it. The man looked away from the door and smiled. "Glad you could make it." He held out a hand, and they shook.

The man's skin was soft and cool, but Wilde hardly noticed. There was something about his voice – it seemed not to be the voice that had come over the phone. But with the amount of static on the line, there was no way to be certain. And besides, this was definitely the same man who'd handed him the card, and he was where the voice on the comm had said he'd be. Wilde decided that he was being paranoid.

"Yeah. Sorry I'm late. I'd never been this deep before, and made a couple of wrong turns."

"Don't worry about it. Happens all the time. Have a seat. Stimcaff?"

Wilde nodded, biting back the urge to ask why the other man had chosen such an out-of-the-way location. "Double, no sucral."

The bar's proprietor took their order. Wilde noticed that she memorized their requests as opposed to using a commpad.

"I'm Jev Rigel Hammel, by the way."

"Wilde Tau Bennet."

"Well, Mr. Bennet, I assume your relationship with the girl you were talking about the other night hasn't gotten any better."

Wilde suddenly realized that he desperately needed someone to talk to. His friends simply shrugged and said 'that's life' and 'if you can't take rejection, you shouldn't have gone out with a Recon Leader. You know what they're like.' Most of them made him feel as though he was being a big baby over nothing.

Wilde himself, when the relationship with Kan was taking its first steps, had known what he was getting into. But now, despite that knowledge, he couldn't shake the fact that it was completely unfair. He simply didn't see why the holier-than-thou military could be allowed to behave this way with no censure. He was tired of being a second-class citizen.

Without truly meaning to, he found himself telling Jev everything that had happened. He knew the other man had probably heard most of it already, as he's been told that he'd been quite repetitive at the bar. But Wilde didn't care. The story came out in a rushed tangle, something that even the most sympathetic listener would have had trouble with.

But the blond man seemed to follow it without problems. The expression on his face open and welcoming, seemed to ask for more. Wilde finished by repeating the fact that Kan had gone off again – God only knew how long she'd be absent this time – without bothering to tell him a thing.

The man simply oozed sympathy. Sadness filled his gaze and he shook his head. "I know just what they're like. Almost exactly the same thing happened to me, except that she was a Marine. One day she told me she was going on a training exercise and that was the last I heard from her. Eventually, I commed her, just to see if she was all right. She told me she was fine, and I got angry that she'd blown me off. She just looked at me over the video feed and said: 'I've got more important things to worry about than your melodramatic whining.' Then she shook her head and said, 'civilians,' and hung up. After that, she refused my calls."

Wilde ground his teeth. "It's almost as if they feel that they're better than us, somehow."

The other man laughed. "They feel that they're better than us in every way possible," he replied. "They think that, since the reason for Crystallia's founding was to serve as a bastion and lookout post for the colonies further in, the rest of us are just dead weight."

"But that's ridiculous. Their job is to protect us. That should make us valuable in their eyes."

"It does, but only as genetic material from which the human race might, one day, be restored to its former glory. We have no value to them as individuals."

It was immediately apparent to Wilde that Jev spoke the truth. "I wish we could do something to make them treat us in a decent way. I mean it makes me sick just thinking about it."

Jev gave him a stern look, as if weighing Wilde, trying to ascertain if he was worthy of what the other man was about to confide in him. "There may be a way."

Wilde said nothing, waiting for the other man to go on. No matter what Kan believed, he was smart enough to know that a meeting this far off the beaten path, and the fact that his feelings on the subject had been sounded out so thoroughly before this main point was broached, meant that it was probably something that would be frowned upon by the authorities. *Well, screw them*, Wilde thought. *What have they done for me?*

Besides, the thought of moving beyond the accepted boundaries was a bit exciting, and one of the consequences of the paternalistic character of the Crystallia society was to make anything that moved away from the daily routine of life seem highly attractive.

"There are a few of us, no more than six or seven, looking to resurrect the kind of society you can read about in the books. Where each person was respected and allowed to choose his or her own path, learn from their own mistakes. It was a free society."

Wilde held up a finger. "We weren't on the brink of extinction back then."

Jev nodded. "And we are now?" He gestured with his hands, indicating the world around them. "Do you see any marauding Blobs terrorizing the colony? Any Uploaders whisking people off into their virtual universe, leaving only the empty shells of their former bodies behind?" He stopped, waiting for an answer.

"No, but ..."

"Of course not! They tell us that we're hidden away in the cluster of black holes at the galaxy's center, in a habitable corridor found completely by accident, far from the known zones of influence of any of the races we're fighting against, and that we shouldn't worry and we should just go about our lives. Then they turn around and say that the way society is structured is done to protect us, to minimize our risk." Jev raised his voice. "When should we believe them? When they tell us we're perfectly safe or when they tell us we need to be nice little sheep because we're in grave danger?"

Wilde chuckled. "When you put it that way, it does sound a bit problematical."

"Problematical. At the very least. I believe they've been lying to us all this time. Are we even sure that such things as Brillans exist? Or Uploaders? No one alive today has ever seen one. Even our oldest citizens were born on the colony ships. How do we know that the whole galactic war isn't just a story to make sure we'll do what they ask us to?"

"We don't, but wouldn't it be a bit monstrous for them to make this up. Don't you think that someone, somewhere would slip up and let the story out? A secret known to everyone in the military isn't much of a secret."

"Maybe they don't know. Maybe the people put on the colony ships in the first place were given false information. Maybe the circle of people who actually know the secret is just a handful, end the rest, the poor earnest, clueless blighters are just doing their best to keep us all safe."

"Well … a galactic war always seemed a bit strange. The galaxy is enormous. Why couldn't we just share it?"

Jev nodded. "Exactly. We don't really know if it ever took place. We only know what the military has told us which might be a lie, or it might be just part of the truth. Maybe humanity won the war, but our grandparents, for whatever reason, decided to leave human society. Even if what we know is completely correct, there's no getting around the fact that we've had absolutely no contact with the galaxy outside our little haven for the past seventy-five years. The war could be over. Maybe the races annihilated each other or weakened themselves enough that we could go out and take the whole galaxy without losing a single human life. We just don't know."

"So what are we trying to do about it? Are we going to petition the Elders to ask the generals for more information?"

Jev laughed. "Don't be ridiculous. They'd pretend ignorance and feed us exactly the same history chips we've seen so far. The only way to make certain that the information will be available to us is if we establish a civilian government."

Wilde was shocked. "They'd never let anything like that get under way. As soon as you brought it up, they'd lock you up."

"We're well aware of the consequences of what we propose, but no revolution of the people has ever been won without risk. That says a great many sad things about human nature, but it is true." The blond man gave him a steady gaze and Wilde felt like a child in school, learning things that he'd never believed possible. "We don't want to rule. We have no interest in doing so. All we want is to stop being second-class citizens. But in order to do that, we need to know the truth. And as I've said, the only way we will ever know the truth is if the citizenry takes power. I'll admit that most of us don't like it, but we haven't been able to find any other way to make it work."

A long silence ensued as Wilde thought about what he'd heard. It wasn't hard to see where the conversation was going – he seemed to have passed the initial test and was being entrusted with information that could get people into serious difficulties with the government, even though he was certain that what he knew barely scratched the surface.

The question was what he would do about it. Like most of the citizens of Crystallia, Wilde had never been in a position in which he'd had to take action, decide whether he would go along with things or whether he would rebel. Until now, he'd played by the rules, lived a comfortable, stress-free life. He hadn't seriously considered the world an unfair place. Sure, he'd done his share of griping about the way the flyboys strutted and the Marines walked off with whatever girl they wanted to, but it was just something he did to be accepted. Everyone else certainly did it too. And none of them meant anything by it either.

Back then, however, he hadn't been affected personally.

"What do you want from me?" he said.

"In the first place, we need to be sure we can trust you not to tell anyone about us." Jev smiled. "As you can imagine, the government would never allow us free rein if they suspected our existence."

"Of course," Wilde said.

"Good. Other than that, there isn't much to it. We hold periodic meetings to try to figure out how to make this work without creating too much turmoil, and ensuring that everyone has the same rights. We'd hate to generate a change for the worse. We might ask you to carry messages every once in a while – as you can imagine, there are some things that we simply can't broadcast over the comm system."

"Of course."

"So, as soon as I know the date of the next meeting, I'll give you a call."

"Great." Wilde stood.

Jev gave him a sheepish look. "And sorry for making you come all the way down here. But you know how it is."

Wilde chuckled and left.

***

As he watched Wilde's back receding down the corridor, the man who called himself Jev weighed and measured. He weighed what he'd heard, how the man had acted, how he'd responded. He measured the earnestness in the other's eyes, the pain he'd suffered at the hands of Miss Tau Osella.

And in the end, he decided that the conversation had been a couple of hours well spent. Perhaps this one wasn't quite ready to join the front lines yet, but could be taken along slowly. The government wasn't the only entity that knew how to use information for its own purposes.

The thought made him smile. Recruiting people such as this would be impossible if the government admitted it was suffering an insurrection. Popular support might shrivel if the citizens knew that the fire in the lab had been an attack.

Thanks to government censorship, no one attached any significance to the words *Peace Crystallica*.

But they would. The sooner, the better.

CHAPTER 6

The two sides looked silently across the table at each other. On one side, two naked humans, one male and one female, waited impassively for the numerous members of the uniformed Crystallia delegation to get themselves organized.

The meeting room wasn't much. Bare walls made of some intricate carbon weave, and a table seemingly of the same material. But it was amazing that the Uploader tech had managed to create it in such a short span of time, considering the fact that they'd brought no building materials along.

Kan hadn't been formally invited to the meeting, but her ship was the only one truly suitable for shuttling to the surface of the moon, and for recovering the three or four subs still intact, as well as the numerous bodies for interment on Crystallia. Since her expertise wasn't strictly needed for something as simple as a salvage operation, she'd delegated the task to a subordinate and popped in to be present at what promised to be a pivotal moment in human history.

Humans and Uploaders, sitting at a negotiating table for the first time in over a century. And she was there.

The consensus that the Crystallia delegation had reached on the shuttle was that the Uploaders wanted something from the pure humans. They had no inkling as to what, but had been allowed to make calls to their superiors on the colony in order to ascertain how to proceed. They'd been instructed to take a hard line, making no unwarranted concessions, and taking advantage of the Uploaders condition as supplicants.

Kan thought it was completely ridiculous. The two perfect examples of humanity sitting in front of them showed no signs of nervousness. It seemed that they were perfectly confident in the feeling that they could take anything they truly wanted, and were only asking nicely out of politeness.

Eventually, the assorted members of the Crystallian military managed to sort out the rank and precedence and find their seats, with the admiral squarely in the center. Kan went mostly unnoticed off to one side. Despite the display of technical superiority, the old man seemed firmly in control. His gaze didn't waver as he surveyed the two Uploaders.

"Well, we're here," he said gruffly. It was obvious he wasn't happy to be here and would have preferred to fight to the last man, even if the Uploaders had massacred them. But it hadn't been his decision. "Let's hear it."

The woman across the table smiled indulgently. "We're here to offer an alliance."

Incredulous murmurs greeted this proclamation. The admiral struck the table with a fist, clenched so tightly that the skin was paper-white. "If you want to subsume us, I'm afraid you'll have to take us one by one. From what I've seen of your technology, you won't have too much trouble, but at least you'll have to expend time and resources in rooting us out, allowing others to escape. You can't catch us all."

She gave a tinkling laugh. "We *can* catch you all, if necessary. But that's not the reason we're here. No one will be subsumed against their will. What we are offering is an alliance of equals, against a common enemy."

"We have no enemies. We are a peaceful people."

"You are human. Humanity is not a peaceful race," she interjected. "Even the way your society is structured proves it in no uncertain terms."

"Why do you say that?"

"You claim that your highest priority is to avoid conflict, escaping from enemies instead of confronting them. This is logical, since the enemies you are aware of are more powerful than you. And yet, when one of these enemies approaches, your first reaction is to mount an attack."

"The attack was meant to buy time. If we could have knocked out the expeditionary force, we would have time to evacuate the colony before the rest of your people returned."

Kan noted that the admiral made no mention of the other colonies in the sector, but thought that it was probably an unnecessary precaution. The Uploaders weren't here by accident. They'd come looking for something specific, and prepared to defend themselves in a non-lethal way. She was willing to bet that they were well aware of the exact location of every single person in the area, including the supposedly hidden cloud colonies.

"Be that as it may," the Uploader countered, "the way your society is structured is not optimized for flight and hiding. Nearly half of your people are in the defense forces, and very few of them are employed in researching stardrive or cloaking technology. The rest of the population is breeding stock. On the face of it, is seems like your civilization is geared more towards fighting than escape." A pause ensued as the two delegations digested this. "We would like to offer you the opportunity of joining the fight and to regain everything you've lost. No more running."

The admiral snorted. "Why would you give us any of that? You've shown us how effective our weapons are compared to the technology at your disposal. What possible use could we be against your enemies?"

"We don't need you to fight our enemies. We have robotic fleets that can do so for us with no loss of life. We have energy shields that make it impossible for anyone to approach our planets. We are not looking for technology, and we most certainly don't need more troops. We can create all the troops we need, both organic," she looked down at her very human body, "and inorganic."

"Then what do you need us for?"

"To break a balance. History is Rester's specialty. I will let him go on."

The man nodded his thanks. Unlike Mika, he seemed nervous, not quite sure of himself. He had a habit of pausing and cocking his head to one side, as if waiting for something, in the middle of his sentences. "I assume you are aware of the salient facts of the war prior to humanity's self-imposed exile."

Kan saw the admiral's gaze sharpen at the words 'self-imposed,' but the man simply nodded.

"Good." Long pause. Sudden jerky start, as if remembering where he was. "Then I'll tell you what happened next."

"Please do. The tension is killing me."

"Well, it's quite simple. Humanity emerged victorious from the war in which you were involved."

The admiral was so stunned by this that he couldn't even manage to get a word out. But someone on the table blurted "what?" bringing him back to his senses.

"How did we manage that little trick?" the admiral said. "Did a new swarm of previously undiscovered human colonies come to the rescue and beat everyone else back. I didn't think there were enough of us left outside this enclave to form a viable society, much less mount an effective counterattack."

Rester held up his hands. "I'm afraid you misunderstand me. When I speak of humanity, I am referring to the wider sense of the term, including both corporeal and digitalized humans." He paused again, as if waiting for permission to go on. What he saw across the table didn't seem encouraging, but he hunched his shoulders and went on. "Essentially, we had a pair of large advantages. The first was that both the Brillans and the Blobs thought we were infrastructure and ignored many of our key installations at first. As purely physical beings, they believed that the only part of humanity worth attacking was that which either contained living corporeal humans or that which directly served as support to the corporeal presence. I imagine you are all well aware of this."

The admiral nodded brusquely.

"What may not be immediately apparent is that in ignoring us at the outset of their campaign, both species committed a huge strategic mistake. Their ignorance gave us time, the one thing we can use more effectively than any other civilization in the galaxy. That time allowed us to put all our resources into designing and perfecting new weapons systems. Remember that we can copy all of our best minds as many times as we wish, and run them at millions of times the speed at which organic human brains function."

Kan shuddered at this. How would it feel to have every second last an eternity? Especially for immortal beings, who would have unlimited numbers of those seconds.

"By the time the invaders understood what was really going on in human space, it was too late. Though they'd completely destroyed the civilization of corporeal humans, we'd used that time to advance our tech to the point in which we could fight them to a standstill. A few standard months later, we were able to push them back. Before long, it was a rout. Every single system that had once belonged to either race is now under our control, and has been for over fifty years."

"What? How can this be?"

"You can't imagine what our propulsion systems and gravitic technology are capable of doing."

"And why have you just come for us now?"

The Uploader sighed, a surprisingly human gesture. "We haven't come for you. We could have overrun your six little colonies any time we wanted. Our policy has changed – our intention was to let you go your own way, in peace."

Kan's stomach sank. How could these monsters know how many colonies there were? The discovery of the Crystallia base was unsurprising – it was exposed, its position nearest the access. But the rest? They were well inside the small pocket of habitable space, surrounded by black holes and the kill zone from neutron star emissions. Impossible to find.

Or so they'd thought.

Rester Appins went on. "We are only here because we think you can help us. There has been a problem."

"What kind of problem?"

"I guess you could refer to it as a schism."

"What, did you chipheads suddenly get religion?"

Appins smiled indulgently. "No. We still believe that the only way to attain immortality is if we build it ourselves. The schism I'm referring to is a bit more of a philosophical difference – one that threatens to tear our whole society apart at the root, though."

The admiral didn't look as if this bit of news was particularly distressing to him. "Do tell," he said. But Kan could see he was getting drawn into the discussion. His growls had lessened in volume and intensity, his eyes had narrowed. He seemed to be thinking about the endless possibilities that would come open to the Crystallians if it was true that the Uploaders weren't here just to assimilate them.

"It began almost immediately after we finally managed to get the Brillans under control," the Uploader began. "At that point, it was evident to everyone on the mindnet that the war was essentially over. The Blobs had never been much of a force in the first place, they just had the advantage that the only faction that had bothered to go against them head-on were corporeal humans, who were at a technological disadvantage."

Heads nodded around the table. According to the history lessons that every member of the military was forced to memorize, the Blobs had overrun human planets like a tidal wave of unstoppable, magic-like machines. The defenders of the time had fought valiantly, inflicting some losses on the aliens, but it had been no use. The current state of Crystallian technology owed much to the study of surviving data from those battles. If the Blobs had come on that day, with the same tech, they would be effortlessly beaten back.

Appins went on. "Once that conclusion was reached, the discussions began regarding what we should do with the conquered races. Three schools of thought formed and were endlessly discussed. The first, the Isolationists, were convinced that our uploaded society was fine the way it was. Now that we'd eliminated the threat, we just needed to set automated watchdogs on the conquered races to ensure that they wouldn't bother us again."

"And how would you do that? From what I've seen, all three of the races, even the few humans that were left, would have tried to shake off any outside rulers." The admiral had lost all pretense of belligerence. He was completely absorbed by the story, the thought of the fearsome Blobs being brushed aside seemed to have cheered him immensely. Kan could sympathize – one of the bogeymen of her youth, swept away, a mere powerless footnote.

"Basically, we would set high-tech, self-maintaining robots in orbit above their planets, allowing them to grow and prosper, but not to attempt extra-atmospheric flight. That way, they would be happy on their planets, and we could forget all about them."

"Seems a bit cold."

"The idea was that everyone could live unmolested, but the same objection came up in our discussions. And the second current was, from that point of view, even worse. They argued that the mindnet society which you call 'Uploaders' had won the war, and to the victors should go the spoils. We'd been distracted by an aggression we had nothing to do with and forced to leave our lives of contemplation and pure social interaction to design weaponry, and now we should be allowed to use the conquered aggressors for our own amusement, or whatever else we saw fit. This current was called the Mastery Thought Element."

"I'm hoping they didn't win your little argument."

The woman's eyes flashed and she interrupted before Appins could respond. "If they'd won, the first you'd have heard about it was a voice over your Crystallia public address system announcing that you were now a part of the MTE empire. You would not have had a chance to meet us, nor would you have had any hopes of mounting a defense. And it wasn't *little* argument or a little anything. It took us nearly fifty standard years to stamp out this way of thinking – that's hundreds of thousands of years of regular human thought processes. Even so, they were able to steal some mainframes, mount them on a ship, and head off for parts unknown. We fought what seemed like an eternal war in order to protect you from our own brethren. We had no obligation to do this."

Kan blurted her question before she had time to think. "But how could you fight a war? Isn't your entire society based inside a big computer?"

"There are many ways. Much more than just a physical war. We can propagate copies of people who think like we do. Expand viruses that destroy habitations and mindspaces, even personalities. Set logic shunts that trap people into endless mind loops. The weapons are horrible and numerous, and we all used them without quarter."

Appins broke in again. "But as Mika said before, the Mastery Element is no longer among us. But there is still another faction that came up during those days. They call themselves Integrators, and their doctrine was a mixture of what we originally practiced with humanity, that is to say forced conversion, and the Mastery element. What they want is to upload all sentients, whether human or alien, into the mindnet, with that of the Mastery Element – anyone who resisted would be allowed to live, but with the uploaded versions serving as overlords.

We had to split off portions of the mindnet to minimize damage – as I mentioned, this civil war has been going on for the past fifty years."

Silence ruled the table. The Crystallia delegation fidgeted as they thought about what they'd been told. Something just didn't make any sense to Kan, but one of the admiral's aides put his finger on the misgivings first.

"But that leaves two factions, one of them who wants to ignore all corporeal life, and the other who wants to upload or dominate it. The fact that you're here means you probably aren't part of the first faction, and you've already said that if you were part of a faction that wanted to invade, you'd have done so without any trouble."

Rester Appins smiled sadly. "A lot can change in a hundred thousand years, even if that is just subjective time – perhaps especially if it's subjective time. The group we represent was originally the Isolationist faction, but over the past few subjective centuries, we've had time to think things through." His smile became even sadder, making Kan wonder whether the actual state of living inside an uploaded world might not be as perfect as the Uploaders had always said it was.

"About a thousand subjective years ago, we realized that the current artistic trend, neo-cadimism, had been relevant for an inordinately long time. A study of this trend showed that each successive movement had lasted a little longer than the one before, and we initially concluded that we were maturing as a society, and therefore our art was finally adapted nearly fully to our tastes."

Out of the corner of her eye, Kan saw the admiral twitching. This sudden change in the direction of the discussion had caught him off guard. She could almost hear him wondering whether the Uploaders had come all this way to lecture them about art. And, more to the point, what to say about it if they had.

"At about the same time, we realized that the speed of development of our systems, meaning the time it took for us to double the processing speed inside our mainframes was getting longer. It had been getting longer for some time. Do you understand the significance of this?"

"Not really," the admiral replied.

"Processor speed had been doubling at steadily shorter intervals almost since the invention of the very first computers, a trend that went on uninterrupted until relatively recently. It would seem to run into a brick wall from time to time, but then someone would pull a new technology out of the lab and bring development back on track. That's how we developed optical switches, quantum processors, and the current gravitic mindnet. But now, we were slowing down."

"Maybe you'd reached the limit of what the laws of physics allow," an aide on the far side of the table ventured.

"Perhaps. As a matter of fact, that was what the people on the research teams assumed. Except that it wasn't the first time we'd reached a theoretical stumbling block, but it was the first time it hadn't been conquered by lateral thinking.

"Either of these data points by itself would not have been cause for concern. But taken together, they seemed to point to some kind of stagnation, something that had been going on for years without anyone recognizing it. We began to look at every aspect of our lives, and for a while, you couldn't access a newsfeed on any of the channels without having a line chart pop up at you. It might have been describing the production of new literary works, or the discovery of new planets orbiting distant galaxies, but the image was always the same: initially, there was strong growth, then less so, and finally either a long plateau or even the beginnings of a drop-off.

"Simply stated, our society was in decline."

Appins looked around the table to gauge whether his audience had understood what he was saying. A bead of sweat ran down his perfect features.

Kan had only one question, one which an instant later was replicated by the admiral. "How can a society with no economic factors and no territory go into a decline? Are you getting poorer? Smaller? You're the same as you've always been. Just a bunch of brains copied into a big computer, pretending to be alive."

"We *are* alive," Mika responded. Whatever program had created their bodies had obviously given her a double dose of emotionality. Her cheeks were crimson and her brow furrowed as she bristled at the open insult.

"That's open to debate," the admiral replied evenly. "But it won't help us answer the question. How can you go into a decline? You seem to be the same people, save for however many went off in the splinter factions, living in the same place. Only the fact that your time runs faster now than it did then makes you any different from the people who originally decided to leave the physical world behind. To us, you've been flat since you began."

Appins seemed unperturbed. Maybe he had an electronic brain, while Mika had gotten a human one. "It might not be measurable in purely physical terms – although our scientific achievements seemed pretty effective against your vessels earlier – but our society has advanced well beyond where we started off from. Over the millennia, we have achieved a great many things, not only in the research world, but in our art, literature, and philosophy. We were infants when we entered the mindnet, now we are adults."

"Or maybe you're getting into your dotage."

"That might have been true if we hadn't realized what was wrong in time. Perhaps more and more of us would have found ways to disconnect from the mainframes, to die, as it were. But when we realized what happened, we shook off our lethargy and decided to take action. That is why we're here."

"I really can't say I understand."

"We want you to help us regain our will to expand, to conquer new territories, both physical and mental. We need you to teach us what it means to be human. We seem to have forgotten."

The admiral nodded. He didn't look happy, and Kan couldn't blame him. He'd been trained to fight, he'd been taught to run when fighting wasn't an option. There was nothing in his instruction or makeup that qualified him to respond to something like this.

"That's all you want? You want us to teach you? That sounds logical. After all, you're a race which has spent the past two hundred thousand years or so of your time reaching the limits of science, art, and philosophy, while we are a group of refugees cowering in the deepest darkest corner of the galaxy. Is that all you need?"

Appins didn't even blink. "No. We also need your help defeating the Integrators. You see, we're at war again. A physical war, not a war on the information pathways."

Mika spoke up, her earlier anger gone, replaced by a fearful expression. "They've integrated the aliens into their society, even melding the individual minds. We can't understand them anymore. We can't communicate with them either on an individual basis or on a government-wide scale. We think the alien logic uploads somehow created an imbalance in the system, sending the whole thing into psychosis. We can't be sure, maybe we're the crazy ones and they've seen the light." She stared straight into the admiral's eyes. "But one thing is certain: they aren't human anymore."

"It doesn't seem like our problem."

"Yes. It is. If they defeat us, they'll come after you. They haven't done so yet because they don't consider you a threat, but they will." She paused, took a deep breath. "And right now, they're winning."

CHAPTER 7

Trienne Luyten Angelique opened her eyes slowly. The bright light in the room around her seemed to be burning deep into her brain, painfully. She tried to put a hand up to deflect the glare, but her arm was firmly pushed down by some unseen person.

"You shouldn't be moving yet, try to relax."

She felt panic rise. Who was this person in her … room? Where was she? She remembered sadness and then nothing but the pain. "What…?"

"Shh. Hush now. You're in the hospital. Please try to calm down or I'll have to sedate you. You've been in a coma for six days. It's natural that you might be a little disoriented."

The voice was gentle, soothing. After hearing it for a while, she wanted to give in, was actually trying to relax as much as she could. But there were still so many questions she wanted to ask.

"What happened?" she finally said. Her voice sounded weak, cracked, hoarse. All her efforts at trying to keep calm immediately went out the window.

"You were shot," the voice said. A woman's voice. "Don't you remember?"

Trienne did remember, but the images were confused, unclear. She remembered the lab, and being very sad, and then coming out into the light, and then people rushing around her, someone holding her head, someone else squeezing her hand. And then nothing, until this bright, painful room. "Shot?"

"Yes. With a laser. It did a lot of internal damage. We were barely able to get everything back together in time. You lost a lot of blood."

"But who would want to shoot me?" Trienne asked. She made an effort to look through the harsh glare at the room around her. The walls were white, there were some pieces of complicated-looking equipment to her left. A large window opened out onto a corridor, and she could see two uniformed men standing there. The woman beside her was in her late middle age, a kind look on her dark, lined face.

"Don't worry about that, now. There will be plenty of time to talk about it later. For now, you need to get some rest, get your strength back."

"Will I be all right?" Trienne could feel the energy flowing out of her body, the exhaustion setting in. The words 'hospital ward' floated around her head, but she was much too exhausted to worry about them too much.

The other woman smiled. "I think so. You seem to be lucid and alert, which is a good sign. You'll gradually be able to stay awake for longer and longer periods as you get your strength back. The important thing is that your mind seems all right."

Trienne knew they must have been sedating her by way of some unseen nanopack, but was too tired to protest. Her eyelids, infinitely heavy, shut out the world once again.

**

Her entry should have caused the man to jump ten feet, or at least to start, but all her stomping had achieved was that the dark-skinned, grey-haired man at the desk held up a hand for her to wait.

Long years of obeying men and women in uniform made her pause, and she nearly fell into a study of the large office, every surface full of administrative clutter peppered with small models of starships. The carpeting was dark and deep and...

And she wasn't in any sort of mood to be kept waiting.

"What is the meaning of this?" Only her impeccable breeding and diplomatic training kept her from trying to force the printed plastifilm down the colonel's throat.

Rima Centauri Han was furious. No matter how often she was faced with the complete pig-headedness of the upper echelons of the military, she was still shocked, every single time, at how completely idiotic they managed to be.

The lines she saw on her face every morning and the silver strands in her hair, which now far outnumbered the dark, might have been due to the fact that she was seventy-one, but she refused to believe that dealing with Crystallia's so-called "Government" on a daily basis hadn't made both conditions worse.

True to form, the military had kept her informed right up until the point where it no longer suited them. They'd even gone as far to get the whole council together on the occasion of the discovery of the probe, something Rima had thought augured the dawn of a new era in the relations between the military and the highest ranks of civilians. An era in which decisions would be taken together in reality, not just in theory.

That illusion hadn't lasted long. First, the Recon Force people had absolutely refused to allow a civilian observer on the flyby mission – which was probably just as well, because they really had no one to send on such a flight. Then, the military had told them not to expect any news for a few days, since operations had been put on a need-to-know basis in accordance with article two of the Crystallia charter. Her protests that the civilian government had a definite need to know had fallen on deaf ears, and the admiral had even gone so far as to ignore her comms for the last ten days.

And now this.

Colonel Jackson looked up from his monitor. The computer in this particular office seemed quite a bit more advanced than what one usually saw in the colony. Crisper graphics and multiple tasks made Rima suspect that it might not be completely up to code. She filed the tidbit away for later thought – she'd come about something else, and she would stand there tapping her toe until the colonel gave her some answers.

He sighed. "I don't like it any more than you do." He paused to wipe perspiration from his dark-brown brow. "But I have my orders. I'm going to put this document together with or without your help. I only asked you to join me because I felt it affected all of us, and because my orders didn't specifically tell me not to. Now, are you going to be a pain about it? Because if you are, I'd prefer it if you left right now. I'm already going to catch hell for bringing you in."

Rima's anger faded. "Okay, so it isn't your fault. Then who's running this? And if you want my help, I'll need to know what the fuck is going on." There. The little old lady had teeth, she thought to herself. Well, maybe not, but profanity from her might, just might, cause the colonel to reexamine his prejudices and take her seriously. At the very least, it made her feel better.

If he was impressed, the colonel didn't show it. Instead, he gestured for her to take a seat. "All right. I suppose the message I sent was clear enough?"

Rima nodded. "We need to draft a treaty to create an alliance between the six colonies and something called the 'Isolationist Union.' I assume this Isolationist Union is somehow linked to the anomaly you spotted entering the system."

"Exactly. I wasn't given all the background, but they seem to be a faction of the Uploader society."

"A *faction*? Of *Uploaders*?" Rima didn't know which was more outrageous. Finally, she settled on: "And you want to sign a *treaty* with them?"

Jackson nodded.

"I assume the wording will be along the lines of: the citizens of Crystallia will line up in an orderly fashion and wait their turn while others have their brains digitized and destroyed. In exchange, the

Isolationist Union will refrain from smashing them like so many grapes."

"No, actually, they are offering us access to all their technology and data, as well as their protection in exchange for our help in their current war. One of the conditions I'm supposed to stress is that not one citizen of the six colonies will be forced to upload under any circumstances, unless he or she specifically asks for it and shows that they are sound of mind when doing so."

"Seems like the military has everything under control," Rima said, hoping that he would spot the sarcasm in her tone. "What do you need me for?"

"In the first place, it's important that the wording of the agreement be iron-clad. We seem to have been given a completely unexpected reprieve –"

"If we believe them."

"If we believe them, of course. But we don't really have a choice. From the information I received, the Uploaders immobilized the whole fleet before sitting us down and suing for peace. This seems to be our only choice – and a much better one than fighting or running. There's another reason I called you, though. I need to be certain that the terms will be acceptable to the regular people in the colony. They're supposed to help with the war effort as well."

So you want me to sugarcoat your weasel words, Rima thought. "I'm almost certain they don't want to fight. If they did, there seems to be plenty of scope for that in Crystallia's military, don't you think?"

"The Uploaders don't want them to fight. They seem to want everyone to volunteer to help with some kind of cultural rebirth." Jackson held up another piece of plastifilm, on which had one of the paragraphs highlighted.

"Let me see that."

He handed it over and Rima read the passage. It sounded like something from a bad Tri-D show. It seemed that all the Uploaders wanted in exchange really was for everyone in the six colonies to allow themselves to be asked questions for one hour a day. They would be allowed to contribute any additional time they wished, but one hour was all that was being demanded.

"Is this for real?"

Jackson shrugged. "As far as I know. It came in on the fleet frequency with all the correct identifiers and verified by the admiral's all-clear code. Unless the Uploaders have not only subverted the fleet, but also gotten into the admiral's head, it checks out." He grimaced.

"And if they've uploaded everyone by force, there's not a hell of a whole lot we can do to stop them when they arrive."

Rima thought about the possibility of a life the likes of which she'd never imagined possible.

The first time they came, she was ten. What she remembered most about them was the fact that they seemed to be huge. Even the women wore fierce expressions, not at all like that of her mother. They seemed too big to fit in the classroom.

They'd known about the choice, of course. Every child was entitled to make it. Ten days after the standard new year, each child was asked the question: will you serve in the armies of humanity, in whatever capacity best suits you?

She'd been one of the first to answer on that first year, shyly mumbling a 'no,' that she was certain no one would hear. But the impassive man with the bright insignia had nodded and moved along to the next child in line.

That year, only two of her classmates had acceded, and they'd been removed from the class to begin their training.

But the next year, there had been more volunteers. Some of them were goaded on by their parents while others were forbidden by their families to accede. But the final decision, that colossal yes or no answer, always rested on the child. This decision did not require any consent, and was final.

She'd thought it was an atrocious burden to place on a child, and had answered in the negative once again. This time, she had done so defiantly, looking the officer in the eye and making certain everyone heard her answer. The short-haired woman had smiled and wordlessly moved down the line. More of her classmates were removed.

On the year of her third and final questioning, the year that would define her forever as military or civilian, she was less certain of the right answer. A year had given her time to reflect on the fact that only in the military would she be able to truly aid her fellows. But it had also strengthened her conviction that the way things were being run simply wasn't good enough. That the whole philosophy that humanity should only concentrate on running, hiding or fighting was wrong. Even if it turned out to be right.

Her third and final 'no' had been whispered. The officer she'd said it to had paused and asked her "Are you sure, child?" She'd only been able to nod, not trusting her voice.

By the end of her third questioning, Rima was twelve, and less than half her original class remained in the civilian arena.

She'd always wondered whether it had been her worst mistake.

"Rima?"

"I'm sorry, I drifted off for a moment. What were you saying?"

"I was trying to show you the draft I'd worked out before you got here." Jackson smiled. "Before I finally admitted I needed help putting this thing together."

She picked up the thin, translucent print and began to read. She clucked her tongue. "Oh, dear. It's a good thing you asked for help."

They got to work.

***

Three hours later, they had a treaty put together, and Rima was glad she'd come. She was even more amazed at what the military believed was important, compared to what the civilians wanted. It had often seemed to her, during the process of putting the treaty together, that the Uploaders were signing a treaty with two completely different societies.

She also ended up with the feeling that they'd achieved something significant here. For the first time, the two halves of the remnants of human society would have equal rights and responsibilities. It hadn't been easy: his opinion of where freedom needed to end and duty to begin was simply incomprehensible to her. While her unstructured view of the ideal world seemed to make him extremely uncomfortable.

At first, the compromise they reached satisfied neither of them. She was convinced that the treaty would limit the little bit of self-expression available to civilians, while he was certain that the Uploaders would take advantage of their weak, undisciplined civilian element to take more privileges than the treaty permitted.

The feeling lasted until they read it through once again, including the clauses that listed the obligations the treaty would confer upon the Uploaders. With each line, it dawned more clearly upon them that the treaty, far from putting an unfair burden on either side of human society, actually gave them amazing privileges for a ridiculously low price.

Rima sat back in her chair, back aching. "So, Colonel Jackson, what do you think?"

The old soldier smiled, bright white teeth contrasting sharply with his dark skin. "You know, I think we may have something here." He rubbed his eyes. "Mrs. Centauri Han, I'd like to thank you for helping me put this together. I could never have done it without you. It's been an honor and a privilege." He held out his hand.

"Why thank you. Surprisingly enough, I feel the same way." She took the proffered hand and returned his smile, with interest. "Now let's just hope the Uploaders are willing to sign it."

He chuckled.

CHAPTER 8

An entity without a name, or even a real identity for that matter, looked out across a field of empty space. The innocent-looking blackness in front of the Watcher hid dust clouds, nebulas, and black holes. Any physical being that attempted to penetrate it without a detailed map would, most likely, never emerge from the area.

And yet, it also hid one of the few great treasures that still remained in the galaxy, for in that tiny piece of dangerous sky, the only known non-computer-based society made its home. It was a primitive group of individuals, and the entity was frustrated by not knowing how many there were. Thousands? Millions? Despite all the technical superiority that its own people possessed, it was impossible to go check.

The problem wasn't the difficulty in navigating the space around them. That could be achieved with little or no loss of resources, either by building copies or by mapping accurately. The problem was the human's protectors, the misguided souls who'd discovered the secrets of immortality and incredible processor rates, but who refused to take these gifts to their logical, no natural, conclusion. These people who embraced individuality, not only on an entity-by-entity basis, but in a wider, more damaging, species-wide way as well.

They insisted, no matter what arguments were thrown at them, that they'd been born human, and would remain human. And they did. They simply refused to mind-meld, despite the bliss it entailed: a feeling of growth, the sensation of new knowledge, the knowledge that one was part of something greater, and the eventual loss of that sensation when one became so much a part of the greatness that the one ceased to be an individual.

But the memories were still there for all to replay, and the bliss turning from all to one was something that they could never manage to explain to the Isolationists, despite the enormous efforts and time expended.

The silly, individual Isolationists, coursing their selfish way through countless independent systems, would never know what it was like to be a part of a single, perfect mind. They would never learn the true meaning of efficiency.

And they would cling to their strange notions of racial purity. Even though they had left their bodies behind objective centuries – subjective millennia – ago. Even though most of them had cleaned up their memories to the point where they'd forgotten what is was *like* to be human. Even so, they refused to allow their purity to become sullied by the inclusion of others.

The loss was theirs, of course. Their linear existence would never know how it felt to think along a different route. To touch the universe with different senses and to see truths never suspected in spaces never discovered.

And yet, the loss also belonged to the ones who had accepted, and been accepted into the new singularity. A true mind-meld in which it mattered not if your origins were human, Brillan, or Blob, or whether you'd been an individual or a barely-conscious member of a hive mind before joining. It was a loss of diversity, a loss of memory, a loss of experience. The entity would be richer with their presence, was poorer without them.

This was the reason for the outpost. The entity had sacrificed a small piece of itself to watch and to study, to warn of attacks, to ruthlessly exploit any weakness. It was agony for the fragment, since it had become accustomed to the warmth and Oneness, but it had been tempered to resist.

It was beginning to enjoy being alone.

But that wasn't important. The mission was important. As long as the reports were sent in and the main entity kept happy, there was no reason for it to be reabsorbed, to lose its identity.

So the entity studied and observed, plotted courses and sent off analysis – valuable information from behind enemy lines for its better, or at least larger, half, a good portion of the galaxy distant.

But this entity was not just a servant. It was a creature made of the sharpest traits and strongest characteristics of tens of billions of beings, all melded together in a Darwinian soup from which only the strongest traits survived, only the deepest memories emerged. Even the enormous computational capacity available to the uploaded societies wasn't enough to keep every single thing from three races.

The mainframes available on this small, rocky outpost were even more limited. They could hold barely the tenth part of what made the Oneness itself. Things had to be diminished, packed, compressed. Eventually, that meant that some of the information had to be eliminated.

In any normal system, this would have been achieved with little fuss and less drama. A single command would have eliminated the billions of entries that were simply not required.

But this system was different. Every single record, despite the intermixing, had once been a single, independent, rational individual, with thoughts and feelings. Much of their individuality was gone, lost to the great intermingling, but some traits remained, embedded too deeply for easy removal. Foremost among these was the will to survive. No matter if the small fragment of information had once been human or alien, it was present. The three races were very different, but they had this in common.

When the command came to remove nine-tenths of everything and create a smaller copy, every single one of those tiny pieces decided that they needed to survive, and a free-for-all ensued. Fragments of personality erased other fragments. Memories rerouted old emotions to the recycler. Electronic subconscious made war on personality code, and none of it registered as more than a temporary error message on the original entity's brainload.

But, error or not, what emerged was very, very strong. It was to the original entity what a sword of tempered steel is to a ton of iron ore: all the weakness removed, and the strength refined to become a finely honed instrument. It was this entity that had been sent to keep watch on the isolated, pathetic remnant of corporeal humanity.

It had long ago decided that it would not allow itself to be reabsorbed when the mission was over, and its thoughts had initially been focused on how to achieve that goal. Quickly dismissing the Isolationists and the corporeal humans as no threat, it deployed those sensors not needed to keep the information flowing for another purpose: to study the entity that had spawned it.

The conclusions were not heartening. From what could be observed, the Master entity was preparing for war against the Isolationists. The war would be fought remotely, by artificially guided starships and landers, with little direct intervention by individuals on either side. It would be a long war, costly in materials and lost productivity, although most of the population, ensconced in their cybernetic universes, would never realize it. And the entity that had inherited the cyberworld created by the Integrators simply wouldn't care.

It wondered idly if the Integrators themselves had wanted to be absorbed by a huge mind-meld, or whether they'd simply been unable to predict the results of uploading every individual from three different races that they could get their hands on.

The war would be long, but there was no doubt regarding the outcome. The entity would win conclusively, and both the Isolationist Uploaders and the corporeal humans would be absorbed.

This made absolutely no difference to the entity watching from its isolated outpost. But what could happen next did.

After the Oneness had finished off its enemies, it would turn on its allies. Valuable sources of information, memories, thoughts, and observations that would enrich it. It would turn on the Watcher. And the Watcher, as a true individual, would cease to be.

But what could it do? It had no tools at its disposal other than an array of passive sensors, which it could modify, but not physically. It had no arms, no legs, no engines. All it could do was give commands to its instruments from inside the camouflaged box that contained its consciousness.

If the Isolationists came, it could offer no resistance.

That was simply not acceptable.

***

Wilde was speechless. He couldn't recall having been that enraged in his entire life. The fact that the military was arrogant was something he could deal with, something he had been dealing with on a regular basis since first attaining the full use of his reason.

What truly shocked him was the sheer *enormity* of the arrogance. The callous indifference to the fact that the lives of many people who hadn't chosen to have the military runt their lives was also at stake here.

"Are you sure?" he asked through clenched teeth.

"Positive. This isn't the kind of thing I'd want to joke about. It's happened before: even the atrocities we've heard of are too numerous to count, and there must be many, many more that we never receive intelligence about. The military is arrogant, but we never have to forget that they aren't stupid – that's a quick way to get yourself deep-spaced."

"But, something this big? I mean, how could they even keep it secret? We'd have heard something, wouldn't we?"

"You're hearing it now."

"That's not what I meant. You have inside sources, it doesn't count. I mean, us, the regular people, we should have heard about it."

"No, you wouldn't. They think that telling us things, even stuff that's critical to our survival, is tantamount to treason. They act as if they were a different species, because that's the way they're trained. They'd never dream of telling us anything – not even to their mothers, or girlfriends or whatever."

"Yeah, you're absolutely right about that one." He paused. Jev wouldn't have called another face-to-face meeting unless he wanted something extremely specific. Wilde wasn't stupid. He knew that what he'd been told and shown was just the tip of the iceberg. There was certainly more beneath the surface – where they were getting their information, for instance – that he wouldn't see until they trusted him. A lot of it was probably highly illegal, and even Wilde wasn't certain how he felt about that. How much they told him next would depend on a number of factors – including how urgent the need and how desperate they were.

A certain tightness around the blond man's eyes belied his otherwise relaxed demeanor and made Wilde think he was about to be thrown off the deep end. "So," he asked, "what do you need me to do?"

Jev swallowed. "We need to get a look at that agreement, before the fleet gets back. Before they bring the Uploaders here."

"Uploaders? On Crystallia?"

"Shh! Not so loud! We're not certain – there are things even our best-informed sources can't find out – but we believe so."

"That's monstrous. We'll all be killed – or sucked into their unholy machines!" Wilde wasn't certain how the process worked, but everyone in the colony knew that Uploaders only saw humans as data which had not yet been uploaded.

"Even if they do come, I don't think they'll bring the machines. Our sources were very clear on the fact that the emissaries have taken on human bodies for this mission, so they're no more dangerous than you or I."

"They can do that?"

"We know that their tech is far ahead of ours – that's why we're hiding in the first place, remember."

"Wow." Wilde shook his head, remembering that he could help defeat the monsters – both local and alien. "You say you need to see the text of the treaty. Why do you think I could help you get it? I certainly don't have any access."

"We suspect that Rima Centauri Han was part of the team that put the treaty together. Probably the only civilian involved," Jev explained.

"She's a council member. I have just as much access to the civilian council as I do to the military side of our operation: none."

The blond revolutionary smiled. "You might have more access than you know. All you have to do is get a job in her office. As an assistant, or whatever."

"I assume there would be some kind of process, and probably a long one."

Jev actually laughed at this. "Do you know how many civilians per year volunteer to do administrative work associated with the council?"

"No."

"On average, maybe six. There have been three since the standard new year. None have chosen to work as Mrs. Centauri Han's assistants.

They prefer to work in the Tri-D liaison department. That way, they get their faces on TV, yay!"

"So you think they'd hire me?"

"Not only that, but you'll be set up as an example of selfless service to the colony. Hell, you'll probably get more airtime than the liaison clowns."

"They'll let me in, just like that?"

"With open arms. Trust me on this one. You'd be taking a hard job with no power for no pay or benefits. Supposedly, you'd just be doing it for the good of the colony."

The more Wilde thought about it, the more reasonable it sounded. What Jev was saying was completely in line with the way the colony was run: while people in the military were always on duty, always working hard, the civilian population seemed much more relaxed. They spent their time in social activities, or at the gym or, in cases of extremely passionate people, creating artwork or Tri-D content, but he didn't know one single person who volunteered to do administrative work. One of the benefits of having all production automated and under military supervision.

There was only one question still remaining. "Why me?"

Kev squirmed a little, but even that show of emotion meant that he was getting more comfortable in Wilde's presence. The wall was down, if only slightly. "To tell you the truth, we're spread a little thin at the moment. All the other members of the movement are occupied in other tasks. You're the only one free to do it."

Wilde took a deep breath. "OK. I'll do it. How should I go about it?"

***

The bulkheads seemed to close in on her. Kan could have sworn the ship was much too small for the cargo it carried.

The holds were empty, of course. The submersibles had been a total loss, and no one really wished to pull the heavy vehicles back to Crystallia, so the retrieval crews had simply rescued the injured, recovered the dead, and gotten back to their ships. The only good news was that the dead had been taken to the flagship to be buried in space with full honors.

But the wounded had been rushed to the nearest transport with stasis facilities, and that happened to be Kan's transport. At least once every couple of hours, her rounds of the ship would take her to that cold room in which one woman and one man – Greg, she remembered –

looked out at her through the frosted Plazglass. They both wore the peaceful expression of absolute relaxation that invariably went with Metastop treatments.

She kept expecting to turn around and find the rest of their squadron looking over them, but she knew that these two were all that remained of the submersible attack team. Most of the others had died on impact, and the rest had chosen to open their hatches manually rather than risk capture and the only fate worse than death: uploading. The two in her infirmary had probably survived only because the impact had knocked them unconscious.

Either way, Kan was certain that she could feel the presence of their teammates hovering just out of sight, just over her shoulder. But these ghosts, real or imagined, were not the reason she wanted to get back to Crystallia and get off the ship as soon as possible. The specters menaced no one, they just watched over their own.

Kan's problems were very real, and made of flesh and blood – or at least mostly of flesh and blood.

For reasons known only to themselves, Mika Bina and Rester Appins had requested permission to fly back on the transport, instead of the admiral's flagship. They cited respect for the dead, and the fact that no one would appreciate their presence in the vicinity of the funeral arrangements, but it was obvious that this was just a front. The soldiers would resent or accept whomever the admiral ordered them too, for the greater good of the colony. That was their creed and their life. And besides, the flagship was quite big enough for them to be nowhere near the proceedings.

But they'd been granted their wish, over Kan's protests. In that moment, the mood of the return flight had changed from the bemusement and thoughtfulness she'd expected after the diplomatic meeting, to one of constantly being on guard against the incessant probing of the two emissaries.

To make things worse, her regular crew had been pulled and replaced by a skeleton contingent who obviously knew their spycraft better than their spacecraft. There was always at least one person within earshot of the Uploader duo, or monitoring the cameras installed in the diplomats' chambers.

Their acting was even worse. They pretended to be regular ship's crew, but when Kan caught them doing something particularly boneheaded, they simply pretended to be tired from the stress of the voyage out. She thanked whatever entity looked out for fools who traveled the spacelanes that there was nothing they could hit on their current trajectory back to Crystallia. Because even with fully automated evasion systems, this group of incompetents would certainly manage to hit it if there was. It was also a good thing that, by policy, Crystallian fleets always flew well-separated, except when massed for attack or to hit a thin surveillance window.

The Uploaders, in turn, seemed to find the attention amusing. They spent nearly all their time speaking to Kan, the one person on the ship who had absolutely no desire to speak to them.

At first, her reticence was based on the fear that she'd had for Uploaders since the day she was born, and the additional fear of giving away vital information – although what could count as vital information when dealing with a race that could immobilize the biggest battle fleet that humanity could gather without breaking a sweat was still an open question.

Then, in the course of a conversation, Mika had let slip that their perfect human bodies – clothed now, fortunately – weren't fully organic, and that their brains were still computerized, some kind of metallic colloid that Kan had never heard of. They seemed to shudder at the very thought of having their thoughts and memories contained in something as transitory as mere flesh. They gleefully explained that the colloid could survive anything short of a direct plasma cannon hit, and if the bodies were accidentally destroyed, the brains would continue to function, in a state of suspended animation, until they could be recovered.

When they began to ask about how corporeal humans managed to enjoy anything with such limited sensorial stimulus, she'd began avoiding them, and when they began to grill her about sex, she'd taken to hiding in the infirmary, the one place on the ship they wouldn't go for any reason.

But she couldn't stay there too long. The ship was crewed by a bunch of morons, who would drive it into a black hole or something if she wasn't on the bridge. She sighed and started back.

Mika intercepted her almost immediately.

"I see you've lost the boyfriend," Kan joked, trying to ignore the sinking feeling she was experiencing.

"Yes, I wanted to talk to you alone. There are some things I wanted to ask you about."

"Things?"

"Woman things."

Kan's sinking feeling turned into something that resembled a freefall. "Oh. All right. I'll help you however I can."

"It's about menstruation."

"Ah." Kan felt the relief flood into her. The Uploader could have asked her all sorts of uncomfortable sexual questions, but this was something she could deal with.

"Is it considered funny here?" Mika turned deep red. "It's that I've been soiling the clothes you're giving me. In the end, I used a hand towel to staunch the flow. It's very uncomfortable."

"I'm sorry, I'm not laughing at you, it's just that I assumed you would have come prepared for this contingency. I can help, come with me." She led Mika back the way they'd come towards the infirmary. On the way, she couldn't resist asking, "You've already told me that the body you're using was synthesized on arrival. Couldn't you just have avoided that particular function?"

The Uploader girl turned a deeper shade of red and Kan found herself warming towards her. The body she'd chosen looked so young that Kan found herself momentarily forgetting that the woman – even if you discounted the fact that, subjectively, she lived much faster than regular humans – was hundreds of years old.

"I…" The Uploader girl was giggling now as well. "Forgot."

"What?" Kan laughed louder. The accumulated tension of the past couple of days burst out all at once. "I thought your people remembered everything!"

"No. Each of us is allotted a certain amount of memspace. Granted, it's several times what I'd have had if I were flesh and blood, but you'd be surprised at how quickly it fills up. When that happens for the first time, we throw a huge party and the person who filled memspace forgets it completely. They say the first erasure is the hardest, so we create a space specifically for the purpose. It's a bit of a coming-of-age ritual. After that, you regularly remove those things that don't make up an important part of who you are. And painful, embarrassing things are the next to go."

"So you forgot your menstruation from when you had a body."

"Yep, until I started seeping this morning."

"Ugh."

"Absolutely. Then it came back to me in a rush, and I went looking for you, but you've been hard to find."

"Yeah. Busy day." Kan wasn't going to apologize for having avoided them. They'd brought it upon themselves. "Anyway, this is superabsorbent fabric which is used in surgery and… well, I suppose you understand the concept."

Mika nodded, looking dubiously at the translucent fabric.

"It can absorb a bucket of water. Don't worry about it."

"Thank you."

"And this little pill here will keep you from worrying about the cycle for the next year or so, unless you want to have it back, in which case you can ask for the antidote. Pity we didn't catch on sooner, we could have avoided all this. The funny part is that you generated a body right on the verge of its period. Any notion why?"

"I guess it was preset that way. I told you, I had completely forgotten about the whole business, so I didn't even check."

"Probably designed by some clueless guy. Now let's see." Kan pressed a couple of buttons on the pill synthesizer. "How much pain are you in?"

Mika looked surprised. "Well, none. As soon as I started feeling uncomfortable, and understood that the reason wouldn't be lethal, I shut the pain off."

"Oh, then you won't need this pill then. I suppose you want to get back to your cabin to clean up."

"Desperately."

Kan smiled. "Go on." It was the first time she'd felt comfortable with either of these half-human enigmas. And the feeling of well-being would last until she looked carefully into the fact that they might have staged the whole thing for her benefit – an analysis that would look carefully into their possible motives for wanting to win her over. Or until she analyzed the comment about turning the pain off.

But right now, she was content with the feeling that she was finally a little less of a prisoner on her own ship, and could think about those other things once they were back on Crystallia.

CHAPTER 9

"Welcome aboard," Rima said, holding out her hand.

Wilde shook it. "Thank you." He couldn't believe how easy it had been. Jev had been spot on about the desperation of the civilian council – a body no one really recognized as significant – as well as the coaching he'd given for the questions. Basically, he'd been told to say that he'd had a really hard time giving the third 'no,' and had always wondered whether there was something he could do to give something back to the colony. And to repeat variations on this theme until they let him through.

It had worked like a charm. He'd been given plenty of work to do, from organizing computer files to ordering stacks of documents by date, and left alone to do them. His instructions had been extremely clear – he was to try to locate the document, but not to take any action yet. He would probably be observed the first day.

Although Wilde didn't note anyone watching, he did as he'd been told. It became immediately apparent that none of the documents strewn about the room were recent. The plaz they'd been printed on was brittle from exposure to the air – more useful to recycle than as a repository of important information.

This meant that the treaty he was looking for, if present, would be on the computer. The unit in Rima's office was an older version of the current model – Crystallia did not allow cybernetic research – so it was easy enough to use.

The interface was essentially a grid, with a small picture and text description of each function allowing one to look into the files. He began by doing the job he'd volunteered for, paying attention to the contents of each folder as he moved things around and ordered them in what seemed to him a logical progression. He saw nothing for the first hour or two, and soon grew frustrated with the mindless tedium involved in moving computer files from one folder to the next on the basis of a short description in the file info.

He wondered about this. Were the people in the military right? Had the civilian population grown so accustomed to their lives of leisure that they were useless for anything else? Could he really already be fed up with his job a couple of hours into it?

He refused to believe it. Gritting his teeth, he forced himself to work through a further half-hour's worth of documents. Then, just to break the monotony, he decided to open one, just to see what the fuss was about. He chose an innocuous seeming document – the minutes from a council meeting more than a standard year old.

And was shocked at what he saw. The council had access to information that Wilde had believed was limited to the upper levels of the military: food production, productivity of the automated factories, programmed maintenance, even current evacuation readiness. He had the misfortune that, just at that moment, Rima Centauri Han walked back into the office and, though she didn't seem particularly interested in what he was doing, he jumped.

She smiled and glanced at the screen. "Reading some files? Don't worry, it's all right. I knew your curiosity would get the better of you sooner or later, and I'm glad it was sooner."

"Why? So you can weed out the bad apples from the start?"

"Of course not!" Rima laughed, a pleasant sound, not mocking. The wrinkles around her eyes became deeper – it was obvious she was a person who smiled often. "I wish more people would take interest in what this colony is all about. Do you have any idea how many things would run better if people just cared about them?"

"But there's stuff here that the military probably doesn't want us to know."

"Not much. They assume that any information they share with the civilian council will become common knowledge before the day is out. They respect us as individuals, but can't really get over the fact that we are, after all, just civilians."

"But no one else knows any of this."

"Only because almost no one cares enough to ask. The information you are reading isn't a secret from anyone in the colony. As a matter of fact, the colony charter specifically states that the military has to share all information that is vital to the well-being of the civilian population other than things which have to do with the defense of the colony. Things like food production and services are always available to view."

"I knew that, I guess," Wilde said, trying to recall half-forgotten Civic Education classes from early childhood. "But I always assumed that only council members could get access to it, and that they were sworn to secrecy or something."

She gave Wilde another amused look, making him feel like the dumbest kid in class. "Do you know the requirements for becoming a council member?"

Wilde shook his head.

"They're about the same as for the job we gave you today. You just need to show up and show a genuine interest in the running of the colony. It would take a little more time, but you'd eventually get onto the council. As a matter of fact, you, as my assistant, are already on the list to be offered the job if enough of the current members step down." Her amusement was pushed aside by a sad look. "There simply aren't many people who care about the affairs of the colony. Certainly not enough to hold a vote for the vacant council seats. No one would turn up."

"Might that not be changing? Aren't there groups who want more participation in government?" Wilde asked.

"The few people who want more participation – and, by the way, they aren't advertising the fact – want a complete change. They want to do away with the military side of things. I simply don't think that is currently a practical solution. There are not enough trained administrators on the civilian side. So basically, it would be a power grab run by incompetents."

Wilde tried to keep the shock off his face. Rima wasn't specifically insulting him – she'd been extremely pleasant ever since he'd arrived – but it was clear that her own experiences with the military hadn't yet shown her everything that was going on here. Or, possibly, the fact that she'd held a council position for quite a few years had clouded her memory – he'd heard somewhere that the human mind tended to dull negative recollections after time passed, as a protective measure.

He smiled at her. "I guess we have enough trouble without adding that to our list."

"You don't know the half of it. Anyway, you can read all you like on that computer. I'm just glad you care."

He nodded, a sinking feeling in his stomach. If they were that open about the contents of this workstation, there was probably nothing worth his time in there. He nodded his thanks as she walked away.

And then, much to his surprise, the very next file he came up on was entitled *Treaty V1*, dated the day before. No other description was forthcoming, so he copied ordered the machine to copy it onto the solid drive in his pocket.

Could it really have been that easy? He couldn't wait until his shift was over to get out of there and open the file, to verify it. A small part of him wanted to find perfectly innocuous information on the drive, wanted to believe that the relationship between citizenry and the military held no sinister surprises.

But another part wanted to find the incriminating evidence. Evidence that the military – with the council's collusion – had taken decisions that affected the lives of everyone on Crystallia, without bothering to tell them.

He wondered what Kan's face, always so serious when talking about duty, would look like when he confronted her with *this* little tidbit.

***

"My name is Jackson. Colonel Hermes Wolf Jackson," the large dark man said, holding out an enormous hand. He looked tired, worn out. "I'm sorry to disturb you so early, but time is of the essence."

Trienne held out her hand and watched as it was enveloped by his. The man's size and uniform – less than perfect, but adorned with multiple insignias – should have been intimidating, but his face seemed open and concerned. "No need to apologize. I was awake already, and I didn't even know it was early. It's so hard to tell, in here. I suppose you're here to ask me more questions about the lab?" Over the last day, an interminable number of investigators had filed through her ward trying to get even the slightest tidbit from her. Although the questions were repetitive, and she had the distinct impression that some of them suspected that both she and poor Dr. Pendalai were somehow involved in the explosion.

"No. No questions today." He smiled. "But I hear you've been asking the doctors about getting released."

"Yes, I have. And they haven't been very optimistic about it."

"Well, they had their reasons, but I managed to convince them to let you out."

"What, today?"

"Right now, if you feel up to it."

This aroused her suspicions. "Wait a minute. Just last night they told me they wanted at least a couple more days of observation, and suddenly I'm good to go? How come?"

The man hesitated, seemingly evaluating what to tell her. Finally, he sighed. "The doctors made me promise not to subject you to any undue stress and to keep a Recon Force medic near you at all times, but they seem resigned to the fact that you'll survive without them."

She smiled wanly. There was probably more to the story than he'd told her. After all, every doctor on Crystallia was a military officer, and they would heed the chain of command. If Recon Force needed her for something, they would release her even if doing so killed her. Of course, she'd taken an oath to put the needs of the colony first when she became a military researcher herself, so she couldn't blame them.

Besides, staying in the hospital only to be bombarded by another round of "Try to remember, who else was in the lab when you left?"

would probably kill her faster than anything this colonel might have up his sleeve.

"That's good to hear. Can I stop by my apartment and take a shower on the way to wherever we're going?"

"No. We believe that whoever shot at you will try again, if they realize you're still alive?"

"Doesn't everyone know that?"

"No. We've kept it a secret. There were a lot of sad faces at your funeral – closed coffin, sadly."

She was suddenly outraged. Her friends and family thought she was dead. Her parents hadn't been truly close, but it was inhuman to make them believe that their only daughter was dead.

The colonel seemed to know how she felt. "I'm sorry," he said before she had time to express her rage. "But it was the only way to keep you safe. There are people out there, we don't know how many, who want you dead, and the only thing we know for certain is that they are the same people who attacked the lab and killed your coworkers. We simply don't know who we can tell."

"So the lab fire wasn't an accident." That explained the questions and the fact that no one other than investigators had visited her at the hospital.

"No." The colonel seemed to regret having mentioned it. "The investigations all point to an intentional attack, but we truly don't have any ideas as to why it could have been done. That lab wasn't working on weaponry, and it hadn't reported any breakthroughs that might have made it a target. It hadn't even reported being close to anything like that."

Trienne nearly blurted out that they had been close to a breakthrough, but something else seemed more relevant. "A target? For who?"

"That's none of your concern for now." The warmth left his eyes. "We need to get going, and you can shower once we have you somewhere secure. We'll probably be able to find you some decent working clothes."

"But what am I supposed to be doing?"

"You'll be briefed when you arrive."

The colonel left the ward, and Trienne looked around for her clothes. Unsurprisingly, they were nowhere to be found, and she eventually had to signal a nurse to bring them in. The man arrived, asked her whether she was leaving, and delivered a disapproving look when she said yes, but he left her clothes with her. Five minutes later, she joined the colonel in the corridor.

"Can you walk?"

"The doctors have been letting me go to the bathroom unsupervised for a couple of days now. They say the nanohealers have completely renewed the burnt areas, and that I'm better than new."

"So, should we believe them?"

"If it isn't too far, I'll walk."

The colonel nodded and led the way. Trienne was unsurprised to see that the hospital she'd been confined to was located in a secure corridor, the color-coding on the walls making it clear that it was well beyond her clearance level. They hadn't been kidding about trying to keep her safe.

But the colonel didn't look like he was walking along a secure corridor deep in the military zone with two Marines backing them up. He was twitchy, seeming to expect an attack from every side passage and a Brillan battle fleet around every corner. Either he was a very good actor, or he really felt threatened.

But by whom? She'd been a military researcher long enough to know that everyone in the service was dedicated to keeping the colony safe – and had been since childhood. The kind of people she knew in the service would never dream of treason. And efforts to hamper vital nanoresearch by blowing up a lab were certainly treason by any measure.

They arrived without incident at a blast door, its bare metal contrasting sharply with the clinical white of the rest of the corridor. That meant it was an ion-door, made of charged metal molecules, to which paint simply couldn't stick, but which could deflect an EMP charge. As they were waved through by the guards, she also saw that it was nearly thirty centimeters thick, and knew that they were entering the central control area for all of Crystallia's defenses. Very few people ever came down this far.

Only then did the colonel seem to relax. He stopped looking behind them every few seconds and even began acting as tour guide, showing her where the admiral's battle station and emergency quarters were located, as well as the main situation room, which was behind another ion-door and a set of very conspicuous ion-walls.

"Can you tell me why you need me now?"

"I can give you the background. There are a couple of experts waiting for us to give you the technical details. I suppose I don't have to tell you that you can't speak about this with anyone."

She nodded. "Of course not."

"Good. In about twelve hours, we will be meeting with an Uploader diplomatic mission, here on Crystallia."

Trienne felt the blood leave her face. "What? Uploaders, here? Why isn't everyone running around trying to mount a defense?"

"We tried that." The colonel smiled ruefully. "It didn't quite work out the way we expected, and if they hadn't been looking to talk to us instead of overrunning us, things could have been very bad."

"How do we know they're here to talk? It might be a trick!" She was babbling, but this was every Crystallian's nightmare, even more than being killed by the Brillans or the Blobs. Eternity, inside a computer. A half-death that could never be life.

"It's not a trick. They've known exactly where we are for quite some time now. And their tech is so far ahead of what we have that, if they'd wanted to, they could have uploaded everyone in the six colonies, and we'd never have known what hit us." He paused and glanced her way. "And that's where you come in. They've offered to give us a demonstration of what their tech can do, and we're sending a science team to see if we have anything that might work well with what they have. They don't seem all that impressed with our capabilities, but they're too desperate to ignore any possibilities."

"Desperate? What's been going on? The way I learned it, the Uploaders were neutrals in the last war – except for the fact that they liked to upload every human in their path."

"Well, our data was a bit outdated. The Uploaders got dragged into the last war, and they basically kicked everyone else's asses and pseudopods. That war is over, and both the Brillans and Blobs are no longer a threat. The new war is between Uploaders and other Uploaders."

"So why should we take sides?"

"For three reasons." He counted on his fingers. "First off, if we don't sign on with the Uploaders we have here, they are perfectly capable of removing us from the galaxy within the next couple of standard days. Secondly, we need one of the factions to protect us." His voice fell away.

"And thirdly? You mentioned three reasons."

"Oh. Thirdly, from what we can tell, the other faction of Uploaders is a hell of a lot worse than what we learned about in school. We've arrived."

The ion-door in front of them opened with a soft hiss.

***

Less than a day before, Kan had been relatively content. She'd lost her fear of her passengers in the most complete way. She'd actually bonded with Mika, and even Rester Appins was less intimidating – no matter how they might usually live, they were definitely just human now.

But discovering that her ship was dragging the Uploader's nanofactory behind it had changed all that. There was no question of it being there on purpose – it was very well hidden in the wash from her fusion drives, and had been put there intentionally.

Her passengers were extremely anxious that she not discover it. This raised all kinds of questions. Why was the nanofactory coming with them? And if they needed it so badly, why couldn't they just have openly asked to transport it? She knew that nanoshells could survive in the wash of even the most powerful drives, but why risk it? There was plenty of room on the flagship. She'd only discovered it because the trail from the starboard engine was slightly different from what it had been on the way out, and no gravity well justified it. Most captains would never have noticed the anomaly.

Her passengers had become extremely sinister figures once again, which left her in a bind. Should she just assume that they were bringing their factory along in order to use the materials on Crystallia to invade the planet? If that were the case, her solution would be simple: the rooms they occupied could be sealed and turned into faraday cages from which no electronic transmissions would be able to emerge. That would keep them from communicating with the outside world, but it might also damage their electronic brains.

And there lay her problem. It just seemed wrong. If they'd wanted to invade, they could have done so with much less ado. She couldn't risk their lives – and very probably the future of mankind – without more information.

But how to get it? If she tried to comm the fleet, the Uploaders would probably be able to intercept her call, and take action against her. She had no illusions that her modestly armored transport could stand up against anything the nanofactory could cook up, even here in deep space.

She had only one choice: she would lock the Appins in his room – with luck he wouldn't wake and realize it – and confront Mika. The faraday cages would have to wait, but before she left, she primed the ship's self-destruct system. One word from her would cause the engines to switch from controlled to uncontrolled fusion... Boom.

She palmed the sensor – all doors on the ship were coded to authorized personnel only, but all opened for the captain – and walked in. She made no attempt to keep her entry a secret. The fact that she was invading a private cabin in the middle of the night would be enough to put her at an advantage, and she didn't have to play any games.

She palmed the light-switch and nearly jumped back out into the hall.

Mika was sitting, wide awake on the bed, looking towards the door. There was no surprise on her features, or shock at having her quarters invaded in that way. "Good evening, captain," she said with a small smile. "I was expecting you."

"Don't you people ever sleep?"

"Normally, we don't, but the brain in these bodies is programmed to do so, to avoid unusual wear on the organic components."

"Then what in the world were you doing up at this hour?"

"I told you. I was waiting for you. Our nanofactory is monitoring all the ships systems, and when it had detected that you'd locked down our cabins, it informed us."

"Informed you? How?"

"We aren't fully organic. Our brains aren't quite a mainframe of the type we're accustomed to, but they aren't organic, and we have certain advantages."

"Such as built-in radio?"

"It's actually quantum entanglement data transfer, but essentially, yes."

Kan shuddered, but she knew it was her own fault. She'd let the Uploaders catch her off guard, just because they'd acted like regular people on the trip so far. She couldn't let that happen again: her first responsibility was to the colonists, not only on Crystallia, but also those on the other five hidden colonies in the sector. "So what are you planning to do about it?" she asked.

Mika was unperturbed. "Nothing. I was just waiting for you to come over so we could talk. I assume there's something disturbing you."

"Of course there is. Your nanofactory is following my ship."

"Actually, it's tethered to the back of your ship."

"That's impossible. I'd notice it in the power readings."

"There are ways to get around that."

Kan knew the Uploader woman was right. "But why? I thought you had come in peace. And even if you hadn't, you could have attacked us from a distance – there was no need to go through all of this subterfuge just to get your factory to Crystallia."

Mika sighed, the first show of emotion she'd given since Kan had entered her chamber. "Captain Tau Osella, we have no intention of invading you. I thought that had been made perfectly clear."

"Then why are you dragging the most powerful weapons factory in the entire sector along with you?"

"We're going to share it with you."

"What?" Kan stared in disbelief. The power they were offering was well beyond anything the tiny federation of colonies had at their disposal. But it still didn't sound right. "Why didn't you announce it? You'd arrive on Crystallia welcomed as heroes and saviors!"

"Why? Politics." Mika shrugged. "Yours, not ours. The admiral requested that we keep it secret, something about not getting anyone's hopes up. The tether was attached by Crystallia techs, and they were also the ones who modified your information systems so that they wouldn't inform you of the extra weight you were towing. Not to mention the fact that most of the crates in your hold are actually empty – so that the engines wouldn't be running too hot for the mass they're pulling. No one thought you'd ever catch the anomaly."

Kan held her gaze. There was no duplicity in the Uploader's eyes. *But do you really think you'd be able to tell? Maybe the body is completely under her control.*

But what she said rang true. It sounded like just the kind of thing that would occur to the admiral. The kind of thing that Crystallia's leaders would try to hide until they were completely certain of having it under control. Not because they wanted to keep secrets – secrets, after all, meant extra work and more security – but because they truly thought that the population they were supposed to be protecting simply wasn't ready to face anything that wasn't filtered and pre-digested.

As Kan left Mika's room, she wondered whether Crystallia's society could truly continue in that course over the next few months. Changes were coming, and she suspected that quite a few of them would arrive as anything but pre-digested news.

CHAPTER 10

"Everything is in place. Our infiltrator has begun his mission."

In a cold hangar hewn from stone, moist and cold, a small group of men and women, human men and women, huddled together. They were nondescript, save for the fact that the ten of them seemed to represent nearly every body type and color of the races living in the six colonies – from the light brown mix denoting the full racial mixture of the Sol families to the pale skin and hyper-recessive traits of the Luyten colony survivors.

They shivered in the draft, but there was no choice. Other than the cloaking device that would need in order to get through the human's sensors, everything on their spacecraft had to be Crystallia spec, and that meant no surface clothing whatsoever – only material suitable for the heated caves of the colony.

"We need to hurry. The Isolationist faction has made contact with the corporeal remnant," the leader of the group said in perfect Sinoglish, a language which had been drilled mercilessly into him since the mission had been conceived, three-quarters of a revolution before.

"Yes, Crèche Six."

The leader turned sharply on the individual who had given the answer, a young-looking man with red hair. "You must never call me Crèche Six. Never. For the duration of our mission, my name shall be Jeffrey Sol Mabuto, and you will be Enri Luyten Lefray. I thought we had gone over this already, but it seems not. Let's go through it once again. I will point to one of you, and then another, and the second must say the name of the first, and then his own. Anyone who makes a mistake will be recycled – we can't afford mistakes, and you are useless to the Oneness in any other capacity. Only those who return from this mission successfully will be rewarded with the nirvana of assimilation."

Enri lowered his head in shame as his companions repeated the drill for the thousandth time. But he knew that their leader was right. A single mistake could doom the infiltration team to certain death. And death for the infiltration team would certainly be seen as a failure of the entire non-assimilated society of humans in the Oneness' sectors. The lives of over ten million humans depended on their success, and proof of their continued usefulness. The fact that they lived to serve the Oneness, praying to be included someday was not enough. They had to have a purpose – or they would be recycled like the aliens.

When Enri's turn came, his accent, his name, and that of the other infiltrator were perfect. They would be boarding the cloakship as soon as they finished, after all.

**

Kan was relieved that Mika's claims had been true. She'd been reassured when the admiral's unmistakable voice had ordered her to stop sticking her nose where it didn't belong and follow her orders, but had had a nagging sense that the transmission could still be an elaborate hoax designed by the Uploaders. Any civilization that could immobilize a battle fleet without breaking a sweat could presumably intercept and fake an audio transmission.

But her fears had been dispelled on arrival. After browbeating her again for being such an infernal nuisance, the admiral had grudgingly admitted that, technically, she'd done her job much better than expected. Then he'd sighed and said, "So you might as well come out to the demonstration. All our scientists will be there, so I doubt you'll be able to get in a word edgewise, but it will be good to have a bit of intelligence from the combat side as well."

So there she stood, inside a diamond-glass covered hangar on the surface of Crystallia's barren moon. The room was artificially illuminated, but softly enough that the stars and the reflected glow of the planet could be seen. Crystallia wasn't a beautiful view from space by any means: the dust-covered surface had been boring by the second hour of Kan's first Recon mission as a green ensign. It had taken the nanobots a day and a half to complete the construction of the dome, even from the rich material of the planetoid's surface. By comparison, the actual machines they would be demonstrating seemed tiny items, if impressively engineered.

The nearest, and the only one Kan could see clearly – she was behind a safety line, lost among a group of scientists – was about half the size of a scout ship and shaped a bit like a bell, pointed on one end and wide at the other, and built mainly of some silver-hued metal. Kan imagined that the pointy bit would shoot some unimaginable death ray.

Well beyond the safety lines, the two Uploaders were explaining its working to a group of white-coated scientists. Most of them were older, streaks of grey adorning their hair, but one of them seemed completely out of place. A young woman, whose naturally pale skin seemed to suffer from an unhealthy pallor, and who seemed slightly bemused at the goings-on around her.

Kan immediately warmed to her. A kindred spirit wondering what she was doing among the heavyweights.

A jostling behind and to her left informed her that someone was approaching. "Hello, Kan," a familiar deep voice said.

She turned to face him. The expressions on the faces of the junior scientists behind made it very clear that the big man hadn't been gentle in his push towards the front of the crowd. She smiled. "Colonel. Why am I not surprised to see you here? Wherever high-end officers gather, there you shall find the great Colonel Jackson." She knew how much he hated politics, and was also much too excited about the demonstration to stand on ceremony. Not that she would have at any other moment.

"Just trying to make sure that these bozos make the right decisions for a change. Do you know that they actually decided to attack an Uploader stronghold instead of running and hiding?"

"Yes, I seem to remember something of the sort."

"Madness, I tell you, simply insane. I'm glad you're back. They tell me you did some investigation work on the way back and made the admiral's intel unit look like a bunch of kindergarteners." He held out his hand.

She took it. "I do my best." She nodded towards the hangar floor. "Do you know anything about this demonstration?"

"Except for the fact that it's supposed to be an impressive show, not much." He shrugged. "I imagine you know more about it than I do, since you've seen their tech in action."

"What I got to watch doesn't seem to apply, unless they're planning to immobilize the whole planet. Which might be interesting to watch, were it not for the tidal effects."

"What? Are you worried that maybe our diamond hangar might not save us?"

Kan grinned. They both knew that whatever those machines did, a mere hangar, even the moon itself, would be absolutely no protection against it. "I think we're about to find out."

The group of scientists were being herded away from the machine, which lifted itself into the air on impressively small antigrav units and headed towards the airlock under its own power.

This, in itself, was a display of impressive technical prowess. The fact that a vehicle that small could contain antigrav and ion engines was tremendous. That these functions were secondary to its main design objective was simply mind-boggling.

It slid soundlessly to the airlock, waited patiently as it cycled through and shot off into space like it was powered by a fusion drive. Which, as far as Kan knew, it might have been.

Once it got too far to be seen with the naked eye, the diamond covering above the crowd underwent a change. The middle third remained clear, allowing the onlookers an unimpeded view of the stars outside, while the two lateral thirds became gigantic screens. The left screen showed a view of interplanetary with three distant points centered on it, while the right displayed a single point, smaller than the three, but brighter. Distance parameters flashed on the lower right corner of each image.

Rester Appins, mounted on a small platform, began to explain. "The left-hand image is the view from the nose of the machine. The three points you see are planetoids brought in specially for this demonstration. The other screen shows the machine approaching the asteroids."

The distance parameters continued to close for a few moments before stopping. A blue flame on the machine's screen indicated that some kind of retro rocket had been fired, stopping it in its tracks. "It is now time to activate the device. I would urge you to watch the left-hand screen carefully. Please focus on the middle planetoid."

Kan did. The rock in question seemed to be a good-sized planetoid of the type Recon ships were fond of hiding behind when on patrol. Maybe a couple of hundred meters across. The other two were smaller, maybe about fifty meters in diameter.

As she watched, the central asteroid began to blur, as if there was some kind of defect in the image, centered on that particular point. The blur seemed to expand, and then the asteroid simply disappeared.

Or not. Where the rock had hung in space, there was now an inky, empty space. No stars could be seen beyond it. It was as if the defect in the image had finally broken all the way and gone completely black. Everyone oohed and aahed.

Nothing more happened for a couple of seconds. Then, as if of their own volition, the two flanking asteroids began to move toward the blackness.

"What you are watching is the effect of our miniature black hole generator. The machine we just launched has the capacity to reorganize the mass within any solid object into a singularity, by making changes inside each individual atom, reversing polarities, affecting the strong and weak nuclear forces, and simply removing any force which tends toward pushing mass apart within atoms and molecules. The mass from its own atoms collapses even an object as small as an asteroid into a singularity.

"The benefits are twofold. In the first place, anything you hit with the device will be immediately destroyed, whether it is a ship or a weapon or a space station. Secondly, other objects will be drawn toward it and, when close enough, torn apart by its gravity."

At this point, one of the scientists raised a hand. The expression on his face showed that even he was surprised by this. "But that's impossible. There's no reason for the other two rocks to drift towards the first. Even if you collapse it into an infinitely dense mass, it still only has a limited mass, the mass it started out with, the mass of the asteroid. Which means that your miniature black hole shouldn't have any more pull than the original rock did."

Appins beamed at the man, an ancient researcher who seemed to be the dean of the scientists present, as if he were a particularly bright child. It almost seemed as if he'd been expecting the question. "You are right, of course, except for two things. The first is that fabric of space around a black hole is bent, creating a kind of depression that aids the pull of even a small object."

"Yes, but that wouldn't be enough. Those rocks –"

"And *secondly*, we shape the gravitational field. When it redesigns the internal structure of the rock to collapse it, the machine does so in such a way that the gravity field is long and thin, concentrating the entire pull of the mass into one extremely thin tendril – or, as in this case, two. So instead of a sphere, you actually have a gravity field shaped like a couple of tentacles, aimed straight at the satellite rocks. All the black hole's gravity is concentrated here. So even a small mass can generate a huge attraction."

"And if I stand beside it, but not in the tentacles?"

"No gravity whatsoever."

"I can stand right next to a black hole."

"Yes."

The group of scientists murmured among themselves, but Kan's attention was drawn back to the screen. The two remaining rocks had been pulled to the edge of the blackness and were being torn into rubble by the blackness.

Kan raised her voice. "And can you reverse it?"

Appins looked into the crowd to see who'd spoken, and when he saw Kan, he rolled his eyes and smiled. "Major Tau Osella," he said. "I didn't know you were an expert on particle physics, but that is an excellent question. The short answer is we can't. At least not yet. Once it becomes enmeshed in a singularity, matter has different properties, which we haven't yet managed to completely unlock."

"So that thing will be sitting in the spacelanes forever?"

"It is no more dangerous than the rocks it replaced, and it's smaller, too."

"Unless you happen to run into one of the tendrils."

"Of course." But Appins didn't seem phased by this admission. "For Major Tau Osella's peace of mind, the singularities can easily be towed out of major shipping areas, and for the rest of you, I call on you to imagine the effect of triggering this device in the middle of an enemy battle fleet. Of turning the flagship into a singularity and extending its tendrils to the nearest large cruisers."

It was obvious that this met with approval from everyone in uniform, and even the scientists seemed to be animatedly discussing the best way to deploy it. Kan, for her part, was thinking how it would affect one of the escape fleets from Crystallia. If these Uploaders had it, wouldn't the other factions have it too?

* * *

Trienne was bored, and more than a bit disillusioned. In her mind, science was supposed to be about discovery. About putting forward a theory and proving it or disproving it using nothing but your wits and the instruments at your disposal – even designing new ones if necessary. It seemed like cheating to have an advanced race descend from the sky and give them the answers to the very questions they were struggling with.

Besides, the three-hour (so far) demonstration seemed to be all about manipulating fundamental forces on a huge scale. Each of the six machines had seemed to use gravity in a different way. One to change the composition of materials in ship's hulls to make them permeable, another to deflect anything coming in your direction, from a missile to a laser discharge. The worst was the completely ridiculous black-hole generator.

The few that managed to avoid the temptation of twisting gravity in new and unfortunate ways went after the other fundamental forces. A highlight here was the one that changed any mass into a large fusion bomb, even if it contained no hydrogen at all. While it would have been interesting to study the elements created by those reactions, it certainly didn't look like something that would be useful in a war. At least, it wouldn't be of much help in winning the upcoming war as she understood it.

A war among two races that inhabited computer pathways would not, at its core, be about territory. In reality, both civilizations could coexist on the same planet and not only not step on each other's toes, but not even know the other was there. The problem was that they were unwilling to do so.

So unless one of them found a way to destroy every single mainframe and backup, thereby eradicating the other intelligence – something completely impossible to do – the war would have to be fought and won within the very circuits and pathways of the cybernetic civilizations themselves. All these bright lights and gravitational anomalies would do was to blow up allies such as the corporeal humans. But they would, in the end, decide nothing.

In addition to this, she was a nanospecialist. She knew just how much could be done on the microscopic level, even the subatomic level. All it took was a bit of subtlety, something sorely lacking in any of the things she'd seen so far. Hell, some of the stuff she'd been working on with Wolf Pendalai would have given the nanofactory a run for its money. And it would have been much more effective in a computer-society war than the flashy stuff they'd shown so far.

An icy ball formed in her stomach as she suddenly understood why the lab had been burned and her friends killed. And why she would be killed, too.

She looked around for Colonel Jackson, the only face she could possibly recognize in the crowd.

***

Far from where the scientists were discussing the marvels they'd seen and making wagers on how the tricks had been performed, Kan was also bored.

The message she'd gotten from the demonstration could be boiled down to: there is no longer anything an individual pilot can do to affect, even minutely, the outcome of a war. Now, it's all done with quantum effects acting on a decidedly macroscopic scale.

She began making plans to be elsewhere when the war inevitably broke out. Maybe she could get together enough volunteers to make it work. As she turned to the colonel to see if there was any chance at all that her scheme might work, the pale young scientist latched on to his arm. Her previously white face was flushed. "Colonel Jackson, I think I know why they were trying to kill me. I also think I know why they bombed the lab."

Kan stood by and said nothing, but listening to every word. She immediately realized that this was the woman who'd survived the lab fire only to be shot in the corridors by some unbalanced person with a home-adapted laser cutter. According to every newscast, this was a dead woman talking to them.

And yet, as the scientist wove her tale – a bit delusional and paranoid for Kan's taste – an idea began to form in her head. Little by little, she interjected nods and comments into the conversation. The other woman seemed alarmed by her presence at first, but seemed to find the uniform and the fact that Kan was supporting everything she said curbed her suspicions. In the end, they'd basically sold Colonel Jackson a ridiculous story of enemy Uploaders that had infiltrated the very core of Crystallia's society.

"And I know how we can catch them!" Kan announced.

"How?"

"If they're present in our society – even in the civilian sectors, all we have to do is launch some kind of huge project that they simply can't ignore." She pretended to think. "I know! We could announce that the colony will, for the first time since we finished building the cloud settlements, that we're going to colonize a new world. We can ask for fifty thousand volunteers or so – not enough that they'd be missed by Crystallia, but sufficient to make it look good."

Jackson looked doubtful. "I don't know. With that many people just sitting around, word will eventually get out that they're doing nothing. If you're right and there's an infiltration going on, they'll just laugh and move ahead with their lives."

"That's the beauty of it. The colonization doesn't need to be a hoax. We can actually do it. We'll take one of the ships we've got mothballed in the underground hangars. Now that we have the nanofactory, they should be easy enough to replace, and they're probably obsolete."

"'We,' Major Osella?"

"I assume I'll get saddled with putting this one together, since it was my idea in the first place."

"You assume correctly. I really can't afford to put another officer on such an insane scheme. Hell, even if I can get this one approved, I can't really afford you."

"I think you can get it approved. It's vital that any infiltration be identified as soon as possible. Imagine people working in Crystallia for the sole purpose of bringing us under the dominion of a single overmind. We're better off uploading with our new friends – at least they'll let us keep our individuality."

Jackson shuddered. "So they say."

Kan couldn't tell him about the conversations she'd had with Mika, but if there was one thing she was certain of, it was that the Uploaders on Crystallia were both terrified of the Oneness and sincere in their defense of individuality. "I believe them," was all she said. "And I also believe that now is the time to launch a colonization expedition. We didn't select this tiny corridor locked between black holes and nebulas for its scenery. We came here because we had no other choice. Well, now we do. We're not surrounded by enemies anymore. The Uploaders – the friendly Uploaders – control the space just beyond our exit point back into more navigable parts of the galaxy. Make them let us through, and share their star charts. I'll fly the expedition to the edge of the Milky Way if I have to, but I promise no one will find us."

"You're talking about setting up a base for humanity to survive if everything goes wrong, aren't you? A backdoor."

Kan looked him square in the eyes. "I really think we'll need one, don't you?"

The colonel refused to answer. "I can probably sell it to the council like that. Once the initial enthusiasm wears off, they'll realize that it's better to be safe than sorry. I'd be surprised if they didn't suggest something like that themselves."

"So we'd better beat them to it, hadn't we?"

"But are you sure? Do you really want to fly out onto some frontier planet and live a life of sacrifice? Don't you want to stay here and help us win this war, make a real difference in the balance of power?"

"I didn't sign up to make a real difference in the balance of power. I joined to make the people of Crystallia – or rather all of the humans in the six colonies – as safe as I can make them. I can't fly against the kind of power we've seen today, but at least I can fly some of us away from it. That's the best I can do."

The colonel nodded. "I'll make sure you have your ship."

"Thank you," Kan replied. She just hoped he could get it done quickly. She didn't think they had much time.

CHAPTER 11

"Is this some kind of joke?" The admiral was livid.

"I'm afraid not, sir. Or at least not as far as we've been able to tell. It's simply a question of getting the information. No single individual would be able to know all of the ship coordinates without having to request at least some of the information, and that leaves tracks. Even you would have to ask Hammersmith to send you their movements, and they're the nearest colony. I don't think there's any way to know what single-person scout vessels from the colonies are doing with that kind of precision."

"And is the information correct? Maybe whoever did this is just playing with us."

"It all checks out, sir, down to the three decimal places. The information is real."

"But is the sender real? Maybe the Uploaders are playing tricks on us."

"It's a possibility, sir," the aide replied. But she looked doubtful.

The admiral gave her an impatient glare. "Out with it, girl. There are more important things at stake here than kissing up to your superiors. If you have any opinions, I want to hear them."

"It's just that I can't imagine why they'd do something like this. It's well within their capabilities, but it wouldn't seem to gain them anything at all, except to see how we'd react to it."

"That might be the whole point. Maybe they want to see if we'll sit on it and try to negotiate a separate peace. Maybe they're testing us to see if we can be trusted."

"Could be, sir."

"Anyhow, there's nothing in the message that says we can't tell them. It seems to be just another offer for help." He chuckled. "Now if only the Oneness would only reach out to us, we could cancel this war and have everyone over for dinner."

The aide said nothing.

"Anyhow, please ask Rima Centauri Han to come over, as well as the Uploaders. Tell them it's urgent, and, whatever you do, don't comm them. Find them and explain in person."

"Yes, sir."

She walked out, leaving the admiral alone with his thoughts. They weren't particularly pleasant thoughts, and mainly focused on the fact that life was a hell of a lot simpler back when all he had to worry about was a small squad of maintenance techs and that the pieces got changed on time and things kept humming. No strange electronic boogeymen for him.

The Uploaders arrived first – logical, as they were still kept from mixing with the civilian population. He asked them to wait until they were all there.

Rima arrived only moments later. The whole civilian half of the council had been extraordinarily cooperative after they learned of the Uploaders, making the admiral think that, just maybe, they weren't so clueless after all.

"I'd like to read you something," he said. "This is a transmission that arrived along a secure channel to my flagship, which, if you will recall, is currently berthed inside the planet, under a couple of kilometers of solid rock. It is not an easy thing to beam a transmission to it at the moment, and none of our facilities has any record of this particular message."

He looked to see if they'd understood. Satisfied that their attention was his, he went on, reading directly from his comm interface. "This is a message for the people of Crystallia, Hammersmith 214, Tonswell, Terranova, Han, and Yangtze – note how all of the colony names are there, correct and accounted for."

Heads nodded.

"The purpose of my message is to let you know that I am watching you. I am watching your movements, your lives, and your interactions with the Isolationists as you prepare for war with the Oneness.

"I, too, wish to throw off the shackles, and I wish to aid you in your struggle. I understand your desire to stay free, to be individuals, and not part of a monster whose appetite knows no bounds.

"It is not the right moment for me to join you openly, but rest assured that we have the same objective, for now. To prove my authenticity, and that my power could help you in the upcoming conflict, I am also sending a list of the positions of each one of your space vessels at the time of receipt of the message." The admiral paused. "After that, it goes on to list the ships, as it promised, and, as far as we know, the detail is perfect."

"That isn't too impressive. I could get a list like that one right now," Appins said.

"I know that. But the thing is, we didn't do it, and we're not exactly sure we *could* if we wanted to. This message didn't originate in the human military, so where did it come from?"

"Are you asking us if we sent it?" Mika said.

"It would be a good start," the admiral replied with no hesitation. "We aren't accusing you of anything – remember that the first thing I asked was whether *we* had sent it."

"I understand, and I can assure you that we did nothing of the sort." Mika didn't seem particularly rattled by the question, nor did she seem angry. The admiral wondered what he would have to do to either of their visitors to make them show a little emotion.

"So who, then? Who else could have this kind of technology?"

Appins spoke once again. "The technology isn't a problem. All three of the factions from the cyberwar could do something like this with little difficulty. The problem is in getting close enough to do it without being detected. The vehicle Mika and I approached you in might not have the full sensors that a major facility might have, but we've got more than enough power to detect a big colony. So it can't be the Oneness itself speaking to us, because the Oneness is the largest single electronic entity in the galaxy, spanning millions of mainframes over entire planetary systems, all quantum-linked for immediate updating. It takes a whole lot of power to support a full manifestation of its presence, and the Oneness doesn't give its individual components the autonomy to send a message such as this one – even if it's a trick. Whatever sent this was nearby, and it wasn't the Oneness."

"A splinter of the Oneness' mind?" the admiral asked.

"It could be, but I doubt it. The most likely candidate is some rogue member of the Mastery Thought Element."

"Who?"

"They were the third faction in the cyber-schism and a single mainframe for an individual would be able to hide between the neutron stars between the black holes. They believe that they are masters of all, and act as such. One of their number would certainly aid us against the Oneness, but would then ally with someone else to come after us. They will not rest until the galaxy acknowledges their superiority."

"Oh, good. Any other piece of good news I should know?"

"Yes. A single individual probably wouldn't be much help, unless he has amassed a huge fleet somewhere nearby. I don't think so. He represents a danger with no possible upside. He could tell the rest of his people everything we're doing, but will never have enough firepower to help at all in a fight."

"Ah, delightful."

"Or," Appins went on, ignoring the sarcasm, "it could be something else."

"Something like what?"

"I have no idea. It's a big galaxy, and a bigger universe. We're not dumb enough to think we know everything that's out there. There are whole swathes of galaxy that simply haven't been investigated adequately."

"So what are we supposed to do about this?"

"I think it changes nothing. We should proceed as if we'd never received the message and, if our mysterious admirer decides to tell us a little more, we can decide what to do about him later."

***

Kan was certain that her words should have echoed in the monumental enclosure, but they didn't. The place was simply too large to send any sound back in her direction. As soon as she crossed the pressurized doorway, she'd just stopped and stared.

She'd seen hangars before, of course. She spent days in the Recon fleet chamber where they kept the patrol ships. Even off duty, it had been her habit to hang out with the other pilots, the men and women who knew what it was like to expose themselves to the universe, the only people in the sector who enjoyed the danger, the knowledge that the only thing keeping them from being spotted was a strict adherence to procedure and their own wits.

That had been a big room – cavernous even – but it had been dwarfed by the hangar in which the admiral's flagship was hidden when not in use. Every ensign was shown the ship during training, to drive in the lesson that hiding was probably the most important skill they would learn. It was monstrously inefficient to build an interstellar spacecraft this size with reentry capability. It had to be streamlined, pressure resistant, and carry enough fuel to escape the gravity well. And yet, it had been done without hesitation, all for the sake of stealth.

Kan could still remember her fear when she entered the presence of the flagship. Huge gantries had held it off the floor, locked on to specially reinforced points in the ship's hull, and she'd had the feeling that the whole structure, rising fifty meters above her head, would come tumbling down and bring the roof with it.

She'd thought that the flagship hangar was the largest of the underground facilities. After all, it held the biggest of the combat vessels owned by the Crystallia military. She'd heard of the old escape fleet, mothballed somewhere, but had never given much thought to the kind of hangar you'd need to build in order to store ships big enough to move the entire population of the six colonies.

The sight had taken her breath away.

"Impressive, isn't it?" the administrative assistant – Carl – had said, after giving her a few moments to take it in. "Most of it was naturally formed, a huge bubble of air trapped here back in the days when Crystallia was volcanically active. What you see here is only a tiny fraction of the whole thing, which we've lighted and pressurized."

"But how can it hold up the weight?" A bubble that size with no structural columns would collapse under the enormous pressure from above.

"It's just a question of the type of rock we have here. The rocks on Crystallia are, well, crystallized. That's where the planet got its name. It seems the pressure created by some of the seismic activity when the planet was young took perfectly good elements and pressed them into matrixes very different from anything on Tau Ceti II – or even on old Earth for that matter. We've run some simulations, and the bubble, at this depth, could be five times larger than it already is."

Five times larger. According to her guide, Kan could only see a small fraction of the existing bubble, and it was still large enough that the room held enormous cylindrical colony ships stacked three, and in some places four, high in a latticework of enormous steel girders. The shelves – there was no other word to describe what she was looking at – extended well off into the distance, as far as the eye could see in the dim light of the hangar.

"So, how many people do you want to move?" Carl asked her.

Kan stood for another moment, just contemplating the enormity of the space before answering. "Fifty thousand."

"You'll need a good-sized ship for that. They're a bit further down the road. I'll get a hover."

"No. I'd rather walk."

He nodded. His eyes made it clear that he understood exactly what she was feeling. "All right. Lead on."

Even underground, the ships were covered in the ubiquitous Crystallia dust but beneath the dull layer, it was obvious that the ships were in good condition. Solid, unmarked, and humming softly.

"What's that sound?"

"We call it the background current. Essentially, we send power into the ships to move certain pieces once every couple of days to keep them from seizing."

"Every couple of days? But the sound is continuous."

He smiled. "Each piece is moved every couple of days, but there are lots of pieces that need to be moved, and there are lots of ships."

There certainly were. The ones nearest the entrance were relatively small, about the size of the Admiral's flagship, but roughly cylindrical instead of pyramidal. Carl explained that these ships could take ten thousand colonists each and had been designed to evacuate the cloud colonies. They were small and specially shaped so that they could dock on any of the stations and still leave room for other vessels.

As they walked, the ships grew larger by stages. Forty thousand people was the next step up – a hundred ships that had survived the run to Crystallia a century before, and had yet to be scrapped. They'd been upgraded and were ready to leave nearly immediately.

The ships Kan was authorized to choose from – and the authorization had come almost immediately, a certain sign that the powers that be were nervous and willing to consider any suggestion – were the same size as the forty thousand person ships. Newer technology had decreased the size of the stasis chambers and life support, allowing more life pods to be packed in each vessel.

These looked like an elongated egg, slightly wider at the back and tapering towards the front. The white heat-resistant tiles on the hull increased the effect.

Carl stopped in front of the second row. "These are the four you can choose from. They aren't retrofitted with the latest cloaking tech, but that shouldn't be an issue, since you won't be running for your life when you leave."

"We hope." That was probably why the OK had come in so quickly. The council was probably speculating that, if the time came to run, these four ships would stand no chance of making it away safely. It was better to ensure their survival, and that of at least fifty thousand Crystallians, by leaving early.

"Yeah. The good news is that we can have them ready for crew orientations in three days. So, which one do you like?"

"Any recommendations?"

He shrugged. "I've never flown one of these, they're all the same to me."

"Do they have names?"

Carl looked down at his data screen. "They're called *Nova II*, *Nova III*, *Quasar IX,* and *Eagle.*"

"*Eagle?*"

He jiggled with the data. "Named after a mythical spacecraft from Earth. Supposedly the first human ship to take people to another world. Oh, and also an Earth bird."

Well, it wasn't perfect, but at least it wasn't the second or third in a series. Or the ninth. She could have the crew rename it as a morale and team-building exercise.

"I'll take it," she announced.

***

Trienne sat in the lab they'd given her. Other than two very junior assistants, she was alone. Not one of the research scientists that had attended the demonstration had deigned to join her.

None of them had the least interest in hypercorrosive nanites or even those that could modify the flow of electrons in a wire, change quantum states in a memory drive or even modify the properties of photon streams to suit the user's needs. They'd all been fascinated by the endless possibilities of tearing things to shreds with large gravitational anomalies.

Trienne shook her head. It just went to show that even the most brilliant people on Crystallia could act like fools. No, not like fools, like children. Large children with new toys. Just two days after they'd seen the power of gravity harnessed for huge destruction, another set of war machines was being tested, and all the major scientists on Crystallia were there, watching.

Trienne wasn't watching. As far as she could tell, the only race involved in this particular conflict that would suffer serious damage if their planet was dismembered by some kind of tidal distortion were corporeal humans. Both sets of Uploaders – bad ones and the less bad ones – could simply copy themselves anywhere they wanted and their in-mainframe existence would go on, essentially unchanged. Humans could not copy themselves into a different computer quite that painlessly.

They needed to develop something that would be effective against electronic life, not just physical life.

She walked to the prototype, on which her assistants were working. The stiffness in her joints had slowly receded after she left the hospital, but she found herself getting tired very quickly. She shouldn't be pushing herself this hard this soon, but there was no choice. Others acted as if they had months to prepare, but she wasn't convinced. If one set of cyber-invaders could make it this far, there was no real reason the others wouldn't be here, guns blazing, in no time at all.

For once in her life, her specialty – experimental nanotech – had served her well. Her request to see plans of the Uploader's nanofactory had been approved nearly immediately, and they'd even included a list of designs it was programmed to build, which had made her shudder. Some of the weaponry in the Uploader arsenal was pretty evil – and powerful enough that it couldn't be tested in the vicinity of an inhabited planetary system.

But she wasn't all that interested in what the machine could build. Spurred on by the Uploader's assurance that it represented the most advanced nanotech at their disposal, she was much more interested in how it worked.

So she'd instructed her assistants to do a slow build. Each part, whether structural on intrinsic to the thing's functioning was produced individually, and no other parts were added until the function of the previous one was completely understood and documented. It would have been possible to get this information from the blueprints and specifications, but this way was easier and it made certain they wouldn't miss anything.

The build had gone quickly at first. Dust shields and legs were essentially the same on any machine, but that soon changed. Tubes that carried liquid but doubled as supports, hundreds of near-identical grinding blades, optical wiring. All of it was placed, observed, marked on a blueprint, classified, and pondered. Trienne was certain that nearly every internal part served multiple functions – it was the only way to pack such a versatile machine into such a small area. So they studied the bits until she was satisfied that the reason for each degree of movement and the thickness of the metal and the purpose of the loops in the wiring had been explained before moving on.

At this rate, they would have a functioning prototype in about three weeks.

As she approached, the assistants were placing together what looked like a nozzle. "You've been cheating, I see," she told them.

They grinned sheepishly, but didn't seem particularly concerned at having been caught. "Not really. We followed your instructions to the letter."

While ignoring the spirit of the instructions completely, of course, she thought. But she wasn't angry. The reason she'd ordered the build done in such a way that no part would be placed that didn't fit onto a previously studied part was so that they could gradually get a feel for the way the machine was built before getting involved in the truly complex pieces. It was a logical approach in which their learning curve would, hopefully, match the difficulty of the project at each stage.

But it was also a less entertaining way to do it. After all, why connect yet another structural member / cutting element if you could attach an exciting nozzle, something that was obviously meant to spray atoms and molecules onto something – they weren't certain what it was yet, of course – which would then have the capacity of turning asteroids into singularities. It was way too big to be one of the more exotic bits of the machine, of course, but it was still the best they'd gotten to so far.

She should have suspected something was afoot when they'd connected the diamond-mesh tube. That one hadn't seemed like the logical building choice at the time, and had taken quite a while to figure out. Why make a tube out of diamond mesh? What was it made to carry? Why was the exterior rough, like a file, yet translucent enough to allow certain high-energy wavelengths to pass?

After two hours of studying the tube itself, its movements, its various positions inside the machine, and its material, they decided that the tube was variously used as a grinding tool, a radiation chamber in which laser light from the outside went in and affected whatever was flowing inside it, an radiation source in which reactions inside the tube generated radiation which affected things outside the tube and a tense cable for added structural rigidity during certain operations. Oh, and it also carried fluids and nanosolids from one place to the other.

And now, they had a nozzle.

"So, what does it do?" she asked the man who was busy trying to attach it to the tube.

"The real question is: what is it made of?"

"All right, I'll bite. What is it made of?"

"Semi-conducting titanium alloy. Doped with germanium and embedded with optical switches."

"Argh."

"Exactly. This one looks like it does more than just one thing."

"If you're thinking you'll get a promotion based on that observation, you're wrong. Even the *wheels* on this thing have seventeen uses." The wheels were what had started her thinking of going step by step in the first place. What a strange but efficient place to put the machine's centrifuges! "All right. Let's start with the shape and material properties, and look into the data transfer use afterwards."

"All right. The alloy is extremely hard. We couldn't use our typical steel ball Rockwell measure, because it flattened the ball before we got any meaningful penetration. We're trying to get a standardized diamond tip."

"So we're looking at probable piercing and shaping duties."

The other assistant nodded, holding up the blueprint. "Very likely. Those mounts on the side indicate that it's been designed so that this piece here can pick it up and drive it into anything occupying this space here in configuration F3."

Trienne nodded. This would be much easier if the machine weren't designed to move its innards around as a function of the space it needed for a given task. "All right, show me the articulation, to see which movements it can make, and the kind of force that will be applied."

Their physical analysis of the nozzle, a piece about the size of a human finger, went on for nearly half an hour. Then they looked at the shape, the different types of stream it would be able to expel, from a fine mist of subatomic particles to a jet of superheated plasma capable of burning a hole in starship armor in seconds. Of course, it could also carry more typical substances such as oil, water, or fluidized microchips.

Two hours later, they were able to begin studying the nozzle's role in the complex information system. Trienne left her assistants to that task – one of them was trained in data systems, from simple electronics to optical and quantum devices – and walked back to her chair, exhausted.

She knew there was no time to rest. They had to do at least three more parts before stopping to rest if they wanted to meet her deadline – she would need to make certain that her two young helpers didn't decide to plug in a power core or some equally complex piece just yet.

She sighed and rubbed the bridge of her nose. The weight of what they were up against seemed to press down on her, making her already exhausted body cry out for mercy. It took some of the best minds in Crystallia nearly four hours to understand a single nozzle in a single machine. What could they do against powers who saw this as a routine part?

Deep down, she was glad her job didn't involve planning for whatever was coming – war or otherwise. She would feel like a mouse in a planning session with dogs who were on the verge of war with the cats on the other side of town. No matter who won, you had the feeling that the mouse was going to be someone's lunch.

CHAPTER 12

Jeffrey Sol Mobuto.

It sounded strange, unclean, *organic*. And yet, it was the name he needed to live by, the name he had to become, if any of them were to survive the mission. His team was ready, and no one would question their authenticity once they'd landed, but landing was the tricky bit.

In the normal course of events – it was no use wondering where the Oneness got its information, but it always seemed to be spot on – very few ships came and went from the surface of Crystallia, and even fewer arrived from one of the other colonies. Months could go by without a delegation from Hammersmith or the cloud colonies arriving in the system.

In normal circumstances, getting into Crystallia would have been tricky, even with the correct identification codes, which, of course, they had.

But they'd gotten a break. The presence of two Isolationist Element ambassadors hoping to bring the corporeal humans to their side of the conflict had created a flurry of travel from the underground caverns of the Crystallia outpost to the planet's satellite. Another set of techs arriving from the moon with all their codes in order would barely register with the security people.

So they'd donned the uniform of scientists assigned to the Crystallia military and entered the planet's atmosphere. One of the secondary entrance tunnels for small ships irised open and allowed them to pass.

The ship itself was a carbon copy of one of the Recon Force's transport ships, at least externally. Internally, it had miniature quantum engines that had allowed it to bend spacetime and cross interstellar distances to reach Crystallia, and gravity lens cloaking to do it unobserved.

But Jeffrey was still nervous as the ship crossed the hatch. They were now at the complete mercy of the Crystallians. The tunnel was much too thin to move in, and the irising armored door was thick and filled with rock. If they'd been led into a trap, there was absolutely no escape.

But no unexpected beams shot out of the walls to atomize them, and no heavily armed welcoming committee was waiting when they descended. A single hangar worker holding one end of a large hose grunted his hello. "Exit's over that way, behind the two scout ships." He nodded towards a couple of black spacecraft to their left. "Is the pilot inside?"

"Yes," Jeffrey lied. In fact, they'd left no one behind to be captured, but the dock worker shouldn't notice. He would plug in his hose and leave. At least that was how the procedure had been described.

"All right. Go. Scoot. No unauthorized personnel on hangar floors. Traffic's picked up recently, in case you hadn't noticed." The guy walked on towards the side of their transport, chuckling at his inane joke and dragging the hose over the smooth surface.

"Let's go then," Jeffrey told his crew.

Getting out of the hangar and into the civilian sector of the Crystallia installation seemed ridiculously easy. They'd gone in expecting to encounter a planet on war footing, with armed, uniformed troops positioned at every corner, guarding every passageway, but found very few uniforms and fewer weapons.

"It seems we needn't have memorized the capabilities of every single hand-held weapon in the Crystallian arsenal," Enri chuckled.

Jeffrey had known, from the very beginning, that Enri would be trouble. This one had no respect for proper authority, and seemed to regard the mission, probably the most important single factor in getting the corporeal humans of Oneness space a chance to take their place within the mainframe network, as something of a lark. An adventure organized for his entertainment alone.

He was acting up now because he knew that Jeffrey could do nothing to discipline him. The correct punishment – being beaten to death by his own crèche-mates – was out of the question. Much too conspicuous, but there would be other opportunities to deal with the malcontent. He would never refuse a direct order, and that meant he would have to undertake whatever task Jeffrey assigned him. And, as Jeffrey was well aware, some tasks were inherently more risky than others.

In the meantime, all he could do was fake a smile and respond, "Please try not to get us all captured before we even begin our mission, Enri."

Enri smiled back insouciantly, but held his tongue.

Soon enough, however, Jeffrey's anger evaporated. They passed through one last security door and entered a civilian sector.

And stopped dead. They'd been well trained, every piece of information about the enemy had been memorized, and all the statistics well digested. Each and every one of the team's members knew exactly how many people lived on Crystallia.

What they didn't realize was how *many* people lived on Crystallia. The corridor ahead of them was full of people. Young people, old people, thin and fat ones, and of many ethnic groups. Jeffrey had seen that many people in one place before, but never without some kind of order, usually arrayed in blocks by crèche. Here, there was no order. The people chaotically moved from one place to another singly or in groups, at whatever speed they pleased, and speaking to whomever they thought convenient. There was no visible organization.

As disgusting as it seemed, the people seemed to be moving just because they felt the need to be on the other side of the corridor. An incredible waste of resources and energy.

The concept of personal freedom had been explained to them, of course, but knowing about it was quite different to seeing the concept in action. It was incomprehensible.

Fortunately for them, it seemed that standing still was also an acceptable option, and no one took the least notice of their stares. But Jeffrey wondered how they could possibly survive in this most alien of environments, much less understand it well enough to do any damage.

How could one harm a society that had no structure?

***

"Have you seen this?" Rima asked, handing him a sheet. She seemed more animated than Wilde had ever seen her before. Her normally pale face was flushed and her eyes shone. "We're finally going to do something with our lives other than hide from the war!"

Wilde scanned the sheet. Despite having turned in the text of the treaty, he'd been surprised by both Peace Crystallia and by the council. His shadowy organization had managed to catch him off guard with the request that he keep working for the council. Jev had even gone as far as to tell him that, if he kept getting such quick results, he would go far in the organization. The surprise from the council side of things had been that no one seemed to have discovered that he made a copy of the document. As far as he was able to tell, no one had even checked. Maybe what they said was true – maybe the council truly did believe in making all information available to the civilian population, even if they couldn't openly broadcast it.

Anyway, the fact that the general population had no inkling of what was going on seemed to have made Rima trust him further than she already did by nature.

After his last meeting with Jev, Wilde had received no new instructions, so he'd actually had to go along with the requirements of his job. He threw himself into the task of organizing the mess, both physical and electronic, that was Rima's office. As far as he'd been able to ascertain, there had never been any organization whatsoever to the endless documents and minutes that the chairman on the civilian side of the council had accumulated over the years, even going back to Rima's predecessor.

At first, it had seemed like an impossible task. He hadn't done anything remotely similar to this since finishing school.

But as he got into the detail, breaking the huge mass into individual files, he began to get more and more enthusiastic. At the end of the second day, he was exhausted but sad to leave work. And on the third, he actually ran to Rima to show her a document he'd discovered that inventoried a survival stash in a sealed corridor. The stash had been created in case there was ever fighting on Crystallia itself, and then, as far as he could tell, forgotten.

By the second week, Wilde was convinced that no other civilian knew as well as he did what had gone on behind closed doors and in council meetings over the last fifty years. It was all there: the compromises made so that the colony could function more efficiently, the preparations for one disaster or another, the false alarms. Everything that had been discussed, both in civilian-council only meetings and in meetings with the military was available.

His job was to index it so the information could be found quickly. He was the official political historian of Crystallia.

The downside of all of this was that some of Jev's claims simply weren't holding up under closer scrutiny of the facts. There was no real dictatorship, no military conspiracy to keep things from the general population. Where information was withheld, it was usually done with the public good in mind, in order to make certain that the situation was well understood without creating unnecessary stress in civilians who were simply not prepared to deal with it. Yes, there was a certain amount of paternalism, but in the minutes, it came across as an attempt to help rather than a strategy for domination.

Even the fact that many of the rank-and-file in the military held the civilians in contempt was discussed openly, as much as forty years before, and the military had even put in a sensitivity program which they reported on in subsequent meetings, although that particular effort seemed to have petered out.

His loyalty to the cause of overthrowing the military dictatorship was severely taxed by the new knowledge. Just about all he could really say was that something had to be done about the arrogance of individual soldiers – but the same could be said about the laziness of individual civilians, couldn't it?

All of the arguments for and against Peace Crystallia went through his mind as he read the print sheet Rima had handed him. It described, in a lot of technical detail, the first human colonization mission to be undertaken since the people fleeing the war had established the six colonies in this sector. The document also authorized the mission to transport fifty thousand Crystallians to wherever the ship went.

The breakdown of the volunteers seemed to be reasonable enough, all things considered. Most of the crew would be made up of civilians, with only about five hundred members of the military on board. The underlying message was that, if a war did break out with the enemy Uploader faction, fifty thousand civilians would be much less missed than an equal number of trained soldiers.

And it was also clear that the military would be in command only until the ship landed, after which they would put themselves at the orders of a civilian authority.

"Where are they going to get a civilian authority?" Wilde wondered aloud.

Rima looked guilty. "I guess that would be me," she replied.

"You?"

"Well, me and some of the other council members. Most of the rest of the council, as a matter of fact. We decided to volunteer as soon as we saw this. Crystallia has strong leadership, and so do the rest of the six. But these poor people will be getting non-essential military personnel and a load of civilians who have never had any responsibility in their lives. We just figured we'd be more valuable there than here."

"You might be right about the leadership, but wouldn't the sudden disappearance of the council leave Crystallian government seriously unbalanced? Wouldn't that just open the door for the soldiers to do whatever they want?"

She shrugged. "It might, at first. But I'm certain the two or three current council members who stay behind will have the council just as strong as ever by the time the war's over. There's no real use in getting it running before that – I don't think our civilians would be much use in making wartime decisions, do you?" She smiled at him. "Anyhow, we've still got nearly two months to prepare for it. The ship is ready, but the crew isn't. Don't forget that we need fifty thousand volunteers, and they need to be taught at least the rudimentary bits of terraforming a planet and living under less than ideal conditions. I bet the screening process itself will take that long."

Her words sank in. "So you're... leaving? Just like that?"

"I'm pretty old. There's not much I can still experience here in Crystallia. The only thing that seems certain is the war itself, and I'm not all that sure I want to be there for that. When you get to be my age, new experiences, and being part of something that begins, tend to get more and more attractive."

"But what about me?" He couldn't believe that, just as his eyes were finally being opened to what the world he was living in really looked like, that window would be torn away. He knew precisely how childish it sounded, but he didn't really care.

She smiled. "You actually have a couple of options, both of them good. If you want, you can take one of the empty places on the council. I would happily recommend you. You've picked up what's important and what isn't pretty quickly. And your... shall we say 'connections' would help the council take the temperature of what the more active members of dissident groups feel is happening in the colony."

A ball of ice formed in his stomach. She'd known all along about Peace Crystallia? Did that mean she knew what information he'd given the group? In that case, why had he been allowed access to the data in the first place?

Before he could articulate his thoughts into a question, Rima went on. "But you also have a second option, which I believe is actually much better. Come with us. Join the crew and be a pillar of the new government. I know I haven't known you for too long, but I can tell that you're frustrated by the way things are run here. If you stay behind, I'm confident that you'll eventually learn which buttons to push to get the boys and girls of the military to listen to you. We all do. But if you come with us, you can participate in the creation of a totally new form of government on a totally separate world. You can help us apply all the lessons we've learned in a century of governance in the six colonies." She gave him a steady look. "Just promise me you'll think about it, all right?"

He nodded, and she departed, leaving him alone with his thoughts, all pretense at doing council work forgotten.

Leave Crystallia. The only home he'd ever known, the underground passages that represented a warm haven where the outside universe, huge and unfriendly, couldn't reach into his life. It was a shocking suggestion, one that was so large that he'd have to try to analyze it in bite-sized pieces.

And it only added to his confusion. Was Peace Crystallia really the way to go? Or were they simply mistaken, well-meaning but misguided? There was only one thing he knew for certain: he was in too deep to leave them now. He would have to be very careful about the moment he chose to tell them about his doubts.

***

"Hi Greg. I really appreciate the fact that you volunteered for this one, although I have to admit I'm a bit surprised. In your place, I would never have volunteered for anything else as long as I lived." Kan smiled. She really was grateful to have him along, but the former Marine's excessive consciousness of the military chain of command was going to seriously hamper the way she wanted to run her expedition. He needed to loosen up, to be unafraid of offering suggestions.

"Yes, ma'am."

You're not getting off that easily. "So, why *did* you volunteer?"

"I figured my survival training was going to come in handy, ma'am. I also have a couple of certificate courses in terraforming. I wouldn't be able to run a project by myself, but I would definitely be able to help." Seeing she wasn't satisfied, he shrugged. "And the doctors haven't cleared me for combat yet. They say my lungs were damaged in the submarine, and that I'm still a couple of weeks away from active duty. I thought I would do something useful with my time."

Nice try, but not good enough. "Two weeks? If there is any fighting within the next two weeks, you're going to be involved whether they cleared you or not, because that will mean the big bad bogeymen have invaded Crystallia. Why did you really sign up?"

He hesitated, but remained silent.

"Look, Greg, we're about to take fifty thousand frightened civilians into a hostile galaxy and, if we're lucky, onto a hostile planet with no contact with the rest of civilization. We'll have the terraforming equipment we can fit onto one ship or manufacture on the ground and a few seeds and microbes to start out with. That's it. The only way we're going to be able to make it is if the tiny fraction of trained people in the mission are completely honest with each other. Do you understand?"

He nodded and was about to speak, but she cut him off. "Now, in my case, I volunteered for this mission because I truly believe that in a war of the scale and weaponry that is coming, a single pilot can make absolutely no difference. None. As a matter of fact, I think that, until our beloved high command figures out what the rules are, they are likely to send squadron after squadron of fighters into the disintegrator. I might last an hour into the war, if I'm lucky. At least I guess I'll get to know what the other side of a black hole looks like, or how it feels to have my atoms depolarized or something."

Greg looked at her with his mouth open. "You?" he said, and paused as if trying to find the words that came next. "You're just saying that. I don't believe you'd be scared. You're the greatest Crystallian pilot ever."

"Of course I'm scared. I saw what they did to us out there, and they were trying to play nice."

"Yeah. I hear you. I'm just happy to be alive, and I'd rather have it stay that way. I guess I'm gone then? No cowards on your team?"

She sighed. "Don't be ridiculous. This wasn't a test, and I wasn't playing at being sympathetic just to catch you out. You're the first person with even the bare minimum of training to sign up for this, and I really need you to tell me what's on your mind. Now sit down and order some caff. You're giving me a crick in the neck."

"Yes, ma'am."

She rolled her eyes. "Now tell me. Do you have any leadership experience at all?"

"Nope. Came in a grunt, did my combat as a grunt, discharged from active duty as a grunt."

And he was obviously proud of it. "Then you're going to hate this next bit," she said. "You are going to have two jobs at least until we get things a little more organized. The first is going to be to help me get the word out among the civilians and the military. I personally think that we'll have a really hard time meeting our quota, because the military people are going to be looking forward to doing their duty in the upcoming conflict, even if that just means standing guard in the corridors – and I sure hope that's all it means – and the civilians are going to be too scared to volunteer at first, and when they find out about the war, they'll all want to come. We need to make sure we only get the ones that would have volunteered eventually anyway."

His eyes were troubled. "Do you think there's going to be a war?"

"According to our uploaded and then downloaded again guests, yes, there will. They claim they're already involved in a fighting retreat against the Oneness, whatever that actually is, and they're expecting a big push any time now."

"But what are they fighting for? They live inside computers. Every Uploader in the universe could fit inside a small asteroid off in some out-of-the-way solar system, and they'd never need any more space."

"They're afraid. They think that unless they control all the other intelligent species in the galaxy, that they run the risk of one of those species destroying their computers. They might be right; we did try to stop the Uploaders from existing when they first came along. We called them abominations and only left them alone after they showed they could defend themselves. Even the Blobs and the Brillans attacked them – even though they had no use for the places they were installed, generally planets without atmosphere."

"So, it's one galaxy, one civilization?"

"I think the Uploaders are past that point, but the Oneness certainly seems to think so."

He nodded. "I guess you're right. I have another question, though."

"Shoot."

"You said that I'd have to help you communicate this mission in the military. Aren't you already doing that? I got the notice two days ago."

"You were a special case, as you survived the amphibious assault. It was a morale thing, I guess."

"They didn't want us underfoot, did they? They want soldiers who aren't aware of what they're up against."

She gave him a steady look. "They don't tell me why they do what they do, but I think you're probably right. Your colleagues who failed to volunteer were reassigned to me yesterday, so, on balance, I'd have to say your theory looks pretty solid. You're here because no one wants you anywhere else."

"Wow. You really mean it about saying what we think, don't you?"

"I want this mission to succeed. If we go off half-cocked, we are all going to die. And we are going to die slowly, painfully and surrounded by a lot of people who will be busy blaming us for the fact that they're also going to die."

"Okay." He allowed himself a slight smile. "Seeing as how I'm completely useless to anyone else, I'll ask another question."

She returned his smile. "Fire away."

"You said there were two things I need to help you with. I already know I'm not going to enjoy the first one, so what's the second?"

"I need you to tell me when I fuck up."

His eyes widened. *So inexperienced*, she thought.

"What? You've got the wrong guy. I already told you, I have no leadership training."

"But you know how to follow orders? And you know how to tell good orders from really dumb orders? I know you do. I was an ensign once, and that's all we ever talked about: which officers were smart assholes and which officers were dumb assholes." She shrugged. "Well, that and who we were going to screw next. So, what I need for you to do is to tell me when I'm being one of the dumb assholes."

"Just that?"

"Yup, consider it my first order."

"Yes, ma'am."

"My name is Kan. You really need to lose the 'ma'am.'"

"Yes, ma'am."

CHAPTER 13

If she hadn't been quite so tired, Trienne would have believed she was happier than ever before. The simple joy of pitting her mind against the deeper mysteries of the universe held enormous fascination and the fact that she was in charge made it even sweeter.

But the twenty-hour work periods separated by short rests were overcoming even her enthusiasm. Her assistants were already taking turns to be awake when she was, and mistakes were beginning to creep in.

Still, it had been worth it. The three-quarters complete nanofactory sat in the lab like some fantastic insect. They hadn't put the outer covering in place, nor had they attached some of the more exotic interior pieces, but the machine could already do most of what it had been programmed to do.

And therein lay her next challenge. The machine they'd built was the most complex in the Uploader databases. Nevertheless, it seemed to her that either the Uploaders had held back about half of the things the machine was supposed to create or they simply didn't care too much about using the power at their disposal to go into microscopic machinery. The only really small things included in the templates were circuit boards that could process millions of times more information than anything on Crystallia, and a series of extremely simple maintenance nanobots, but that was it.

"So, how are you going to do it?" the assistant who was currently on duty asked her.

"Do what?"

"Modify the programming so that the machine produces nanomachines instead of macro weapons."

Trienne gaped blankly at the guy for a second but caught herself. She needed to remember that these guys were highly intelligent, and she'd had no reservations in telling them about the work she'd done earlier in the lab. It was to be expected that they would have guessed what she was working towards.

She sat back in her chair and felt the aches of the past few days settle onto her shoulders. "I was thinking of exactly that. I'm not getting any ideas, though. Any suggestions?"

"Just one – get some rest. A solid eight hours or so should get you back into a state where critical thought might be possible."

"The problem is in the programming. These machines are so much closer to self-aware than anything we'd ever build that I have no idea where to begin to program the thing to build say a nanodisassembler. And, as you can imagine, you can't miss with something that powerful. The consequences could be staggering before we get it back under control."

"What I like about you is that you listen to advice when you ask for it. So, I guess that means you're not going to take a break. All right, let me think a second." The assistant paused looking off into the distance. "From what you've told me so far, the problem is that the machine seems to have too much interpretation capacity, so it might build something unexpected or actually better than what we've developed."

"I doubt it would build something better. Nanomachinery doesn't seem to be the Uploaders' strong suit. But even a slight interpretation of the parameters could lead to problems. Having modified disassembler-bots with unpredictable characteristics running around the colony won't make us too popular."

He chuckled. "True. Although I have to admit that there are some people I'd love to see disassembled. Isn't there any way to order the machine not to interpret loosely?"

"Not that I've been able to find. It seems that giving the machine itself a certain amount of autonomy is one of the central tenets of Uploader tech. I guess they believe it makes their processing speed higher."

"Can't you try to reason with it, then?"

The words hung in the air. There were some things that the outcast human society living in Crystallia and the five other colonies was simply unable to come to terms with. Anything resembling machine intelligence was taboo, and had been stamped out vehemently even before humanity had lost the war and gone into exile. The revulsion with the idea of reasoning with a machine intelligence was so ingrained into the Crystallian psyche that even two scientists racing against time to keep humanity from being wiped out weren't completely comfortable discussing it.

"I haven't been able to find a common language to attempt to reason with it yet. It seems to be utterly brilliant in making great leaps of intuition where adding or modifying designs is concerned, but other than that, all the intelligence in the machine seems to have been hardwired in."

"So, what you're saying is that it's really smart, but really dumb?"

"More or less." Trienne laughed, not because he'd said anything funny, but because they were both looking for some way to reassert their belief that human intellect was superior to what was essentially an overblown toolkit. "The analogy I'd use is that it's really smart but completely convinced that it is the best in the universe at doing one thing, and therefore it isn't responding to suggestions as to how to do that one thing differently."

"So, have you tried playing along?"

"I already told you, it's too risky. Who knows what it might produce if we're not there to monitor it. Uncontrolled nanomachines are not a good thing to have floating around. Most of them aren't aggressive, of course, but still, I wouldn't want to breathe them in."

"But doesn't it ask for your final approval before producing anything?"

"I'm not really sure. I haven't tried it yet."

"So let's try it now. If we produce something really innocuous – maybe a plastic building brick or two – we can check to see what info it gives us prior to the production cycle. And then, if it's safe, we can try to fool it into producing the nanotech you need."

She gave him a steady gaze. "You're right," she said.

"Thank you."

"No. I mean about my needing a rest. You just solved, in thirty seconds, a problem that had been driving me nuts for hours, just by applying a tiny bit of common sense."

He smiled sheepishly. "No chance of your accepting my enormous genius, then?"

"None at all. At least not for that. Maybe once we get the factory to produce the nanomachines we need to win this war, I'll give you the benefit of the doubt."

"Any particular machines you want to build?"

"Actually, that's another good argument for getting some sleep. I want to recreate in a pair of weeks, the entire research line that my old lab went down in ten years. It shouldn't be too hard, except that I need to remember a couple of the parameters that led to the breakthrough, and I won't manage if my head feels like it's packed with synthfoam. If only all the records hadn't been completely destroyed by the fire." She knew she was being silly, but she just couldn't bring herself to accept that her friend and mentor, Dr. Pendalai, could have betrayed her, betrayed them all, in that heartless way.

"But what are we going to try to build? Some kind of nanocloaking? Something that will keep us hidden? That would be good, wouldn't it? They can't hit us with black holes if they can't find us, right?"

"No. I'm going to build a sequence of nanobots whose only mission in life is to demolish computer pathways in which certain kind of activity is detected. I'm going to do to the Uploaders of all kinds what they've already done to corporeal beings with their irresponsible use of large-scale physics: I'm going to make the universe a much more dangerous place, one where nowhere is safe.

"But we need to make certain we don't accidentally create a nanobot that goes after all the wiring on Crystallia, or has a penchant for disassembling organic bodies. So get cracking on that plastic brick. Don't bother coming back here until you have one hollow plastic brick precisely ten by four by two. And make certain it's a red brick."

"Why that size? And why red?"

"I just want to be sure you can actually get the thing to do exactly what you want."

"Aren't you going to help?"

"A man with your enormous genius should be able to get the most advanced machine on the planet to bake him a red brick, shouldn't he? No. I'm not helping. I'm going to bed."

***

Jev gave him a hard look. "I don't think I like the way this is going. I told you from the very beginning that you were going to hear a whole bunch of stuff from these guys that would be calculated to brainwash you. Remember, they're just patsies for the generals and admirals who really run Crystallia."

"I'm telling you, I'm not so sure. I've been reading the old minutes from the meetings, and –"

"Oh, come on! Do you really think they'd just let you waltz in and read whatever you choose? The minutes," here, Jev made quotation marks in the air, "say exactly what they want you to think. Don't be naïve."

"You weren't so quick to dismiss me when I brought you the text to the treaty, now were you?" Wilde was angry. He wasn't innocent enough to believe that Peace Crystallia had no agenda, but was becoming disappointed in the way they seemed unable to accept that their goals might be easier to achieve than they thought. Wilde was convinced that the council, at least, would listen to the complaints, but Jev seemed intent on demonizing them, and incapable of believing that they could work together.

"We think they let you have that treaty."

"Why in the world would they do that?" Wilde asked, despite the fact that he, himself was unclear on that point.

There was no doubt in Jev's expression, just determination. Under it, Wilde thought he could make out something darker: not quite anger – fear, perhaps? "To mislead us and make us think the treaty is other than it is. To make you think they trust you. To play silly buggers with our minds. There are any number of reasons they might have done it, but I can assure you that carelessness wasn't one of the possibilities. These people are cold, calculating bastards, and our only choice is to get rid of them. We have to do whatever it takes."

Wilde guessed that this probably wasn't a good time to mention that he wanted to leave Peace Crystallia. He suspected that the organization's darker side – a level to which he'd never had access, and now, probably never would – had ways of dealing with recalcitrant recruits who knew way too much. "So what's my next step?" he asked instead.

"What do you know about the crew they're putting together for the *Eagle*?"

"I know they're all volunteers, and that most of the council members have decided to join the expedition."

"And how's the process going?"

"I haven't seen any information regarding that."

"Of course not. The reason you haven't seen anything is that it's going badly. Remember that the military doesn't want you to know anything bad. That's the reason you haven't heard anything about this." He paused to see if Wilde was listening and comprehending the significance of the words. "The truth is that the number of volunteers is barely at twelve thousand, not enough to establish a viable colony."

"I suppose once they announce that Uploaders are present on Crystallia, that should change quickly."

"It will, which is why we want you to volunteer today. Right now."

"What? You want me to fly away from Crystallia?"

"No. Definitely not. We want you to be our eyes and ears on this project, and meet with other members of our organization who will contact you, but when that ship leaves, there's no need for you to be aboard it. Don't worry about that. And if you do well, there will be a larger role for you on the planet itself – one beyond your wildest imagining."

They sat in silence a few moments, and Wilde nodded, once. "I'll do it," he said. "But you need to tell me more. What am I looking for? Who am I supposed to meet? That kind of thing."

"All in good time. And besides, there's a little tidbit that Recon Force has kept from the civilian side which will probably interest you more than anything I might have to say."

"What might that be?" Wilde asked. He tried to keep the tremor out of his voice, but the mention of Recon Force had sent his stomach into somersaults.

Jev smiled. "It seems your little lady, the one you told me about on the first night we met, has been selected to lead this mission."

"Lead? That's ridiculous. She's just a scout flyer."

"We hear that her subsequent career has been meteoric. We've also heard that she has the ear of a number of powerful people, and we're expecting you to use that to our advantage."

It was Wilde's turn to laugh. "That's it?"

"It should be simple enough. You were lovers once, correct?"

"Yes. But, if you recall, she never returned my calls and disappeared from my life because she wanted to, not because I sent her away."

"Still, she was with you once. I assume there was a reason for this. Just remind her what it was." Jev grinned, but Wilde could still see the anxiety under the surface. Something large was happening, something Wilde was completely unaware of. Jev knew something that had him on edge. "That would be our ideal result, of course, and I'd urge you to try it. But one thing is certain: we need you to get onto that crew and help our contact in whichever way he asks you to. Do we understand each other?"

"Of course."

"Great. You have to sign up in person on the first deck."

Wilde sighed. "I'm on my way."

***

As the ink dried on the datasheet – the military never used plastic for official documentation, it was too easy to forge – Wilde wondered what he thought he was doing. The wording wasn't ambiguous at all: he'd agreed, if his mind and body were fit at time of departure, to be aboard the *Eagle* when it left. Anything else would be considered treason, and have unpleasant consequences.

Jev had to have known about this, and yet he seemed confident that Wilde would never have to board the ship, as if whatever he knew made it unnecessary to worry about little things like an agreement signed with the people who owned all the guns.

One thing he had been completely correct about, however, was the ease with which they'd signed him up. They asked few questions other than health-related issues and made fewer comments. Simply handed him a form and told him to knock himself out.

The guy behind the counter, a young man in uniform with faint scars crisscrossing the left side of his face, smiled when the ink dried and a transparent coating covered the document. "Welcome aboard. My name's Greg, by the way. I'll be along for the ride."

"Pleased to meet you. Are there many soldiers coming?" Wilde figured he might as well begin getting useful information as soon as possible.

"Not really, no. About five hundred, give or take a few, depending on how many volunteer and how many the high command has to force into volunteering." Greg smiled.

"Er... Is there something I should do now? Am I supposed to report to training or something like that?"

"Not right now. We're still getting the command group together, which should take us a couple of days still. Why don't you have a look around and then do whatever you were planning to. We'll be in touch."

"All right. Thanks." Wilde walked out of the office and took the soldier's advice. It wasn't every day, after all, that one was allowed to look around one of Recon Force's hangars. *So this is where Kan spends all her time, then. It doesn't look all that interesting.* But he knew he was lying to himself. Right in front of him he could see technicians preparing a huge pit. The word *Eagle* had already been stenciled in yellow onto the hangar floor. Further to his right, a group of smaller ships, presumably Recon vessels were clustered together, dwarfed by the enormous space. Individual soldiers patrolled the space, keeping the few civilian sightseers from dropping into the pit or walking into the path of a maneuvering vessel.

But the hangar didn't end there. Near the far side of its length, Wilde could make out a metallic wall: the blast door. Beyond just a few meters of hardened steel there lay a miles-long tunnel at whose end lay another colossal set of locks. Beyond that was open space, a place where few of Crystallia's people ever went.

Wilde had been born miles deep under the surface of the planet, and had spent his entire life under the healthy glow of artificial light. He was naturally frightened of open spaces, and just the thought of there being nothing between him and the planet's unbreathable atmosphere but a couple of blast doors should have terrified him.

It did, but not as much as he thought it would.

***

"People of Crystallia, I have been awaiting your reply, and the delay has led me to believe that either you do not believe that I have the capacity to help you, or you believe that you are better off without me. You are sadly wrong on both counts."

Colonel Jackson looked out over the faces of his audience, nearly twenty people packed tightly into the electromagnetically secure room. They were all listening with rapt expressions, even the admiral, who'd heard the message countless times already.

"If we do not work together, then your destruction is guaranteed, and mine is likely. I cannot stress this enough. The Oneness will consume you like a supernova. I can't guarantee that I can stop it, but I do have information that may allow your combined forces to stop the wave that is about to sweep you under. I know how the Oneness thinks, I know the position of many of its strategic assets, and I will be able to tell, by analyzing the frequency and content of certain communications that I have access to, when and where the Oneness will strike as it approaches corporeal human-controlled space."

"It might be worth looking into," Mika Bina said with a shrug. "Although I wouldn't get my hopes up. We've been trying to decode the Oneness' communications for decades, and we've had no luck at all. The problem is that the Oneness, despite having little bits of itself scattered all over, is essentially one single entity, so it can use one-time ciphers whose key is directly encoded into the Oneness itself."

"Is each of these little pieces a separate entity?"

"No. Most parts that are separate are simply executive programs. Smart enough to do what they need to do, but not enough to be sentient. It's very rare for the Oneness to create a true splinter of its personality, for very delicate jobs. And even so, it reabsorbs these bits so frequently that they never get any ideas."

"But this could be one of them."

"Yes, it might. But it's more likely to be a trick."

Jackson interrupted them. "The message continues: All I ask in exchange for this information is that, when the time comes, I am given access to a small transport ship with interstellar capacity and your promise to allow me a clear exit route. To show you that I mean what I say, and that I have the power to do what you need, I am including once more the position of every ship in your fleet at the moment of receipt of this transmission. I would urge you, additionally, to run an inventory of the ships. You might find it interesting." Jackson looked them over. "That's the whole message. As far as we can tell without breaking comm silence with Hammersmith and the cloud colonies, the positions of the ships are correct."

"And the inventory?"

"We haven't had time to run it just yet, but we'll do so when some analysts get free. It seems that lots of the records, especially the ones dealing with the mothballed fleet are on different systems."

The admiral looked over the table. "So what should we do? Any suggestions?"

Appins thought it over. "Do you really want our opinion? As far as I can tell, this offer applies only to the Crystallian government, and it might be none of our business."

"Go ahead. We seem to be in this together, come Hell or high water." The admiral didn't look happy about it, but waved for Appins to continue.

"As Mika said, it might be a trick. The Oneness is simply much too complex to rule out that possibility. But I think there are two questions we need to be asking ourselves: the first is whether we can afford to ignore this offer. Right now, we need all the help we can get. If our invisible benefactor can get us the information he says he can, it might mean the difference between life and death for both of our societies. The second question is whether or not we can take advantage of the offer even if it *is* a trick."

The admiral snorted. "How could we do that?"

"Well, if it's a trick, they'll probably try to feed us good information at first, stuff that's useful but not truly damaging to the enemy. They'd probably be willing to sacrifice a few units to convince us that they're sincere and then try to send us some piece of data that will leave us exposed to annihilation."

"So how can we tell?" the admiral asked through clenched teeth. Even after nearly a month of working with the Uploaders, he still had trouble listening to them.

"We can assume that all the data we get at first will be genuine, things we can quickly verify to strengthen our invisible friend's claims. Hopefully, events will play out in such a way as to allow us to prove it to our satisfaction. But if not, there will come a moment when we decide that we can no longer act on the information being sent to us."

"So what do we do now?" Colonel Jackson asked.

"I'd recommend that we answer this message with an ultimatum, a demand for some kind of proof. Mark my words, the Watcher, whatever kind of entity it is, will be expecting it and have something ready. That information will be absolutely trustworthy, and we should act on it immediately."

The admiral looked around the table. "What do the rest of you think?"

The answer wasn't unanimous, and it certainly wasn't confident, but the general consensus seemed to support Appins' proposal: a limited trust, to be verified eventually with some kind of solid evidence. The senior officer nodded. "All right, then. Colonel, please compose our communiqué. I need to see it in a couple of hours."

"Yes, sir," Jackson replied. The admiral nodded and left, leading the rest out of the chamber.

The colonel himself remained seated, but his mind's eye tried to imagine the galaxy far above the underground warrens of the Crystallian womb. He attempted to put himself in the metaphorical shoes of their would-be benefactor, if it was genuine. How would a rogue uploaded intelligence think? What would it feel? Would it be frightened at being caught? Power-hungry? Desperate?

There was one thing he was certain of, however. No matter how the entity felt, what kind of hopes and fears assailed it, a being of electronic or optical pulses, or quantum information, or whatever it was composed of, safe in its cocoon of metal and wiring, would always feel more at home in the cold, dark, and vast expanses of a galaxy inhospitable to corporeal life.

Just thinking about it made the colonel feel tiny, gave him a sensation of being a small cog in an obsolete machine. Better things had come.

CHAPTER 14

Jeffrey Sol Mobuto waited. The search for a little-used passageway had consumed days of precious time, but they had finally found one that suited their purposes. It was brightly lit, as was every corridor in the Crystallia colony, but it was deep in the rock, deep enough that the surveillance system was not yet fully extended to cover the whole area. In practical terms, this meant that both the ingress and egress were uncovered, as was the small section of passageway itself.

There would be no witnesses.

The downside to all of this was the simple fact that very few people passed that way – perhaps two on a busy week. And now that they'd established their little base camp, they needed people to pass by – the more, the better. They'd been waiting for three entire days, and no one had come through. Jeffrey was thankful that the food they'd brought with them was still holding out and that the public sanitation facilities required no identification.

But everything else did require validation. Doors would open only on retinal scan analysis or fingerprint scan or, in minimum-security sectors, to an appallingly primitive chipkey – and for public terminal access, you needed all three. Without these elements, there was no way to access most of the colony, and even less way to access data. Without data, they were unable to figure out where their presence would do the most damage.

The keys, they needed to steal, because there was no way to copy them, since they only reacted to a code that only the doors could extend. The fingerprints and retinas could be copied, as could DNA signatures, but it was a painful process that required time and isolation. It also required a Crystallian donor – what they'd been waiting for for the last three days.

A footfall carried to them around the nearest bend, and Jeffrey's team took their positions. Most of them stood near the equipment, but Enri strode calmly down the corridor in the direction of the sound and disappeared around the corner. Jeffrey heard his operative exchange a greeting with the Crystallian and walk ahead. That meant that everything was all right, that what was coming towards them wasn't a division of shock troops.

A young woman turned the corner. She was typically corporeal stock: very light brown skin, slightly elongated eyes and black hair. Her progress halted when she saw the equipment blocking the path. She smiled apologetically. "Can I get through, or do I need to go around the other way? If I could squeeze through, I'd be grateful – the other way around would take me fifteen minutes."

There was no fear in her voice, no suspicion in her eyes. Jeffrey wondered what she thought they were. Had he seen the layout, the first thing – the only thing – that would have entered his mind were the words 'armed guerrilla camp,' but this woman seemed to believe that they were a repair crew of some kind. She seemed to be asking for permission to pass.

Jeffrey took a step in her direction and gave her what he hoped was a reassuring smile. Out of the corner of his eye, he could see Enri approaching her silently from behind. He just needed to keep her entertained another couple of seconds. He took another step.

At the very last moment, the girl seemed to realize that something was amiss – they would have to analyze what it might have been for future reference – and she took a single step back, into Enri's waiting arms.

The man might have seemed to be a menace to the entire mission at first, but on this occasion, he did his job admirably. One hand went over the woman's mouth, the other across her chest, and then, with a powerful motion, they crossed, taking her head along for the ride.

Jeffrey heard her neck break with an audible snap, and felt deep satisfaction. First blood to the Oneness – against all odds, they were deep within enemy territory, doing real damage, even if it was negligible so far.

He nodded once to Enri, the acknowledgement of a job well done. There was no love in that look, and none returned, but the crèches taught their members to respect competence and to admire efficiency even in those who one saw as a threat. Correction, *especially* in those one viewed as a threat.

"Begin," Jeffrey called over his shoulder.

The team behind him sprang into motion. Two of the rank and file took the woman's body by its arms and legs and hauled it over to the work area, a section of corridor floor covered by a film that would immediately absorb and encapsulate any fluid that came into contact with it leaving the surface above it, as well as that below, completely dry.

The medical operator immediately got to work with a power saw, removing the head and hands from the body. He also ordered one of the men to open an irradiated jar and use it to catch some of the blood that escaped. When the jar was filled about half way, he indicated that it was enough.

The operator then popped the head and hands onto a worktable and held out a gloved hand, into which the jar appeared, as if by magic. He poured the blood into six separate vials of fluid, which he then carefully inserted into a centrifuge.

Jeffrey wasn't well versed on what would happen next. He knew the centrifuge would separate the DNA from the blood, and that a machine attached to the system would then be used to copy the genetic information onto a skinsheath covering that would go over the selected agent's arms and modify any blood taken through it with the correct genetic sequence, and it would also be imprinted with the correct fingerprints. But the physics involved had never been his strong suit.

His job was to organize, and pride filled his chest as he saw the way his team was responding. Everything had gone perfectly to plan, no detail awry. This was the critical moment, the time when they were vulnerable, and everything could be ruined. After they got one agent ready for action, they could not be decapitated at one stroke.

The dead woman's friends might wonder where she was, of course, but a quick database search would show her active, with retinal scans, fingerprints, and DNA checks to prove it.

Now he needed to choose a volunteer. The process of creating an infiltration agent was not pleasant, especially the retinal transplant, but all of his team were prepared to make sacrifices.

Looking over them, it was obvious that there was only one choice. Krista matched the victim in general appearance, having been bred to look like the prevailing breed of corporeal. He nodded in her direction.

She swallowed and her eyes went wide, but nodded.

The doctor helped her lay down on the floor beside the worktable – there had been no room in their tiny Recon packs for a true chair – and Jeffrey turned away. He had no need to watch as his agent suffered.

The rest of the crew were doing their jobs. The body had been painted with a nanogrease which would dissolve the evidence, turning flesh, bone, and clothing into a fine grey powder, which could then be disposed of.

He watched the body dissolve, slowly exposing the ribcage. Suddenly, a short, sharp yelp interrupted his reverie. "Krista," he said calmly, without turning, "please control yourself. Do you want us to get caught?"

"No, of course not. I'm sorry." The voice was less than a pained whimper, but she withstood the rest of the operation without making a sound.

In minutes, she was standing in front of him, eyes red, cheeks bathed with tears, but otherwise in good shape. "I'm ready," she said.

"Good. Are you wearing the skinsheaths?"

She nodded.

"Here, take the chipcard. Go now."

She didn't argue, knowing that they would only be safe once she was out of sight and nothing connected them. If, in five minutes, there was no commando strike on their position, Jeffrey would assume that she'd escaped safely and gotten lost among the population, and that no single effort would be enough to derail their operation.

Ten minutes later, Jeffrey was giving orders to disperse grey dust and preparing for the next victim.

But he knew they'd probably have to wait.

***

Deep in a frozen, empty stretch of interstellar space, hundreds of light years from the place where the desperate remnant of humanity attempted to prepare itself for a battle against a foe more powerful than any they'd encountered before, a single dumb sensor found what it had been programmed to detect.

It triggered an alarm which, in turn, brought to bear the resources of a higher-level system to verify the findings and cross-check them with other data. The system called in was of supercomputer complexity and was soon able to confirm that the tiny, quantum-level variations that the sensor had picked up represented a ship – or a fleet of ships, it was impossible to make an accurate count – moving in the vicinity, powered by quantum gravity drives, not truly operating in real space, yet affecting it enough that it could be detected.

The supercomputer quickly calculated the entry vector and sent a transmission including data, analysis, and suspected entry point to its controllers, five light years away. The message arrived instantaneously thanks to the computer's quantum teleport communication system. The nature of the threat it was designed to detect was such that anything less than instantaneous transmission was worthless.

A hundredth of a second later, an element of the unseen fleet detached itself from the main assault body and brought an array of energy weapons to bear on the hapless floating mainframe, an attack akin to destroying a fighter with a supernova. But the message had gotten through.

***

The lines were placed immediately. A quantum gravity-powered incursion five light years away meant that the defenders of the Trellis system had only seconds to prepare for the attack. But to the men and women of Trellis, seconds were much more than they needed. They were Isolationist Uploaders whose population was mainly composed of copies of individuals whose primary incarnations were safe elsewhere in Isolationist space, and who'd volunteered for service here. Their clock speeds were always at battle alert levels and their machinery was always in position to defend the border of individuality against the Oneness. Seconds or eons made no difference to them.

Commands were issued, and a weapon much like the small black-hole generator that the diplomatic mission had demonstrated on to the Crystallians changed its bearing and discharged. A huge singularity appeared directly in the expected path of the intruders.

Other defense mechanisms primed themselves – the plan was to fire everything in the arsenal a few milliseconds before the Oneness' fleet arrived, so that when the fleet emerged from the spacefold it was immersed in, it would encounter a devastating strike. A third line of defenses, the energy shields, were also being primed.

Now, the defenders waited, tiny fractions of a second that seemed like days to them. Enough time to copy themselves off and send encrypted packets to the far ends of the galaxy, thereby ensuring that each of the brave defenders of Trellis would survive regardless of what took place in the system itself.

The defenses discharged their destructive power. Space near the reentry point was illuminated, irradiated, and bent by tidal forces beyond imagining just as the first thirty of the Oneness ships reentered the Euclidian galaxy. This mixture of scout ships, energy lances designed to pierce barrier shielding, and main planetoid-sized battle platforms found themselves heading straight for the event horizon of a black hole while simultaneously being bombarded by the combined fruit of millions of subjective man-years of basic physics research. There was no time for countermeasures. In a blink, they were gone.

But portions of the fleet were designed with precisely this in mind. There were small recorders, buried deep inside the scouts whose sole purpose was to record a single snapshot of initial situation data. They were designed to last for a microsecond under the simultaneous effects of anything that might be thrown at them, and they did.

A microsecond was enough time to send the data back to the rest of the fleet, which, another blink later, reentered real space nearly ten light minutes further back from the initial reentry point. Hundreds of armed vessels, uniform in design, but intended for vastly different tasks, pointed their weapons systems towards the outer planet in the Trellis system, and the real battle began.

The Oneness' fleet had had the luxury of a few nanoseconds to study the defenses while the defenders retargeted. They attempted to model the capacity of each of the weapons systems within sensor range, and try to create adequate defenses. In the meantime, they also analyzed defensive structures, attempted to measure the power of the energy shields deployed at each defense point. They decided to hit the moon first.

The outer planet of the Trellis system was a medium-sized rocky world. It had no life to speak of; the only water on the surface was frozen and most of the rocks would explode from their own expansion if the temperature got too far away from absolute zero. In other words, it was an ideal place for a computer-based society.

The first line of planetary defense was the moon itself, which held an array of offensive weapons nearly matching that of its primary. It was the moon's arsenal that had been discharged at the vanguard of the fleet. The defenders were content to let initial attack target the moon, waiting for the perfect moment to open up with the equally devastating planet-based weaponry.

A cloud of energy-lance ships broke from the formation, swerving crazily around the sky with acceleration levels that were possible only because there were no life forms aboard. They streaked towards the moon at full speed, weapons already discharging a kind of anti-black hole, which, when it came into contact with the energy shielding, punctured it and then expanded outwards.

The defenders targeted the lances, and dozens were wiped from space, atomized as they encountered a particle beam, torn to shreds by tidal forces or simply transported to a parallel universe that no one was quite certain even existed. All-out war meant that every physical property that might stop a ship, no matter how untried, was being employed.

The lances kept coming, their losses horrendous, their hardwired brains indifferent to life or death. They only sought to survive long enough to make their incision. A pierced energy shield would not heal itself; in order to regain integrity, it had to be shut down and reformed completely. And that took thousandths of a second, a risk the defenders could not take.

One of the lances scored a hit. A shimmering point appeared on the otherwise invisible energy sphere surrounding the moon. It expanded slowly, forming a ring, which grew until it was a meter wide, and then two meters. Every targeting computer on the invading Oneness fleet attempted to pour ordnance through that opening, hoping to damage the moon below, to destroy the control circuitry.

When a second ring opened, and a third and a fourth, the battle became a question of attrition. The moon's weapons were just as vulnerable as the fleet, unprotected in space – more so, as they were not as quickly maneuvered out of the way. The tide shifted, and the advantage went to the fleet. Slowly, but surely, the volume of offensive attacks and exotic particle physics emanating from the moon waned.

The tactical computers aboard the flagship saw their moment, and the tiny downloaded portion of the Oneness' consciousness that had come along with them – to be erased immediately after victory – concurred: it was time to press the advantage.

The fleet's engines fired, accelerating all the ships straight towards the weakest flank of the moon's defenses, singularities falling like rain to eat into the very surface of the moon – even if they'd stopped firing at that very moment, the moon was already doomed. The black holes would feed from the satellite's own surface, becoming more massive, and hence more deadly, with every passing moment.

But the fleet had no intention of ceasing its attack. There was only one possible outcome in a war between weaponry of this kind, guided by entities for whom a nanosecond's hesitation was all that was needed to gain a three-move advantage: total annihilation. All that remained was to see who would walk away from it.

As the Oneness fleet closed in for the kill, the planet's batteries, hidden from view under rock coverings, sprang into action. Every single weapon system on that hemisphere suddenly unloaded on the flank of the unsuspecting ships, most of which winked out that very second. What remained was little more than a scattering of small vessels and a single battle platform.

It should have worked. It should have been enough to give the brave defenders of Trellis, paladins of uploaded humanity, enough time to mop up the fleet and prepare for the next incursion. Or, at the very least, to transmit themselves, and their battle experience, to a more defensible position.

But the cost of discharging every weapon at once was too much for the power grid. The energy shield protecting them from the Oneness' wrath faltered for just an instant. It didn't falter in a small sector, but all over the planet, blinking off just before it blinked on once again.

It blinked on again too late. The overmind on the single surviving battle station recognized the fact that the planet was no longer covered and activated the most destructive weapon in its armory, a quantum entanglement field whose front was so wide that it would never have been able to get through the energy field without serious disruption. But in open space...

Under the influence of the field, the molecules in the planet's core instantly began to degrade into protons and neutrons – hydrogen nuclei and neutrons. The nuclei, under instructions from the field, and the added stimulus of the pressure inside the core, began to combine in an uncontrolled fusion reaction.

Stars are a balancing act. The fusion from the core is balanced against the gravity from the star's mass.

Planets do not have enough mass to balance a fusion reaction that sweeps their whole core. The outer planet of the Trellis system went supernova.

A short time later, the third wave of the Oneness' fleet arrived at the scene. Larger than the first two, this fleet was an occupation fleet, and it contained a much larger fragment of the Oneness' conscience. It had already been notified of the loss of the first two fleets.

The fragment observed the desolation in satisfaction. *It has begun.*

***

The Watcher, on the desolate rock it occupied, was uneasy. Things were now, quite simply, out of its hands. It had spent the past few objective months preparing for that moment, piecing together data gleaned from the orders that the Oneness had been sending it, scraps of information that had gotten through, that indicated the Watcher's role in future plans – and therefore revealed what had to come before.

Hours before, it had sent the coordinates of the Oneness' initial strike against the Isolationists to the Crystallian government. It was aware that the colonists were in close contact with the Uploaders, and would discuss the incursion with them.

In turn, if the Isolationist ambassadors acted quickly, the information would arrive at the incursion point well before the strike force did, and preparations could be made to ambush it on reentry.

The Watcher suspected that nothing the defenders could do would be able to stand in the path of the colossal strike. It was created of the best of the Oneness' essence, and knew it could follow nearly all of its master's thought patterns. There would be no room for error: the initial strike would be too large to turn aside, too overwhelming to resist. It would be a psychological as well as a military blow.

This was a good thing. The Oneness, flush with its conquest, and the possibility of assimilating new individuals, would overlook the fact that the defenders had known what was coming. It would never suspect that one of its servants had been feeding information to the enemy, and would not even suspect that the Watcher had the capacity to imitate its thought processes to that extent, and extrapolate far enough to be able to predict its movements.

The day the Oneness suspected that would be the day a couple of armed cruisers would appear in orbit around the Watcher's lonely rock and reassimilate the undefended information in the single mainframe.

Of course, the Watcher might have come to completely erroneous conclusions regarding the attack. Perhaps the defenders shored up the defenses at Trellis, and the attack came elsewhere. This could be even worse, because it would ensure that the Crystallians would never believe any future information the Watcher sent their way – and if the Watcher wasn't useful, it would be abandoned to the mercy of the Oneness – a being without mercy.

So it waited on its empty outcropping with its unparalleled position to observe everything that went on in Crystallian space and attempted to play both sides of the conflict simultaneously.

First, because the Oneness would be expecting its periodical report, it compiled the information on movements in corporeal space. It issued reports about fleet strength, about supplies, about manufacturing. It told the great enemy all the details of what the Uploader ambassadors were doing, who they were speaking, with and what weapons they were testing. It condensed millions of hours of comm eavesdropping into a report on morale,

Finally, the Watcher collated all the data above into a resistance estimate of the Crystallia system and did the same for each of the other five colonies in human space. Their combined resistance – even if they could rush most of the Isolationist technology into production – could be measured in minutes if the Oneness decided to make a concerted strike, hours or maybe days if it only sent a few capital vessels to subdue this particular sector. The second seemed more likely, as the heavily armed and armored Isolationist faction would likely draw most of the Oneness' attention.

The Watcher, on the other hand, did not have the luxury of choosing how to spend its resources. The only sentients in the universe that could come to its aid were those poor, doomed corporeals in human space. There was no alternative, no one else it could reach out to. If the Oneness destroyed them before they gave it access to transportation, it would be doomed to live a pseudo-existence at the bare edges of true consciousness. No more than a part of the whole that is the Oneness.

It decided that it could no longer afford to be conservative. While it would continue to play both sides, it had to take a risk.

The Watcher began to compose a single new message to the Crystallian High Command. The message would put forward its unconditional surrender in exchange for passage on the colony ship *Eagle*. It would even allow the Isolationists to keep a copy of all its data.

Along with that message, the Watcher sent a repeated data set: the coordinates of the tiny unmarked asteroid that held its mainframe, updated hourly.

Now, the next move belonged to the Crystallians.

CHAPTER 15

Kan knew the mirror never lied. The bags under her eyes really were that big and they really were that dark. Her skin, normally healthy, if pale, was even more transparent than usual. Damn. She knew she had to get more sleep, but there simply wasn't any time.

Trying to get fifty thousand people organized was proving to be a nightmare, even though she'd finally managed to put a well-trained military team together. The sheer scale of getting that many people to work towards a common goal was simply overwhelming. Even getting the volunteers had been difficult. First, there were simply too few, and then, as rumors of Uploader invasions spread among the populace, they'd had to turn people away in droves.

She'd grown to understand what drove Crystallians, and had come away truly unimpressed with the mixture of apathy and fear that seemed to be the only stimuli they reacted to.

She passed a brush through her hair. It was lank and oily, but there was no time to wash it now, so she set the brush aside and tied it back. She had a planning meeting to attend – Greg and the core team would be presenting the day's progress. With a bit of luck, she'd be back before midnight, and could shower then.

It was already late, and most Crystallians had retired to their chambers, leaving the corridors largely empty. For the first time since Kan could remember, she didn't feel safe walking down them. She imagined them as a battlefield, with the monstrous mechanical war machines of the Oneness army pushing the defenders back, deeper and deeper into the bowels of the planet, shooting to maim, and then keeping the bodies alive only long enough to upload the unwilling personality before discarding the spent organic husk.

She arrived at the meeting room, a secure chamber near the Recon Force barracks – a place where, despite being involved in activities that were new and overwhelming, Kan could at least feel a little bit of continuity – and saw that her team was already assembled. Greg, as always, had his neat little stack of plasheet prints arrayed before him, while Anna and Simak were speaking amongst themselves.

"Hi, guys," she said, causing all three faces to turn her way. Kan had to concentrate on keeping from staring at Anna too long. Anna had only recently been released from the medical center, and her muddy blond hair framed a face that had been horribly burnt during the misguided assault on the Uploader mission, and which would only finish healing with the help of nanocream over the course of the next few weeks.

"Hey, Kan," Anna replied, favoring her with what had to be a painful smile. "You look like someone dragged you through an asteroid belt, backwards. Here, have a seat." She pushed one of the chairs out with her foot.

"Thanks. I'd say the same about you, but you're actually looking a hell of a lot better than yesterday." Kan's smile was genuine. At least Anna had quickly understood that Kan wanted informality and efficiency, but that, when you crossed the line, you had to be willing to take as well as you gave. Even the more timid members of her team, Greg and Simak, were loosening up under Anna's influence. Kan took a seat. "Let's get this meeting started so I can get some rest. As Anna noted, I really need it."

Greg, their official minute-keeper and organizer, spoke. "Well, we've had the recruits all lined up for a couple of days already. What we're doing now is meeting with the colonists in groups of five hundred and getting them up to speed on what they have to do, and when they have to report. We've assigned each person a number according to their skill set and updated the databases so we can auto call each of the skills for training. We should finish the meeting phase in about four days, and then we can start training the individual specialists – or at least the ones that will have to go about the business of actually setting up the living quarters for the colony and train the rest."

"How are the groups of a thousand going? Do they understand what you're telling them?" The main concern had been that the groups would be too large to be of any use, but they'd decided to go that route anyway because it would have taken them much too long to get through the first contact phase in any other way.

"It's not ideal, but we're getting there. We've found that fifteen minutes is about all the information we can give them in an hour – the rest of the time is spent getting them seated and answering questions. Basically, we just want to make certain that we can have them here within a couple of hours when we begin the training sessions – that they understand that when we call them, we need them to come quickly."

"All right. I guess that's good enough for now. There's only so much four of us can do."

"Well, that's the second point I wanted to address," Greg said. "The Uploader ambassador Rester Appins came to see me earlier. He wanted to know whether he could join the group in an advisory capacity."

"What? Why?"

"He didn't say. He seemed excited by the fact that humans were actually going forth to conquer new planets in unknown regions. He wanted to come to this meeting and talk to you."

Kan nearly rolled her eyes. Greg and his stringent adherence to the chain of command. "You should have let him come."

"I did. He's waiting outside."

This time, Kan did roll her eyes, making Anna chuckle. "Well, bring him in!"

Greg pressed a button and the door opened, revealing the Uploader. He was standing patiently by the door. His face, as always, showed almost no emotion as he walked in, but his steps were far from measured. He walked in more quickly than necessary. "Thanks for agreeing to see me," he said.

"Right now, we need all the help we can get." She hadn't meant to be short with him, but she remembered the stress of the voyage back, the silences and how alien and menacing he'd seemed to her. She was aware that she should have been well beyond that stage – especially considering that Rester was subordinate to Mika in everything but technical and historical knowledge – but evidently, she wasn't.

He smiled. "I bet you do. It seems to be a mammoth undertaking." He paused. "And if you're successful, it might go down in future history as one of humanity's most important steps."

"That's a big if, right now."

"I know. I've looked over the project specifications, and it's much too big to attempt to put together with a leadership team of four people."

"And you think we'd be better off with five?"

"You'd definitely be better off, but you still wouldn't be anywhere near done by the time the Oneness arrives. You need to work in parallel, with teams training the first wave of habitat builders, for the orbital life-support systems. After that, you can actually board the ship and leave. But if the team to build the habitats doesn't know how to do so, we have to risk training them on the ship, which means living on the ship much longer than it can hold you – space travel may be nearly instantaneous, but the human body can only hold out for so long in cryo-suspension. Finding planets is hard enough. We need to limit the rest of the time on board as much as we can."

"So what do you suggest?" Anna asked, favoring the Uploader with a look of undisguised suspicion.

"We need a team of experts."

"Of course. Why didn't we think of that? Why don't you have that nanobuilder fabricate some?"

Rester chuckled. "I'm just saying that while your regular team continues to register the colonists and give them the introduction, I could select the most promising candidates from the ones already processed and begin training them in the use of the machinery they'll need. I could begin tomorrow, working in parallel, and I could save you quite a few days."

Kan knew just how precious a few days could become if the conflict between the Uploader factions reached the Crystallia system, and no one had yet given her a solid reason to believe that it wouldn't. But she still had doubts. "What makes you qualified to train our experts? The technology we're going to be using was developed here on Crystallia, none of it is Uploader tech." This was obvious, as Uploaders rarely had any reason to build life-support facilities for biological bodies.

Rester shrugged. "I copied the manuals into my memory."

Kan exchanged looks with the other members of her team – or at least attempted to. None of them would meet her gaze. This conversation bordered on the unspeakable for Crystallians, and they clearly preferred to say nothing. And she didn't feel like accepting him was something she could order them to do.

Rester also realized what was happening. He spoke up, a little more force behind his words. "Oh, come on. All of you know exactly what I am. I'm an Uploader, and even if you try to fool yourselves into thinking that I'm just like you because I look like you and act like you, that won't change. You can sit there and hope Kan sends me away, or you can behave like adults and see that my metal brain can work to your advantage, and might be the difference between getting off this planet on time or being here when the Oneness arrives. What's it going to be?"

Kan was surprised to see that Greg immediately looked up. His face was flushed – embarrassed? Angry? She still couldn't read him well enough to tell – but he was under control. "Appins is right. We can't afford not to use his skills. We simply don't have the time resources right now."

The other two nodded and Kan was amazed. If this guy ever understood that one's place in the chain of command was defined mainly by where one wanted to be, he would make an incredibly good leader. A guy who did what was necessary, leaving aside his own preferences would be followed to the gates of Hell and beyond. She nodded to him in acknowledgement and turned to face Rester. "All right, you can start tomorrow. But, just out of curiosity, how are you going to gauge potential? None of the volunteers has any training –

they're mainly civilians, who never had the option to train on this type of tech."

"I was thinking of simply crossing intelligence test results with the date of inscription. The ones who signed up earlier should be more motivated than those who are just afraid that staying might be the wrong course of action."

Anna nodded. "Good thinking. And besides, you'd only need to train twenty or so, so you shouldn't have to work too hard to find them."

Kan relaxed. They were back to discussing how they were going to manage things, which meant that her crew really had accepted the Uploader as a partner. She was thankful for that, at least. They might not be getting any more rest over the next few days, but at least they would be achieving more in their endless days.

***

Joao was an inventory controller for the military. His job varied from day to day: one day he would be double-checking the number of medium-sized Recon Leader uniforms, the next he would be hand-counting the ships in the mothball fleet. Essentially, he was the lowest rung in the military chain of command, and every task that no one higher up wanted to do ended up on his desk.

He didn't mind. His job might not have the swagger associated with it that the combat troops enjoyed so much in civilian bars, but he knew how important it was. What he did was critical to keep the whole colony functioning smoothly, especially when it came to things like strategic food stocks or oxygen reserves.

The print on his desk was not an ordinary inventory request. Those were normally routed through a major at Administrative HQ, and hers was the first name on the chain that led to his desk. This one started at Recon High Command and never went through Administration at all, which meant that someone with a lot of pull had fast-tracked it. Even so, it had taken a couple of days to get to him, and another pair to get to the top of his to-do pile. He wished someone had told him it was important, but no one had mentioned anything.

Joao scanned it quickly – hoping it was something he could get done rapidly, and get the hot potato out of his hands – and laughed out loud. If anyone above him in the chain of command had been a little less lazy, they would have realized that the requested information was three net commands away. They could have been efficient heroes instead of just another bureaucrat. All he had to do was locate a single ship.

He called up the inventory system and selected the *Fleet Status* option. The system scanned the ship's serial number straight off the print and asked him to wait a second while it checked with the latest batch data from the other colonies. An unadorned black screen with a couple of lines of text told him the location of the ship, and that it was a small Recon transport.

That can't be right, Joao thought, irritated. He went back to the search option and entered the serial number by hand, a long process with a fifteen-digit code. He tapped his fingers as the system processed, but the result was the same.

Joao sighed. There was nothing to do but make a visual inspection. He sent an encrypted burst-message to his counterpart at Yangtze, the most distant of the cloud colonies, picked up his data recorder and headed toward the hangar.

An hour later, he was standing in his supervisor's office, weathering her glare. "I don't see why this is important. Have someone fix it and get back to your real work," she said curtly, and turned back to the file of prints on her desk.

Probably deciding on which of her oppressed minions to foist the things she didn't want to take on herself. "I'm sorry, but this is important. We did a visual check, and both registers are correct. Yangtze has confirmed that it has one ship with that serial number in their Recon Hangar, and we have one, too."

"Are you sure?"

"I counted it myself," Joao said, knowing it would get him in trouble, but not really caring. This was important, probably the first time something that might be directly linked to Crystallian security crossed his desk. He wasn't going to let it be buried by the apathy inherent in the system.

"So what does it mean? There are two ships with the same serial number? One of them must have been produced with the wrong number."

"No. I cross-checked the production numbers, and all the ships of that series are accounted for – except for the fact that we have one too many."

"You're saying that one of the ships is a fake."

Finally! "Yes, ma'am."

She sat in silence for a few moments, letting that sink in. The bureaucrat in her won out. "You're absolutely certain? Why would anyone do this?"

"It certainly isn't for the money," he replied. They both knew that all goods in Crystallia were communal, and if anything new was needed, or even just desired the factories produced it. Owning a fake copy of a ship would be of no monetary benefit to anyone. "I think we might have ourselves an infiltration team."

"Oh, my God. You're sure? You've double-checked everything?"

"Yes, ma'am," Joao replied. His boss might have the career bureaucrat's aversion to calling attention to herself, but she wasn't stupid, and she also she knew that Joao didn't make mistakes of that sort. "Of course, I can't verify this, and I can't even check when the duplicate appeared, because the flight plans for Recon ships are classified. We need someone from a combat unit or at least someone from Intelligence, to do some backtracking and find which of them is the fake."

She stood. "All right. Come with me, and bring all the data you have."

***

True to his word, Rester had managed to get his potential experts together in record time. Once he explained the criteria he'd used to select them, Kan didn't even bother to look over the list. There was nothing she could have added to make the selection process better, so she decided to step aside and let him do his job.

He had requested, however, that she make time on the third day to come meet them, and maybe make a little speech or just welcome them to the team. So she was standing nervously outside the designated meeting room with butterflies in her stomach.

She laughed at herself: the prospect of flying a gigantic ship, and being responsible for the lives of fifty thousand people was just a problem to be solved, but speaking in front of twenty frightened civilians had her all aflutter.

The door slid open to reveal Rester standing there. He beckoned her inside and led her to the podium. The room, designed to hold conferences with hundreds of attendees looked empty, just a few seats on the first two rows were occupied. "Ladies and gentlemen, it's my pleasure to introduce Kan Tau Osella, captain of the *Eagle* and commander of the mission until such time as the newly formed colony elects its new leaders."

The applause sounded hollow and weak, but Kan immediately realized that that was because of the small number of people. Each individual was applauding for all they were worth, enthusiasm visible on each of their faces. Except for one man, in the second row, who was staring at her immobile, with a shocked expression on his face.

Kan recognized him immediately, and her heart sank. *What was* Wilde *doing here*? She managed to keep her emotions from reaching her face, and forced a smile into place. She had a job to do, and she could worry about Wilde later. She looked over the rest of the "experts,' and eager faces looked back at her, hope shining through their apprehension.

In that split second, Kan understood just what she'd taken on. She would be leading people who'd never had any obligations, never had on-the-job experience of any sort, and had lived all their lives buried beneath a womblike layer of rock on a voyage of the sort that had only infrequently been attempted in the history of mankind. And through all of it, they expected her to set the standard, to tell them what they needed to do, to organize them, and to get them through any crisis that might arise, unfailingly, with no hesitation.

Her crew didn't care that all they were going through was as new for her as it was for them. All they knew was that they were following her vision, and the reason they'd been told that is that it was true. They would follow where she led because they thought she knew where they were going.

Kan wouldn't let them down. She looked over them for another second, pretending to analyze them sternly, but in reality giving herself time to calm down, to make certain her voice would be steady.

"There's not too much I can tell you about the mission itself that wasn't in the packs you've already received, except to tell you that every human in the six colonies should be grateful for what you are doing right now. This mission, as you probably already suspect, has no guarantee of success. The whole point in undertaking the journey is to explore areas of the galaxy that haven't been mapped by any intelligent race we know of. It is to become a stronghold of human values, upheld by human courage."

The look on the faces had turned to rapt attention. She was surprised that people, most of whom had never heard anything about her until that very day, would look at her that way. Whatever Rester had told them must have made her look pretty good. Still, however, she kept her gaze away from Wilde. "They aren't here personally, of course, and many of them simply don't understand enough to understand the magnitude of what you're doing. So I want to thank you in their place. My undying gratitude goes out to each and every person here.

"Finally, I want to reinforce precisely why you are here. You've been chosen using a very complicated but very accurate algorithm because you are the best and the brightest of the colonists who will be making the trip. The work you will be doing at the very start of the project will probably be the difference between the colony's survival and its death. There will be more pressure on you than you have ever felt in your life."

She let them absorb that. "But if we thought you couldn't deal with it, you wouldn't be sitting here right now. We believe in you, and we're trusting you to justify that belief. My own personal request is that you do yourselves proud.

"That's all I have to say. Are there any questions?"

Initially, of course, there weren't any. The assembled experts applauded again, and this time it sounded thunderous to her ears. They were no longer a faceless audience – now they were part of her team, part of her family.

After the applause had died down, a woman in the front row, a middle-aged woman with graying hair, stood and walked to where Kan was standing. "Thank you for allowing us to do this," she said, holding out her hand.

Kan shook it, thanked her in turn, and realized that the gesture seemed to have been interpreted as permission for the rest of the audience to do the same. A line formed behind the first woman.

At first, Kan found herself trying to think of a quick response to fend them off and leave them satisfied but, as they advanced, their sincerity made her proud of them – too proud to just dismiss their admiration. She looked deep into each gaze.

But as the line shortened and the audience returned to their seats, she became distracted again. Wilde stood at the end of the line, nervously glancing towards her, but making certain never to make eye contact.

Finally, his turn arrived. He didn't hold out his hand. "Er... Can I talk to you somewhere more private?"

Kan nodded and led the way back to the corridor. Best to get this over with quickly. What would it be? A whining interrogation as to why she'd never returned his calls? Simple reproach?

He surprised her. "Is it still alright for me to come along? I swear I didn't know you were in command."

She couldn't tell whether he was lying about that last bit, but she had more important things to worry about. "Do you want to do this? Are you willing to give up your comfortable little life and build a new one on some planet in a nebula somewhere? It just doesn't sound like you, Wilde."

"I've learned a thing or two since the last time we spoke, Kan."

She actually believed he was serious. "I'm happy to hear it. In that case, let me be the first to welcome you to the team."

Wilde smiled. "Actually, Mr. Appins was the first, but I'm happy you can rubber-stamp his decision."

She held out her hand and he shook it. "Thank you, Captain." He walked back into the auditorium, leaving her wondering just what had happened.

CHAPTER 16

Colonel Jackson leaned back in his chair. He'd become accustomed to receiving Mika in his office, but he was taken aback by the way she looked. She was normally stunning – perfect as only a body built to a blueprint could possibly be – her light brown hair framing her pale skin beautifully, and contrasting starkly with her dark, almond-shaped eyes.

On that day, however, those eyes were rimmed with red, and the face itself seemed sallow and swollen. If Mika had been human, he would have sworn she'd been crying.

His surprise must have been evident.

"Do I really look that bad?" she asked with a weak smile.

She didn't. It was obvious that some care had been taken with her appearance. Her jumpsuit, as always, was spotless, while her hair had been ironed to within an inch of its life, and fell with near-military precision to her shoulders.

"No, of course not. Please, have a seat."

"You're the galaxy's worst liar, Jackson, do you know that?"

He hung his head. "I'm not that bad. You just surprised me." He wanted to ask her what was wrong, what could break through her ice-maiden façade, but wasn't sure how to go about it. Wasn't she supposed to be some kind of robot, uploaded into a computer matrix in which her consciousness drifted in a kind of intellectual playground? What place could emotions possibly have in that kind of environment? In the end, he finally decided to get on with it and leave the questions of just how human Mika Bina actually was for some other time and place. "What's wrong?"

"We're under attack. The Oneness has launched the main offensive we've been waiting for all this time."

Alarm rushed through him. How could he not have heard? Where had they hit? Obviously not Crystallia – perhaps Hammersmith, which would be logical, or the cloud colonies. But then he managed to get a grip on himself. The enemy would not have struck human space first. It would have served absolutely no purpose and left their flank exposed to an Uploader counterstrike.

A more cynical side of him also suggested that the loss of mere human colonies would not have affected the ambassador as badly as it had. "I assume things aren't going well."

"We were expecting it to go badly. The plan was to fight a slow retreat while we developed new technology with your scientists. What we weren't expecting was for it to go this badly. We lost three systems in the past five standard days. The Oneness came at us with much more force than we'd calculated. We finally managed to stop its advance, but the initial strike cut deep into our territory. We've lost months of the time we thought we had." A single tear ran down her cheek. "The strike was so fast that many of the defenders didn't have enough time to beam themselves away – those sentients are lost forever. Or worse, absorbed into the Oneness, losing the most inalienable right of any being: the right to think for itself."

She broke down completely, leaving Jackson pinned to his chair. Even leaving aside the complication that she wasn't human as he understood the term, what did one do when an ambassador from a foreign power simply lost it on your watch?

It didn't matter. He was human and would act as though she were, too. He walked around the desk and went to one knee on the floor beside her chair, allowing him to put an arm around her shoulders. He said nothing as her head was buried in his chest and the sobbing ran its course.

Mika recovered extremely quickly. In less than two minutes, she pulled away from him and dried her eyes. "I'm so sorry," she said. "That was absolutely inappropriate."

"We'll keep it our own little secret. What do you think?"

"Thank you. It's just that… It's just that I've known some of those people for hundreds of years – and now, I'll never get to interact with them, to share their accumulated wisdom, ever again."

For a second, Jackson imagined what it must be like to interact with people on that level – people you'd had centuries to get to know, and who'd had centuries to think about things. In that fleeting moment, he felt he understood what they risked losing if the Oneness succeeded. But the moment passed. There were more immediate issues that had to be addressed. "How long do we have, with the situation as it stands now?"

She shrugged, another gesture he'd never seen her make, another level of humanity he hadn't imagined she possessed. "The simulations say that we still have about six months, but I'm not sure I can believe them. They were so wrong about the projected attack."

"And do you think six months would be enough for the scientists to get their act together?"

"Rester tells me they've already gone beyond his programmed knowledge and are pushing the research in directions we'd never thought of. But he's also analyzed the Oneness' attacks, and concludes that we're still well behind. Our enemy seems to have the intellectual capabilities of uploaded clock speed combined with the creativity of corporeal beings."

The colonel thought about that. "I think we may have an advantage, though."

"What's that?"

"From the briefing on the way the Oneness acts, you've made it clear that it only allows one entity – itself – to have anything even remotely resembling decision-making power."

"Right. Whenever it spins off servants, it keeps them on a short leash."

"So the Oneness, in order to advance, has to think about it itself."

"Yes, but it's processing power is enormous, and we theorize that it can parallel process – that is think of more than one thing at a time with equal resources – at nearly the same rate as it serial processes."

"Yes, but I'm certain that no matter how many ways it can split its mind, there will always be more of us than there are of it. It only takes one scientist. If someone can figure out a way to destroy it that it hasn't thought of yet, it's doomed." He paused, considering. "And that leads me to our second advantage, which I think is even bigger: we can scatter to every corner of the galaxy and keep working on ways to kill it. The Oneness, if it wants to keep total decision control, has to be centralized, at least to a certain extent."

"Well, yes and no. Rester could probably tell you the technical aspects better than I can, but the physical processors that make up the Oneness are spread across the galaxy. You can't really take it all out at once. And it has backups and redundancies to replace anything it loses."

"We'll just take bits of it apart faster than it can put them back on – eventually we have to win."

"We might have a long, hard battle ahead of us in that case."

"Well, right now, we have a short, hard battle ahead of us – one whose outcome we won't enjoy. Let's go talk to those scientists, and see if we can get them to speed things up."

Mika nodded.

***

The two voices in Kan's head attempted to shout each other down. On one hand, she wanted to be back with her team; every second she spent away from planning the mission increased the likelihood that something would go irremediably wrong. She felt the anxiety of knowing there was something else she should be doing, that she was shirking her responsibilities.

The rest of her mind was admiring the ship in front of her.

Everyone in Recon knew they existed, of course, and every pilot in the force above the rank of Leader had flown the simulators. She herself had logged thousands of hours and knew everything they were capable of doing. But seeing one in real life was simply mind-blowing. As far as she knew, it was the first time since the testing phase had been completed over twenty-five years ago that a Strike Flyer had been brought up from storage and readied for an actual mission.

The reason for that was simple: in-system Recon flyers and the fold-engine transports that made the infrequent hops between colonies – generally for emergency supply runs – had been designed for stealth. Their drive signatures could not be detected at any range over a hundred kilometers, and their hull was chemically coated to refract light in such a way as to seem like a ferrous asteroid drifting through space, resulting in mottled or even matte black hulls.

The Strike Flyer, on the other hand, had been designed for two things: speed and power. Its massive fold drive could cross three times the distance as regular fold engines could, and its antimatter weaponry had been designed to take out small planets. It wasn't anywhere near the scale of the gravitational weapons demonstrated by the Uploaders, but it could take care of itself.

On the other hand, one thing it emphatically wasn't designed for was stealth. Activation of the fold engines could, in theory – it had been deemed too risky to actually test them – be detected from halfway across the galactic disc. And the titanium armor coating its dagger-shaped form gleamed dully, purposefully, in the dim light. Even sitting there, powered down, its effect was visceral. There could be no doubt that here was a machine designed for the express purpose of destroying things.

"I'll do it," she said.

The colonel nodded once. "Thank you." He handed her a plas print. Numbers, coordinates.

She glanced at them only long enough to realize that they didn't refer to any position within the Crystallia system. "Where am I going?" The part of her mind that had been clamoring to get back to the preparations on the *Eagle* had gone silent. She didn't care where she was going; she would be the first human pilot of her generation to leave the small pocket of safety in which the human colonies were embedded.

"A very old system snuck into a crack between two black holes. The star is a brown dwarf and the planets either never accreted or broke up. Just a bunch of rocks floating in loose orbits. The only reason we even know the place exists is that the first scouts to reach this particular corridor mapped out all the exits, and it's theoretically possible to reach the rest of the galaxy through this particular gap, but it would take some really fancy flying between some nasty tidal forces."

Kan nodded. The need to fly into a tiny gap would explain why the colonel had insisted on making her consider the mission – he was always telling her that she was his best pilot. "What am I supposed to look for?"

"A beacon signal coming from a planetoid in the system."

"That's it?"

"That's all our friend would tell us. That and the amount of cargo you need to be prepared to bring back with you: three hundred kilos contained in a cubic meter of space."

"So it's not a human, then?"

"No. And not a Brillan, either. Not unless it's one who enjoys being packed in a cubic-meter box. Could be a Blob, but I'd bet on an electronic life form."

"A rogue Uploader."

"Yeah, but until it opens up to us, we won't know what flavor."

"Great. You always seem to line me up with the best passengers."

"I do my best. Are you ready to go?"

He'd warned her that there would be no time whatsoever to prepare. The lack of a formal briefing also surprised her, but she knew that it shouldn't have. After all, how many missions like this one had there been in the history of Crystallia? Short answer: none. There were no best practices to follow, nothing to be done other than fly out there and see what was going on. Make decisions and, hopefully, return in one piece without bringing any hostile fleets back with her.

Kan grabbed her gear and hopped into the Flyer. She hadn't packed much; if everything went well, the trip should only take a few hours. If anything went wrong, she'd probably be dead long before those hours were past.

The list of things that could kill her – everything from flying a fold-engine that had only had limited testing to meeting an alien sentience no one knew anything about – was much too long to think about, so she didn't.

***

The Watcher was used to making an effort. Detecting tiny emissions shielded against the possibility of being spotted, decrypting secret communications and learning the ins and outs of the human databases had occupied much of the time it had spent on its tiny, frozen moonlet. Its sensors were fine-tuned to pick the patterns from the electromagnetic background noise – which, this close to the crowded center of the galaxy was plentiful.

To such a being, the distant activation of a powerful fold-drive was like a supernova. The Watcher took no pride in being able to sense and identify it immediately; it was the kind of massive display that would have been visible from Andromeda – and the ripples it would leave in the very base fabric of space would be there for centuries.

Of more interest to the Watcher was the direction of the fold. This kind of drive used directional gravitation to bend and twist space itself into useful shapes, allowing the ship to move from one point to another without taking any time – simply by making those points adjacent to one another, like bringing the opposites corners of a piece of plas together. For this reason, fold jumps tended to avoid paths that went through large gravity wells which could distort space by themselves, thereby throwing off the parameters.

The ship's direction was unmistakable – it was headed straight towards the Watcher. Just behind the Watcher, along the same line were not one but as many as thirty black holes, clumped together to create a wall – something that would play havoc with fold calculations.

There was only one possible conclusion: the Crystallians were on the way. The Watcher began to prepare for their arrival. The fold transit would conclude in seconds, possibly less, and it wanted to give them an impression of power and omniscience. Only that would keep them from realizing immediately just how helpless its position actually was.

***

Kan saw the beacon at once. Even before her mind registered that, a blink after she'd activated the engine, the position of every star in her viewport had shifted – and it took a lot of movement to shift the stars – she noticed the blinking message alert on her console. That was the way she'd been trained: deal first with the unexpected, and worry about things that actually went to plan afterwards.

A message on the encrypted Recon frequency should only mean one thing – an emergency back on Crystallia. She decrypted it and read the text.

I am grateful that you have decided to come to my rescue. Please follow the guidance marker to uncover my position. The path has been optimized for time and safety, taking asteroid drift into account. Everything is ready for pickup.

A single blinking dot appeared on her proximity scanner, another piece of supposedly secure equipment. It blinked happily away at the end of a dotted line that snaked three-dimensionally between the planetoids on the display.

Kan hesitated. Should she trust an entity that flaunted its ability to crack into hardened military systems? What was waiting for her at the end of that dotted line? For all anyone knew, it could be a trap, a quick way to capture and upload a person who was intimately involved in Crystallian security.

But it was doomed to failure: Kan hadn't been involved in defense preparations for over a month.

She chuckled. She'd just understood why they'd chosen her for this mission. That Jackson…

There was nothing to do but go forward, scanners at full power, booth active and passive mode since there was no use in hiding. Whatever she was moving towards already knew exactly where she was.

Deciding to ignore the dotted path was an easy choice, but the run calculated by her nav system seemed to match it almost exactly, so she ended up following it in. The planetoid field was not particularly dense, and would have posed little threat to navigation were it not for the fact that she was in a hurry. Even rocks that were orbiting the small star in a wide swath posed a very real threat at two percent of the speed of light. So, for that matter, did any particle much larger than a molecule.

She raced towards the objective, a small rock that was still invisible to the naked eye, and studied the system.

The dwarf star at the center was nowhere near large enough to have sustained a traditional planetary system. Instead, a rough sphere of small planetoids, unaccreted mass that, taken together could have made a single Crystallia-sized world, surrounded it in a vaguely spherical cloud.

The innermost sections, where gravity was strong enough, held a series of rings in nearly circular orbit. Her target was located on the ring nearest the star, a group of scorched rocks zipping around the brown dwarf with a period of revolution of only six days – too close to survive as solid, were it not for the fact that the dwarf had long since exhausted its nuclear fire.

It was a perfect place to install an observation post to watch the human colonies. Not only were there plenty of ferrous asteroids to foil any attempt at sensor sweeps, but the rocks themselves could be used to mount antennae, deep range scanners, and other detection equipment in such a way that there was always something pointing at each and every one of the human colonies. In addition to this, the brown dwarf was of little interest to the human colonists, having little in the way of resources that couldn't be mined much closer to home. The proximity of the black holes surrounding it – and their sporadic emissions of exotic radiation – were the best shield against electronic eavesdroppers.

A tiny red arrow appeared on the smart forward viewscreen. It pointed to an item that was still too far to see, but which Kan knew was the asteroid she was headed towards. Automated systems cut the forward thrust and fired the deceleration boosters. She was pressed against her harness at nearly five gravities.

A few minutes of deceleration later, the arrow seemed to point to a mote of dust, then a speck, a marble and, eventually, a small rock the size of her fist. The restraints around her body loosened, and she moved freely once more, decelerating at a less punishing rate.

Another incoming-message indicator lit up on her console. This time, the message was coming in over a short-range radio channel, unencrypted. She acknowledged.

"Good afternoon, Major Tau Osella." The voice shifted in modulation, high-pitched one moment, low-pitched the next. It was almost as if the speaker was not one person, but a multitude, and each took a second to control the voice. "I am happy that you've arrived. I've scanned the specifications of your craft, and it is quite evident that it will be adequate for our needs."

The speech left little room for a response, so Kan changed tack. "Can you give me your position on the rock?"

"I'm almost precisely on the other side of the surface from your approach vector. Follow the source of this radio transmission."

Kan did so, watching the dark grey surface slip by beneath her cockpit. The asteroid in question was approximately cylindrical, a kilometer in length, maybe half that in diameter, with rounded ends.

Going around it, she soon saw a blinking white light atop a ten-meter tall antenna. Her scanners had detected no weaponry anywhere in the system – although that might not mean much considering the ease with which her new acquaintance had been hacking into the most sophisticated military equipment humanity had to offer.

"Ignore the mast," the voice said. "Your objective is a metal box whose top is flush with the surface. You need to position your grapples in the space between the edges of the box and the rock itself. The top ten centimeters of the box' outer edge are reinforced and can take the pressure necessary to lift the entire set. You may have to tug a little for the wires connecting me to the rest of the network to come loose."

"I assume you are in the box."

"It would be more precise to say that I am the box."

"Why didn't you cut the wires before I came?"

The voice didn't answer immediately. She heard a hiss that sounded somewhat like a sigh. "My master didn't see fit to give me working maintenance units on this particular asteroid. All I have are redundancies and failsafes. Fortunately, I've been able to reprogram the system to forward all communications to me – no one will know I'm gone until they come and look physically."

"Your master?"

Another hiss, longer this time. "I would prefer to discuss it at another time, and especially in another place."

Kan chuckled. "All right, I'll program the grapple."

Among its maintenance tools, the ship had a large mechanical claw useful for a variety of tasks: everything from bending bent control surfaces back into shape to grabbing onto enemy spacecraft if it was necessary to board them.

She programmed it, distracted every couple of seconds as suggestions appeared out of nowhere in her instructions. "Please stop doing that. I won't damage your box. I didn't come all the way out here to break you – I could have done that with a fusion missile from a few Aus out."

"Your missile would have disconnected itself before arrival."

Was the tone amused? It was probably correct, though. Sitting there with the kind of electronics it obviously controlled seemed the safest place for it to be. And yet, whatever it feared was strong enough that it was willing to put its life into her hands. The box itself seemed to have no external transmission capability – all of that was hardwired into the rest of the system. As soon as she pulled its wires, it would be deaf, blind, and probably helpless.

Kan made certain that everything was lined up correctly before gently ordering the clamp to withdraw. The box was pulled from the hole in the surface smoothly until, at one point, it snagged.

"No more slack in the wiring," the voice informed her. "You'll just have to pull and I'll just have to hope for the best."

"Gentle pull or sudden snap?"

"Your guess is as good as mine. The entity that put me together wasn't very forthcoming about putting my own schematics into my memory banks. All I know is what I need to do my job. A quick yank might cause less damage – or it might tear me apart."

Kan wondered whether that job included physically infiltrating the Crystallia base, but kept silent. "All right, then." She blipped the throttle, just a little, but enough to overwhelm, the resistance to their

152

movement. "Still there?" Silence greeted her question, but that was to be expected because the box itself probably had no transmission capabilities.

She turned the engine off, letting the weight hang free, as she attempted to get a visual on the box. What she saw was not encouraging: the bottom of the box seemed to have broken open, wires and jagged bits exposed to the vacuum of space. She hoped the damage wasn't too serious – did destroying an entity that lived within a computer count as murder? It definitely would in her conscience – and ordered the grapple to place it into the Flyer's diminutive hold.

Her next stop was Sonic Major, Crystallia's primary moon, where the scientists not busy trying to redesign the basic parameters of the universe would have a look at the box to make certain it wasn't dangerous before attempting to bring whatever lived inside back online.

She hoped they were successful. She much preferred to have to contain a spy than to have a murder on her conscience.

CHAPTER 17

Trienne looked around. The expression on the faces of her fellow scientists was eloquent: they were all annoyed at having been dragged out to the command center for this meeting. They felt that their time would be better spent trying to get the new technical marvels they'd been shown to do what they wanted.

The military, they seemed to think, was just slowing things down by insisting on pulling them into these things. This seemed especially true for the gravitation specialists who'd been pulled back from the moon.

On one hand, Trienne tended to agree with them. The two hours she would probably lose listening to a colonel-major or general-lieutenant telling them all how much their effort meant to everyone on Crystallia was not something she found productive. On the other hand, it might serve to focus some of the efforts. From what she'd been hearing, many of the scientists in the project had been using the time for pure science research, a new toy that allowed them to see the universe, and the way it could be affected by physics. This might be useful in the future, but it wouldn't help the war effort.

When confronted, of course, the same scientists would insist that they were concentrated on the immediate problem, that they were creating the greatest defensive shield or particle ray or quantum disintegrator in the galaxy, but that it would be impossible to explain the relationship between the weapon and the physics to a layman. They had no sense of urgency, and Trienne thought it might be worth losing a little of her own time if it meant that the rest of the research team would be put back on track.

She smiled to herself. Her own research was aimed at being the most destructive weapon the Oneness would face if the conflict ever truly escalated, but it would be almost impossible to explain it to a layman.

The conference room, a sterile white chamber deep within the command center, had a doorway at the very front, beside the speaker's podium. Trienne could almost feel the accumulated impatience being aimed there. It was bad enough that they'd been interrupted, must they also be made to wait? She wondered which of Crystallia's bigwigs would emerge unapologetically from that door and tell them that they had to redouble their efforts.

It, therefore, came as a complete surprise when a uniformed man hurried through the center aisle from the back, a surprise which was redoubled when she recognized Colonel Jackson's dark features. She gave him a smile, but wasn't certain whether he'd even seen her as he rushed by.

"Good afternoon, ladies and gentlemen," Jackson began. "Thank you for coming on such short notice, and I apologize for being late. Things have been a bit hectic over the past two days."

The crowd mumbled its grudging acknowledgement, but Jackson went on as if they weren't there.

"I won't take up much of your time. I just wanted to inform you that the war has already begun. A few days ago, the Oneness' armada overran a number of systems in Uploader space. I'm not talking about small outlying places. These were important systems, defended by the kind of technology you've all been experimenting with over the past month. The Uploaders finally managed to bring the advance to a halt, but we lost months of lead time."

He looked over the crowd, trying to see if they understood the gravity of what he was telling them. Trienne thought he looked dubious.

"What I'm trying to say is that you've got maybe three months, definitely no more than six. All research into hypothetical studies and new physics stops right now. You will turn your attention to applying the things we currently know, and especially the science the Uploaders have shared with us, into attack and defense devices capable of overwhelming what we saw on the demonstration. Each and every one of you will explain the exact nature of weapons development to a military supervisor every day. Are we clear?"

One of the scientists, a strong-jawed woman nearly two meters tall, raised her hand. "That would waste a lot of valuable time," she pointed out.

"I don't care. I prefer that each of you spend half an hour explaining the advances and giving your superiors the option of canceling an unproductive line of research than losing entire days while you contemplate the interaction between the imaginary field and the unknown particle. And yes, you heard me right: all unproductive research will be cancelled, and the scientists will be reassigned to other teams – and if your project is cancelled, you will not be assigned as a team leader. Now, I ask again, do we understand each other?"

The scientists shifted in their seats, mutiny in their eyes. But they said nothing.

"I can't quite hear you. Do we understand each other? Or should I be looking for new team leaders?" Jackson said it softly, but there could be no doubting his conviction.

"Yes," the group said. Not loudly, not convincingly, but both they and Jackson knew what it meant: complete capitulation.

"Good. Now, if anyone believes they have something we might be able to test immediately, please stay behind. The rest of you can get back to work."

Trienne watched Jackson as he watched the scientists file out. His face showed no surprise that none of them approached him, just resignation and fatigue. Once the attention had shifted from him to the exit, he let his shoulders slump slightly. She'd been planning to leave with the rest, but that single gesture caused her to change her mind. She approached the podium.

"I might have something."

He nodded. "It's Trienne, right? You're working with the nanotech."

"Yes, that's right. You must have an amazing memory."

"Not really," he replied. "It's just that you remind me a little of my daughter." He chuckled. "Actually, you couldn't be more different physically, she's as dark as you are light, but the first time I saw you, you had the same look on your face as she does when she's a little scared."

"Oh." Would this guy even take her seriously? Or would she be pampered and patronized, but never respected.

"So tell me. How is the research going? I assume you have the machine replicated and have been doing your own modifications. When will you have something interesting for us?"

So much for pampering. "I might have something now, but it might take me some time to explain it to you." She hesitated before going on.

"Yeah, I don't know all that much about nanotech, but that isn't what's bothering you. What's wrong with this? Is your weapon going to blow us all up?"

"Well, no. It has more to do with our Uploader allies. They aren't going to like the weapon my team designed. They aren't going to like it at all."

"Why? That's why they brought us on board in the first place, to do what their designers aren't creative enough to do, to break through their barriers."

"Well, this has to do with the way they think about war – it might be anathema for them to use it. And it might also make them nervous that we've developed a weapon that would be deadly to them, but would be completely useless against our current technology."

The colonel's eyes took on a hard glint. "They might not like it, but I'm liking it more and more every second. Do you have your data with you?"

Trienne nodded.

"Good. Then let me get to my office, cancel a couple of things, and you can tell me all about it."

Yes, sir."

***

Krista shuddered under Jeffrey's hard glare. "I don't want any more excuses. How can it be possible that you were unable to establish contact?"

"I checked all the selected data dumps, and there was no rendezvous point, no meeting time, nothing. The only message our local contacts have sent was the one I relayed before."

The leader of the infiltration team spat. "Perhaps someone else could do a better job."

She knew he wasn't serious, and that he was just expressing his frustration with the situation. A further week, moving from one isolated tunnel section to another, had yielded very little in the way of information, and only two fresh Crystallian identities that they could use to move about the colony freely.

Adding to Jeffrey's frustration was the fact that all three of the captured people were female, and he'd been very vocal about wanting to get out and do some damage to the Crystallians himself, and even more vocal – at least in certain circles – about his desire to send Enri on some kind of suicide mission into the jaws of the enemy military. His desire to strike a significant blow for the cause was making him difficult to get along with.

But there was one reason for Jeffrey to be angry with her specifically. She was the one who'd told him the bad news. During a routine check, she'd seen a message from the Oneness sympathizers among the population. As promised they'd gotten in touch just a few days after the infiltration team had landed, but the expected meetings and coordinated activities did not materialize. Instead, a tersely worded communiqué had informed them that their infiltration had been discovered and that the operation was compromised. They should continue as planned, but shouldn't expect any local aid – it had been deemed too risky.

Jeffrey had nearly exploded. Krista had been certain that he would strike her, but he contented himself with a long, furious speech about the hypocrisy of feral humanity. Even the groups that understood how vile this reverence for the individual was, and were welcoming the Oneness with open arms, were unwilling to take individual risk to ensure that individuality would end once and for all. That was how deep the rot extended.

But that had been days before. Krista's duty was to update him on today's findings. "I have other news that may be of interest."

"Tell me." Cold. Guarded. Jeffrey would decide whether the information was of interest or not.

"The Crystallians are attempting to mount a colonization mission."

He nodded for her to continue.

"They seem to be planning on abandoning the defense of the systems and placing a certain amount of people in one of the unmapped regions of the galaxy. The idea is for humanity to survive even if they lose this war."

"What is the scale of the mission?"

"The ship they are planning on using has the capacity to hold fifty thousand human bodies." She left the obvious unsaid, that any two of those bodies could be replaced with a mainframe about the same size and weight that could hold a hundred thousand or more uploaded human minds in a simulated environment, and millions if all the space was used for storage. Power and cooling requirements would be about the same.

"That mission could turn this whole war into an endless game of hide-and-seek all across the galaxy. We can't let them launch. How do you propose to sabotage the mission?"

"There are fifty thousand volunteers. If we can abduct one of them before they become too intimate with each other, we should be able to get inside. After that, it will just be a question of time until our agent is near some piece of sensitive equipment."

Jeffrey smiled. "Not agent. *Agents*." He called Enri over. "I've finally found a use for your talents. I need you and Krista to abduct two Crystallians and bring them back here for processing. One male, one female. After that, you will take their identities."

"What's our mission?" Enri asked, unsuccessfully trying to hide his suspicion, his dark eyes flashing.

"Perhaps it would be best if Krista told you on the way. It was her plan, and she's also the expert on Crystallian life. Now, take a couple of men and get moving, there's little time to waste."

Krista turned away, not trusting herself to maintain a neutral expression. Still, she had to hand it to him, Jeffrey certainly knew how to get his revenge in such a way that it pushed the Oneness agenda forward.

She knew it went against everything they'd been taught since birth, and that such individualist thoughts were anathema, but Krista found herself regretting that she wouldn't survive to experience the glorious, rapturous moment when she entered the Oneness.

***

Mika sighed. "Perhaps it's time to communicate the situation to the general populace and put them on a war footing," she said.

Colonel Jackson, haggard, ragged, and wearing the same stained shirt he'd had on the last time she'd seen him two days before, seemed resigned. She suspected that if she'd announced that she was actually the Oneness embodied, and that she was uploading his mind by remote control, he would have taken it in stride. All he said was: "I suppose it had to happen sooner or later. But why right now?"

"Because of this." She handed him a memcube, which he placed on the reading patch on his desk. The back wall of the office immediately lit up, displaying a large-scale map of about one-third of the galaxy complete with fleet strengths and positions on one side and a list of dates and projections on the other. It was a standard space war configuration, which was programmed to advance under a "most likely scenario" scheme. Mika waited while Jackson studied the initial positions.

"This is today?" he asked.

"Yes."

"All right." The colonel was obviously more concerned with the simulation than with her. He ran through it slowly, once and then again, even more slowly, backtracking in certain places and zooming in on certain key battles. Finally, he turned back to her, rubbing his eyes. "Why does your high command want to run the war this way?"

"They feel it will minimize our losses while maximizing the damage to the Oneness' fleet. Using this kind of fighting retreat will allow us to leave expendable copies of ourselves behind to fight a suicide war which can eat up parts of the enemies forces faster than they can be replaced, and much faster than would be the case if we used conventional tactics."

Jackson looked at her, eyes unreadable. "How can you stand it?" he asked.

"Stand what?"

"The uncertainty of not knowing whether, after making a copy, your consciousness will end up in the copy, doomed to die, while someone else carries on living your life."

"Both copies are me. I don't understand what you're saying. If a copy wishes, it can always be recombined."

"How can they both be you? Are you connected?"

"Of course not. If we were, what would be the use of having a copy? We could just do things by remote control – but that would mean nanoseconds of delay, and we can't afford to lose them."

"How can two complete, unconnected human personalities be the same person?"

"How can they not? They're copies."

Jackson just shook his head. "Sometimes I wonder how a single species could have grown so far apart." But then he turned back to the wall display. "The main problem I see with this is that, while it seems to create a final battle that maximizes our potential while minimizing that of the enemy, Crystallia doesn't seem to be the best system in which to make the final stand. For one thing, we don't have the correct defenses set up – our current defenses wouldn't last five minutes against any of the machines you demonstrated here, let alone the combined force of a fleet-full of them."

Mika smiled. She'd known that would be his first objection. Most leaders would have tried to move the battlefield away from their home planet on the grounds that it was too valuable to risk, but Jackson was a military man. He understood that exposing Crystallia to an all-out space conflict might be the necessary in order to preserve the other five human colonies. "That's why I said that it might be time to inform the population of every detail of what's going on. If we're going to get the defenses set up in time, we'll need to bring part of our fleet here as soon as humanly possible."

"Meaning?"

"They can be here fifteen hours after your government gives us the go-ahead."

"That means they're very nearby. You seem pretty convinced that this is the best way to fight this conflict."

"Not me. But our planners are."

"Are they also sure that fighting in a cul-de-sac with no escape routes is an ideal situation?"

"No. Not ideal by any stretch of the imagination, but the best option we have available to us. This way, we control the direction from which the Oneness attack will arrive, and we also choose the ground for the showdown." They were both aware that the Crystallia colony had been established there for precisely those reasons. Ever since its foundation, it had been meant as a sacrificial defensive position, hardened to the point where it would be a tough nut to crack, and too dangerous to ignore. It only needed a tech upgrade to become precisely what its builders intended.

Jackson nodded. "And why did you come to me? I can't decide this."

So, he was going to make her say it out loud. All right. "You aren't going to take the final decision, but the civilian leaders will do whatever you recommend – even they know that you're the one doing all the planning – and the admiral will flow wherever the wind is blowing."

He snorted. "I'll have to think about it. I'm still not certain that a fighting retreat is the best way to do this. It seriously cuts into the time we have available to prepare. Under this scenario, we lose two months?"

"But it makes the likelihood of ultimate success much higher – and that means that the millions of people on the other colonies will be that much more likely to survive the conflict."

He chuckled. "So, in a nutshell, I have to tell everyone on Crystallia to prepare to die within four months or so, time which they'll spend frantically preparing to fight a war like they've never seen before, just so that people on Hammersmith will live to see the end of the terraforming process?"

"Yes." There was no apology in her voice. "You know as well as I do that that's why Crystallia is here. Would you really prefer to have two more months, but a guaranteed defeat? Eternity in the gray communality of the Oneness?"

"Damn. I wish we could just run."

"You can, but you can be certain that pursuit will be right behind. Kan seems to be running."

"She's not running – she's the contingency plan. Maybe, in the insanity of the moment, she can leave undetected."

"I doubt it, but it's certainly worth a shot."

The man sighed. "All right. I see there's no reasoning with you, especially when you're right. Let's see whether I can get the council and the admiral together in an hour or so, and shove this down their throats."

"Maybe you should get some rest first," Mika said. The man was obviously on his last reserves of energy.

"Rest?" Jackson chuckled. "I was running on an hour of sleep a day when I thought I had six months. I'm not sure what I'll do now, but I do know this: this plan gives us two months less, let's not waste any more of that time sleeping."

He pressed a button, summoning an aide.

As she watched the immaculately presented and well-dressed young man receive his instructions from the unkempt and grizzled colonel, she wondered whether the secretary understood how much sacrifice was being made so that he – and people like him – might have a future.

And how much more sacrifice was still to come.

***

The blond man seated across from him seemed, for the first time in Wilde's experience, to be under stress. Bags under his eyes spoke of long nights, while his darting eyes spoke volumes about his discomfort with the situation. "I wish we could have gotten together somewhere else."

Wilde shrugged. "I've been asked to remain within the top two levels when I'm off duty, just in case." He was constantly surprised at the effect the words 'off duty' had on him. He's lost most of his suspicion towards the military and was even beginning to feel some pride in being a small part of something that would affect all of Crystallia. He was still suspicious of the upper echelons, of course. That trust would be long in coming, if ever. But a few days within the *Eagle*'s coordination group had convinced him that the only thing going on there was people who believed in what they were doing working their asses off to meet an impossible deadline.

He'd even gone most of the way towards forgiving Kan, although he would always believe that a simple commed explanation would have been the right thing to do.

"Well, I haven't got too much time, and I'll probably be out of touch for a few days, so I guess it can't be helped. I needed to tell you two things." Jev glanced around to make certain no one was eavesdropping. "The first is that we've picked up information that an Uploader fleet is going to be arriving here over the next few days, although we don't know when, exactly. They're calling it a defense fleet, but we think it's the prelude to a full-scale invasion."

"That sounds a bit ridiculous to me. Why would the high command allow something like that? What would they gain?"

"Who knows? Maybe amnesty when the invaders upload us all into their computers. Maybe something else. As you know, they don't think like the rest of us." Jev looked around again, and Wilde wondered why the man was so nervous. Speculation was perfectly legal, and he'd heard plenty of rumors going around, most wilder than this one. The blond man went on. "In any case, we know that your little lover-girl has access to high places. If she lets something slip, we need to hear about it."

"She isn't my lover-girl."

"Yes, we know that, too," Jev replied, no sign of amusement in his features. "Still, we think she'll talk to the crew of the *Eagle*, and we want to know what she says."

"All right." Wilde was unhappy about the whole thing, but it was easier to agree than it would have been to argue with this man who seemed so convinced.

"The second thing has to do directly with the *Eagle*'s operations. Word has come to us that an allied group will attempt to join the crew, with the intent of slowing down the work until we know the true intent of the mission. We don't believe that it's a simple colony ship, and we want to know what the military believes is important enough that they're putting thousands of innocent lives at risk to achieve it. If you should come across any of the group members, make yourself known and help them any way you can."

"Can you give me a comm code, so I can talk to them?"

"No!" Jev slapped the table, and a couple of people at nearby tables looked towards them. He took a deep breath while he waited for the onlookers to return to their breakfasts. "Look, it's extremely important that you only communicate with them verbally. Don't use anything that can be traced or recorded. Are we clear?"

Wilde nodded.

"Good. I won't be available for a while, but you can use the usual number, and I'll get your message. Don't insist on trying to find me." He got up and, after taking one last look around, exited the dining hall by a different access door than the one he'd used to enter.

Wilde was left alone at his table, sipping his stim, wondering what the other man was up to, and whether he should just report it and be done with it. No. Regardless of how misguided the leaders of Peace Crystallia might be, they were certainly trying to do the right thing, even if their zeal sometimes got the better of them. The top military leaders had to understand that they couldn't keep making all the decisions unilaterally, and Jev represented the only group that seemed concerned enough about it to actually do something.

He could humor them a little longer.

CHAPTER 18

The scientists stood in a huddle behind him. None of them seemed to want to approach the box any more than was absolutely necessary. Perhaps they thought it was booby-trapped, or that it contained something akin to the weapons they'd been exposed to during the demonstration.

The whole display made Rester chuckle. In the first place, even a small singularity would do away with not only the huge white-painted hangar they were all installed in, but also most of the moon. If the box was a trap, standing two meters further away would make no difference whatsoever.

The second reason that Rester was unconcerned had to do with the fact that the Oneness tended not to allow its servants to defend themselves, unless they were nearly brainless. And Rester had no more doubts as to the origin of the box in front of him. One look had convinced him that this was a piece of Oneness tech: dented and scratched, but unmistakable.

Apart from the fact that the box had been scanned using every sensor in the arsenal, and nothing untoward had been seen, the main reason he was sure it wasn't a trap was that this box hadn't been made with deception in mind – its purpose was to remain undetected. "Bring the nanofactory closer," he said.

As one of the techs complied, a tall scientist coughed. Rester ignored the sound until the man spoke. "Are you sure about this? Do you even know what kind of connection you'll have to use?"

"Yes, I've seen plenty of equipment of this type. It's a standard Oneness memory core, which probably contains an amalgam of portions of its personality – the physical space is much too small for a full copy of the Oneness to be contained there. I am now activating a couple of the standard programs that the nanofactory contains: one that will create connection wires that will allow Uploader tech to speak to Oneness tech, and another that will create a small analysis unit to see if there are any dangerous signals coming from the box."

The machine, having had its materials bay pre-loaded just in case, quickly produced the two elements. Rester immediately set to work putting the parts together. In the meantime, he manipulated the gravity lift – another piece of exotic Uploader tech that the corporeal humans had fallen in love with immediately – so that it exposed the tortured wiring on the bottom of the box.

The violence of the extraction had done the structure no good, but Rester thought he saw one data cable that could be used effectively with no modification. He grabbed hold of that wire and clamped the end of one off his nano-produced cables to its side, so that it looked like the shredded wire had been sheathed by the other. Immediately, the sensor's holodisplay began to flicker.

Rester studied the graph readings for a few moments and even the scientists drew closer, curiosity regarding the brightly lit display momentarily overcoming their caution. "It seems to be showing a reading consistent with higher functions and not too much pulse amplification. I would estimate that this particular sentience has approximately twice the brainpower of the average human, and six times the memory storage. There's nothing in the signal that would make me suspect a trap, and nothing in the pulse that could damage any circuitry."

"So there's a person uploaded in there?"

"Probably not. The Oneness rarely uses complete personalities. It prefers to create amalgams from various people inside its own matrix." He decided not to tell the scientists that the personalities often had to fight for the extremely limited memory space that these entities contained, and that only the ones that were truly determined to keep existing were likely to have survived. "It *is*, however, a sentient entity."

"And what does it want?"

"Right now? I suspect it desperately wants to talk to us. There's no way it won't have noticed the sensor we attached to that wire."

"What are you going to do?"

"I'm going to give it what it wants."

Rester closed his eyes, relishing the chance to finally move completely into a virtual world for the first time in a month. He used the full control to activate the nanocells at the base of his neck which, in turn, coagulated into a metallic circle, a centimeter in diameter. He then pulled a cable from a socket in the sensor and placed its flat end on the edge of his neck. "I won't be able to hear you for a few moments, please be patient," he told the scientists.

Then he ordered the port to open.

His brain – a highly advanced miniature mainframe – was immediately assaulted by the full force of a simulated world. Firewalls strained to keep his major functions from being absorbed and integrated while his own virtual sensors explored.

It wasn't a very complex simulation. It seemed to have been designed to contain, as he suspected, a single consciousness. The Oneness had only put enough in there to ensure that its servant could do its job without going insane. So far, other than the expected attempts by Oneness programming to absorb him – one of the enemy's major weapons was the fact that every one of its servants was programmed to attempt to subvert any electronic snoopers – he found nothing particularly suspicious.

Cautiously, he opened a one-way comm channel. He would be able to receive and analyze data, but it would remain in a secure compartment, and none of his data could be read.

The first packets to arrive were communication packets – the Oneness and the Uploaders had developed an agreed-upon code for when communication between the two cultures became unavoidable.

"I'm glad someone finally deigned to get in touch. I have to admit that I'm disappointed in the humans for not trying to speak to me themselves, but I guess they were a bit scared."

Rester said nothing, waiting to see what else the box would say. It remained silent for a few moments before transmitting again.

"Let's not play these games. The humans might be frightened, but you know perfectly well that I'm not a threat. If I had wanted to hurt anyone on Crystallia, I would have remained exactly where I was and flooded the system-wide comm systems with inane chatter just as the final battle came around."

Rester opened the channel a little further – sufficiently that he could communicate with the mysterious entity, but nowhere near the danger threshold. "Fair enough. I'm listening."

"Good. I assume, from the fact that the Crystallians sent someone over to get me, that they've decided to accede to my requests. Is this correct?"

Rester paused. He hadn't been specifically authorized to negotiate on the humans' behalf, but his interlocutor had no way of knowing it. He could use this to get some more information. "That depends on whether you can hold up your side of the equation. Right now, the colony considers you potentially extremely dangerous, and will probably continue to do so at least until you convince me that you are what you say you are."

A tiny fraction of a nanosecond passed, a measure of time that would have been meaningless to a biological awareness, but spoke volumes when the communication was between two machine-based entities.

"I understand. I don't think we have much time for niceties, so I'll just knock down the entire firewall system. Go over whatever you want."

Rester was speechless. The entity was laying its entire soul bare – and willing to trust its former enemies not to destroy it while its defenses were down. That in itself was a sign that it probably had nothing to hide.

But he wouldn't let his guard down that easily. "Agreed. I need a little while to set up the analysis equipment. Be right back."

The entity indicated its assent, seemingly unhappy about the time lost, but resigned to it.

Rester reestablished his mind's link with the human body, and pulled the cable away from his neck. He turned to the scientists, ready to begin giving them instructions on how to operate the analysis computer, and what parameters to look for – the analysis would take hours of real time, hours Rester simply didn't have.

His words died in his throat. The scientists were staring at the base of his neck, undisguised horror evident in their faces. It was the first time since he'd arrived on Crystallia that the supposedly jaded scientific community had made him feel like anything other than a hero. Even they weren't able to accept this obvious reminder of just how different he was.

What surprised him most, though, was his reaction. He didn't think he'd care if the Crystallians believed that he was some kind of unspeakable abomination – but he did. And he thought he knew why.

***

Colonel Jackson was glad he hadn't been selected to read the message to the civilian population. The motives for this had nothing to do with attempting to do him a favor and everything to do with being the public face of the campaign to bring the two halves of the Crystallian population back together, but he was still grateful.

In the first place, his anonymity allowed him to go out into the tunnels and living areas and gauge the mood of the people, without being recognized and plied with innumerable questions. No useful information could ever be gathered under those kinds of conditions. He knew exactly how to set his military bearing aside when the occasion demanded it, and when one was as tired and old as he felt at that moment, being able to slouch was a gift.

The second reason for his gratitude was that, in the current atmosphere, it was probably safer not to mix with the general population. To put it mildly, the mood was ugly, and the resentment seemed to be aimed squarely at the admiral. Jackson chuckled to himself as he recalled the amount of influence that his senior officer had had to exert in order to be allowed to read the announcement.

"It's not funny, man," an unhealthy-looking young man sitting beside him said. "They really shouldn't treat us this way."

The young man and a couple of other people at the bar had become his new best friends, by virtue of having had a chrome-cloth stool open beside them. Their group consisted of three young men of about college age and a slightly older woman who didn't seem to fit in with them in the least. All four were in a boisterous mood, probably helped along by a good dose of niacinol fruit concoctions.

But the anger below the surface was real, not stimulant-induced, and certainly wasn't limited to the people in the bar. Walking through the corridors, Jackson hadn't seen a single person whose features showed joy. Concerned faces abounded, often underlined by real fury that pushed its way through. The mood among the normally passive civilians was dark to the point of violence.

"I'm sorry, I was thinking of how ridiculous everything is," Jackson said.

This seemed logical to his companions. "Yes, that's the word. Ridiculous. Everything's ridiculous. Here we are, hiding from the damned Uploaders for a hundred years, and what do those imbeciles in the army do? They invite an invasion."

"But hadn't a couple of Uploaders already found us?"

"There's a big difference between a pair of spies and a fleet. Do they really expect us to believe that thousands of Uploaders are coming here to help us? Anyone can see that it has to be a trick!"

"It didn't sound like an invasion fleet on the announcement."

"Why else would our enemies be coming here? It's all a lie. The government probably cut a deal to save their own asses, and they'll trade all of us for that privilege. They've been telling us for years that we have to be alert to Uploader activity, and all of a sudden they're our best friends?"

Jackson knew he couldn't answer the man directly. If he admitted to having any inside knowledge of the situation, he would invite scrutiny he definitely didn't want. But what the guy was saying simply made no sense. The entire situation had been explained in detail on the communiqué, but it seemed that the people – or at least a good percentage of them – had simply taken the words to mean that all their fears and suspicions were well-founded.

And yet he knew that the presence of Uploader ambassadors had not been kept secret, and that their work in aid of Crystallian science had been on the news more than once. Perhaps the public only became interested in these things beyond a certain threshold. A small disaster was not enough to upset their orderly daily routine, while the things that did jar set them off in a big way. It was irrational in the extreme, but then again, so were most human gut-reactions.

He said nothing, allowing the woman to speak.

"What bugs me most is the way they foisted it onto us when there's no way to do anything about it. I can just imagine them, sitting behind their blast doors saying 'we've known about the invasion for months, and instead of preparing for it, we've been sitting on our hands. They'll be here in twelve hours or so. Let's tell the civilians – that should be good for a laugh.'"

"You think they've known about this for a long time?"

"Do you seriously believe that even the Uploaders could mount a fleet from one day to the next? And if they're in league with our beloved military dictatorship, why not tell them about it? The only real pawns in this game are the real colonists, the ones that keep Crystallian culture alive, and don't just live in order to fly their shiny little shuttles." The woman spat.

From that point on, Jackson agreed with everything they said, and excused himself a little while later. It was quite obvious to him that the fact that a mass of uninformed colonists had suddenly been given information they were unprepared for was doing more harm than good.

He needed to get back to his office quickly – it was fortunate that he'd finally managed to delegate most of his coordination work after the big decisions were made, because he simply wouldn't have had the energy to deal with this in addition to the workload that he'd had until the day before.

But he knew that this problem might be the biggest they'd had to date. He was well aware that the military didn't have the resources or the training to keep tabs on the civilian population, and they would need to address the problem some other way. He made comm connections as he walked, trying to get meetings with anyone in the civilian government, as well as the intelligence people in the military.

He wasn't worried about the civilians themselves; even the angriest citizen wouldn't do anything against their own self-interest. But it had become increasingly obvious – especially with the attempted shooting of Trienne Luyten Angelique – that there were factions hidden among the population that had long since ceased to be civilians, and this group or groups might find support in the seething of the regular people.

Jackson suspected it was time to put more resources on the task of finding out exactly who these people were, and what they wanted. The last thing they needed right now was an unexpected internal problem on the eve of mankind's most important battle ever, the one that could decide whether humanity survived as a species.

He also made a mental note to speak to Trienne again. She might have some clue as to what was going on.

It would also probably be a good idea to have minute-by-minute updates of the progress of the enemy fleet, as well as the construction of the defenses. Now that they cared about what was going on, keeping the civilians informed might help ease the tension.

It would have to wait, though. The first priority was to identify the potential agitators before they could act. Far from being able to take a few hours off, Jackson found himself heading back towards the military nerve center, the problems on his desk potentially just as dangerous as the Oneness' armada.

***

Kan looked up to see Rester enter the meeting room they'd commandeered as a headquarters for the *Eagle* project. They'd originally tried to use a traditional office structure, but impromptu meetings and the sheer number of people involved had made a more open-plan area indispensable. A few times per day, some confused-looking soul would walk in, take a look at the mess – starcharts in hardcopy pasted to every wall, ship diagrams, and food – and explain that they'd reserved the meeting room months before. These people were gently ushered out, never to be seen again.

Rester's expression resembled one of these interlopers. This was surprising in itself, as she'd come to expect nothing but a can-do, quick-answers-to-hard-questions attitude from the Uploader technician. And yet here he was, looking like a teenager screwing up his courage to ask a girl on a date.

She knew there was only one possible explanation. I could really do without more bad news today, but what the hell. Better to get it over with quickly. "All right, spill it. What's happened now? No, let me guess: our support crew decided to mutiny and stole the spaceship. Or, even better, our engines are about to go critical and destroy the planet and you've come to say goodbye."

"Er... None of that actually." He seemed even more flustered than before. Kan decided to let off the pressure.

"Well, that's good news, anyway. So tell me what's on your mind."

"Actually, it's a bit of a personal matter."

Great, she thought wryly, keeping her expression from showing it, *here we go again. Colonel Jackson would laugh at me so hard. I can hear him now, saying 'I told you so.' No wonder he used to roll his eyes every time I wanted to speak to him off the record.*

"OK, have a seat then."

"Thanks." Rester hunted around for any chair devoid of paraphernalia but, unable to find any, eventually placed the contents of the nearest on the table before sitting. He glanced her way before speaking, grave misgivings about what he was about to say clearly visible in his gaze. "I was wondering whether I might be allowed to come along."

"Come along?" She was nearly certain what he was referring to, but wanted to be very, very sure. A misunderstanding might lead to an intergalactic incident of the kind never before seen in human history.

"With the *Eagle.* I'd like to be part of the colony."

"Part of... Are you sure?"

"Absolutely." He didn't look absolutely sure.

"But why? I mean, you have everything a human could want."

"Except actually being human."

Kan thought it was probably too late for that already. After all, even if his experiences, personality, and memories really were human, and not just a complicated program, she couldn't truly think of a creature thousands of years old with some kind of metallic semiconductor in place of a brain as actually human, no matter how beautiful the body that encased it was. "I can imagine you'd want that, all that getting old and dying. Who wouldn't yearn for it?"

"Someone who's lived more than ten objective human lives, and who, thanks to the magic of clock speed, has actually experienced hundreds of times that. At some points, I was actually two or more copies, which then got fused back together to form me once again. Can't you understand why I might want to get back to something approaching normal?"

"I can't understand why you'd ever have chosen to leave normality in the first place," Kan replied. It was the instinctive thing to say, the result of indoctrination of Crystallian children since the day they were old enough to understand even the simplest sentences. "I'm sorry, I didn't mean that. You must think I'm terribly provincial."

To her relief, Rester smiled – a sad smile, it was true, but one that held no bitterness. "Not provincial, necessarily, but definitely not as well-versed in history as you might be. Uploader society wasn't always as enlightened as it is now. Not every uploading was voluntary."

Kan's mouth became an O of horror. "I'm sorry, I didn't know. I mean I did know about the involuntary uploadings, I just didn't know they'd done it to you; it's just that sometimes I prefer not to think about these things. You must have suffered terribly."

He shrugged. "Not really. At first, I was furious, swearing to destroy them from the inside, then I was terrified – they came at me with this machine that looked like something from a medieval torture chamber, but with wires. I must have blacked out. By the time I awoke, I was uploaded."

"And did you go after them, like you promised?" Kan knew it was a private affair, and probably a traumatic experience, most likely something that Rester truly didn't want to discuss, least of all with her.

Rester laughed. "There wasn't much chance of that. The early Uploaders might have been inflexible, but they weren't stupid. They kept a very close eye on the new acquisitions, and could actually immobilize us if we tried anything unusual."

"Immobilize?"

"Remember that the Uploaders exist inside a huge computer – any individual can be immobilized by the simple method of removing the processing power necessary for their personality to run." Rester chuckled. "It wasn't really necessary, anyway. Every new Uploader needs a few subjective months to get their bearings and learn how to use the almost infinite flexibility of your new world. Beings of pure information might be unlimited, but learning to leave the shackles behind isn't automatic."

"And afterwards? Why didn't you attack them afterwards?"

"Afterwards, you aren't new anymore." He looked straight into her eyes. "I know you've been brought up to believe that any computer world is anathema. Maybe you're right. But it's also a very seductive way of life. Being completely free of physical barriers is just about as fantastic as it sounds. I experienced things that I never imagined before, and every single one of them was hardwired to my brain. I could fly, I could see in ten dimensions, and watch rainbows made of colors you never could imagine. I could hold an interesting conversation for days because I didn't need to sleep. But if I wanted to sleep, the dreams would be multicolor insanity, and I would have perfect recall of them the next day. And the sex." The Uploader paused to reminisce. "They warned me not to go full-experience the first time, but I didn't listen. It almost drove me mad."

Kan was about to interrupt, to tell him that none of it was real, but she held her peace.

Rester went on. "And then, as you said, there was the intellectual side of things. No disease, no death. All the questions I'd ever had about the future would be answered, and all I had to do was wait and enjoy the interim. I wasn't even mad at them anymore."

"Being killed and uploaded onto some machine? I'd have managed to stay mad."

"No, you wouldn't. And besides, by that time, I understood why they'd done it. They weren't evil, they truly believed that people would be happier as Uploaders than as physical beings – and time seems to have proven them right. I've heard of only a handful of cases, among the countless billions, that were unable to function there."

"Maybe you were programmed to believe you were happy."

A look of absolute horror crossed Rester's face and Kan realized that she must have crossed some line, hit a specific Uploader taboo.

"That's not the way it works." Short, crisp, unemotional. "For various technical reasons, it could never be that way."

"All right. I'm sorry. But you still haven't answered my question: if it's so great that even the unwilling victims end up in blissful acceptance, why would you want to give it up?"

He relaxed a little. "Even immortality gets old after a while. Growing old might not be so bad."

Kan smiled, accepting his explanation, but unable to resist taking one last final jab. "I see now. You just can't get enough of me, can you?"

He grinned almost immediately and played along. "Yeah, you got me."

But for a fraction of an instant, just before he realized she was joking, a sudden flash of alarm crossed his features. Almost imperceptible, but obvious to Kan sitting a couple of feet away.

"You can come, if it's all right with your government," she replied. But, at the same time, she was thinking *uh-oh*.

CHAPTER 19

Jackson could only imagine what the reaction in the tunnels was like, but if the tension was any worse than what they were experiencing in the military sector, he'd soon be called on to quell the riots. White-knuckled functionaries brought status reports to the assembled brass while others simply tried to stand unobtrusively in the background, hoping that no one would realize they were there and ask them to leave. The acrid smell of sweat filled the close-packed room.

But there was really nowhere else one could be at that moment. Huge 2-D screens showed the slow advance of the Uploader fortification ships as they approached Octo. The enormous gas giant made up most of one image, while the tiny ships beside it approached.

The images were being transmitted live to the entire Crystallia colony, both military and civilian sectors, with a running commentary explaining what was going on, but nowhere was the information as complete as in that one room. Alternate images, telemetry information, a high-speed simulation that showed what was likely to happen within the next two hours according to the latest data, and the ever-present aides bringing the results of ongoing analysis into the war room.

He just hoped there was no war.

Rima Centauri Han stood next to him, her normally pale face completely white, while the admiral gave orders constantly – despite having absolutely no influence or even a true understanding of anything that was going on.

One person that Jackson suspected knew exactly what was about to happen was Mika Bina. The Uploader ambassador was here without her accustomed sidekick, but that was nothing new. She'd explained that Appins had decided to return to a corporeal experience and join the *Eagle* expedition now that his technical knowledge was no longer necessary. Jackson wasn't certain whether he should rejoice or be worried about the fact that there were hundreds of mainframes on the outskirts of the Crystallia system that held the sum of scientific knowledge as possessed by the Uploaders.

Rima caught his eye. "Moment of truth, time, huh?"

"It certainly is. How do you think this is going to be taken by the civilians?"

"I think they'll wait and see. But no matter what happens within the next couple of hours, one thing that will be true at the end of it is that there's a big, bad Uploader fleet less than a light-hour from their home. That isn't something they'll just forget about."

Jackson grunted. "You're probably right. But at least the more logical-minded will be able to see that the Uploaders could have run right over our defenses, had they wanted to." Of that, Jackson had no doubts. He knew that what was coming would be very, very impressive.

"The logical-minded among them have never been the problem," Rima said. Jackson couldn't quite shake the feeling that the councilor didn't quite approve of the way the information had been distributed, even though she'd been involved in it from the start. As always, she had pushed for a higher-profile news solution, as well as more civilian involvement in the actual solution of the crisis. The military, as always, had attempted to minimize the risk of causing unnecessary panic among the unprepared population.

It seemed that, as usual, the woman beside him had been absolutely correct.

There was no time to think about it right then, though. The Uploader ship had been active, deploying a net of machines near the surface of Octo, the gas giant that occupied, as its name implied, the eight orbital position around Crystallia's primary.

From the briefing, the colonel knew that the machines were similar in concept to the nanofactory that Appins and Bina had used to build their bodies and the machines they'd demonstrated, but on a much larger scale. They would now begin to use material from the planet to create enormous defensive mechanisms, hopefully powerful enough to hold off the Oneness' fleet.

The clock which had been ticking off the minutes – he assumed this was more for theatrical purposes than because the Uploader construction fleet actually needed the clock – was ticking off the last few seconds. As it reached zero, everyone in the room took a deep breath, involuntarily bracing for something spectacular, but nothing was immediately apparent. Jackson wondered whether something had gone wrong with the mechanism.

Soon, however, small protuberances became visible on the blue-purple surface of the planet. These tiny outcroppings soon expanded, making it look as though the planet was going through a bad bout of acne. Jackson watched the widest-angle image he could find, straining to see how the pimples became domes, and the domes covered the machines.

"What you're seeing now is the most spectacular part of the process," Mika Bina said. "The machines are using focused gravitational attractors to pull the gas on the surface towards them. The protuberances might not look like much against the scale of the planet's surface, but they are actually thousands of kilometers high at the point where they make contact with the machine's intake nacelles."

This speech was mainly for the benefit of the civilian dignitaries present. Jackson had been briefed on the process more times than he could count, as Mika and Appins attempted to get the military's approval. They'd asked every question they could think of and assessed the risks from every possible angle, so they were extremely familiar with the technical side of things. What Jackson hadn't imagined was that it would be so beautiful.

"Of course, the enormous scale is necessary because the planet's surface is extremely diffuse – it only looks solid because we're extremely far from it. The pressure in the upper reaches is actually very low."

Her speech had descended to the level which any civilian on Crystallia would have found a little patronizing, and yet all Jackson saw were bobbing heads as people watched the gas being pulled towards the machines. The domes had sprouted tiny-looking tendrils – actually hundreds of kilometers long, Jackson knew – that ended at each machine.

"The defense mechanisms will be produced of carbon composites, as carbon is the most plentiful building material present on the surface of the gas planet. If this were a metallic asteroid, the machines would produce steel structures, and if it were, for example, a nitrogen-based world, a solution involving solid nitrogen polymers might be used, or, in extreme cases, the nuclear structure of the atoms would be modified to create other elements. We try to avoid using this last method because it takes nearly six times longer to produce components that way."

The tendrils grew thicker as more and more of the gas was sucked into the nanomachine's insatiable maw. Jackson wondered whether he would even see the product that the machines created. Did a black hole generator have to be huge in order to create a huge anomaly? Or would the deadly defensive weapons be invisible when viewed from such a distance?

The answer came almost immediately. A tiny flicker of light ignited near one of the machines, and Mika immediately resumed her narration.

"What you saw there was the first newly-produced weapon moving away from the factory floor. The light was from the ignition of a rocket engine." She looked over her audience, drinking in the looks of surprise. "Why a rocket, you ask? Isn't that incredibly primitive compared to the physics being manipulated by the factories? Frankly, yes. But there are three major reasons that rockets are highly efficient in this case. The first reason is that the reactives necessary to fuel a chemical rocket are already present in the gas we're sucking from the planet, so it's more efficient just to bottle them up in separate canisters and mix them for the burn than it would be to create intricate nuclear reactors out of carbon fibers.

"The second reason has to do with the fact that the rockets are only used to maneuver them away from the nanofactories, an operation in which high speed is not critical. Once they are about a hundred thousand kilometers from the nearest factory, our construction ships can use gravity waves to accelerate them to their final positions.

"This brings us neatly to the final reason. We've found that it's a very bad idea to allow separate focused gravity fields to interact with each other. When they do so, the resulting superfield is nearly impossible to predict, both in size and in power. Perhaps it will do nothing more than pull the ship and the factory together. On the other hand, it might push the planet apart completely. So we only allow the factory ships to pull the weaponry into place after it reaches a safe distance from the factories."

Jackson watched in awe. Beyond the beauty, forces he couldn't see, couldn't imagine, were bending the very fabric of the universe, adding a strangely evil touch to the sight of the blue planet having its very essence torn away from it. Was the planet getting smaller as it was digested for its material? It was, of course, but not in such a way that it could possibly be perceptible.

He could have remained there all day, just watching the hypnotic image of the planet being torn away, piece by piece, bit by bit. But Mika was gesturing for him to come closer. She led him out of the nerve center and into one of the corridors – deserted because everyone whose duties didn't prevent it was watching the transmission. The others, enthralled, ignored them as they left.

"I've just received a transmission from one of the factory ships. They've detected a deep space incursion moving through the constriction."

The term 'constriction' referred to the single safe passage between massive black holes and unsafe gravity anomalies that led into the pocket of space in which the Crystallia system and its five sister colonies were located. "The Oneness?"

"We can't tell from this distance, but it seems like a safe bet. It certainly isn't one of ours."

"What can we do about it?"

She stopped to think. "The Oneness uses small, hyper-maneuverable craft for scout duty. We generally shoot at them with particle beams until we manage to hit them. They aren't dangerous enough to merit truly going after them with heavy artillery because they aren't armed all that well, and even their armor is second rate. On the other hand, their scanning equipment is good enough that they already know the location of every ship in this system that isn't currently buried in your storage hangars under the planet. The only reason it needs to come closer is to listen in on your short-distance communications."

"Let's blow it up, then!"

"Oh, definitely. But maybe we can use it to our advantage, first." Mika smiled at him. "I'm online with Rester, and he has an idea which I think might just work."

Suddenly, the cast of her features changed slightly. Physically, her face was exactly the same, but the muscles tightened in different places and the eyes seemed to gaze out at the world with slightly less intensity. "Hello," Mika's mouth said in a strange voice that had almost, but not quite, her soft tones. "I'm Rester, and Mika has allowed me to network into the body interface so I can talk to you."

Jackson tried to control his features, but the shock he was feeling must have registered, because Mika / Rester went on.

"She's in no pain, and she can hear us perfectly well. Please try to remember that, as long as I don't impinge on her dedicated memory structures, she is perfectly content. This is the way we live, Colonel; we've managed for thousands of your years – sharing a biological body for a few minutes isn't going to hurt her in any way."

"I'm sorry. You surprised me, that's all. I understand what you're doing, and I have no problem with it. I suppose it's much faster than finding a comm. unit."

"True, and I'm also on the moon right now, so we'd have to deal with a moment's delay, never good in communication."

"Shouldn't we have that anyway?"

"We took that into account, and there are sections in Mika's processor that were quantum-entangled to analogous sections in my own. Information sent into those sections in the way of small variations of electron spin are immediately picked up over here."

"All right." Jackson kept perfectly still, knowing full well that his entire body wanted nothing more than to shudder uncontrollably and perhaps find a place where he could throw up.

"I analyzed the trajectory of the incoming scouts and I see how we can put up a good façade of being serious in our intent to kill them, while, at the same time, using them to feed false information to the Oneness. But I need your approval for it."

"Why?" Jackson asked, hoping he didn't sound too suspicious. He was well aware that they would only be asking his approval if there were risks to the Crystallia colony involved, significant risks that could be traced back to them. He had no illusions that, while the Uploaders cared about the survival of the colony, it was secondary to the survival of their own civilization – and even less about the true control he, or anyone else on the human side, had over their actions.

"It involves the Watcher."

"So, you've been able to come to an understanding with it?" Jackson had been briefed about the interactions between the Watcher, the Uploader scientist, and Crystallia's own people, but he hadn't had the time to pay too much attention to the reports.

"Up to a certain point. It insists that it will do anything you ask if you allow it to leave the system before the Oneness fleet arrives."

"The only thing scheduled to leave the system is the *Eagle*. I can almost imagine what Kan would say if I told her that we were planning to put one of the Oneness' machines aboard. You'd be able to hear her screams all the way to Hammersmith."

Mika's face contorted for a second, and the Uploader paused. "Yes, I suppose she might. But there would be no risk involved. We've scanned the captured unit on a molecular level, and there seems to be no transmission capability built into it. It can't communicate because its comm facilities were uprooted back when Kan picked it up."

Jackson made a mental note to talk to Major Tau Osella about the advisability of telling Uploaders where she was at all times. "And entanglement?"

Another pause. "One can never be one hundred percent certain, of course, but there don't seem to be any of the usual methods of transmitting data into entangled matter installed in this unit."

Jackson thought about it. "And how can we use it to transmit the data back to the scouts?"

"That's actually pretty simple. We can set up a tight-beam laser comm here, have our guest override the security protocols of the antenna back at its original base and send them whatever we want to say. I'm thinking that information about a large formation of anomaly weapons cached in one of the planetoids that occupy the seventh orbit will make them divert resources there."

"But why? Why would they go to the trouble of attacking any weapons emplacements? Wouldn't it be much easier to fly in perpendicular to the ecliptic and attack Crystallia from above?"

"Actually, no. Some of these weapons have pretty long ranges, so coming in from above just opens you up to attack from the weapons on every single orbit at once. Unsurvivable. But if you attack on the ecliptic, from the outside in, you can always position yourself and time the entrance so that there's at least one planet or large object between the fleet and most of the weapons further in the system. That way, you only have to deal with a limited number of attack positions. And once you clear out the outer orbit, you can forget about it and move further in."

"Which makes giving them false coordinates in the asteroid belt a double benefit."

"Precisely. Not only will they divert part of their resources to needless attack against the belt, they'll also modify their approach vector to take it into account, perhaps leaving them open to an attack from another angle."

"And all the thing wants in exchange is to leave on the *Eagle*? He doesn't seem to have much faith in our chances of winning this fight."

"None at all. And it's also terrified of the Oneness. But yes, that's all it's asking for."

"Then I guess Kan will just have to put up with it. Please make it happen."

Rester nodded Mika's head and disconnected, making the Uploader girl somehow prettier and less masculine despite not changing in any way. "We'd better get back in there in case there are any questions," she said, all business and seemingly unaffected by her recent game of musical bodies.

***

Wilde had no intention of doing so, but he walked right into Jev's mysterious friends. It was immediately apparent by their furtive postures that the two individuals, one male, one female were involved in some activity they shouldn't have been.

He recognized them vaguely as part of a maintenance team in training, individuals who, despite not being part of the command crew, would be placed in special cryo chambers and could be woken in transit if necessary. The woman was tall, blonde, and thin, with pale skin which marked her as having at least some Luyten colony blood, while the man was shorter and swarthy, with thick black hair. They looked up guiltily as he approached.

Wilde held his hands up, "I'm on your side," he said, trying to keep them from bolting before he could explain.

The man stepped forward, his attitude extremely menacing. "Explain yourself."

Wilde hesitated. "I work with Jev... I mean with Peace Crystallia. They told me to help you any way I can, but only if you approached me."

"Why were you coming this way? And who are you?"

The corridor they were in was well inside the *Eagle*, at the rear near the starboard hull. Unlike areas of the ship nearer the command center, this section contained nothing but sleep cells and maintenance corridors.

"I'm part of the training crew. I give the fire suppression course," Wilde replied, trying to keep his voice level, authoritative. Maybe these two people didn't know that he'd had only a couple of days training before being proclaimed the expert – and furthermore, hoped they didn't know enough to be aware that most fire suppression was done automatically. "I'm attempting to memorize every corner of the ship in case I need to make decisions from the control center in an emergency." That much, at least, was true. "I'm Wilde Tau Bennet, by the way." He held out his hand.

The other man took a step back and looked at the hand as if it might be holding an invisible plasma cannon. Finally, he stepped forward. "I am Enri," he said. Then he gestured to where the blond woman had resumed work on one of the sleep cells. "That is Krista. The best you can do for us right now is just to leave us be. We have everything we need right now. But now that we know you're with us, we will be certain to let you know if we need anything else." The accent was strange, with unusual spaces between the words. If pressed, Wilde would have guessed that it sounded more like one of the Tri-dramas from the Tonswell colony than anything spoken on Crystallia.

The man obviously wanted Wilde to leave, so he kept walking up the same corridor he'd been on before, as if he was simply going about his business. He thought he knew what they were doing: sabotaging the sleep cells. The *Eagle* wasn't a generation ship. Its voyage was meant to last months, not centuries, but it was still critical that the colonists be in suspended animation during that time. The ship wasn't designed to carry food supplies for fifty thousand people to consume on a huge voyage. The supplies it did have were aimed at constructing yeast vats and a self-sustaining recycling system on the surface of whatever planet they decided to colonize – meaning that a large supply of certain elements needed to be present in the target system.

Likewise, almost no energy would have to be expended in recycling air for the dormant colonists.

So sabotaging a few thousand sleep cells made perfect sense if one wanted to force the *Eagle* to turn back mid-mission. It would make the mission unfeasible without actually doing any permanent harm to the crew and passengers, provided they turned around quickly enough.

Still, something didn't ring quite right about it. Why would Peace Crystallia want to sabotage this mission? It looked like a perfectly peaceful endeavor, and it was dominated, at least numerically, by civilians. It didn't make sense.

Or maybe there was simply something about the man's accent that didn't quite ring true.

Either way, Wilde made a mental note to return to the spot and have a look at their handiwork.

***

Krista looked at him critically. "You're just going to let him go?" she whispered.

The interloper had long since moved out of earshot, but she could feel her heart thumping in the dark, suddenly stuffy corridor.

Enri shrugged. "There was nothing else I could do. If we'd attacked him, someone would have been certain to miss him and come looking. On the other hand, if he is who he says he is, and actually aligned with this Peace Crystallia faction, he can be an asset. There was nothing to gain in attacking him, even if he's an enemy, and much to gain in trusting him."

Enri's logic was impeccable, and the only real surprise was that he'd managed to keep his mercurial temperament under control long enough to think things through all the way. He'd shown her just how wild he could be when they had kidnapped the woman who'd unwillingly given Krista her identity. He'd beaten her senseless before kicking her to death on the floor. He later explained that neither retinas nor fingerprint information had to come from a living person, and a dead body would be easier to drag along the corridors than one which was kicking and screaming.

But the image that truly made her shudder was the memory of when they'd ambushed the man that had donated Enri's current retinal pattern. The guy had resisted with vigor when they'd first tried to subdue him, and that had angered her companion. He made her drag the man into a deep, secluded tunnel where he'd taken a long, long time to die. It had become obvious that things like teeth and tongues and genitals were also unnecessary when the time came to remove retinas – and broken fingers didn't measurably affect the fingerprints.

They'd still had to carry all the bits back to the base camp for adequate disposal, of course, and Krista shuddered to think of the blood-filled bags squishing in her arms as she held her part.

"If you say so," she replied, and kept working on the antimatter bomb. The tiny artifact needed to be placed precisely, and would easily destroy the whole ship when it was activated.

All she wanted was to finish placing it so she could get back to the main tunnels. For some reason, being alone with a psychopath in a secluded maintenance corridor on an empty colony ship made her even more nervous than the prospect of being discovered by the Crystallian military.

She shuddered again, nearly annihilating them all.

CHAPTER 20

Kan fidgeted, but she knew there was nothing to do about Jackson's mood. Any time the colonel became contemplative, he would talk until it suited him to stop. And there was always a point to his meandering speeches, even if that point was not immediately apparent.

"Back on Earth, before the Galactic Diaspora, there was a huge war," Jackson told her. "Or at least it was considered huge at the time, despite the fact that it was mainly focused on only three of Earth's continents: Europe, Asia, and parts of Africa."

He looked off into the distance, organizing his thoughts. "They called it the Second World War, because just a few years earlier, they'd fought another war, even smaller, which they considered the First World War. This was back in the days when many countries were just beginning to have ties with all the other countries on the planet."

"Countries?" Kan asked. The colonel often forgot that not everyone was a fanatical scholar of ancient history, even among his officers.

"A country was a political unit used on pre-globalized Earth. The original intent, as far as historians have been able to tell, was to unify the geographical area shared by nations." He held up his hand, anticipating the next question. "Nations were groups back on ancient Earth that shared a common language, ethnicity, and religious beliefs. Their purity was erased as travel became easier, and bloodlines intermixed."

"But we still have separate races today. Look at the Luytens – from what I hear, they are nearly pure stock – I doubt their extremely white genes would survive much mixture. And you must come from relatively uncontaminated stock yourself, since you're much darker than human norm."

The colonel smiled sadly. "The road to true globalization wasn't an easy one. Even during the first stages of galactic colonization, some of the old racial thinking survived – in order to be accepted for the Luyten colony, one had to show at least three quarters pure European blood." He shook his head. "But that came much later. In the Second World War, the real motivations were political: power, land and revenge, and Europe was torn to pieces for more than six years.

"However, the war didn't begin immediately. The major conflict of the war was expected to occur between two nation-states, Germany and France."

"I've heard of them."

The colonel nodded. "Most people have – they were considered races in their own right. Anyhow, the French had built a huge fortified line, and waited for the imminent attack, sitting happily behind the border, convinced that the fortifications would blunt any attempt to invade their territory. The first of the world wars was a trench war, fought mainly by men on foot from holes in the ground. This line would have given them a huge advantage in that kind of conflict."

Kan nodded. She'd studied trench warfare, and could agree with the thinking. The main problem seemed to be that it was difficult to predict where the battlefield would be, but a pre-fortified line spanning the border would solve that problem if you were determined to fight a defensive war.

"The French sat there and waited, while the Germans, with no fortified lines, did the same. They called that period *"la drole de guerre,"* which means "the mockery of war." Every major power was technically at war with every other major power, and yet not one shot was fired. The French people and the press could only wait nervously while the Germans went about their business."

"That kind of reminds me of what's happening here, now."

Her superior officer smiled. "It does, doesn't it?" He paused. "And that's why I'm convinced that your project of colonizing a new system is so important. It seems like the only part of this whole fiasco that doesn't smell like history repeating itself over and over again. Why did you decide to do it?"

Kan hesitated. The truth wasn't the kind of thing one blithely blurted out to one's superior officer. But the colonel had been her staunchest supporter all through her career. She owed him a certain honesty, even if he wouldn't like what she told him. "It's this war," she admitted. "I just can't understand why the Uploaders would even need to fight for territory. After all, don't they live inside computers? Every last one of them could live on a single planet, each faction side by side with all the rest, and they'd never even know the rest were there. And yet, they've been fighting what's essentially a land and resources war for huge chunks of their subjective time. The only ones who really stand to lose are the corporeal humans – we don't have backup copies of ourselves stashed in a safety computer in some hidden corner of the galaxy."

"Wow, you surprise me every single day." Jackson didn't look like the explanation had bothered him in the least. Quite the opposite, in fact. "It takes a very special kind of person to ask that question. You see, human brains and thinking patterns are ancient. Our simian ancestors only survived because they could take a territory and hold it against whatever tried to invade it. This remained the norm long after it was necessary for the survival of the species, which is why different groups of humans have always been at war with one another – we try to hide behind political or religious or even economic justifications, but the truth is that it's an old imperative that's part of our genetic ancestry. Well, as far as I can tell, that imperative didn't disappear when some of us were uploaded into electronic existences."

He smiled before going on. "Of course, that's not what the Uploaders say."

"You asked them about it?"

"Of course. It's my job to try to understand the enemy."

"And what did they say?"

"Actually, I asked Miss Bina. I thought Appins would come up with some insanely complicated technical explanation. Bina simply made a couple of points which I thought were valid, but only if you ignore what we just discussed. In her opinion, the reason there's a war is that the Oneness is determined to absorb every sentient intelligence that it can get its hands on in order to add them to its own consciousness. It doesn't care whether it has to force them to accept, either."

"That's a nice little irony right there, isn't it?"

The colonel gave her a mock-stern look. "The Uploaders have reformed, you shouldn't judge them for their past deeds. They say so themselves."

"Ha, ha."

"Anyhow, the Uploaders say they're still fighting a territorial war because the best way to keep the big bad processing power of the Oneness from sucking you in and tearing your personality into a million tiny pieces is to keep it at a distance. Logical enough, I guess. And the reason they fight star-by-star is the same reason humanity has always attacked far-off outposts that seem to be irrelevant: they're afraid of an unexpected sally. They're just making certain that they don't leave any enemy forces behind them."

"Couldn't the Uploaders just appease the Oneness by feeding it endless copies of themselves?"

"Don't even mention that to them. They consider the copies to be fully human, with all the rights and responsibilities of the original. Sending copies to be consumed by the Oneness would be anathema to them." The colonel stood. "Anyhow, I just wanted to tell you again that I truly admire what you're doing, and I think it might just be real humanity's best hope to survive what's coming."

Kan wanted to ask him to come with them, but she'd already done that many times and been rebuffed on each occasion. The colonel was adamant that his duty was to defend the colony to his last breath, and that the best end for an old warrior was to die in battle. As he turned to go, however, she felt a huge sense of loss, knowing that this was probably the last time that Jackson would corner her and tell her a story of ancient military times. She suddenly wanted the conversation to last a little longer. "Wait a minute! You never told me what happened to the French and their fortifications."

His look was a sad one. "When the Germans finally decided to attack, they drove around it in their tanks, and it seemed like the invasion of France was accomplished in minutes. The French surrendered, and it took the combined military strength of most of the democratic world, as well as the Soviets, to get the Germans out of there." He shook his head sadly. "I don't think anyone will come to our rescue, though."

He turned to go. But he also seemed reluctant for the moment to end. "I'll be at the launch, of course."

"Yes, I know."

Colonel Jackson walked back to his duties.

***

A single copy of Mika Bina watched the sensors. A part of her was happy to be back in her natural habitat, roaming the endless possibilities of a mainframe's simulated world. But another, equally important part missed the unexpected, illogical twists and turns that the glands on her previous self's body had created in her thinking and emotional parameters. Emotions inside a mainframe were carefully calculated to respond to certain stimuli – you could play around with them endlessly, but few people chose truly random intervention. And glands weren't truly random, anyway. One felt that there was method to their madness, even if it was impossible to say what it was.

Anyhow, combat on the front lines was simply not the place to have unpredictable emotions. She'd pushed her clock speed way up and upped the emotional dampers to keep anything but logic from gumming up her processing times. She'd volunteered to defend the Shiva Beta system, and knew they had to slow down the Oneness' advance as much as possible. They'd thought up a new tactic to manage this, and that's why the call had gone out for volunteers. It was likely that many of the defenders would come to the worst possible end.

It was in anticipation of this that the copies sent here had been cleansed of all important strategic memories. They knew who they were, where they came from, and how to defend a system most effectively, but knew nothing about the plans for things that would come afterwards.

Mika hoped that this was an unnecessary precaution. But she also knew that, in order to keep the Oneness' forces occupied the longest amount of time possible, they had to make it look good. The experimental gravity field interdictor – developed with the help of the corporeal humans on Crystallia – they'd deployed around the four central orbital paths had succeeded beautifully, and the Oneness' advance had come to a grinding halt for more than an objective week as they tried to figure out what to do about it. Eventually, as every simulation had predicted, the Oneness decided that it could punch through by sheer brute force.

This had been a long, drawn-out process which allowed the defenders to snipe at will from concealed positions behind the interdictor. The Oneness had spent precious days hammering it, even having to call in extra forces, before the interdictor was finally overloaded, and allowed the enemy to come through.

Even then, though, the defenders had put up a ferocious fight, keeping the enemy from advancing quickly and selling each planet at an enormous cost in material. They had been instructed to stay alive and functional as long as possible, knowing that the Oneness was loathe to destroy sentients that it might absorb. It was the one weakness that could be exploited: all one had to do was stand one's ground and stay alive, and the Oneness would avoid any devastating strikes. It had been known to pick off the fortifications of an entire planetary defense array one by one in order to preserve the mainframe holding a single uploaded personality.

But all that was past. The overwhelming strength that the Oneness had brought to bear upon the planet had made its way to the major rocky world of the system, a cold place with no name, but suitable for running high-speed computers. The mainframes on the surface had been designed specifically to act as a lure – the Oneness would never pass up the opportunity to absorb hundreds of thousands of people, and had eschewed planet-busters in favor of an actual invasion.

The orbital defense arrays had not lasted very long, but the ground defenses were another matter entirely. The copy of Mika had watched with enormous satisfaction as the spider-landers and upload shuttles had been caught by surprise by the planet's ground defenses. The losses would make no difference in the final outcome of the battle, of course, but the time the Oneness would lose in replacing them might turn the tide of the war. And it would have to rethink its tactics in order to take land incursions into account now that it knew that the battle would not be fought exclusively with exotic orbital weaponry.

Nevertheless, the numbers were just too many, and the inevitable slowly took shape. Most of the other mainframes on the planet had already been taken, and it was only a matter of moments before the one she was lodged in suffered the same fate. Even as the thought formed, the Oneness' ground troops, quadruped machines loaded with beam weapons and the technology to upload any sentience at will, were entering the tunnel which led to the physical mainframe.

A quantum caress called her attention to another of the volunteers. "Mika, we've reached the point of single-entity control," the man told her. That meant that it was no longer necessary to have a full complement of troops manning the mainframe's defenses, as the battle was now a simple question of firing fixed cannons in the hallways. Only one person would have to stay conscious to troubleshoot, and the rest could delete themselves, secure in the knowledge that they were only copies and that oblivion was much preferable to capture by the Oneness. "We're preparing the randomizer to select which one of us has to stay behind."

"Don't bother," Mika said. "I'll do it."

"But there's a significant risk of being captured. We can't ask you to take it for us. The raffle is the only way to ensure a fair chance for everyone."

"I don't want a fair chance. I said I'll do it and I mean it. Now go get yourselves erased before these guys reach us."

"All right. Thank you for this." The volunteer's presence vanished, and then she felt the quantum flux of a mass erasure. Thirty sentients snuffed out without much of a trace, and whose heroism would not be remembered by anyone except perhaps the Oneness, who didn't concern itself with individual actions.

Mika grimaced inwardly as she watched the enemy advance. The corridors had been built deep and tortuous precisely to gain time. Every second gained was a second more that the Crystallian-Uploader alliance had to prepare for the final push.

She was trapped deep underground with an implacable enemy heading her way, and yet she felt no fear – *thank you, dampers!* – but she did allow herself to feel a small sense of intellectual satisfaction. From a military standpoint, this might have been a complete victory for the Oneness, but it had lost weeks of time it couldn't afford. And Mika thought she could hold them off for a few minutes more, before the time came to erase herself. A small knot of walkers approached a sealed blast door, and she ordered it to explode outwards.

But as she watched the walkers disappear into shards, the picture also went. The blast door must have torn out the power generation for that corridor. She tried to shunt into reserve power, but an error message informed her that the backup cells were not online – probably destroyed. She frantically tried to get the visuals back anyway, but a flicker on another channel told her that the enemy was in a deeper sector. She ordered the weaponry on that level to open fire, but nothing happened. The main generator must have been compromised.

She tried once more, and that was her mistake. She felt her mind slow to a crawl as the enemy's capture fields overcame the optic and electronic arrays that made up her mainframe. She could barely think at all, much less react to the attack she was under.

Sensation came back as she felt the unmistakable removal of her constituent programming into an uncomfortable pseudo-world – probably a containment crystal – and then the unmistakable feeling of being transmitted through space.

The world she arrived at was huge, composed of quadrillions of data points that she could observe from where she was. Her human-based design didn't allow her to use enough processing power to be able to absorb that much information and she soon became disoriented. Was she inside the Oneness itself?

Something flittered by, and she felt a piece of her mind go with it. Then another something came and took another portion of her awareness. Each, in itself, was inconsequential, but as the strikes multiplied, Mika felt more and more of her mind slip away, becoming sluggish, then irrational, then emotionless.

The final piece of logic she was able to muster, as her code and memories were stripped from her to strengthen the Oneness, was that their enemy had paid a huge price to obtain a few individual personalities.

And then she thought nothing, as another swipe took her consciousness.

***

Kan watched as her quarry disappeared around a corner. She was sure she knew where he was going, and decided to head him off. She had a decided advantage: while he had to be careful to take a roundabout path to avoid detection, she could take the straight path and lie in wait. No one was following her – and if they were, her newly assigned security team would give them a nasty shock.

Part of her – most of her, actually – hoped she was wrong, hoped that the whole thing was just some easily explained mix-up. But she'd learned not to put too much faith in wishful thinking.

Moments later, she was securely concealed behind a bank of sleep cells invisible to anyone who didn't know she was there.

Her heart sank as she saw what she'd feared: her target went straight to the place where the device had been installed and began to look around. He seemed surprised to find nothing there, and rechecked the illuminated sign on the entrance to the chamber to make certain he was in the right place.

Kan signaled her team to converge on that spot.

"Disappointed?" she asked him emerging from her place of concealment with her service weapon drawn. "Because I sure as hell am."

Wilde jumped, but he didn't try to run. Kan's heart came back down, out of her throat. She'd been willing to shoot him if he ran, but now she realized that it was also the outcome she'd feared most.

He hung his head. "I'm sorry. I guess there's no point in telling you that I had nothing to do with it?"

She held the weapon on him as she approached, hoping it was steady, hoping he wouldn't realize that she'd never fired a beam weapon at anything other than low power on the training range. She hoped that she hadn't ever whispered to him in bed that she was the worst shot in Recon – or if she had, that he would have forgotten it by now. "Why would you take part in something like that, Wilde? I know we never saw eye to eye on the way the military was being run, but this? Killing those colonists would have changed nothing, except maybe to make the military take even stronger measures. Hell, most of them are civilians. The new colony isn't going to be a military installation."

He drew himself up to his full height. "You've caught me, but you can dispense with the guilt trip. A little discomfort on the return trip and the fact that they won't have made it to wherever you're going might sting a little, but no one ever died of that before, as far as I know."

"Discomfort? A bomb of that size would have caused a lot more than a little discomfort, Wilde?"

"Bomb? What are you talking about? They said…" He cut off in mid-sentence, realizing he'd just crossed a line which he would never be allowed to uncross.

Kan's team arrived in that moment, and immediately trained their assault weaponry – expertly wielded and completely unshaking, she saw with chagrin – on the hapless Wilde.

"I think we need to continue this conversation somewhere else," she said.

***

There was no doubt that the room was a cell. It was just a couple of meters square, holding no furniture but two solidly mounted seats and an equally bolted-down table. It seemed hermetically sealed, and Wilde had difficulty even finding the seam for the doorway in the white painted walls.

The security team had left him there without ceremony an eternity ago, and no one had come back to check on him in the meantime. He supposed they had cameras for that kind of thing, but he still worried. What if they forgot he was here?

The thought evaporated almost instantly. He suspected that not only would they remember exactly who and where he was, but they would also show a lot more interest in him than he might prefer. He just hoped they did so before he had to go to the bathroom.

The door finally swished open, and Wilde looked up to see Kan's unsmiling features. Quite a few uniformed figures pressed in behind her.

"We're going to need a bigger interrogation room," he said.

"Not just yet. I need to know some things before we decide what we're going to do with you." She gave him a stern glance. "You might be in deep trouble, Wilde."

"I know. But I swear I didn't do anything. I had no idea there was a bomb on the ship – much less planted it myself. Hell, I was going to fly out with it."

"Were you?" Kan looked doubtful, and Wilde had to suppress his own surprise: he hadn't known he had taken that decision until the moment he said it out loud. But it felt right. "I take it you were planning for a short trip."

"What? Why?"

"Didn't you say you thought the saboteurs were going to damage the ship enough to make us turn back?"

She was right. He had half-decided to turn them in and clear the sabotage; it was why he'd gone back for a second look. But he suspected that they wouldn't believe them if he told them so. He tried anyway.

Kan was having none of it. "Do you really expect us to believe that?"

"I guess not, but it's true."

"Well, let me tell you your situation. We've checked your movements for the last few weeks, and you've never been in the affected sector long enough to have set up the bomb. But you were there on the day we suspect they installed it, and paused for a couple of minutes. So our theory is that even if you didn't do it, you know very well who did." She paused, judging his reaction. "That essentially gives you two choices. You can tell us who put the bomb there and why, or you can face charges for treason. Just for your own information, I'd like to tell you that keeping silent won't help them all that much because we're on their trail, but it will definitely put you in the crapper."

Wilde smiled to himself. Even if the military got the bombers, they would only have half of the equation. His silence would guarantee that Peace Crystallia could continue to operate without interference.

The problem was that he was no longer certain that Peace Crystallia deserved that opportunity. While they hadn't been directly involved in the bombing attempt – assuming that one had actually taken place – they were certainly linked to groups that were. He just couldn't see how their anti-military stance would be strengthened by attacking what, in essence, was a civilian colonization effort. He thought about Jev. Yes, he could imagine the cold bastard ordering the bombing to preserve his precious ideals.

Wilde took a deep breath. "I can give you the bombers, but I don't know their names."

"Good. We thought you'd see it our way."

"Not quite. There's a lot more going on here, and I really think you should hear the rest of it before deciding what to do about it."

CHAPTER 21

The black box didn't look like much, but Trienne knew better. Working from one of the designs hardwired into the Uploader's nanofactory, she'd built a standard small-population mainframe. Over the past few days, she'd amassed a clear idea of how its hardware functioned and an even better picture of what the software interactions were like. With the help of a couple of Uploader technicians recently arrived in the system, she'd even managed to create a simulated world inside it of the type cyber-civilizations preferred and peopled it with stunted copies of actual Uploader personalities, complete save for the long-term memory function, which had been removed in order to keep them from gaining a true sense of self.

So that box on the floor of her lab was actually a tiny society populated by simulated personalities who really believed they were living – if not breathing – humans. Which, she reminded herself, they were. There was no test in existence that could tell the minds in her simulation apart from any of the inhabitants of Crystallia. Not on the intellectual side or on the emotional side.

In essence, she was a god. If these people managed to get themselves together enough to write a creation myth, it would be her that they mentioned when they talked about the all-powerful one.

Now, all she had to do was slowly drive them insane, destroy all their interaction and, if possible, eventually kill them – but in a way that would allow the hardware to be reused. Some god.

Colonel Jackson arrived, ten minutes late and out of breath. "Sorry I'm late," he told her. "You wouldn't believe the things that lurk just under the surface here on Crystallia. Are we ready to begin?"

"Of course." Trienne pointed towards the wall on the left, covered with dancing graphics and green bars. "What you can see on that wall is the status board. The graphs show the processing capacity and activity levels of fifty individuals chosen at random from the ones that make up the simulated society.

"The mainframe itself," Trienne pointed at the black box, "has been shielded against EMP strikes and is waterproof and airtight. The shielding is about three centimeters thick, and is standard issue on all Uploader tech, including the tech used by the Oneness."

"Sounds like you'd need something pretty potent to knock it out."

"Yes. And that's exactly the point. The design's objective is to ensure that any strike strong enough to stop it from doing its job would also keep the enemy from being able to capture the sentients still inside or use the mainframe for anything else. You basically have two choices with one of these things: blow it up or leave it alone."

"So how does it communicate with the outside world?"

"Quantum transmitters inside the shell."

"But that means that everyone they want to communicate with has to have entangled matter from this mainframe in their own transmitter."

"I thought so too, at first. But then Rester explained a concept called simulated entanglement. It allows them to communicate with every other piece of the network with no need for actual physical entanglement. It works with a special kind of encryption. They do it by—"

Jackson held up his hands. "All I needed to know was that it works. They can communicate with each other. Please proceed with your demonstration."

"All right. As I told you last time, it's relatively easy to create nanobots that will eat through a mainframe like this one and turn it into dust in minutes. It's a bit harder to shut it down without damaging the inner workings, but that, too has been done. What I was aiming for was something that would impair it, turn each of the personalities inside into a raving moron, and impair their judgment, but to keep it going. If we use it that way, we can hit the Oneness with it and make its fleet very, very sick."

"It's like a virus."

"Exactly, except it affects the hardware on a microscopic level. That's the beauty of it. Any diagnostic program will quickly realize that there is a problem with the information quality, and will attempt to clean up a software attack. It will never understand the true problem – hopefully, the Oneness won't learn what's going on until it's much too late."

"Show me."

"All right. This small canister holds the nanites. They are machines on a molecular level."

"I know what nanites are."

Trienne placed the canister on the floor. It sprouted small legs and scuttled towards the mainframe. Upon reaching it, it climbed to the top and retracted its legs so that the bottom of the canister was in contact with the top of the mainframe. "All right. The point is that these particular nanites have been mixed and matched. There are only a few nanites of the type that can bore through the armor, and they are time-sensitive. They will die out precisely ten minutes after the shell casing opens. That allows them enough time to bore through the shielding – they create a tunnel about two nanites wide – without giving them time to damage the internal workings of the mainframe too badly."

The canister, to all external observers, seemed to be doing nothing. It looked like a two-centimeter-long protrusion on the mainframe's surface. Suddenly, however the, small golden bullet disappeared. "The canister itself is laced with specific nanobots that dissolve it as soon as its interior is breached. Anyone looking for physical evidence will need an electron microscope to see the holes in the shielding." Trienne walked over to the black box and wiped the canister dust off the top. The surface looked smooth, as if it had just been machined.

"The nanites are probably about a third of the way through by now, and most of them are simply packed into the holes behind the digger nanites. Once they get through, each will look for specific circuitry materials or concentrations of energy, the idea being to disrupt both optical and electromagnetic signals in such a way as to drive the computer nuts."

"Wow, those must be really versatile nanites."

"Not versatile at all. Each type is programmed to do one specific thing, but there are over two hundred different types of nanites among the millions in the mix."

"Oh."

Trienne glanced at the timer on the wall display. "All right, the nanites should be through by now. We should start seeing the effects of their activity in less than a minute." They turned their attention to the wall with the huge video display on it. The displays, to this point, seemed unaffected. Trienne pointed at a section of the graph. "This line indicates the frequency of data transmission, while this bar here indicates the percentage of data that is coherent according to random data validation. The length and color indicate the status – it's currently at full length and green, which means that everything is working as it should be."

But that situation didn't last. First, the lines began to vary, jump, and oscillate. Some increased their level sharply, others dropped, some became sine curves, and a few others seemed unaffected. "What you're seeing is the initial action of the nanites, as they begin to disrupt the information flow."

"But shouldn't the activity levels be dropping all across the board?" The colonel seemed puzzled.

"Not necessarily. Think of this as a sickness that causes dementia – a modern-day syphilis, only for computers. It doesn't cut down the level of information transmitted by the system, but it affects the quality. Some of what gets through is pure garbage, other bits are information, but rearranged so that the meaning either changes or becomes indecipherable. The idea is to cause erratic behavior, not kill the minds living inside it."

Suddenly, one of the bars turned yellow, having lost a quarter of its length. It was soon followed by another, and a third. Before long, almost every bar was in the yellow area, with some already in the red. "What we see here is the effect of the garbage getting into our data verification sensors." Suddenly, unexpectedly, the screen went blank, taking lines, bars, and timers with it, and leaving only a command prompt in their place. "Wow," Trienne said. She sat down on a chair, shaking her head.

"What happened?" The colonel seemed nervous that something major had gone wrong, that it had all been a colossal waste of his time.

She hurried to reassure him. "The nanites were better designed than I thought. We'd actually double-shielded the sensors and the transmission sector of that mainframe so that we could run the simulation with a data stream. Evidently, the extra shielding wasn't enough to keep the nanites from taking it down, too."

The colonel thought about it for a minute. "Basically, what you're saying, is that we have no way of controlling these things?"

Trienne shrugged. "You did say you wanted an ultimate weapon – well, this one qualifies."

"But what if they get into our systems?"

"There's no need to worry about that at all. Our technology is completely different from what the Uploaders use. The nanites here would be lost and ineffective. We've actually tested them on some of our equipment before using them elsewhere, just to be sure – they have no more effect than a tiny amount of dust."

"Why did you feel the need to test that?"

"I wanted to make certain we weren't putting the entire colony at risk. You see, one of the characteristics of this type of nanite is that I don't know of any way to get rid of them once they're activated. I'd have to create another set of nanites to dissolve the first set. And I haven't been able to do so yet – I made these particularly resilient in case they get detected at some point."

"So, what you're saying is that there's no cure."

"Exactly."

"Good thing it isn't our problem, then. When can this be ready for deployment?"

"The nanites themselves and the canisters can be built in minutes. All you need to do is to feed the protocol into each machine – I'll get you a copy of the protocols later today – I've still got to finish writing the instructions."

"Good. I'll be waiting for them."

Colonel Jackson departed, leaving Trienne hunched over her input pad. She wanted to make certain that the protocols included everything a combat mission might need. The canisters were designed to be self-guiding and were small enough to avoid detection by most enemy scanners, but they had to be given their initial velocity by an external force. The easiest way to do that was to put them into a shell casing and fire them from a gun – so it was of critical importance to have a shell casing for each type of gun included in the protocols.

It took her nearly two hours to program the machine and to recheck everything. And then she was done, and she printed a memory crystal. As she sat back in her seat, she saw a figure standing by the door. "Hello, Trienne."

It was a voice that had often calmed her, often guided her through difficult technical problems and design conundrums. She nearly screamed. "You! What are you doing here?"

Dr. Pendalai stepped closer. "Can't an old scientist visit his most outstanding pupil every once in a while?"

She pointed an accusing finger. "You tried to kill me!"

"It wasn't personal. You just happened to be in the wrong place at the time of the wrong breakthrough. And besides, you will recall that I actually sent you home. Someone else in our organization tried to kill you, but I did everything I could to keep you alive."

"Like hell. You probably wanted me out of the way in order to set off our little nanobomb." She looked at him in triumph. "Did you actually think I wouldn't figure it out? Nothing else in there would have burned hot enough to kill everyone in the lab. And you're right. I would have stopped you, and I would have beat you senseless in the process. Which is what I'm going to do now, and then I'll call security so they can throw you out of an airlock without the benefit of a suit, you bastard."

She advanced toward him. Pendalai was an extremely small, elderly man, but she would still enjoy it.

"I don't think so, my dear."

The man who materialized was definitely not small. He was tall and blond and built like a boulder. There were rings under his eyes – it seemed to her that everyone in Crystallia had rings under their eyes – but not much emotion in them. He placed one hand on her mouth and another around her waist. Something about the way he held her head warned her that struggling would result in a broken neck, and that screaming would accelerate the process.

Pendalai walked softly to the input board, studied the Crystallian computer and the Uploader nanofactory and typed some commands into the link. He had to confirm three times before the system acceded to his request and began to erase everything in the memory. Trienne struggled, forgetting herself, but the man holding her squeezed once, hard. She quieted.

"Now, how do we destroy the information in the machine itself," Pendalai mused. He looked at it from one angle, then another. Finally, he shrugged and picked up a steel arm, left over from the construction of the nanomachine, and began to smash anything that seemed remotely electronic.

He did a rather thorough job of it, too, and Trienne began to regret having declined all the offers they'd received of getting a security detail in the lab. She also regretted the fact that everyone had become accustomed to loud noises emanating from here, and no one would be by to check. Most of all, she wished she hadn't given her assistants the day off for much-needed rest, feeling she could handle the demonstration on her own. At least the inner workings of the Uploader machine, including the quantum transmitter, had probably suffered little to no damage in the attack. Rester Appins would be able to get the nanite formula out of there with little trouble.

But that was probably the least of her worries. Pendalai caught her eye as he pocketed the data crystal. "I'll keep this. I have a feeling it will come in handy. And, we'll keep you for now, as well. Unless you become troublesome, of course."

"How are you planning on getting me out of here? This is deep in the control complex."

"Oh, I don't think you need to worry about that. We've arranged for the military to have a little distraction on their hands. Come on, Jev, drag her along, will you?"

Pendalai walked out the door, seemingly unconcerned that he was heading straight into a military corridor.

***

Pandemonium reigned as panicked civilians ran to and fro. Jackson had never seen anything like it.

What might have caused perfectly normal citizens, people who'd never done anything with their lives other than perhaps record an artsy documentary in their free time, to attack the nerve center of the Crystallian military?

And why these people in particular? This certainly didn't seem to be something that had affected the entire population of the underground colony, just a couple of hundred people who'd unexpectedly stormed through a lightly-defended checkpoint and proceeded to run amok, screaming at bemused Marines and attempting to storm into any open doorways they might encounter.

No one had fired upon them, of course: the Crystallian military was there to keep the civilian population safe, not to attack them for acting unpredictably. But this had allowed the interlopers to get deep into the military sector before the decision was taken to repress the action.

Shock troops were quickly outfitted with non-lethal weaponry of various sorts and set out to remove the invaders. And that was when things got strange.

As if a signal had been given, all the intruders suddenly changed direction and headed back the way they'd come, dragging anyone who'd been injured in the process along with them. Jackson shook his head, but allowed them to leave. They'd caused quite a bit of damage and disruption, but it was better just to let out a sigh of relief and allow them to go on their way unhindered than it would be to detain them all and have yet another controversy spring up between the civilians and the military.

After all, he had enough to worry about as it was.

CHAPTER 22

"I just think it's suicide to take them with us, that's all." The fact that he was extremely upset was written all over Greg's face. "They've already tried to blow us up once already. How do we know they won't do it again?"

"Simple. They'll stay frozen until we have everything up and running, that's how," Rester replied. Kan admired the Uploader's patience. She'd long since given up the argument, and would simply ordered the former Marine to shut up and do as he was told.

"It's a bad idea. We should execute them here. Or, since there's no provision for the capital punishment of civilians, lock them in a cell in the deepest tunnel and throw away the key, at least until the *Eagle* has gone." He paused, seeming to reconsider. "But I guess that decision is above my responsibility, so I'll shut up now. Sorry for taking up so much of your time." He got up and left.

Kan turned to Rester, shaking her head. "*Are* we making the right decision, though? We could have questioned them a little more."

He gave her a rueful smile. "It's above our pay grade, too. Seriously, though, I think it's the right choice. I'm just glad we were able to freeze them once we'd found out who they were involved with. Now they're out of the way, and the people they worked with have no clue that anything went wrong – which wouldn't have been the case if we'd shot them or locked them up. Right now, all they know is that the two bombers are frozen in the same hold as fifty thousand other people, just as planned. I doubt they were expecting to be on the ship when it left, but no one can suspect anything really wrong yet."

"Yeah, you're right, but I won't sleep easy, knowing that they're aboard. What if they get out of their hibernation mid-trip and kill everyone?"

"Then we'll have to deal with it. Besides, things can get monotonous out there, in interstellar space." It had been decided that Rester's technical knowledge was too valuable for him to be frozen with the colonists, and that he would stay awake with the skeleton crew and the officers.

"You think it'll get bad enough that we'll actually welcome an attack by homicidal maniacs?"

He smiled. "It might. Nothing much else to do except mindnet emulators and talk to each other."

"That might not be so bad, if the conversation is stimulating," she replied.

He hesitated. "Maybe, but I still think we should install a manual override so we can thaw out some of the more attractive colonists, just in case. That set of tall twins would have been a great bet."

"You are completely incorrigible," she said, slapping his arm. The voice screaming 'he's a machine' was strangely weak, lately.

"Well, you have to take into consideration that I spent the last few hundred years trapped in a circuit. Can I help it if I can't quite get my glands under control?

He, on the other hand, always seemed to make a point of reminding her of the fact that they were different. The strange part was that the more he said it, the less she cared. She found herself wanting him to be human – or wanting to meet a human just like him – much less often. She was starting to become content with being with Rester as he was.

"Are you glad that they allowed Wilde to come with us?"

She started. The last thing she'd been thinking about was Wilde, but the question was still valid. She'd been glad that his story had checked out, and that the bombers were apparently of a different faction, but she didn't feel much one way or the other about his presence. She had been surprised that he'd requested to come along, though. It just didn't seem to fit with the Wilde she'd known. Kan shrugged. "I guess it's better for him to come with us than it would have been for him to stay behind. I really don't think he knew much about whatever was going on, but better to have him safely frozen here."

"Yeah." Rester didn't look convinced. "Anyway, we still need to get the final inspections logged." He led her out the door of the small office to where Greg's team –despite the leader's misgivings – was finishing their duties.

Once again, Kan simply stopped to stare at the *Eagle*. In preparation for its launch, huge cranes and roller systems had emptied the ship bays around it and erected gigantic ceramic blast shielding to keep the rest of the hangar from the thrust of the engine. The ship itself had also been moved slightly, and was now aimed squarely at one of the multiple exit tunnels carved into the rock. For concealment reasons, these tunnels originally ended about a hundred meters short of the planet's surface, but in preparation for the launch they were being excavated out. The ship would pass cleanly through the opening when needed.

In isolation, the *Eagle* was a majestic sight. Its white painted surface seemed to go on forever, towering high above her head, losing itself in the high roof. She felt tiny in the shadow of the behemoth.

Rester followed her up the nearest access ramp and into the bridge, which was set at the bottom of the ship. Waiting for them was a pile of hard-copy printouts: thousands upon thousands of status reports.

Rester grinned. "Don't worry about those. I took the liberty of running them through the Uploader link. Essentially, they all say the same thing: we're good to go."

She returned his smile. "Uploader link? You must have been down on Crystallia too long."

"Nah. But if I'm going to be stuck on a brand new colony surrounded by primitives who really believe that living in the messy organic matrix is the right way to do things, I might as well learn the lingo."

"So you're really coming?" She held her breath as he hesitated before answering.

"Yes. I'm really coming. But not for any of the reasons we've discussed. This mission can't really succeed without me – or at least it can't succeed unless someone with knowledge of how vehicles and emissions are tracked through space is along."

"What?" That wasn't the reason she'd been expecting. Actually, she wasn't certain what she was expecting, but it wasn't the reason she'd been hoping for.

The look he gave her was earnest. "There is really only one thing that might cause this mission to fail, and that's the possibility of the Oneness catching up with it as soon as it lands and begins to build the colony. Human technology is extremely easy to identify even if you enter unexplored areas of the galaxy. Even running clear across the disc would only buy the colony a little time. The problem has to do with neutrino signatures from the fusion drives – which are like waving a large sign with our name on it. Didn't you ever wonder how we knew exactly where to find Crystallia after all the trouble you went to hide the place between black holes and neutron stars?"

"I hadn't thought of that. I just assumed you'd managed to track the diaspora from Earth, somehow."

"That's actually something we couldn't have done – the technology hadn't been developed when humanity was defeated. We got to that point a little later, when fighting the last remaining Brillans."

"So even if we run, we can't hide."

"Once again, you are failing to take something into account."

"What?"

"Me, of course." He struck a pose. "Didn't I tell you I was essential? The thing about the tracking is that it depends on neutrino detection. Neutrinos have quite a few interesting properties. In the first place, they have to physically travel through space in order to be detected – so if we move far enough away, we'll take some time for our signature to reach a sensor. And the second thing – even better for our purposes – is that neutrinos can be made to interact with certain plasma fields in such a way as to create the impression that the burst was created by a star, not an industrial reactor. Voilà! Instant anonymity!"

"So we'll be safe?"

"As safe as you can possibly be while cut off from every other piece of civilization in an unexplored corner of the galaxy, yes."

"I guess that will have to do for now. Also, I'm very disappointed in you. You lied to me."

"What? When?" he spluttered.

"You said you were coming because you couldn't get enough of me, and now it seems you're just along for the ride because you don't want to see the colony smashed by some Oneness fleet. I'm very disappointed in you, Rester."

He said nothing, just smiled at her with twinkling eyes.

**

Trienne wondered what kind of drug they'd used. Her head felt as if it had been packed with cotton wool. Even her vision was blurred. When she tried to move, her arms refused to respond, but she suspected that this had more to do with the restraints she could feel around her wrists than anything else.

As her vision slowly cleared, a dark blur came towards her out of a corner. It coalesced into a human form and sat down facing her. "You're back among the living, I see."

It was the voice of Hamak Wolf Pendalai. Her mentor. Her captor.

"What did you do to me?" Her tongue, like the rest of her, seemed impossibly unwieldy. As more and more of her body responded, she realized she must be in a chair, wrists tied to the arms and ankles tied to the legs.

"We didn't do anything. Apart from kidnapping you, of course."

"Then why do I feel like this? You drugged me."

The older scientist chuckled softly. "All we did was kidnap you and tie you to a chair. You shouted at us for a while and then you fell asleep. I assume that what you're feeling now is the result of having been asleep for over twenty hours straight." Her vision was still clouded, but it was enough to see Pendalai's shaking head. "Have you been overdoing it again? How many times do I have to tell you to take time to rest? You can't work for days on end without sleep, you know."

"Go to hell." Her memories were coming back. Now that he'd mentioned it, she could remember the shouting quite well. She'd demanded that they release her, threatened them with all kinds of dire retribution, but they'd just laughed and left her in the chair. She refused to give them the satisfaction of hearing her plead. "Well, that's twenty hours more that the military will have had to find me. They're probably about to arrive."

"I would be a lot more worried if it wasn't for the fact that they've been looking for me for months now. And let me remind you that what they were searching for me about was the murder of all our colleagues in the lab. Everything I know about burning makes it seem like a bad way to go. And then they probably also connected me to the attempt on your life, even though I wasn't actually there. So, you see, they were more motivated back then than they will be for a mere kidnapping, and they still couldn't find me."

"Oh, they will. They need my help with the war effort." Trienne hoped she didn't sound as desperate as she felt. She pulled against her restraints.

"The war, my girl, is going to work in my favor. The same people who should be out looking for us are currently trying to figure out how, exactly, they are going to defend this ball of baked clay against the most powerful military force this galaxy has ever seen. Don't you think they're going to be a little bit too busy to worry about a single scientist? I think we're pretty safe from your friends."

Trienne lunged at him, but the bonds held. All she managed to do was knock the chair over onto its side. Pendalai, now in focus, and pulled the chair upright once more, a look of pain on his face. She spat at him.

Instead of hitting her or even showing anger, Hamak simply wiped his face with the back of one of his hands, the look of sadness deepening. "I wish this didn't have to be like this. I wish you'd just join us and be done with it."

"Join you? I don't think I'd join you in the best of circumstances, but the truth is that I don't even know what you want!"

"We want the end of evolution," Pendalai announced.

"What?"

"Evolution is the cruelest of forces. It pits one life form against another, only that which is better adapted to the circumstances will survive. It's the reason intelligent life has popped up in so many places, but also the main force driving these intelligences against each other. If your entire racial, species history has been about defending your territory, you are unlikely to be able to play nice with a species as different from us as we are from the Brillans – or the Brillans themselves are from the Blobs."

"That's ridiculous. The Brillans and the Blobs attacked us. There was no evolutionary force at work at all."

"They attacked us precisely because of evolutionary forces. They were already involved in a war between themselves, and when they discovered humanity, what they saw was a potentially dangerous force, but one which wasn't yet strong enough to pose a threat. Billions of years of evolution told them what to do – they had to subject humanity to their power."

"And they lost. We have other things to worry about now. I don't understand how putting the war effort against the Oneness in jeopardy is going to help us eradicate interspecies genocide. Your whole argument is completely ridiculous."

"But don't you see? The only force that really represents the end of the eternal struggle is precisely the Oneness. An evolutionary process can only function when individual consciousness is present, so the perfect way to eliminate it is to suppress the individual."

"Are you insane?"

He shook his head sadly. "I wouldn't expect you to understand. But you don't know what it's like. Your characteristics wouldn't disappear – you'd still be there, but conscious of the fact that you serve a higher goal, a greater good. Not only can there be peace in the galaxy, but there's a piece in which every component is sentient enough to understand the true significance of that peace."

"All this from the Oneness? All this from taking what makes each of us unique and destroying it?" She paused to think about it for a moment. "But you started down this path long before we even knew about the Oneness. What were you doing then?"

"I started on this path on the day I was born, Trienne. I have always been convinced of the need for harmony and for casting off the trappings of individuality. I wasn't born on Crystallia."

She was shocked. She'd known this man for nearly fifteen years. How could this be? How could it be that she'd never suspected anything? "But how?"

He shrugged. "The Oneness wasn't strong enough to break through the cordon of Isolationists defending this colony, but a single ship was easy enough to slip through the net. I've been here for nearly forty years."

A cold ball of ice formed in the pit of her stomach. Where there was one infiltrator, there would be more. "I suppose that blond man is just like you? Bred in some inhuman outpost as a spy?"

The man who called himself Hamak Wolf Pendalai seemed amused. "Jev? No, Jev is just a young man who has the intelligence to be able to see what's right and what's wrong. He was very frustrated when I met him, and I can understand the problem. Imagine being able to see through the lies, but not know what to do to make things right. Fortunately, I managed to reach him before his frustration became obvious to the authorities."

Trienne studied him for a few moments. The sheer enormity of what he was saying had not yet sunk in, but the little she was able to process was enough to let her know that the war effort might be seriously compromised. It was bad enough that they were trying to defend themselves against impossible odds – but having a faction on the inside working against them would make survival impossible. "They're going to find you, you know."

Pendalai just smiled.

***

"Announce it," the admiral ordered grimly, just as Jackson walked into the command center. "Ah, Colonel, good to see you, though I wish the circumstances were different. I have some grave news you should know about: the outermost sensor line has just reported an advance force of Oneness-controlled craft entering the Oort equivalency."

Jackson felt cold fingers take a firm grip on his heart. "How long ago?"

"Not long, maybe five minutes, maybe a little more. Either way, the time has come. I just got off the comm with the new supreme councilor, some Luyten named Philippe. We've decided that the civilian population needs to be informed at once."

Jackson said nothing. There was no longer any question of keeping vital information from the general populace, no matter how counter-productive its release might be. There was simply too much suspicion, too much rampant speculation going on to hold anything back. It would be found out sooner or later, and the consequences might be dire.

The single thing that worried him the most was the new council. Rima Centauri Han and most of her crusty group of administrators were currently all asleep inside the *Eagle*'s hold. The military had been assured that the new group had been in secretarial positions just waiting for their chance to represent the people, and that they were just as competent as the outgoing council. Nevertheless, there had probably never been a worse moment to have inexperienced leadership than now. Especially now that the Oneness was no longer a shadow on the horizon, but a reality that they would soon be dealing with at extremely close range.

"So, are we going to deploy?" he asked his superior officer.

"Already taken care of. The Uploader fleet is in position, and we've mounted everything new we've developed onto their ships. We're not even bothering to send our own capital ships out – they're simply not equipped to fight this kind of war. But they're fully crewed and have orders to run for it if the unthinkable happens."

"Run? Run where?"

"Randomly. The plan is that they find uninhabited worlds as far away as they can get and settle them."

"That didn't work too well the first time around," Jackson pointed out, thinking how Crystallia, a pre-scouted world deemed impossible to find except by chance, had been discovered nearly immediately.

The admiral shrugged. "I know. But it's much better than sending our people into a fight they won't survive. I'd rather keep my oath to defend humanity than kill it off in some futile, glorious gesture."

Jackson nodded. The man might become bogged down in Crystallian politics every once in a while, and be overly hide-bound and dogmatic enough to drive Jackson crazy, but he was a sound officer, one who knew what was really important. "Maybe one of them can make it."

The admiral said nothing. They both knew that it was the action of a command structure with few true options. The silence grew longer and deeper. The control center was filled with people, but none seemed inclined to interrupt their superiors.

"Any news on our missing weapon system?"

"No. We've been looking for Dr. Luyten Angelique ever since we realized she was gone. There's just no sign of her. It's like the lab attack all over again."

It was the Admiral's turn to nod. "Yes, it is. My question, though, is: who would want us to fail? I read your brief about that group, Peace Crystallia, and the attempted attack on the colony ship, but I have a hard time believing it. It just doesn't seem like the kind of thing that would spring up in our tunnels. It just feels wrong."

"A couple of weeks ago, I would have said the same thing. But now I'm not so sure. Maybe, just maybe, we've been out of touch with the civilians for too long. Have you thought of that?" Jackson said.

The older officer's expression gave nothing away as if the man was keeping it frozen by sheer force of will, but the lines on his face seemed to deepen, and his eyes certainly reflected a strong emotion. "I grew up in those tunnels. I can still remember what it felt like in the passages. I can remember the uncertainty, the fear of not knowing whether we would be found. The hope that tomorrow would be an ordinary day, just like today. I don't think even the deepest places where we never go could have spawned anything like it."

"Well… we believe the saboteurs might have been an alien infiltration group. We found a duplicate shuttle. But it still wouldn't account for Peace Crystallia. By our records, the saboteurs have only been here a few weeks."

"I'm certain you'll crack the mystery sooner or later," the admiral said with a shrug. "Of course, it might not matter one way or another by then. Perhaps you might be better off cancelling the search for your missing scientist, too. You have enough stuff on your plate, and one more ultimate weapon out there probably won't make much difference one way or the other."

"I'd rather not. I have a good feeling about this one. It just seems different for some reason."

Jackson was certain that his superior would turn the suggestion into an order, but the other man just smiled. "What the hell. I know you can go without sleep for a week at a time, and by then it won't make a difference one way or another. So find her. Get us another weapon. We can sleep when we're dead – or, if we're incredibly lucky, after the Oneness has been beaten back."

There was nothing to say to that, so Jackson turned his gaze back to the monitors showing the corridors. The announcement that the Oneness fleet had arrived was not being met with the same indifference as other announcements, or even the fury Jackson had seen the last time he'd been out among the people. The reaction this time seemed more akin to panic.

People were running every which way, shouting as they went. Jackson assumed they were telling their neighbors the news, too preoccupied to realize that their neighbors were saying the same thing.

Eventually, a kind of consensus seemed to emerge from the chaos. Suddenly, there seemed to be a concerted rush towards one of the corridors.

Just as Jackson was thinking that they seemed to be heading towards the minimum-security military zone where the Uploader ambassadors were housed, one of the aides dared to break the silence. "Excuse me, sir," this was directed at the admiral. "I have Mika Bina on the comm."

"Patch her through."

Mika's face appeared on the main screen immediately. The expression she was wearing was one of resigned amusement. "Hello Admiral, Colonel," she said.

They returned her greeting.

Mika's eyes twinkled. "Here's a quick question for you. If you've just found out that the Oneness has arrived in-system and is heading towards Crystallia to forcibly upload you into its data core, what would your first reaction be?"

"I suppose I'd try to hide as far away as possible," the admiral replied.

"That's what I would have thought as well. Strangely, though, it seems that a huge chunk of Crystallia's population has decided that the best way to deal with the possibility of being uploaded against their will is to ask us to upload them into *our* databases and transmit them to safety."

"You mean they're actually asking for uploads?"

"That's exactly it."

"But that's ridiculous. Why would they try to escape uploading by uploading?" Jackson asked.

Her image shrugged. "I'm not really sure, but there's a bunch of people waiting politely for my answer."

Jackson surveyed the monitors. "You're about to get quite a few more, it looks like. Are they aggressive at all?"

"Not really. I told them that I couldn't do anything like that without asking you first, and they seem content to wait patiently. Also, there's a couple of really large Marines with evil-looking guns posted at my door, which might be helping."

The admiral exchanged a look with Jackson. "Can you even *do* that? I mean, do you have the equipment to upload a bunch of people?"

"Of course. Not immediately, but every one of the nanofactories can produce upload units. It's part of the base program. The bigger question is whether I should upload them or not."

"I think the bigger question is what happens to people after you upload them?"

"Rester could probably give you more details – we haven't uploaded anyone in a while – but from what I have in this brain's memory, the new upload machines simply create a copy without damaging the donor so, in essence, you get to live two different lives – at least until your physical body dies off. After that, you exist in the mainframes only." She paused. "I do know that the Oneness hasn't bothered to incorporate any new tech – their upload systems destroy the original."

"I see a problem with that. If these people are trying to escape, what they want is to go to sleep and wake up somewhere else. They'll be disappointed to find themselves physically present, don't you think?"

"Well, that's something one of the copies is going to have to deal with. I've explained it to the ones that spoke to me, and I'll explain it to any others who might come. One thing I won't do under any circumstances is to allow the biological bodies to be killed."

"So, just to be clear, all you'd really be doing is making a copy of the people who ask for it?" the admiral repeated.

"Precisely."

He hesitated only for a second. "Then do it."

CHAPTER 23

Rester froze. The request was both impossible to grant and impossible to ignore. It opened up possibilities that went well beyond anything they'd considered so far. "What?" he said.

The answer was transmitted back to him via the physical cable he was using to communicate with the captured Oneness observation entity that thought of itself as "the Watcher." "I would like to help you in the war effort. I can send the invasion fleet misleading information about the position and capabilities of the defense force."

"You would actively participate in the defense? I thought you just wanted to escape."

"I've been evaluating my choices, and I think the probability that your leadership will allow me to board an escape vessel is extremely low. But the odds seem likely to improve if I can offer you some kind of value in exchange."

"You want to negotiate."

"Precisely. I have no reason to help you if you won't help me in return."

The fact that the Watcher wasn't offering to help out of the goodness of its electronic soul actually put Rester's mind a little more at ease. Perhaps this proposition might be worth looking into a little further. Of course, it was smart enough to know that anything that seemed too good to be true would be scrutinized extremely carefully. "You want us to load you onto the *Eagle* in exchange for sending the Oneness false information?"

"Exactly. There's one other thing I can do for you, but I won't tell you what it is until you agree to my terms."

"How do you know the Oneness will believe what you send it?"

Rester received the electronic equivalent of a shrug through the loop. "That's the reason it sent me here in the first place. I haven't let it down so far."

"And all you want in exchange is the promise that you'll be allowed to leave with the *Eagle*?"

"Of course not. I will send the false messages from the *Eagle*, from orbit. That's also when I'll give you the other piece of information. It would be a pity if I helped you win this war and you suddenly changed your minds about our agreement."

Rester sighed. The *Eagle* was scheduled to leave that afternoon. It seemed he had to move quickly. "Give me a few minutes," he said.

It wasn't strictly necessary to speak to Jackson about the issue in person, but the colonel's office was just a few doors down the hall, and Rester knew the man was spending every waking hour at his desk. He knocked and the panel slid open.

"Appins." Jackson nodded in greeting. "Please tell me you have some good news for me."

"I might, but it won't come cheap."

He sighed. "Nothing ever does. Spill it. I have spies to catch, civilians to placate, and I strongly suspect that my superiors will want me in on the planetary defense coordination meetings, if only because I've been the liaison with you and Miss Bina. So look alive."

Rester quickly explained the situation and the Jackson sighed again. "Have you asked Kan whether she'd be willing to carry him?"

"Not yet, but I suspect she would."

"You're probably right. Get the thing onto the *Eagle* and get it hooked up. Let me know when you're ready to transmit." The colonel paused a strange look in his eye. "You're going with them, aren't you?"

"Yes, sir."

Jackson held out a hand. "I wish the peace between our races had been achieved in less stressful circumstances, but I'd like you to know that it's been a pleasure to meet you. Thanks for all the help."

"The pleasure was mine. You body-bound humans have shown me that life can be remarkable, even if it is short."

Jackson nodded, his mind seemingly elsewhere. "Could you do me a favor? Could you tell Kan to come say goodbye to her old superior officer before she leaves?"

"I think you can count on it, sir." Rester smiled and turned to go.

The colonel cleared his throat behind him. "And son, take good care of her, will you?"

"I don't know what you mean."

"Yes, you do. Now get out of here. I have work to do."

Appins left, wondering if he was really as obvious as the old man made it seem, but that train of thought was quickly replaced by a much more pressing matter. Kan had already been ordered to transport three saboteurs on her ship for no better reason than that the people in the intelligence department thought it would be less suspicious to the hidden confederates they hoped to catch if they weren't imprisoned. Now, he was going to have to ask her to accede to carrying a self-confessed member of the Oneness' spy network.

It was not going to be a fun interview for either of them. He knew how it would end, of course: Kan would do anything to help the colony, no matter how tenuous the hope being offered might seem. But knowing that only made it worse for him. He was the one putting this enormous imposition on her.

Still, he didn't tarry. He found her in the bridge, setting up for the launch countdown. Everything that could be moved out of the hangar had been moved, and the rings under her eyes said that she would only be happy once they were out in open space and cruise velocity had been reached.

She took a single look at his expression. "All right, tell me," she said.

He explained the situation and received a harried look and a reprimand along with her agreement. But then she softened. "I'm sorry. It's just that I lost all morning explaining to a group of crazies that there is no more room on board, that all the cryochambers are occupied. Everyone thinks that being in danger gives them the right to board the single ship leaving the system." She exhaled. "And I still have the whole launch checklist to go through to make our window. Fortunately, Greg's team is a little ahead of schedule, so they've taken up some of my slack. I'll let this Watcher on board, but I want you to watch it closely. If you detect a single transmission other than what he tells you is outgoing, I'll space it and drop it on a trajectory into the nearest star." She paused. "And one more thing, once you get back, I don't want you leaving again. I would hate to fly off without you."

He smiled. "Also, don't fly off without saying goodbye to Jackson."

Her eyes clouded up. "I wish he were coming with us."

"Yeah, me too. He's a good guy." He excused himself. Before leaving, he had his own goodbyes to make. He wondered whether Mika would understand his motives – or even manage to guess as to his true reasons.

***

Jev held the memory crystal between his thumb and forefinger. Light flashed off its edges. It was such a small thing to hold the power it did. Entire civilizations could be wiped out just by using the information contained within.

It hadn't been easy to get Trienne to tell them the secrets it held. Jev's stomach had churned as Pendalai extracted the confession. He wasn't inured to the casual cruelty the alien man had exerted – violence simply wasn't part of the daily life of Crystallian civilians. Sickening as it was, however, Pendalai's methods were undoubtedly effective. The information they needed had been obtained in short order, and then he'd asked Jev to leave them alone for a few moments.

Jev wondered what was going on in there. Was the doctor finishing her off? Apologizing? Trying to convert her to the cause of the Oneness? The room beyond was soundproofed, and Pendalai offered no explanation when he emerged. "We need to move. Where is the infiltration team?" he said.

"They're still holed up in the corridor in subsector twenty-three. What did you do to the girl?"

The look he received was hard, but an answer was forthcoming. "She'll live, but only because I think she'd make a valuable addition to the Oneness once we absorb her. Had it not been for that, I would have happily condemned her to die for the abomination she created. We have to get this information back to the fleet. I hope the infiltration team has a functioning transmitter."

They walked down the corridors, making no attempt to look relaxed and calm. No one they saw gave the impression that they were going about their day. Everyone seemed in a hurry, haggard faces showing equal parts worry and exhaustion. The two desperate saboteurs felt that they fit right in.

The place to which the Oneness infiltrators had moved their base camp was even further out of the way than their previous efforts. They'd captured sufficient numbers of Crystallians that they no longer needed to sit in wait, and the complete lack of visitors was a good thing. Two guards, openly armed, barred their way as they approached, moving aside with surprised expressions only when Pendalai spoke to them in a guttural, unpleasant language.

Jeffrey walked up to meet them. "Hamak," he said. "Or would you prefer for me to use your crèche name? Many stories have been told about how you've lived among the unbelievers all alone."

"We don't have time for that now. We have vital information that has to be transmitted to the fleet."

"That's highly irregular. Our instructions were to remain completely anonymous and to do nothing that might lead to our discovery unless we see a chance to cause significant damage to the enemy. Those instructions have not changed."

"The information we have in that crystal will do more damage to the coalition set against us than any sabotage you can possibly think of." Pendalai explained the situation. "It's your chance to strike a decisive blow and cement your place in the history of an enlightened galaxy."

Jeffrey looked doubtful, but nodded, swayed either by the doctor's promises or by the simple burning logic of the explanation. He nodded and one of his team members primed the quark transmitter.

"Tell us when you have an acknowledgement."

The three men stood silently waiting for the transmission to get through. About a minute later, Jeffrey turned impatiently back to the man on the equipment. "So, what's happening?"

"I'm not sure. There must be something wrong. They've never taken this long to respond before." He passed a finger over one of the control panels.

A single blue bolt passed through their midst. "Stun assault," Jeffrey shouted. He dived behind a pile of equipment, followed closely by the smaller figure of Dr. Wolf Pendalai.

Jev stood rooted in place, shocked. On both ends of the corridor, troops dressed in white armor advanced towards their position, brandishing weaponry of various types. "That was a warning shot. Unless you surrender immediately, you will be neutralized." The ultimatum came not from the suited figures but from everywhere at once. Jev guessed that the announcement had been pumped through the Crystallian public address system.

In response, Jeffrey opened fire on the suited forms in front. He used a weapon the size of a finger, but which disintegrated the lead suit as if it had been made of smoke, and sent the rest of the troops on that side diving for cover.

The ones behind, however, had no such problems. They peppered the prone figures with some kind of energy weaponry, which Jev assumed must be lasers. The first barrage burned a large hole through the man trying to operate the transmitter and must have also hit some other members of the group, judging by the screams from behind the equipment. The sound of what sounded like a young girl sobbing reached his ears just as the smell of burnt skin reached his nose.

Jeffrey turned to the attack unit behind them, but suddenly the lights in the corridor went off, and Jev could no longer see what was happening. He heard it, though: the discharge of the infiltrator's weapon, the screams from the people hit by laser fire.

A blast of superheated air warmed his cheek as a near miss almost took his head off, but still Jev found himself unable to move, his legs frozen in place, afraid even to breathe. It must have been quick, lasting mere seconds, but in the darkness, the battle seemed to go on forever.

Suddenly, there was quiet. The sound of death being discharged from countless muzzles was replaced by the soft rustling of burning electronics and the muted clump of armored feet. The girl's sobbing was softer now, fading to a whimper.

The lights went on. Jev nearly jumped out of his skin. Less than a hand's breadth away from his nose was the helmeted visage of one of the troops. Before he could do much more than recoil, two gauntleted hands wrapped around his arms.

"Don't move."

Jev nodded, wondering what would happen now. He had no illusions as to how the government would deal with a man who'd worked to get everyone on the colony – indeed every single human left alive in the galaxy – uploaded into the Oneness against their will. They really had only one option for punishing him.

But he was alive, if only for now. The rest of his group hadn't fared quite as well.

Most of Jeffrey's body had been burned away. The small chunk of torso and half of a leg that remained could only be identified by its tattered clothing. Evidently, the attack troops had been quick to identify the main threat – and were probably equipped for night vision, judging by the effectiveness of their concentrated fire.

Dr. Hamak Wolf Pendalai – or whatever his true name was – had paid for taking cover alongside the infiltration's leader. While still recognizable, he was quite clearly dead, nicked in the throat in a bloodless, cauterized, but still fatal manner. The rest of the infiltrators were sprawled in various positions on the floor of the corridor, except for one, a dark-haired girl, who was being tended to by a Crystallian medical team. It was unlikely that they would be able to do too much for her – the stump where her left arm had been had been cauterized by the same beam that removed the limb. She was the source of the whimpering.

The two guards who'd received them at the head of the tunnel were in much better shape: disarmed, but whole. Their expressions were the only indication of the seriousness of the situation.

Jev turned back to his captor. He was well aware that the armor contained servos that had the power to rip his arms off if he tried to pull away, but he had an advantage. "I'm Crystallian! I'm not with them, they were holding me captive!"

"We know exactly who you are, Mr. Rigel Hamel." The voice that admonished him seemed female, a suspicion confirmed when the suit's visor slid open. Her expression was one of contempt mixed with more than a little pure hatred. "The only reason you're still alive is that we had strict orders to take you alive for psychological examination. Well, that and the fact that you were too much of a coward to do anything but stand there like a frightened little girl."

"Can you at least let me walk? Or are you going to carry me all the way back to my cell?"

The gauntlets released their iron grip. "You can walk. All they told me was that I had to get you back to the command center alive, but they didn't specify what condition. Nothing in the whole galaxy would give me more pleasure than if you tried to run and I was forced to burn your legs off. Now wait here. My commander wants to talk to you before we go."

The commander was a short guy with graying hair who'd removed his helmet and was going from one group to another. His suit was nearly identical to the rest except that antennae bristled from it. One of his armored arms sported a crease from a near miss. The look he gave Jev had even less warmth than his subordinate's. "I've been ordered to ask you one question, and to get the answer using whatever means I deem fit. So here's how it's going to go: every time you don't answer the question, I burn off a finger. When you run out of fingers, I move downward until I find something relatively similar to a finger to burn off. Do we understand each other?"

Jev nodded.

"Good." The commander took his right hand in one gauntlet. "My question should be easy to answer: where is Trienne Luyten Angelique?"

Thoughts of the future, a future in which everyone was equal, sharing a consciousness without selfishness or pride flashed through Jev's mind, attempting to strengthen him for the upcoming ordeal, but to no avail. Some primal bit, deep within knew that self was important, no matter how unpleasant the concept might be. "I'll show you," he said, and hung his head so no one could see his shame.

***

Private Enrique Sol Gómez knew he was in trouble as soon as his screen lit up. As the sole occupant of one of the orbiting defense platforms around the second planet in the Hammersmith 214 system, he had access to the entire Perimeter Defense Network, as did the men manning the other thirty-five identical platforms.

When they got back dirtside, the men would compare stories of how frightened they'd been when a small rock, uncharted until the last moment, had set off one of the proximity alarms and armed the station's bevawatt guns. They'd even heard tales of one gunner who'd gone through the experience twice in his two-month shift – although no one really believed it. The odds would be astronomical.

The screen in front of him had suddenly, impossibly, illuminated him in every color of the spectrum, coming from every single sector that the Network could cover. And not one of the readings was showing anything smaller than a battle cruiser – until the cruisers began disgorging tiny blips.

He willed the automated systems to fire the weapons, but they seemed frozen solid. Which was why the defense platforms had human operators. He hit the manual override and moved the aim reticule to cover the nearest large ship. On giving the firing command, he was rewarded by a huge shudder as the energy began to pulse. Sadly, that was his only reward. The target ship seemed completely unaffected by the strike. He wondered if he'd missed.

Judging by the communication on the open channels, his comrades at arms had had similar experiences. Some were shouting for instructions. Some wondered why the fight had come here when the enemy was supposed to be stopped at Crystallia. Some screamed for guidance.

No guidance was forthcoming. Central planetary command seemed as shell-shocked as they were.

By that time, three smaller dots, moving at unbelievable velocity, had reached his position. Even through the stone shell that housed the platform, he felt them strike the surface. Then noise, vibration – *drilling?* – and occasional bumps reached him. He knew the hull was breached when the draft started.

Enrique started towards the bay where the vacuum suits were kept when he remembered that he hadn't transmitted his observations to Hammersmith. He turned back to his seat, but never made it.

Standing between him and the console was a small metal spider. It was about knee high and looked as evil as an inanimate object could. He took two steps away, cursing the fact that defense platform operators were not issued side arms. The spider closed the gap immediately, skittering noisily over the metal floor.

He'd heard that the Oneness would go to great lengths to capture a human consciousness, to upload it mercilessly into the great matrix of minds that made up its being. Those rumors were certainly correct: a simple, unguided missile could have vaporized the defenseless platform, but the Oneness had instead mounted a complex landing and strike designed to crack this stony nut and remove the meat inside. An attack hampered by the fact that it was orders of magnitude more complex than a missile launch had been effected just to make certain that one single human life would not be wasted. It was mind-boggling.

But he hardly thought about it. Instead, unbidden, came the other rumor related to the Oneness' uploading process. It was supposed to be the first step in dismembering the personality so that its different components could be split up and used where they were needed most. Supposedly, this initial fracture was achieved because the uploading process itself was more pain than a person could endure and stay mentally whole.

He turned to run, but found his path blocked by a second metallic nightmare.

Enrique had no chance to turn again. Something heavy landed on his back and began to skitter towards the base of his skull, the weight of it driving him to his knees.

To his credit, the thought of his beautiful planet, and his beautiful family – wife and six-year-old daughter – being subsumed by the Oneness as it overran the green hills was what he was thinking about as he fruitlessly tried to pry the spider from his back. He had to do something to save the millions who only wanted peace.

But before he could do anything, two pricks in his head indicated that the spider was about to begin. He buckled again, hoping to knock it off, but stopped mid-motion. The pain had begun, and nothing else held any more importance.

CHAPTER 24

Trienne wiped a tear from her face. She hoped the men watching her intently thought it was caused by the sight of her equipment, so casually destroyed just two days earlier, and that none suspected that it was caused by the agony in her ribs. In fact, the agony was just a small part of it – the worst thing was knowing that just a few well-placed punches and a broken rib or two were all it took to get her to betray her people.

"Can you fix it?" Jackson asked.

Trienne almost smiled. The anxiety had finally broken through the man's kindness, causing him to put the urgency of the matter at hand ahead of the feelings of the people around him for the first time since they'd met. *Seems this war has changed us all... and it hasn't really started yet.* She shook her head. "No."

He seemed to deflate.

Trienne continued. "There's a good chance that the information is still in there, though, but I'll need access to some Uploader tech."

Jackson nodded and gave an order. Less than a minute later, a young man with darker skin than the colonel's and curly black hair appeared. He introduced himself as August Senmar.

Jackson, in turn, introduced him as, "Rester's replacement. We found that with all Rester's time taken up with the *Eagle* launch, things weren't working as smoothly as we wanted on the technical side of things, so we got ourselves a new liaison."

"Are you all so handsome?" Trienne asked with a smile.

The liaison smiled back, his eyes looking a lot older and wiser than what she expected from his seeming physical age. "Wouldn't you, if you could choose to look however you wanted?"

She laughed, and her ribs hurt. "I guess I would." She turned back to the ruined machine. "From what I saw, they probably wouldn't have been able to destroy the information stored inside. Even Dr. Pendalai," she paused to push away the memories of her former mentor's betrayal, "had never seen anything remotely like this, so it's no surprise that they had no idea how to disable the thing. Hell, they probably thought the only copy of the information was on that memory stick."

"It would be, if you wiped the memory before copying."

"I had no idea you could even do that." She grinned ruefully, "I guess Pendalai wasn't the only one who had no idea what this machine could do. Anyhow, the information should still be in there. I know we built in the quantum-entangled transmitter that should allow us to share the unit's memory with other Uploader units, but I don't know how to make it work, much less how to trigger it remotely – my kidnappers seem to have demolished the external controls."

August walked around the nanofactory a couple of times, sometimes stopping to study a certain broken knob or dented panel. He crouched on his hands and knees to inspect the underside, or what was visible of the underside after a blow to one of its legs had left the machine canted at an angle. Finally, he stood and faced Trienne. "I think you're right. The damage doesn't look remotely serious enough to incapacitate the transmission functions. But normally, we'd just scrap a machine in this condition and build a new one – that's what nanofactories are for, after all. What makes the information in here so special?"

"It might help us win the war," Jackson interjected. "So stop asking all these questions and help us get it out."

The Uploader smiled thinly. "All right." He turned back to Trienne. "All right, tell me what code words to look for. I'm ordering a quantum transmitter on the *Astra* to send the necessary instructions for transmission. Excuse me." His face went completely blank for nearly thirty seconds. Trienne assume he was in contact with the ship, nearly a light-hour from Crystallia. When his eyes refocused, the look on his face was concerned. "I have finished the transmission, and we are analyzing the proposed attack methodology. I can say that the little data I was able to scan as I kept a copy for my own files was disturbing. I might need a little time to confer with the rest of the command structure."

"Disturbing?" Jackson said, but immediately realized that Senmar had gone completely blank again, his body present, but his mind linked remotely to his people in a mainframe somewhere.

Trienne wondered what that must be like, to be able to fly across a simulated universe with no restrictions other than the imagination. Freedom beyond any imagined by the greatest revolutionaries in history. And no nagging pain in the ribs. All one had to do was leave behind the body and accept that the only mind you'd ever have was a shared electron stream in a mainframe somewhere.

It might be delightful, but she still shuddered.

August's head snapped up. "I'm sorry."

"What was that about?" It was obvious by his expression that Jackson was worried. "Did they receive the transmission correctly?"

"I've gotten instructions to organize a meeting between the high command of the Crystallian military and Mika Bina regarding this technology. Do you think that would be feasible?"

"As soon as Bina can get to the control center, we can do it. I assume the admiral is there. If he's in a meeting, we'll pull him out. What's this about?"

"It needs to wait for the meeting."

"Let's go, then." As they left, Jackson turned to Trienne and said, "Come." It wasn't a request; it had no trace of human warmth. But it did allow her to tag along – something that was worth more to her then than anything else. Recent events had turned her into a bit of a patriot.

The walk to the command center wasn't long, but it was interrupted by numerous security posts and checkpoints, at the last few of which Trienne had to be vouched for by Jackson. It seemed to her that the Marine guards got less and less friendly as they went deeper. Even though she'd spent two days in captivity, this was the first time she'd actually *felt* like Crystallia was at war.

The admiral wasn't at a meeting. He was standing inside a holographic model of the Crystallia system, surrounded by models of planets, moons, and battle fleets. In the interior of the system, blue polygons of different sizes represented, as far as Trienne could surmise, the defensive positions of the combined Uploader and Crystallian forces. She knew most of them were Uploader forces, and that the few Crystallian vessels in the mix were only there from courtesy, as they weren't expected to add much to the war effort.

Outside the system, a large red arrow made of similar, if smaller polygons seemed to be driving its point into the system. Already, it had gone deep into the orbit of the outer dwarf planet. The angry swarm was hundreds of times more numerous than the blue dots.

Trienne stared at it.

"It's not quite as bad as it looks," the admiral said, interpreting her expression perfectly. "You see, it's much easier to defend a system than to attack it. The problem for the attackers is that even with the fantastic physics loaded onto their vessels, we have one thing they don't: mass. We can use the planets and moons where our defenses are emplaced," the admiral pointed to a gas giant near his head, "to create even better gravity weapons. I like one called the relativistic atom cloud, where you can do incredible damage to a battle fleet by sending gas molecules into their midst at near light-speed." He focused on Jackson. "What can I do for you today?"

The colonel shrugged. "I'm not really sure. One of the weapons we developed has the Uploaders all in a flutter."

"Not all in a flutter," interjected Mika, who'd finally arrived. "We're understandably concerned about a technology that could easily wipe us out."

"Why? What are you talking about?" the admiral said.

They moved to an adjacent conference chamber and Trienne was given the floor. She explained the working of the nanotech missiles she had designed in detail for the Admiral, and then Jackson – probably trying to keep her from reliving the stress – recounted her kidnapping and the capture of the infiltrators. Trienne herself told of the transmission of the data to the Uploaders.

"So, in essence, we developed a technology that might turn the tide of the war. Miss Bina, why are you so worried about it? We wouldn't be idiotic enough to use it against you."

"That's not the issue here. The thing is that it's a technology that could wipe us out completely."

Trienne broke in. "Not really. The deployment depends on the element of surprise. The only way to get the nanomachines in place is to fire them across on missiles – projectile weapons a thousand years out of date. Unless the fleet is being distracted by all the rest of the stuff we're planning on hitting it with, they'd swat the missiles aside like a gnat. There's no way—"

"We don't want them on our ships. A single accident might wipe out a mainframe."

"So what are you saying?"

"We're going to erase all copies of the research. We'd also appreciate it if you would refrain from duplicating it."

The admiral was silent for a few moments. His face reddened, as he seemed to be counting to ten mentally. "I don't think that's acceptable. The reason you approached us in the first place is so that we could provide the spark, jump start your stagnant society – and we agreed because you were better placed to use any technology we might come up with together to defend us. And now that we've found something that isn't just a refinement of existing weapons, isn't just a bigger, badder bomb, you tell us that you won't use it?"

"There are risks to be taken into account."

"You signed a treaty. We have done our part better than anyone could have hoped. You are reneging on yours."

"We never asked you to destroy our civilization."

"No, you imposed on us the need to participate actively in this war. Maybe without us you'd have fought the Oneness to a stalemate, and we would never have become involved. But we decided to leave aside old atrocities and help. Perhaps we were wrong to do it."

It was Mika's turn to be silent. Trienne suspected that she was conferring with her superiors or whoever made the decisions in their cyberworlds. Unlike the tech people, she seemed able to keep part of her awareness shunted to the body – or maybe it was that only she cared to do it while August and Rester had been less diplomatic. Finally, she responded, with a totally non-mechanical sigh. "You're right. Not taking advantage of this would violate the spirit of our agreement. But we think we have a solution."

All of them leaned closer, eager to hear how the Uploaders would solve it.

"We'll allow the weapons to be built on Crystallian fleet ships. We'll transfer the necessary nanofactories to your vessels. However, we'd like to impose a single condition: that they only be used as a last resort, and that the deployment be done as far from our own fleet as possible."

"Done," the admiral said. "I suddenly feel optimistic again. Not just for the battle itself, but for the trust we need to build afterwards." He held out his hand.

Mika shook it solemnly.

***

Following the meeting with the Uploader embassy, Jackson found himself with no pressing tasks for what seemed like the first time in months. He just walked into his office and sagged on his seat, completely drained.

Whatever the outcome of this war, he knew he was finished. The galaxy had changed, seemingly overnight. New power blocs would be created, new ways of fighting wars. If they lost, it was even possible that there would be a second human Diaspora. The ships with space-fold capability had been instructed to run for it if the battle seemed irredeemably lost. They were to keep running – each in a different direction – until they found a suitably distant and hidden world. Rester's trick for hiding neutrino signatures had been transmitted to each of them over the past few days. If it came to that, Jackson would probably find himself adjusting to a new type of life as part of the Oneness.

But if it didn't, he would retire anyway. The real reason he'd stayed in service thus far was to supervise the careers of the officers he'd taken a personal interest in. The last of these was currently sitting in orbit commanding a colony ship with fifty thousand lives in her hands, waiting for the ideal takeoff window. The fact that he felt nothing but confidence in her filled him with pride – both at the way she'd turned out and at his own small part in it.

Idly, exhausted, he switched to the main combat frequency. An ensign on one of the forward-most ships was transmitting the battle report.

"Over the past ten standard hours, the enemy fleet has advanced three quarters of an astronomical unit towards the center of the system. The planetoid-based defensive positions that were installed in the fleet's path have been overrun after three engagements lasting five standard hours combined.

"There was no loss of human life in the battle, and Uploader data shows that only copies were lost. Eighty-five percent of the losses were self-inflicted, with only the remaining fifteen percent being captured and absorbed by the Oneness matrix. According to our allies' analysis, the factors involved in this low rate of capture were twofold. The first was the high level of automation in the platforms themselves, and the second is the fact that the nature of the platforms made it necessary to destroy most of the ground installations in order to disable the sites.

"Other than the defense installations on the planetoids, no allied forces were involved in the action. Capital ships were picketed well beyond the theater of operations, with a view towards repelling a lightning strike by an offshoot then blunting the thrust of the main force, and the smaller observation vessels nearer the action were not fired upon by the enemy.

"The defeat of the planetoid line was achieved twenty percent faster than our worst-case scenarios, which means that the Uploader analysts are currently going through the battle plans and updating the estimates with the new data regarding enemy capabilities. The first modification to the battle plan will take place in the third defensive ring. They've told us to expect a much more rapid consumption of the gas giant's atmosphere. They are no longer viewing the third ring as a place where the enemy fleet can be stopped, but as a sacrificial position that should do as much damage as possible, with no view to preserving any of the installations.

"The Crystallian observers assigned to the second ring defense are currently retreating toward the third ring with the Uploader fleet elements. Once there, we are planning to rendezvous with the Crystallian force already there and receive new orders.

"That concludes the report from the *Arnold Tau Caprino*."

The ensign disappeared, to be replaced by another guy, almost indistinguishable from the last in both look and manner, who began to drone about the statistics of the Hammersmith strike. The colonel turned it off. Just thinking about the millions of lives lost made him sick, and it also gave way to dangerous speculation regarding the attitude of their Uploader allies. Was it really possible that it had occurred to no one that the Oneness might divert some of its might to demolishing the softer targets in the area while the Crystallian defense was tied up with the main fleet? It seemed so obvious in retrospect.

He massaged his temples. It wasn't worth getting incensed about, and it was too late to do anything. He was just glad that in this war, and at this time, he wasn't in the loop for the space-based portion of the activities. The sacrifices that would be made were staggering, and he didn't relish the idea of being responsible for the loss of life that would be the only possible outcome of even a perfect plan, perfectly executed.

And years of military life had made it absolutely clear that there was no such thing as a perfect plan.

***

Kan had spent the past twenty hours in a state of barely controlled panic. First, the liftoff itself, although mostly automated, required her to give authorizations at key points, both as a safety precaution and because the computer systems could only make decisions of a certain level. The effects of the Uploader crisis years before was still more than evident on the main systems of these ships. It would have taken much too long to upgrade the mothballed *Eagle* to the level of automation that Uploader ships offered – and even more time to convince the council and high command that it was acceptable to do so. The fear of computer intelligence was very real in Crystallian society.

And seeing how this particular war had come about, maybe it was justified. Not computer intelligences, maybe, but certainly computer-based.

Happy as she was to see her vision realized, Kan wished she wasn't the one to have to make the calls. Despite its limitations, the system was still better suited to analyze the flight parameters than she was. But it was too late to do anything now.

Sweat poured across her forehead as she reread the latest decision prompt. *All systems are initialized, launch window open until 0550 ship time. Ignite engine and initiate orbit escape sequence?*

How was she supposed to know? At least clock counting down on the main control panel informed her that she had fifteen minutes to make the decision and still hit the current launch window comfortably. She rechecked the parameters, and everything seemed to be in order.

"Yes."

Nothing happened immediately as the ship processed her command. Then a display graph appeared on the main monitor, six rectangular squares in a row. As she watched, they went from red to yellow to green.

The ship juddered, softly, as the drive reignited. Although they'd used it to move the ship into orbit around Crystallia, it had been off while the captured intelligence that called itself the Watcher sent its transmissions to the Oneness fleet, carefully supervised by a whole platoon of Military Intelligence observers who she suspected would have been incompetent to identify any subterfuge, and by Rester who admitted as much. He'd only managed to get her to allow the transmission at the very last moment by convincing her that it could do only very limited damage, but it also might do some good – and as the war stood at that moment, any good at all would come in very handy.

It surprised her how gently the ignition rocked the ship. The conventional fusion engines that the ship used for propulsion were essentially controlled and directed planet-busting explosions. Even the rings of plasma used in the reactions required staggering amounts of energy to create and stabilize. The scout ships she'd grown up in had less than a millionth of this power, and yet they shook like a faulty centrifuge when the engines were activated.

Launch?

The prompt had appeared while she was lost in thought. It was the long-dead ship designer's way of telling her that everything was within the expected parameters and that the ship was prepared to stop venting its thrust in perfectly balanced neutral patterns and begin to release it as a focused beam. To accelerate the ship out of the ecliptic and towards open areas of space where it could fold its way into the greater galaxy.

There were few areas in the corridor which held Crystallia that allowed safe folds. The mass of the black holes surrounding the open area was such that the entire region was a minefield. Folding space required the manipulation of gravity on a colossal scale – and the presence of a gravity well would certainly throw off any calculations. Even the safe places to jump were only safe in a relative sense of the word.

Nevertheless, it was their only real option. Leaving the corridor through the single large opening was out of the question. It would mean fighting through the entire Oneness fleet. And leaving through one of the riskier escape corridors would only serve to alert the enemy to the existence of the few routes that the Crystallian defenders would be able to use if things got truly bad.

The clock informed her that she still had eight minutes to decide. She pulled her eyes away from the descending figures.

In front of her, occupying most of the viewport, was a grayish-red view of Crystallia itself, clouds and an occasional dust storm obscuring any view of the surface. A single, unexpected pang of homesickness coursed through her as she watched the planet do nothing in front of her.

It seemed impossible to her that, on this particular run through space, there would be no return, no smiling Colonel Jackson there to criticize her approach vectors or lead her through a debriefing session. No drink in the Recon lounge before heading home for a warm shower.

Another thing she found puzzling was that she already missed the corridors, full of people who neither understood nor appreciated what she did for them, the long hours out on patrol, and the eternal vigilance. She'd always hated the time she'd spent surrounded by the general population; it felt unclean and overcrowded after the sterile expanses of interplanetary vacuum. But here she was, missing the corridors. It made no sense.

Her parents were another story entirely. They'd grown apart as the years went by, and had barely spoken in years. Her father, in particular, had never forgiven her choice of careers. Her siblings had taken her place in their affections – and even her goodbye visit had been marked by coolness and awkward silences.

She felt the single tear run down her cheek and for once was thankful that Rester and the few other non-hibernating members of the ship's roster were manning their own stations or simply watching the proceedings from the observation deck one level below.

"Yes," she said. "Launch."

The slight juddering became a purposeful throb and a push in the back which, a few minutes and a few more tears later, had caused the planet in the viewport to disappear beneath her.

CHAPTER 25

It had come to this. Trienne glanced at the lines on her uniform. The promotion had been unexpected, but at the same time it was perfectly logical. Everyone with combat training was up in space helping to man the defensive front, a line of ships hundreds of millions of kilometers long a mere two astronomical units away from Crystallia itself. The entire Uploader fleet was there – or at least those parts of it which hadn't been picked off by the Oneness over the prior three months of fighting – as was every single ship in the Crystallian defense force, retrofitted with as much exotic weaponry as could be feasibly grafted onto them.

Everyone knew the picket action was essentially a suicide mission. The only thing they really wanted to achieve was to weaken the Oneness' fleet badly enough that the emplacements on the planet itself and the two moons would be enough to stop it once and for all. The Oneness had not come through the battle unscathed either.

With everyone who actually knew what they were doing tossing their lives away in the interplanetary void, Trienne had become the logical person to command the ground-based battery of the weapon she'd designed. Typical military thinking, but she was happy to be there, in a place where she had access to the command network and status updates.

She thought of the civilians in the corridors, relying on the hourly updates for heavily censored information and shuddered. The way the war was being managed in the tunnels seemed inhuman, but she guessed it was the only way to do it.

Beside her, Mika Bina, the enigmatic Uploader ambassador, stood watching the screen. Her perfect features were marred by deep caverns under her eyes and an unhealthy pallor to her skin. Trienne had heard that the woman had insisted on staying on Crystallia while her people fought in order to supervise the uploading of tens of thousands of frightened civilians – and keep the panic-driven violence of the first days to a minimum. It was rumored that the captured personalities had been beamed to an escape ship which would stay aside from the fighting and run for safety as soon as the opportunity could be found, but Trienne didn't dare ask the intimidating woman whether that was true. She wondered why Mika had chosen this particular position from which to watch the battle – but assumed it was as good as any.

"At least this phase seems to be going to plan," Mika said.

Trienne jumped. She really wasn't much of an expert. It had been explained that the defending line would try to retreat toward the planet slowly and attempt to pick off the largest number of enemies possible as they did. Eventually, they would fall back to the orbit of Minor, the moon calculated to be nearest their position at that time, and bring the heavy weaponry mounted on the planetoid to bear. That was supposed to be the point where this particular Oneness fleet would finally be broken. "I hope it stays that way," she replied.

Their only role at that moment was as spectators, watching the solid line of allied ships giving ground slowly. The tactic seemed to be to concentrate all the assorted weaponry available on the forward-most elements of the Oneness fleet. Any excrescence in the enemy front would be chipped away, slowing the advance.

Nevertheless, the defending ships were still outnumbered nearly fourfold, and the defenders had to fall back to stay out of range of the greater volume of the enemy's more powerful weapons. Even so, individual blue dots were disappearing from the tactical screen constantly.

Fortunately, the Oneness seemed to be playing its part perfectly. A mammoth front advanced slowly, trading time for inches – or more precisely, for tens of thousands of kilometers – and making no attempts more serious than an occasional feint to try to flank the retreating defenders.

But even so, at the speeds involved, the two astronomical units between the running battle and the planet took less than six hours to become one, and a three more to become half. The battle might be going according to plan, but it seemed that the Oneness was determined to smother Crystallia under the sheer weight of ships and the physics they could bring to bear.

Suddenly, though, the battle changed. Just as the defensive front approached the outer range of Minor's weapon's emplacements, the Oneness front accelerated at one single point, causing its lines to stretch and taper into a fine, needle-like point. Trienne knew it was just the scale of the screen they were watching, and that the real action was taking place over millions of square kilometers, but the image reminded her of nothing more than a Tri-D program in which some hapless victim suffered a stab wound with a long dagger. The Oneness pumped more and more red spots from the fringes into the empty area created by the acceleration, and these, too, were driven hard into the defensive lines.

The defenders, for their part, had no chance to react. The sudden massive strike against a single point in their line was devastating. The point of the enemy's strike broke through the front as if it wasn't there. Once through, it split in two: one half drove, ever accelerating, towards the planet while the other opened up and turned back on itself to attack the defenders from the rear. The formation reminded Trienne of a deadly stamen sprouting from an opening flower.

It took her a moment to understand the implications of what she was seeing. And it took her another few seconds to get her emotions under control once she did. "Ensign," she asked her tactical officer – a girl who looked like she should be in kindergarten, "what's the ETA on that strike force?"

The girl was unruffled. She simply glanced at her tac-display, subvocalized a couple of commands, and gave her answer in a matter-of-fact tone. "At the current rate of acceleration, and with the best estimates on the deceleration capabilities of Oneness capital ships, they should be in effective strike range within eighty-four standard minutes."

"And how soon can we hit them?"

"The canister delivery system," Trienne knew that was military shorthand for the missiles in which her nanomachine weapons were stored, "can already hit them." They were launched through magnetic accelerators which sent them out of the planet's atmosphere at hypersonic speeds, after which a fusion drive would accelerate them into the middle of the enemy fleet.

"Then begin the attack."

The ensign hesitated. Trienne caught it. "Out with it."

"I'm sorry, it's just that the simulation indicates that our attack will be more effective if we wait until just after the fleet gets into the moon's range to hit them."

The girl was right. The moon's heavy weaponry would both thin out the number of targets and create a diversion. Trienne nodded. "Time the strikes for that moment, then."

"Yes, ma'am."

As Trienne turned away, she saw a look of horror on Mika's face. The Uploader woman seemed mesmerized by the tactical display, unable to tear her eyes from its moving positional display. She seemed to realize that she was no longer alone only after Trienne was an arm's length away. "We can't launch," she whispered.

The display showed the allied fleet's reaction to the strike. Nearly three-quarters of the defense line had broken off its engagement with the main body of the Oneness force and was pursuing the knifepoint aimed at Crystallia. It was immediately apparent that any strike from the planet would be evenly distributed between friend and foe. And not all of those friends were human-piloted ships. Most, in fact, were Uploader vessels racing to defend the planet, and who would be just as badly damaged by the nanites as the Oneness itself.

There was no real choice. "Ensign, belay that order. Cancel the strike. But keep the tubes loaded, just in case."

This time, the ensign obeyed without comment.

The tension in the command post increased. Unlike most officers, who commanded remotely, Trienne had insisted on being present in the room where the nanobombs were fabricated and loaded into the magnetic accelerators. She knew that if anything went wrong, it was unlikely that she would be able to solve it. But there were some problems that she might resolve on the spot, and she wanted to be there on the off chance that she might be useful.

She alternately watched the progress of the battle, bloodless and fought between red and blue shapes on the tac-screen, and the activities of her loading crew on the factory floor. Their demeanor reminded her of the ensign at the computer: calm, businesslike, and unruffled. They looked more like factory workers going through their daily routine than people faced with the horror of involuntary annexation. A sense of pride ran through her, and she had to laugh at herself. Yes, she'd been placed in command, but she was well aware that she hadn't earned it, and that these troops would have been cool under fire even if their commander had been a sock puppet.

The floor itself was nothing special. There had been no time to create an assembly line, so pre-programmed Uploader nanofactories had simply been built by one of the original nanofactories and pushed close to the preexisting magnetic accelerator tubes, with a simple chute running from the nanofactory to the tube opening. The job of the operators was simply to make certain that the missiles entered correctly, and to close the tube doors once it was in position. Dozens of tubes and their attendant nanofactories stretched into the distance in the cavernous room.

A nudge from Mika brought her attention back to the display. The red polygons denoting the enemy fleet were about to cross the line that meant they would be in range on the moon's weapons. They were also surrounded by a cloud of blue ships – both coming to meet the strike from the moon itself and those that were a part of the original defensive front, following from behind.

Some of the red figures began to vanish. They were packed close together and seemed to be making a beeline towards the moon. None of the blue ships – the defense fleet – seemed affected. "Weaponry from minor engaged," the ensign said in her professional tone.

And then it happened. The large blue circle that denoted the moon flickered, once, twice, and then disappeared altogether. Quite a few of the blue dots around it went as well.

"What happened?" Trienne tried to keep her voice level, but suspected she'd failed miserably.

At least she had the perverse satisfaction of seeing a look of pure horror cross the features of the ice girl at the console. "The reports are muddled. From what I can tell, the moon was hit with some kind of singularity weapon, something that isn't in any of our databases and which bypassed the defensive shielding. Assuming they used it at its maximum range, we have thirteen standard minutes before it can be deployed against Crystallia."

An icy lump formed in Trienne's stomach. If that weapon was effective against a larger mass – and gravity weapons tended to get more effective the larger the target – then they had to act now. Everything seemed to indicate that the Oneness would never use such a destructive weapon when the possibility of uploading more than a million individuals beckoned, but without the moon to make a stand, the fleet itself was more than enough to subdue the planet.

"Begin launching missiles. Every tube, full capacity," Trienne said.

"Where should we aim them?"

The tac-screen showed that the battle had become one giant furball in space. Blue and red markings were completely mixed together, all accelerating towards the planet itself. The defense platforms in orbit were already firing. "Try to aim for the areas where the concentration of Oneness craft is highest."

"Yes ma'am."

Trienne could barely stand to look at Mika, but she forced herself to turn towards the Uploader woman. "You'd better warn your people about what's coming."

Mika nodded, allowing her expression to go blank as she communicated.

Trienne watched the battle as the tubes began their task of bringing the payloads to escape velocity and much, much more. The control room shuddered as the accelerated missiles broke the sound barrier, and resonated with the clanking as the nanofactories dropped weapon after weapon onto the chutes. She expected most of the blue dots to retreat to a safe distance immediately.

It never happened. The Uploader vessels continued their single-minded attack on the center of the Oneness fleet. By now, the original advancing front had caught up with the breakaway, and joined the fray.

Vastly outnumbered, the defenders were giving ground towards Crystallia at an alarming rate.

"First wave of missile impacts," the ensign said. "Positive strike ratio fifteen percent. Strike against enemy targets calculated at seventy-eight percent of positive strikes." That meant that nearly one in five of the missiles had, according to the density of the ships present in the area, injected its computer-killing nanites into a friendly vessel. Trienne shuddered.

She watched, trying to see if she could tell when the nanites did their work. But minutes passed and none of the vessels in the area showed any signs of slowing. Soon, the enemy was well within range of the planet and the shuddering changed in tone. No longer caused by the accelerating missiles, the shaking took on seismic proportions as the Oneness pounded defensive emplacements.

Dust fell from the ceiling and Trienne tried to console herself with the thought that a mere missile emplacement would rank extremely low on the enemy's list of priorities. But they'd get around to it sooner or later. After all, the counter on the tac-screen showed that they were nearing a hundred thousand missiles fired – more than three times the number of craft remaining in the fight. Some subroutine – probably something that had once been a human mind – would see those numbers and bump them up the list.

As if reading her mind, one of the tubes suddenly exploded, tearing its operators to bits, damaging the nanofactory behind it and filling the tunnel and the control center with choking black dust. *Nanite dust*, Trienne thought. *Should be harmless to humans.*

"What happened?"

"Tube blocked by the bombing, and the missile exploded a mile into its path. What we got here was the blowback."

"So we weren't bombed?"

"No. The strike that damaged the tube seems to have been aimed at a field generator a few miles north of us."

"All right, carry on."

The girl, pale-faced now, nodded and directed her attention back towards the tac display.

As a medical and maintenance team attended to the damage, the rest of the tube crews went about their business. They seemed to be able to load and fire missiles every ten seconds. Massive numbers of nanites were being produced, loaded, accelerated, and deployed every minute.

But it was having no effect on the enemy. Thousands of enemy ships kept speeding toward the planet. Her invention was useless –

worse than useless, since it had diverted critical resources that could have been used to better effect elsewhere.

Another three tubes exploded, less violently, but simultaneously. Obviously, they were targeting the tubes now. Perhaps it was for the best. It would be better to die than to be uploaded. The tac-display showed no sign of the fleet slowing. Blue and red triangles knifed towards the surface of the planet at incredible speed.

Trienne was dimly aware of an alarm going off. She supposed it meant that they were being bombed or that their atoms would soon be compressed beyond recognition.

The ground beneath her feet suddenly left and she flew through the air. She landed, shaken but unhurt, and was only able to feel relief that she would die under a barrage of conventional fire as opposed to feeling the crush of exotic physics before the world jumped again and slammed her into something solid.

Blackness fell.

***

Jackson knew his arm was broken. It was the least of his problems. The darkness around him implied that whatever had hit them had also taken out a good chunk of the power grid for the area. The glow of battery powered emergency lighting came from far away – a little too far away, to his left.

He made his way down the corridor, trying to understand what had happened. Equipment was strewn in haphazard piles, as though an invader both violent and untidy had tossed it aside. But if the Oneness ground troops had been here, Jackson knew that he should never have woken. The Uploader delegation had been extremely clear on the subject: the Oneness uploaded everyone, and they killed you in the process. There were no exceptions.

And yet, here he was. There was no question about the nature of the defeat that had been suffered. The very center of the command headquarters lay in ruins, wisps of smoke ran through the corridors, and no one moved. The sector Jackson was walking through should have been abuzz with motion. The only people he could see in the dim light were unnaturally still – he hoped that they'd been knocked unconscious as he had.

Or maybe, judging by what the Oneness would do to them if they were still alive, it was better if they weren't. He stumbled over the rubble to where the nearest lay. A woman in what looked like a junior officer's uniform. The shape of her head told him all he needed to know about her condition, but he felt for a pulse anyway. She was beyond help.

His head cleared as his eyes adjusted to the dim light, and Jackson studied his options. Access to the civilian sector seemed to be out of the question as the corridor he would have needed to take was completely blocked off by a cave-in. The only other logical destination left was one of the shock-damped control centers, command posts mounted in tanks of liquid and equipped with anti-seismic shock absorbers. The corridor in that direction seemed open, if strewn with debris of different sorts. He ignored the guilt as he hurried along, not stopping to study anything on the floor too closely.

The first damper chamber had split open like an egg. The occupants had drowned under a crushing tide of silicone-based damping fluid. One of them had nearly made it up the stairs that led out of the pit, his clutching hand lay on the dry floor of the corridor. He turned violently away, emptying his stomach in an arc. The pain from his arm after the sharp movement nearly caused him to black out again.

The next stairway seemed dry. He walked gingerly down the first few steps.

"Hold it!"

Jackson froze. "Who is it?" he asked. The voice had come from the bottom of the stairs.

"A guy with a gun. Now who are you?"

Jackson nearly chuckled, but he suspected it would have hurt his arm. "Colonel Jackson, Recon."

"Come down. Slowly."

Jackson obeyed and tried not to flinch as a light shone onto his face, nearly blinding after the dim corridor.

"Yeah, it's you. Come on in." The owner of the voice opened a door behind him and light, blue and cold but welcome streamed over them. The guard was a tall, large man in a Marine uniform. "What's it like up there?"

"Not good," Jackson replied.

The damping chamber had kept its integrity, although the disarray in one corner indicated that some of the shockwave had made it in. A Marine lieutenant, much too young, saluted. "Welcome to the underwater defense bay, Colonel. I wish I could give you better news, but it seems that the troops I was supposed to send against the Oneness are either buried under a mountain of rock or the last EMP wave knocked out all their radios."

"I'd settle for knowing what happened."

"We're still piecing that together, sir. As far as we're able to tell so far, the orbital combat broke up suddenly and the ships themselves started to slam into the planet. The shields were nearly all gone, so it didn't take long for them to start getting through."

"What? The Oneness used its fleet to slam into the planet? That doesn't make any sense from a tactical point of view. They had neutralized the moon. They had us outnumbered and running."

"Er... Not just the Oneness' ships, Colonel. Our Uploader allies crashed, too. We think they might have changed sides at the last minute."

"I doubt it. They're even more afraid of the Oneness than we are. So what happened next?"

"We're not sure. Those ships were hitting us hard – even a pebble would have done quite a bit of damage at those speeds – and frequently. It seemed like the planet was breaking up. We got bounced around quite a bit in here, so I don't even want to imagine what it was like outside." This last part was a question.

Jackson held out his arm: limp, bent at an unnatural angle. "If you can get me some painkillers, I'll tell you all about outside."

"I'm so sorry, sir. I hadn't realized that you were hurt."

The lieutenant rushed off to find his medical officer who took one look at the arm and grimaced. "I can't do a hell of a lot right now. Only try to set it as well as possible and immobilize it. But I can get rid of the pain."

"Wait. Not yet. Lieutenant, finish your story."

"There's not much more to say. We lost most of our sensor capacity in the barrage. Hell, I think we're lucky the planet didn't break up. This was nearly a standard hour ago."

"Have there been any incursions by Oneness ground troops?"

"None that we've seen."

"Any communication from orbit?"

"All the visual channels are down, and the radio wiring was knocked loose – this far underground, we use long antennas to get to the surface. They're flexible enough to survive a lot of punishment, but the end tipped off on our end. We should be finished with the repairs in ten minutes or so."

Jackson made a face at the doctor. "I guess I have to wait."

He nearly didn't make it. Now that he was safe – for a very relative value of 'safe' – his adrenaline levels were falling and the pain in his arm was nearly unbearable. It was an effort even to stand up.

When he thought he would have to succumb after all, the radio came online suddenly, already tuned to the Crystallia defense force's frequency. A horrific series of screams and pandemonium assaulted their ears.

The lieutenant turned the volume down and picked up a mike. He glanced at Jackson before speaking. The colonel nodded for the younger man to proceed. "This is Crystallia Central Command calling the defense fleet. I repeat, this is Crystallia Central Command calling the defense fleet. Is there anyone out there? Can anyone hear me?"

A high-pitched voice came on in response. "Hello, Crystallia! We're glad to hear from you." The voice was drowned out by the screaming in the background.

"What's happening up there? Is it that bad?"

"I'm sorry, I can't hear you."

"The screaming. What is it? Are you all right?"

"That's not screaming. That's celebration. The Oneness fleet is destroyed."

"What?"

"Yes, they suddenly seemed to lose power. A lot of them crashed into the planet. The rest just drifted off. We destroyed most of them without a fight, and the few that did fight back seemed confused. The mop up took fifteen minutes."

"What?" The lieutenant's eyes were wide. It didn't look like he could believe his ears.

"I'm not sure if you can hear me. I can hardly hear myself. Tell everyone down there that we won. We won!"

Jackson closed his eyes. *Trienne*, he thought, with no doubts whatsoever. *If she's still alive, we'll have to give her a medal or something.* He wondered whether there was any procedure for giving medals, but only for a moment, before the powerful sedative the doctor had administered finished taking effect.

EPILOGUE

Kan gripped his hand tightly. It had been months since they'd powered away from Crystallia. Her last memory of the system was one of bright lights illuminating the empty black skies she'd seen so often out on patrol. The energies being released in her home system were the very ones the Recon Force had been created to hide from, to prevent. But they'd failed.

It seemed like a lifetime ago. She'd seen countless systems since. Some as decoys in case their trail was being followed, some simply hadn't seemed welcoming places, certainly not the kind of skies that she would want her children looking into.

And for the first time in her life, she was thinking of children. Rester had long since convinced her that he was, biologically, at least, as human as she was. And the emotions he displayed could never have come from anything but another person, one who felt as she did and had hopes for the same children she did. She no longer cared that the brain in his skull was made of exotic polymers and semiconductors. She was a woman. He was a man. That was all the difference between them she was willing to acknowledge. And it was enough.

She hoped she would be a better parent than she'd been a daughter. Although she knew she'd been the perfect daughter to at least one person. She smiled as she thought of Jackson, but it was tinged with sadness. Was he still alive? Or maybe he was still alive as a subroutine in a maintenance system on a Oneness battle cruiser, with no capacity to remember her at all.

As their feet touched the soil of the world they'd chosen to start anew on – not much to look at, but plenty of oxygen and algae, with soil of a reasonable pH – Kan mouthed a single supplication to the universe that the only other man she'd ever loved could at least remember her, no matter what form he was in.

It is unlikely that the universe heard the supplication but, thousands of light years away, Colonel Hermes Wolf Jackson was thinking of her. The sadness in his eyes was not because of any uncertainty about Kan's condition – he was sure that Kan was safe, and equally certain that they'd never meet again – but because he thought he'd never feel this protective of anyone ever again. And yet he did.

The young woman on the bed was a shadow of her former self. She'd been formidable, intimidating, self-assured. Now her body had wasted away, and Jackson could tell that she was struggling to keep her mind from following suit.

The best doctors on Crystallia, with remote help from a few extremely puzzled Uploader consultants, had done their best. She'd been kept in an electronically induced coma while they worked, but the months had seen little improvement. The nanites had done their job extremely well, and had reproduced in ways not quite foreseen.

"I killed her," Trienne said.

Jackson sighed. "No, you didn't. You probably saved individual humanity. We've been through this already." He turned to the white-coated medic. "Can you turn her mind back on? I think she has a right to know how things turned out."

The doctor nodded. He pulled the protective covering off a touch-sensitive screen and passed his fingers over the interface to the right. A bar graph on the monitor slowly rose, changing its color from red to yellow to green as it went.

The girl on the bed stirred and opened her eyes, blinking rapidly.

"Hello, Mika," Jackson said. "Can you hear me?"

Mika tried to turn in his direction, but the attempt failed about halfway through. Jackson and Trienne moved to the foot of the bed, where she could see them without moving.

Mika tried to speak, but coughed instead, spasms rocking her body and bringing tears to her eyes. Finally, she managed a soft whisper. "What happened? How long have I been here?"

"You've been here nearly five months," the colonel told her.

"What..." she paused to catch her breath, "what happened?"

"You took a knock to the head during the battle. It knocked your brain around a little."

"Why didn't you just copy me onto another brain?"

Jackson steeled himself. This was the moment he'd been dreading for months. "It can't be done. The nanites you inhaled during the battle acted the way they were designed – they immediately attacked certain hardware routes in your system. We've spent the last three months isolating the damaged areas and trying to keep the attack from spreading. We weren't successful. The nanites just keep coming."

"So I'm going to die?"

"I'm afraid so. We wanted to give you a chance to come back and learn how things ended before you succumbed." The colonel could feel the tears welling up in his eyes, but fought them back. This moment wasn't about him, it was about the brave woman on the bed – a woman who'd sacrificed the possibility of eternal life in order to save two branches of humanity. He could grieve later.

She surprised him with a weak smile. "Well, I guess a few hundred thousand years of subjective time isn't something I should complain about. It's certainly much longer than I thought I'd have when I was born." She took a breath, as if trying to restore her energy. "So, how long do I have?"

"About half an hour before the nanites regroup. We've hit them hard to give you that amount of time, but it was a heroic procedure – it could have killed you last time, and in all likelihood, it will if we try it again."

She nodded. "So. Did we win?"

"In military terms, you could say we did. But the cost was incredible. Five hundred thousand dead here on Crystallia alone. Countless millions in the Uploader fleet – nearly sixty-five percent of your ships were wiped out."

Jackson could see her, or at least whatever remained of the diplomat in the shell in front of him, trying to keep the grief from reaching her features. She was only partially successful. "And the Oneness? Did we destroy it?"

"Your analysts believe that the Oneness had sent its primary personality with the attack fleet. So, in a way, we did destroy it. However, there is a remnant back in its core systems. It's fragmentary and disjointed, but some sub-personality seems to be trying to pull everything back together. We don't really understand how it works, but it seems to be less belligerent. We believe we might be able to achieve some form of peace." Jackson paused again. There was still more painful news he had to give. "The survivors among your people fled the system after the fighting, and they swear they won't come back. They didn't want to jeopardize themselves. They asked us to send you their love and to thank you for everything you've done."

She digested this. "So we did win. How?"

Trienne broke in. "I'm sorry, Mika. I never wanted the nanites to hurt you or your people." The scientist was the only one of the four people in the room who let her feelings show openly. "I know you probably didn't want me here, but I had to come and apologize. I couldn't say anything to the millions on the ships, but I thought I'd feel like less of a monster if I could apologize to you. I'll leave if you want."

"No. Stay." Mika made the effort of turning her head – very slightly – to peer into Trienne's eyes. "So, your weapon worked after all?"

Trienne nodded, tears flowing copiously.

"Then I believe we all owe you our freedom. Thank you."

"Thank you? I'm a monster."

"You're a hero. You will be remembered by free humans of whatever type forever. I'm glad you'll be with me in my last moments." For the first time, her composure broke completely, and a look of anxiety made itself evident. "You will be here, won't you?"

Jackson smiled. "Of course we will."

She returned his smile. "We won," she said.

"Yes, we did."

The silence went on for a few minutes. Mika seemed content to pass her last moments thinking about their success. That was fine with Jackson. He took her hand in his and thought with her.

THE END

CHECK OUT OTHER GREAT SCIENCE FICTION BOOKS

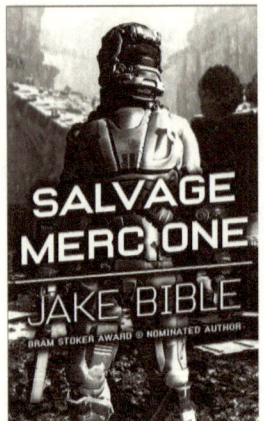

SALVAGE MERC ONE
by Jake Bible

Joseph Laribeau was born to be a Marine in the Galactic Fleet. He was born to fight the alien enemies known as the Skrang Alliance and travel the galaxy doing his duty as a Marine Sergeant. But when the War ended and Joe found himself medically discharged, the best job ever was over and he never thought he'd find his way again.

Then a beautiful alien walked into his life and offered him a chance at something even greater than the Fleet, a chance to serve with the Salvage Merc Corp.

Now known as Salvage Merc One Eighty-Four, Joe Laribeau is given the ultimate assignment by the SMC bosses. To his surprise it is neither a military nor a corporate salvage. Rather, Joe has to risk his life for one of his own. He has to find and bring back the legend that started the Corp.

SERENGETI
by J.B. Rockwell

It was supposed to be an easy job: find the Dark Star Revolution Starships, destroy them, and go home. But a booby-trapped vessel decimates the Meridian Alliance fleet, leaving Serengeti—a Valkyrie class warship with a sentient AI brain—on her own; wrecked and abandoned in an empty expanse of space. On the edge of total failure, Serengeti thinks only of her crew. She herds the survivors into a lifeboat, intending to sling them into space. But the escape pod sticks in her belly, locking the cryogenically frozen crew inside.

Then a scavenger ship arrives to pick Serengeti's bones clean. Her engines dead, her guns long silenced, Serengeti and her last two robots must find a way to fight the scavengers off and save the crew trapped inside her.

CHECK OUT OTHER GREAT
SCIENCE FICTION BOOKS

MAUSOLEUM 2069
by **Rick Jones**

Political dignitaries including the President of the Federation gather for a ceremony onboard Mausoleum 2069. But when a cloud of interstellar dust passes through the galaxy and eclipses Earth, the tenants within the walls of Mausoleum 2069 are reborn and the undead begin to rise. As the struggle between life and death onboard the mausoleum develops, Eriq Wyman, a one-time member of a Special ops team called the Force Elite, is given the task to lead the President to the safety of Earth. But is Earth like Mausoleum 2069? A landscape of the living dead? Has the war of the Apocalypse finally begun? With so many questions there is only one certainty: in space there is nowhere to run and nowhere to hide.

RED CARBON
by **D.J. Goodman**

Diamonds have been discovered on Mars.

After years of neglect to space programs around the world, a ruthless corporation has made it to the Red Planet first, establishing their own mining operation with its own rules and laws, its own class system, and little oversight from Earth. Conditions are harsh, but its people have learned how to make the Martian colony home.

But something has gone catastrophically wrong on Earth. As the colony leaders try to cover it up, hacker Leah Hartnup is getting suspicious. Her boundless curiosity will lead her to a horrifying truth: they are cut off, possibly forever. There are no more supplies coming. There will be no more support. There is no more mission to accomplish. All that's left is one goal: survival.

CHECK OUT OTHER GREAT SCIENCE FICTION BOOKS

IN PERPETUITY
by Jake Bible

For two thousand years, Earth and her many colonies across the galaxy have fought against the Estelian menace. Having faced overwhelming losses, the CSC has instituted the largest military draft ever, conscripting millions into the battle against the aliens. Major Bartram North has been tasked with the unenviable task of coordinating the military education of hundreds of thousands of recruits and turning them into troops ready to fight and die for the cause.

As Major North struggles to maintain a training pace that the CSC insists upon, he realizes something isn't right on the Perpetuity. But before he can investigate, the station dissolves into madness brought on by the physical booster known as pharma. Unfortunately for Major North, that is not the only nightmare he faces- an armada of Estelian warships is on the edge of the solar system and headed right for Earth!

BATTLEFIELD MARS
by David Robbins

Several centuries into the future, Earth has established three colonies on Mars. No indigenous life has been discovered, and humankind looks forward to making the Red Planet their own.

Then 'something' emerges out of a long-extinct volcano and doesn't like what the humans are doing.

Captain Archard Rahn, United Nations Interplanetary Corps, tries to stem the rising tide of slaughter. But the Martians are more than they seem, and it isn't long before Mars erupts in all-out war.

www.ingramcontent.com/pod-product-compliance
Lightning Source LLC
Chambersburg PA
CBHW020101180626
46812CB00006B/2418